Liz and Luther

By: Jessica Terry

I0672792

LIZ AND LUTHER

First edition. November 9, 2025.

Copyright © 2025 Jessica Terry.

ISBN: 979-8999506931

Written by Jessica Terry.

To my family, my friends, my readers, my fellow authors...y'all are dope and I appreciate you.

Chapter 1

• • • •

LIZ TATE OPENED HER eyes in the middle of the plush canopy bed, immediately turning her face towards the sunlight streaming in through the picture window. She smiled when she remembered she was in Belize, and grabbed one of the thick down pillows, hugging it to her chest before suddenly shooting her arms into the air with an excited whoop.

"I'm forty, bitches!"

She'd taken the solo trip to celebrate her birthday, and it had been amazing so far. For three days, she'd gone ziplining, cave tubing, did plenty of lounging on the beach, and ate whatever the hell she desired, because that was what she wanted to do. It was the reason she loved traveling by herself because she didn't have to worry about catering or succumbing to anyone's wishes; she could go and come as she pleased. And any flings she chose to have remained her business.

But as suddenly as her euphoria came, it dimmed. A yearning started to creep over her body and she found herself saddening at the realization that it was her birthday morning and she was alone. It was like a light switch, as suddenly as it happened; Liz wished she was there with someone special.

It had been years since she'd been in an actual relationship. Not because she was hurt over some past breakup or was too focused on her career; over time, she'd just preferred to keep her dalliances with men short. She dated, but kept it casual. When she traveled, she had her fun with men then left them where she found them, having no desire to keep in touch once she left. And if she didn't want to be bothered, she wasn't. That was what she had established for herself and she'd been just fine with it.

So she couldn't understand what was causing this feeling of dejection and loneliness that was spreading as if it was being slowly poured over her from a spout.

"Ugh, is this what comes with turning forty?" she muttered to herself, her arms dropping to the bed with a thump. "I wish someone had warned me."

Springing out of bed, Liz strutted to the bathroom in the white Simone Pérèle bra and panty set she'd treated herself to, telling herself to shake it off. She wasn't going to let this foolishness ruin her vacation, especially since she would be heading home in a couple of days. Then it would be back to work, back to headaches, back to life.

After enjoying a luxurious breakfast via room service, she showered, styled her short black hair, and got dressed in a pair of rag & bone jeans, sandals, and a metallic silver shirt that left her midriff and back exposed. After applying plenty of sunscreen and light makeup, she smiled at her reflection, already feeling better. She chalked up her earlier yearning as a momentary lapse and put it out of her mind, heading out to enjoy her day.

Liz enjoyed exploring the island on her rented golf cart, indulging in Fry Jacks and even booking an impromptu spa day. And as usual, she couldn't resist doing some shopping, telling herself not to overdo it like she tended to do. She loved fashion and it wasn't always the easiest to limit herself when she came across things that she loved, especially if they weren't available back home. She almost always brought luggage just for her new purchases.

She was heading back to her golf cart after gorging on some rum cake at Sol Café when she happened to look up and see the first man that actually made her knees weak.

"Good *god*..." she muttered under her breath, her brow arching in appreciation. Her hand flew to her fluttering stomach. Butterflies were actually a thing? Liz thought that was something that only happened in the sappy movies her heart-eyed sister liked to watch.

Then he turned and saw her, and a slow smile spread across his lips. He eyed her up and down just like she was doing him, and she found herself hoping he liked what he saw, which was another unfamiliar feeling.

Did they put something in the water in this country??

Her heart thumped faster in her chest when he started heading her way. He had to be about six-four, skin the color of dark caramel, a trimmed salt-and-pepper beard, *and* he had the nerve to be bow-legged. His muscles showed he was no stranger to the gym. And the way his eyes stayed on hers as he approached had Liz squirming where she stood.

So much for these expensive panties...

"I hope you don't mind me coming over," he said once he was standing in front of her, his citrus and sandalwood aroma reaching her first, "But there was no way I couldn't."

He was still eyeing her and Liz couldn't tear her eyes away from his if she wanted to. Good thing she didn't.

"I'm glad you did," she replied, relieved that her voice wasn't as shaky as her insides.

He offered his hand. "What's your name, gorgeous?"

She placed her hand in his, feeling an instant *something*. Every nerve in her body felt as if it was lit on fire.

"I'm Liz."

"I'm Luther."

They stood there staring at each other, their hands joined and hanging between them. Somehow they were standing closer than they had been a moment before but Liz didn't mind at all. As far as she was concerned, they weren't close enough.

"Am I keeping you from anything?" he asked her. His voice was low but Liz could still hear him perfectly well despite all the noise around them.

"Not at all. I'm exactly where I want to be right now."

He flashed her a smile, and Liz had to resist the urge to just jump into his arms. She had never, ever been this instantly or this insanely attracted to a man before. This birthday was turning out better and better.

"Would it be presumptuous to say I'd like to spend the day with you?" He licked his bottom lip before capturing it between his teeth. "I know we've only exchanged first names so far..."

"That's plenty for now." Liz grinned at him. "And I wasn't ready to leave you yet, anyway."

"We're on the same page then, Liz. Because I'm damn sure not ready to leave you, either."

• • • •

THEY DIDN'T LEAVE EACH other's side for the rest of the day, falling into an easy rapport with conversation that didn't feel at all forced or tedious, as it sometimes did for Liz when she met someone. All the getting-to-know-you stuff oftentimes felt like an unnecessary burden for a fling, regardless of how lengthy it turned out to be. But Liz didn't feel that with Luther. She was actually interested in what he had to say, already smitten with the sound of his baritone voice. His questions didn't make her want to roll her eyes. And when he grabbed her hand as they walked, her fingers automatically linked with his as if it was the most natural thing in the world to do.

As good a time as she was having, though, Liz made sure to keep things at a somewhat-surface level. Whenever Luther attempted to give her any super-personal information – like his last name – or asked the same of her, she deflected. She didn't even let him know it was her birthday.

"Don't tell me you're on the run from the law," he joked after she sidestepped answering what she did for a living. "I'm not with law enforcement in any way, if it puts your mind at ease."

Liz smiled, liking him even more for not getting upset over her evasiveness. "It's nothing like that."

"Are you married?"

"No. That's one thing I'm more than willing to answer. I'm not married and never have been."

"So why are you being so mysterious, gorgeous? Since I'm not even sure I should assume 'Liz' is your real name, at this point."

"Liz is my real name. But I can understand why you'd think it might not be, with the way I've been steering the conversation. I guess I'll leave it up to you whether you want to believe me on that or not."

He just eyed her, his deep brown eyes narrowed slightly with intrigue.

"You might think this is silly, but I'd rather not learn the deep intricate details about you, get all attached, and then never see you again after I leave here," Liz continued. "I'm loving this, what we're doing here. But to make it easier on myself later, I'd like to just keep it...*here*."

His chin lifted slightly in understanding. "What makes you think you can do that?"

She frowned slightly. "What do you mean?"

"Do you sincerely think not knowing my last name or where I live will keep you from thinking about me once we part ways?"

"I...that's a valid point, I admit." Her eyes dropped to their hands that were loosely joined on top of the wrought iron table they were sitting at. "But the more I know about you, the worse it will be."

"I get it. But speaking for myself, you're going to be on my mind long after I get on that plane and go home. And I don't think it would be arrogant to say it would be mutual. Honestly, I don't think you should assume we'd never see each other again after this."

"Luther...as hot as you are, I don't do long-distance relationships. Tried it, hated it, never again."

"I'm not a fan of those, either. My point is, you never know." He brought her hand to his lips, planting a kiss that had her pressing her legs together underneath the table. "A connection like this can't go to waste."

Liz released a small breath, but chose not to respond. Fate wasn't something she was a huge believer in. She'd never seen Luther before in her life, so there was no reason to believe she'd suddenly run across him after they left Belize. And despite the ache she already felt at the prospect of not seeing him again, she meant it when she said she didn't do long-distance relationships. If she couldn't have this man all day every day, she'd rather not have him at all.

Sensing that she probably didn't agree with what he said, Luther planted another kiss to her honey brown skin and lowered her hand back to the table. "But I'll respect where you're coming from. I truly believe I'll be proven right when it's all said and done."

"I like your confidence."

"And I like *you*."

Her grin was automatic. "Enough to spend the day with me tomorrow? It'll be the last one before I leave."

"I'm all yours, gorgeous."

It was a few hours later when Luther finally escorted Liz to her hotel room door. As Liz debated whether she'd invite him in or not, he pressed a kiss to her forehead and told her he'd see her in the morning. She was slightly disappointed but reminded herself that she'd be seeing him again in a matter of hours. She stepped inside her hotel room and leaned against the closed door, missing him already.

"Happy birthday to me," she muttered.

She woke up the next morning like a kid on Christmas, shooting out of bed an hour before her alarm. It had been a night of tossing and turning in sexual frustration, and hating that she didn't have any of her sex toys with her. But part of her didn't want to bother with any of those, anyway; she wanted the man that had set her body on fire with nothing more than a kiss to the forehead.

Luther was waiting for her in the hotel lobby at their agreed-upon time, and Liz's feet automatically started moving faster to get to him. He stood there in a muscle-hugging t-shirt, dark jeans, and gray Timberland boots. A stylish fedora was on his head, sending his sexiness to another level. Liz happened to like men in hats.

They grinned at each other in anticipation as if they were long-lost lovers, coming together in a firm hug that had Luther lifting Liz slightly off her feet.

"How was your night?" he asked, his face still in the crook of her neck.

"Lonely."

"Something we have in common." He set her back to her feet but kept his hold on her waist. "Part of me was kicking myself for being such a gentleman and leaving you at your door last night."

"Well..." Her hands slid up his hard chest as she looked boldly into his eyes. "There's still tonight."

His eyes darkened. "Indeed there is."

They stood there staring at each other for several moments before they seemed to snap out of it at the same time, with Liz sliding a hand down the back of her tapered haircut and Luther clearing his throat.

"I guess we should get out of this lobby," Liz muttered, her face flushed. She still couldn't wrap her head around the intensity of the affect this man had on her.

"Yeah. First, though," his hand drifted to her chin. "May I kiss you?"

Liz's eyes darted around them. "Right here?"

"It can wait, if you're uncomfortable."

His hand started to drop but Liz caught it. "I'd rather not wait anymore, thank you."

Luther gave a half-smile that faded as he lowered his face to hers. Liz moaned when their lips met, and he pulled her closer by the waist, grunting. Everyone around them disappeared as Liz gently grasped his dark gray silk t-shirt in her hands, leaning into him. She couldn't get close enough. His hands splayed across her back and pressing her against him just felt right.

Their kiss was exploratory but not explicit. Liz felt just the light brushes of his tongue against hers as they got acclimated with each other in this way, and she felt herself fill from foot to head with desire. Not just sexual desire; desire for everything about Luther. He had somehow permeated her in less than a day.

The realization made her step back and place a hand on her heaving chest. This was crazy; she didn't even know this man. Part of her thought she should go back to her room, alone, and quit while she was ahead. But of course, her feet wouldn't move. She could feel his eyes on her but kept hers averted, part of her starting to feel a little silly. What was happening?

"Shall we go?"

Luther was holding his hand out to her, giving her a look that relayed no pressure. Liz felt some of her sudden anxiety melt. There was no way she could walk away from him right now, whether that would be the sensible thing to do or not.

"Yes."

She took his hand, their fingers automatically linking together again as they turned and headed for the door.

· · · ·

LIZ TRIED TO TELL HERSELF this was just one last fling. That the intensity she was feeling towards Luther was meaningless.

Her sister Lovey was the one that believed in stuff like love at first sight and kismet, and people being made for each other, and was what she felt she had in her husband, Roland. And Liz could buy that, for *them*. But for her, not so much. She always figured whenever she did decide to settle down with someone, it would be a decision of practicality more than anything else; whichever man that checked the most of her boxes and get on her nerves the least long-term would be it.

But deep, *deep* in Liz's heart and mind, she knew Luther was different. She felt it. As little as she really knew about him, she wanted *him* to be the one she ended up with indefinitely. It both freaked her out and excited her. And trying to reduce their time together to just a fling wasn't invigorating as it usually was; it was disheartening.

She tried to push all of that out of her mind as they roamed around Belize together, spending the majority of the day in San Pedro. They shopped, made chocolate, and just enjoyed roaming and sightseeing together. But Liz wasn't as focused on what they were doing as she was the bond that was growing between them with each passing minute. And she sensed he felt it, too, with how he looked at her, catered to her, protected her. Something as simple as him firmly holding her hand to his chest as he led her through a crowd of people had her swooning like a schoolgirl.

Once nightfall came, they headed back to Liz's hotel, strolling in silence as their hands swung between them. Liz's mind was racing with conflicting thoughts and feelings. The smart thing to do would be to send him away once they got to her hotel room door. As wonderful as their time together had been, she still hadn't allowed their conversation to delve too deeply, as her way of protecting herself. It was going to be hard enough leaving the next day, knowing she'd never see him again.

But when they faced each other in front of her hotel room door and shared the gaze of fated mates, Liz knew sending him away wouldn't be happening.

Damn that.

"You want to come in?" she asked, anticipation already building in her chest.

"Only if you're sure you want me to."

All doubt left the building. "I'm absolutely sure."

She turned and slid her key card into the door slot with shaky hands, taking a sharp intake of breath when she felt his hands on her hips. His body heat warmed her, despite the goosebumps that were sprouting on her arms.

Every inch of her body tingled once they walked into the spacious hotel suite. Luther waited as Liz put her bags down and kept her back to him, seeming to be collecting herself. He hung back, giving her the moment she apparently needed before stepping closer and reclaiming his hold on her hips.

"No pressure tonight, Liz," he assured her, his lips close to her ear. "Nothing will happen that you don't want to happen. It's enough for me that I'm here with you."

She turned in his arms, her eyes roaming the face she knew she'd be having dreams about for longer than she'd like. "I appreciate you saying that. But that's not enough for *me*."

Leaning up, she pressed her lips to his. He immediately returned the kiss as their arms wrapped around each other, the intensity building instantly. This wasn't like their gentle kiss in the lobby earlier. This one was filled with the heat and longing they'd both carried around since they met. Their hands ventured to more intimate areas, and between Luther's touch and his kisses and his groans of pleasure, Liz had almost no composure left.

"Make love to me, Luther," she pleaded against his lips. Her hands slid underneath his shirt and feeling his chiseled body was like gasoline on the flame of her desire for him. "Please."

"I want nothing more, baby." He removed his hat, tossing it onto the nearby desk. "Damn, Liz, you have no idea how much I want you."

They stepped back from each other long enough to simultaneously pull their respective shirts over their heads before clamping back together in another round of deep, heated kisses. It was like they couldn't stand to not touch each other for too long. Once they were both finally undressed, Luther grasped Liz's hands in his, marveling at her toned 5'9 frame.

"Fuck, Liz..."

She was just as busy ogling him. The muscles this man had were ridiculous. "My sentiments exactly. I hope you don't have anywhere to be."

"Trust me." His eyes met hers with jarring intensity. "I'm not going anywhere."

Liz didn't let herself wonder how intently he meant that. She just let him snatch her up and take her to the bed with him.

Sex with Luther didn't feel like *just sex*, regardless of what Liz tried to tell herself. As soon as he covered himself and entered her, she knew nothing else would ever feel like what she felt in that moment. The way they fit together felt too right, too perfect.

Am I dreaming all this? This can't be real. It just doesn't happen like this.

"Liz..." Luther grunted, his face buried in the crook of her neck as he moved in and out of her, their hands linked above her head.

"Yes, Luther...*fuck*, yes..."

He lifted his head and turned her face to his, planting a deep grunt-filled kiss on her. It was intense but not desperate; they were like lovers that shared a bond cemented by time, when it hadn't even been two days. Liz's legs lifted around his waist as she matched his rhythm, her hands sliding to his back and her nails digging into this skin.

"Yeah, let me know you're feeling this," he whispered against her lips. "Know that this means something, Liz. I want you to feel what I'm feeling, baby."

And she did. She felt like she was making love to her man, not having sex with a random on vacation.

They couldn't get enough of each other. It was intense, focused, intentional lovemaking that left Liz feeling both full and empty. It was almost unfair that she'd only get to experience that, experience *him*, for just that one night.

Liz slept the best sleep of her life on Luther's chest, but come morning, she remembered that she'd be getting on a plane back home in a matter of hours. Crying wasn't something she did much of but she felt the tears when he started to get dressed after their shower together.

"Hey, hey," he said softly, crossing the room and taking her chin in his hand. He lifted her face and waited for her eyes to meet his. "No sad faces, all right? This isn't good-bye, Liz."

She shook her head slowly. "How can you possibly say that?"

"Call me a romantic, but I feel it in my heart." He briefly placed a hand over his chest before pulling her closer. "You might not want to hear this, but I've already fallen for you."

"Luther," she sighed. "Please don't..."

"You don't feel anything for me?"

"Yes." Her eyes held his. "As crazy as it is, I feel something for you that I haven't felt for anyone. But-"

"No, we're gonna leave it at that, baby." He pressed a finger to her lips. "That's all that needs to be said."

"Luther, I don't want to ruin the vibe, but I don't believe in fate like that. For all I know, you live clear across the country from me. If you even live in the *same* country as me. As much as I've loved this time with you, I can't make myself buy that we'll somehow magically see each other again just like that."

"I'll believe it for the both of us, then."

She just looked at him, clear skepticism in her eyes.

"Look, I absolutely get how farfetched this sounds," Luther continued. "It's definitely a first for me. But I'm not running from it. Liz, you...I can't just see you this one time and that's it. I just refuse to believe that God blessed us with this amazing connection only to rip us apart and have us never come together again."

"Please tell me you're not some kind of religious nut."

He laughed. "I'm spiritual, yes, but not religious. And don't think I don't recognize that you're deflecting right now. But like I said, I get it. When you see me again, you'll know. I told you, a connection like ours can't go to waste."

He leaned in and kissed her before she could refute anything, wrapping her tightly in his arms. Liz returned his kiss with all the fervor he was giving her, wishing she could match his optimism but knowing her realism wouldn't let her.

When he finally left, Liz squeezed her eyes shut as she leaned against the door, telling herself it was silly to cry over a man she just met. This had to be a vacation haze she was under; as soon as she got on the plane to head home, she'd snap out of it and come to her senses. In a matter of days, she'd forget all about Luther...whatever his last name was.

But as she went about getting her things packed, she knew she didn't believe that any more than she believed the sky was green.

Chapter 2

• • • •

"ARE YOU ALL RIGHT, ma'am?"

Liz looked up at the concerned flight attendant. "Um, yes, I'm fine. Thanks."

"Is there anything I can get you?"

"Anything with alcohol in it."

Liz hadn't felt like herself since the moment Luther walked out of her hotel room. She felt like she was moving through mud as she packed her bags, rode to the airport, and boarded the plane. Her mind was already replaying her time with Luther as she sat slumped in her seat, her body aching with longing. It was ridiculous how much she missed him already. She even found herself anxiously eying the other passengers as they boarded the plane, hoping there was a chance they were on the same flight. Every time she got her hopes up at seeing a tall Black man and then realized it wasn't him, she just got more dejected. No wonder the flight attendants kept checking on her.

She had never been this sprung over a man. This was what her sister Lovey did, not her. But she sensed that the ache in her chest from being away from him wasn't going away any time soon. It almost made her angry; meeting what felt like the man of her dreams on vacation only to get one measly night with him.

Once the plane landed back home, Liz called a rideshare and started to head to her place, but knew she'd do nothing but sit and sulk over Luther, so she asked the driver to take her to Lovey's house instead. Being around her sister and her niece and nephews would be a great distraction from what was clouding her mind, however temporarily. She texted Lovey to see if it was all right to come over and her little sister immediately replied with an emphatic invitation to come on by.

"Welcome home!" Lovey greeted once Liz arrived, giving her a firm hug. Liz smiled, grateful for the warm welcome. "I missed you; come on in!"

Liz stepped inside Lovey's brick colonial house, lugging her suitcases behind her. She could hear a television going as she followed Lovey into the den where her three-year-old nephew Xavier and his year-old twin siblings Gillian and Easton were playing in a huge playpen. Lovey removed some children's books from the couch and pushed aside a few toys with her foot before patting the sofa cushion with a grin at Liz. "Have a seat. Are you hungry?"

"If I were, I wouldn't tell you. I've told you a hundred times you don't have to wait on me when I come over here."

"Stop. I can order you something, if you want."

"I ate on the plane, Lovey. I'm fine. Now hand me one of those babies."

Lovey grinned harder as she lifted Gillian from the playpen, since her brothers were playing with blocks together. She planted a quick kiss to her daughter's cheek before handing her over to Liz, who immediately lifted her in a playful swing before pulling her close to her chest.

"I cannot believe how fast they're growing," she marveled as Gillian became occupied with her necklace. "It seems like they're all bigger than they were the last time I saw them."

"I know, right? It's blowing my mind that Xavier will be four soon. And it won't be all that long before the twins are two."

"That's so crazy. How are you and Roland managing? Where is he, by the way?"

"He had to run some errands and go by 845 to check on something for an event that's being held there tonight," Lovey replied, referring to one of the clubs Roland owned with his brother, E.J. "He should be back pretty soon. In answer to your question, though, we're managing pretty well. It's can be tiring, having three young children but I wouldn't trade it for anything. And we have plenty of help when we need it, thankfully."

Liz played with her niece and nephews, glad to occupy her mind with something else. Roland came home a little while later and he greeted Liz with a friendly hug before pulling Lovey to him and giving her a long, deep kiss. Liz eyed them with uncharacteristic jealousy. Lovey and Roland were still so in love and lust for each other after over four years of marriage, and clearly having three babies in the house didn't tamp down their fire one bit.

While Roland played with the kids, Lovey pulled Liz into the kitchen.

"Tell me about your trip," she requested as she pulled a couple of bottles of water from the refrigerator and slid one over to Liz across the kitchen island. "How was Belize?"

"It was great."

"That's it?"

Liz shrugged a shoulder, determined to remain vague. "I enjoyed getting away, as usual. Got some beautiful new clothes..."

"As if you need any more clothes."

"Can never have enough."

"I still can't believe you were out of the country for your fortieth birthday and we couldn't celebrate with you. I wanted to throw you a party or at least have something for you here at the house."

"There wasn't any need to go through all that trouble for me. I appreciate it, but I had this trip planned for months. Wanted to close my thirties out with a bang."

"Uh-huh. And just how much *banging* did you do while you were there?"

Liz's face immediately flushed, and it was one time she was glad she wasn't as fair-skinned as her sister. "I don't know what you're talking about."

"Don't do that, Liz. You're always so evasive about your yummy overseas dalliances."

"Because there's no need in rehashing temporary stuff. What happens on vacation stays there."

Her chest constricted as she said those words, thinking of Luther. It was a philosophy she lived by and spouted often but this was one time she wished it wasn't true.

"Hey, you okay?" Lovey asked, concerned. She placed her hand over Liz's. "You look so sad all of a sudden."

Liz hadn't even realized she'd let her expression change. Usually she had a better handle on her emotions than that.

Sitting up straighter, she forced a smile and nodded. "Yeah, girl, I'm fine. Just...there's some things on my mind, is all."

"What's going on?"

"I, um..." Liz couldn't believe she was about to admit this but found herself wanting to confide in her sister. "I've been feeling like I want to settle down with someone. When I woke up alone on my birthday, it...it didn't feel great. It was like I was over the single life as soon as I hit 4-0."

Gasping excitedly, Lovey clapped her hands. "Liz! I am so glad to hear you say that!"

"It's nothing to throw a parade over, Lovey, calm down," Liz chuckled.

"You've always said that you didn't need any man in your face all the time and I respected that, but I've always hoped you'd come out of that way of thinking. There's just nothing like being in love."

"I don't know," Liz's smile faded slightly. "Something like what you and Roland have is rare."

"It's not as rare as you think. Look at our loved ones; Mama Elyse and Daddy Darius, Natalia and E.J., Desiree and Lorenzo. Our parents, before they passed. Heck, all three of Desiree's sisters are happily married. There are so many examples of partnership that we're blessed to see. You just have to be open to it once you find it."

Luther's face flashed through Liz's mind. "Perhaps."

"Let me fix you up."

"Oh...I don't know about that, Lovey..."

"Why not? I can think of a few men that might be good for you, if you give them a chance. And I'll fully take into account your preference for older men."

"It's a preference, not a requirement."

Lovey eyed her with a grin. "Is that a yes?"

Hesitating, Liz finally threw up a conceding hand. "What the hell. Sure."

"Yay!"

Liz couldn't help but laugh at her little sister actually jumping up and down in excitement, her long ponytail bouncing. She tried to tell herself that this was a good thing; meeting someone else would help her get over Luther faster, which she needed because she was already missing him something terrible. Part of her kicked herself for declining his offer to exchange contact information. Every inch of her wanted to hear his voice right then.

But she had to accept that their time was over. It was amazing and mind-blowing and life-altering, but it was over. And she had to find a way to move on. The sooner the better.

• • • •

LUTHER HAD NO SUCH desire to move on. He hadn't been able to get Liz out of his head since he walked out of her hotel room, and he hated that he didn't insist harder that they exchange some kind of contact information. He could have discreetly snuck his business card into her bag or something, but he'd told her and himself that he'd respect her wishes. It didn't matter, though, because they'd be seeing each other again.

He knew she didn't believe it and it wasn't lost on him how crazy it probably sounded. All they really knew about each other were their first names and some basic information like food preferences and countries they'd visited, and opinions on things that didn't matter much, as interesting as they might've been. She'd wanted to keep things light, but he suspected her efforts to not get attached to him were futile, given how dejected she looked before he left. And he'd been no more eager to leave her than she was for him to leave. Thinking of her woke up everything in him.

But he hadn't been lying when he said he was a romantic. And he just couldn't let himself believe that a connection as potent and soul-gripping as the one he'd shared with Liz was something that was here today, gone tomorrow. Even though he had no clue where in the world she was, he'd get his woman back. And in his heart, Liz was already his woman.

But he knew he'd have to go on about his business until they crossed paths again. He'd drive himself crazy if he didn't.

As good a time as he had in Belize, Luther was looking forward to getting home. He'd finally have a chance to enjoy his house that he bought a while back but hardly stayed in due to traveling so much, and looked forward to taking a couple more days to enjoy finally having everything unpacked and decorated like he wanted. The vacation was a treat to himself after months of moving headaches while running his business and training clients, and the last thing he had on his mind was meeting anyone. Meeting Liz turned out to be an extra special bonus.

When his rideshare from the airport pulled up to his house and he saw a familiar Audi in his driveway, Luther groaned. He really wasn't in the mood for company.

He thanked the driver before getting out and grabbing his bags, rolling his suitcase behind him and pausing at his unannounced visitor's driver side window, shaking his head. A voluptuous woman with sepia skin and long luxurious black hair grinned at him before pushing open the door and stepping out of the car, her blue wrap shirt accentuating her 40DD breasts.

"How was your trip?" she asked him.

"It was amazing. What are you doing here, Jules?"

"Geesh, what a greeting for your ex-wife. You aren't even a little glad to see me?"

"I might be if I'd had time to chill before you got here. *Oh*, and if I knew you were coming. You know I'm not a fan of the random visits."

"Okay, you're right," she acquiesced, holding up a hand. "I should've called first. Want me to come back?"

"You're here now." Luther continued to his front door and unlocked it, allowing Jules to precede him into the house. She looked around as he removed his fedora and went to stash his suitcase in his room.

"It is really nice in here, Luther," Jules observed, running a hand over his camel aniline leather couch. "I can't believe all the art you've accumulated over the years from all your traveling. And to think we only went to Miami for our honeymoon."

"Don't try that. That's where you *wanted* to go, Jules."

"Uh-huh. Just figures you'd get all fancy after we divorced."

"I was celebrating my freedom."

They shared a laugh before enveloping each other in a friendly hug. The two of them always teased each other like that, having transitioned to an easy friendship after their marriage ended several years earlier.

"So I know you didn't come by for no reason, so what's up?" Luther moved over to the bar and grabbed a bottle of sparkling water. "You want something?"

"No, I'm good. And I want to hear about your trip but I mostly came by to warn you about your daughter."

Luther groaned as he took a long swig. "What now?"

"She's talking about applying to *another* graduate program. And you know she's gonna come to you begging. I need you to not give in to her this time, Luther."

"You say that as if I'm some kind of pushover."

"You say that as if you're not."

"I'm *not*."

"When it comes to her, you can be. She's your only daughter and she's adorable, and when she turns on those big puppy dog eyes and starts whining '*daddyyyyy*' you turn to pure putty. And I know she stood you up *again* for your daddy-daughter brunch thing you two like to do before you left."

"You are really exaggerating. I absolutely know how to tell Churi 'no' when I need to. And as for her standing me up, I just tell myself she has a good reason so I don't get too affronted."

"Uh-huh. Another example of how you're a softie for her 'cause you wouldn't put up with that from anybody else. I'd surely have told her about herself, if it were me."

"I'm familiar with you."

"You need to tell her 'no' this time, about funding her graduate program. That girl is determined to stay in school just so she can avoid having to get a real job and take care of herself. And I've already told her not to bother asking me to foot her bills anymore. If she wants to keep getting degrees she's not gonna use, she can get a job at the same time, like I did."

"All right, I'll keep that in mind, if she even asks me. She might surprise us and find a way to take care of everything herself."

"Right. And this is my natural hair."

"Anyway," Luther couldn't help but chuckle.

"So, how was Belize?" Jules asked, dropping onto the couch and mindlessly twirling her ankle, her patent leather Nine West pumps reflecting the light. "I'm still mad that you went without me."

"It's still there. You can go tomorrow."

"Stop trying to be funny and tell me how the damn trip went."

"You're fun to mess with," Luther teased, sitting on the other end of the couch. "The trip was great, though. Beautiful weather, scenery, great cuisine. It was a much-needed wind-down from the hectic past few months I've had."

"I bet. I'm glad you got to go and rejuvenate. Meet anybody interesting?"

His mind immediately going to Liz, Luther couldn't help the smile that shot across his face. "I did, actually."

"Well, hot damn," Jules grinned, sitting forward slightly. "Who is she? What's her name?"

"Her name is Liz. And Jules, as soon as I saw her, it was like everything around us faded out. She became my focus and...I just *had* to meet her."

"Wow, Luther. Did you go over there and fall in love?"

Looking thoughtfully at some art on the far wall, Luther dragged his bottom lip between his teeth. "Crazy as it sounds, I feel like I did. We instantly connected and any plans I had after that disappeared. I wanted to stay by her side for as long as she wanted me there."

"And *did* she want you there? Was she feeling you as much as you were feeling her?"

"I believe she was. There was no playing coy or hard-to-get; we expressed our interest mutually. That's one of the things I loved about it; no ambiguity, no second-guessing. Everything was intentional. I just hated I only got a day and a half with her."

"Damn. So not only did you get to go off to Belize alone but you got sprung over somebody, too," Jules summarized good-naturedly. "I wish you could see the look in your eyes when you talk about this woman; you are smitten, my friend."

"I'm not denying it."

"So when are you gonna see her again?"

Luther's smile faded slightly. "Who knows."

"What?"

"I have no way of contacting her. Don't know where she lives. She didn't want to exchange contact information or last names. Hell, I had to take her word for it that Liz was even her real first name."

"I'm confused, Luther..."

"Our attraction was instant and mutual; I'd be willing to bet my house that nothing about her feelings towards me were anything but genuine. And it's because of that that she asked that we keep things light and not exchange any personal information; the less we knew about each other, the easier it would be to move on. And she was adamant about not being interested in anything long distance."

"I guess I can understand that but...I just hope to high heaven that you didn't get catfished. Wait, is it still catfishing if you actually met the person but is just unsure of who they really are? You didn't give her any money, did you? Did you check your wallet before you left?"

"Jules." Luther threw her an amused look. "All valid concerns, I admit, but she didn't steal anything from me. And I acknowledge that I could be wrong about all of this but I just have a gut feeling that everything she told me was sincere."

"You think she's one of those women who've been burned so many times that they're not trying to take a chance on love anymore, and let fear send them running every time they meet someone they're interested in? I can't *tell* you how many books I've read lately with that shit in it."

"Honestly, I don't think that's what it is. I think if we happened to meet while living in the same city, she wouldn't have those concerns. But she didn't want us to get all embedded into each other only to end up hundreds or thousands of miles apart, which I understand but it doesn't deter me like it did her."

"So you're going to try to find her, I take it?"

"I wish I could but no. I don't have much of anything to go on and my sleuthing skills are subpar, anyway. If we're meant to come together again, we will. And I believe we are. As for when?" He threw up a hand. "I have no way of knowing."

"You always were a big ol' romantic," Jules marveled. "Even back in college. I thought you were just putting on when we first got together with all the poems and grand gestures and talk about soul ties, but it turned out that's how you really are."

He hunched a shoulder. "Guilty."

"I know I teased you a lot for it but it really was one of the things I liked most about you. And I'm sure this Liz – *if* that's her real name – will be kicking herself for running scared as soon as she spends her first night back in an empty bed. Y'all could've at least had cyber sex."

"Jules...go home."

"You know I'm right." Jules stood from the couch and tossed her hair over her shoulder before planting her hands on her wide hips. "You should've 'accidentally' left one of your business cards in her room or something. I *bet* she would've been glad you did after the fact, despite what she said."

"I guess we'll never know."

"You were probably trying to be a damn gentleman and respect her wishes, weren't you? I'm not mad at it. I guess. Seriously, though, I hope you get what you want, Lu-Lu."

He winced as he stood to walk her out. "We've had this conversation. I do not love that nickname."

"I know."

· · · ·

THE NEXT DAY, LUTHER met up with his brother Carter at the gym for a training session. He wasn't exactly looking forward to it, as Carter tended to complain a lot even though he practically begged Luther to train him for the physique competition he signed up for, since Luther was a former champion bodybuilder himself.

"Do you torture all your clients like this?" Carter griped through gritted teeth as he did his last couple reps of shoulder presses.

Luther rolled his eyes. "Just the ones that pay me to."

"You'd think I'd get a little slack, being your little brother and all."

"I'm sorry. I thought you actually wanted to *win* the competition. You know, like I did. Multiple times."

"Yeah, yeah, I get it. You the man." Carter finished his set and plopped onto a nearby weight bench, sweat pouring down his brown face. He squeezed his eyes shut before blindly reaching for the towel hanging from his waistband to wipe the sweat out of them. "Who else you training today?"

"You're it. I told you, most of my time is going towards my hat business. I only train clients when I want to."

"I guess I should be flattered that you're making time for little ol' me then, huh?"

"You actually should. Come on, front raises next. Let's move."

"Drill sergeant," Carter muttered, pushing himself off the bench.

Luther shook his head but didn't comment as Carter went over and grabbed his weights. What Luther didn't bother to add was that brother or not, he wouldn't even bother training Carter if he wasn't getting paid.

The workout continued, with Carter doing his usual grumbling and Luther tuning him out when Carter suddenly remembered to ask about Luther's trip.

"It was cool; I enjoyed myself," Luther replied nonchalantly.

"That's it? You don't have anything more to say about it than that?"

Shrugging a shoulder, Luther kept his eyes on the message he was checking on his phone. "Not really."

There was no way Luther was going to confide in Carter the way he confided in Jules, especially about Liz. Carter would no doubt try to clown him for catching feelings for a woman he didn't know much about, not to mention his belief that he and Liz would eventually meet again. Then Luther would get pissed off, despite himself, and curse his brother out, and then they'd be at odds for however long until Luther felt like letting it go. He and Carter usually got along fine but they weren't terribly close. Partially because they were seventeen years apart in age, but mostly because Carter tended to be a little more immature than Luther's patience could tolerate. Carter was thirty-eight but still wanted to act like a college student at times.

"Hey, how's my niece?" Carter asked once they finished. He took a long swig from his water bottle before wiping his mouth with the back of his hand.

"Churi's fine. Still ticked at you for intimidating that boy you saw her out with that time. He never did call her back after that, she said."

"I make no apologies. I know a punk-ass when I see one."

"I'm not complaining. Knowing you've got her back as much as I do eases my mind some because Churi's discernment when it comes to guys is far from stellar."

"No doubt. Nobody's getting over on my niece if *I* can help it. Oh, I was thinking about going to check out that new cigar bar across town this weekend. I've heard it's supposed to be the spot. I bet there's all kinds of ass I haven't tapped yet in there."

Another reason Luther didn't love hanging with Carter; he fancied himself a player. It was yet another thing the brothers didn't have in common.

Not bothering to give admonishment that would just fall on deaf ears anyway, Luther just shrugged a shoulder and took his own sip of water. "Enjoy."

"You wanna go?"

"Ehh, I don't know. I'll probably make it over there eventually but I don't know if it'll be this weekend."

"You should hang with your little bro, man. We can be each other's wingmen. When is the last time you even had any?"

Luther had to fight to keep the smile off his face, remembering his amazing lovemaking with Liz in Belize. It was next to impossible to stop thinking about kissing her, touching her, sexing her. How she shivered when he took her nipples into his mouth. The sensual wind of her hips as she rode him. If he tried hard enough, he could still feel her nails digging into his back.

He could feel his body reacting to the memories and told himself to calm down; standing in the middle of the gym was one of the last places he wanted to get an erection.

"It's been recent enough," he finally answered, managing to keep his face even. "Go and have a good time; you don't need any help from me. I'm not trying to meet anybody right now, anyway."

"You found the Lord?"

"Shut up, Carter."

Luther had no interest in trolling for women. While he wasn't putting his life on hold waiting for another chance meeting with Liz, he also wasn't looking for a placeholder. He sincerely missed Liz, and going to bed at night and recalling their short time together was something he looked forward to. For the time being, he could be satisfied with that.

Chapter 3

• • • •

IT HAD BEEN A WEEK since her vacation and Liz had hoped that going back to work and falling back into the chaos that sometimes came with her job as creative director for a fashion brand would help take her mind off Luther, but no such luck. He was still on her mind as much as he'd been when he walked out of her hotel room before she left Belize.

Liz wasn't used to this at all. Her vacation flings were usually filed away in the 'fun but forgettable' portion of her mind right after they were over. Even when she was in actual relationships, once they were over, she moved on. There was none of this yearning and aching that she was experiencing over Luther. His hard body, his salt-and-pepper beard, his lips, he way he looked at her...all of it invaded her mind day in and day out.

But as good as the physical things were, it was deeper than that. Liz missed being around him, talking to him, his positive energy. He didn't feel like a stranger to her, even right after they met. She couldn't help but wonder what he was doing at any given moment, and if he had forgotten about her already, despite what he'd said.

"Ugh!" she grunted loudly, tossing the pen she'd been holding onto her desk and burying her face in her hands. "I am gonna drive myself crazy if I don't get a handle on this. I don't have time to be pining over this man."

She was supposed to be working on concepts for the showcase that was coming up in a few months. The theme was Corporate Diva, focusing on sexy funky workplace attire, and Liz was still looking for another element that would really make the designs pop. She and her team had been batting around ideas for a couple of weeks but nothing felt right so far. *That's* what she needed to be focused on, because this showcase was a big deal and she needed knock it out of the park.

It was late afternoon and Liz was just coming out of a meeting when her phone rang. She smiled with relief when she saw it was her friend Kinsley.

"Hey there," Liz greeted, going into her office and closing the door.

"Hey girl. Have you had lunch yet?"

"Of course not."

"Can you get away?"

Liz pulled up her calendar on the iPad she was carrying as she crossed over to her desk. "Dammit...I have an appointment in thirty minutes but if you can hold off until after that, I can meet you somewhere nearby. It would do me some good to get out for a minute."

"Girl, my stomach is growling *now*. All I had this morning was some cold pizza."

"Well, then I don't know what to tell you, Kinsley. Go on without me if you need to."

"No, no, I can wait. There's something I wanted to talk to you about and you know I'm too impatient to wait until later tonight or another day. I think I have a pack of fruit snacks in my purse somewhere. That should tide me over some."

Liz shook her head distractedly, an amused tilt to her lips as she read an email that had just come in. "I'll let you know when I'm done. You good with The Flying Biscuit that's down the street from here?"

"Yeah, that's fine."

By the time Liz headed to the restaurant to meet Kinsley, her stomach was growling, too. Kinsley stood and waved her over, and they shared a brief hug before Liz removed her jacket and slid into her side of the booth, ordering some fried green tomatoes and a tropical mimosa as soon as the server approached their table.

"You said you had something you wanted to talk to me about?" Liz asked once their server left.

"Oh yeah." Kinsley tucked some of her dyed fire engine red hair behind her ear. Liz knew she could never pull off that color but it looked great against Kinsley's toasted coconut brown skin. "You remember Orson?"

Liz frowned slightly. "The name sounds familiar. Remind me who that is?"

"Former fuck buddy."

"Oh. No wonder I didn't remember. You have so many of those."

"Ha ha. Anyway, I heard through the grapevine that he's getting married. *Married!* Can you believe that?"

"I feel like there's something I'm missing here..."

"He was running up behind me just a few months ago and now he's already about to run off and get hitched to somebody else. You don't see anything wrong with that?"

"Kinsley, so what? You didn't want the man, remember? I've known you for almost seven years and the whole time, you've insisted that you weren't trying to be locked down to anyone. Why do you even care?"

"Because..." Kinsley tapped her oval-shaped nails on the table. "I think it's about time I get serious and find my boo. You know, do the whole commitment thing. I've been getting some signs that it's time."

"What kind of signs?"

"Well, for starters, my former conquests all taking themselves off the market. The last couple times I tried to hit one of them up, he told me he had a girlfriend now. So many of the good men are getting snatched off the playing field."

"I see. Okay, what else?"

"You know how I used to never want to hear sappy songs or watch romantic movies, and how I'd roll my eyes at all those proposal posts on Instagram? I actually don't mind watching those now."

Liz told herself not to laugh. "Yeah?"

"The last guy I was with, I would've let him spend the night if he'd asked. Now you know that's usually a no-no for me."

"Right."

"And I've been feeling lonely. That's not something I've *ever* felt before now. I've always been fine by myself as long as I knew I had my file of men I could pull from when I needed to, but now that file is dwindling. Hell, it's damn near empty. And I don't want to end up out here by myself."

Liz nodded thoughtfully, her mind wandering to Luther again. "I suppose I can understand that. If I'm honest...I've had thoughts recently of settling down, myself."

"Really??" Kinsley screeched excitedly. "See, this is just another sign! We can help each other. You can help look for someone for me and I can be on the lookout for you, because we surely don't have the same taste in men. You're into those old dudes."

"Actually," Liz shook her head, "I met someone already."

"You did, dammit?? See how everyone is getting boo'd up but me??"

"Girl, calm down. I am not boo'd up with anybody. Luther is someone I met during my vacay in Belize and as crazy as it sounds...he has me open. We didn't even get much time together but I haven't been able to get him off my mind."

"Wow. You're feenin' for one of your vacation flings? That's not like you."

"I know. But this didn't feel like a fling at all. It felt like the real deal, but..." Liz heaved a long sigh. "I probably won't even see him again."

"Why not?"

"Because I made a big deal about not exchanging contact information. Figured we should make a clean break and leave what happened in Belize in Belize."

"Liz, girl, don't even sweat that. Just give me his last name and I'll track him down better than the FBI."

"Yeah...I didn't get his last name, either."

Kinsley reared. "What the hell, Liz?"

"I didn't want the temptation of looking him up and torturing myself. It made sense in my head at the time but now...I'm kinda regretting it. But there's nothing I can do about it now."

"So, what, you're just gonna forget about him?"

"That hasn't happened so far, despite my best efforts. But let him tell it, we're going to see each other again. Said the connection we had can't be wasted."

"He sounds kinda corny."

"Excuse me?" Liz frowned, sitting forward. "Don't go there, Kinsley. You don't know him like that to be calling him anything!"

"Damn, girl, my bad! I take it back, then. You must *really* be into this man 'cause you were straight ready to buck."

Liz told herself to calm down as she snatched her glass of water and took a sip. She was surprised that just happened. Liz had always been quick to defend people she loved, but Luther certainly didn't fall into that category. She cared for him, even had feelings for him. But that's as far as it went.

At least, that's what she was forcing herself to believe. Because falling in love that quickly...it just couldn't have happened. Not to her.

"Sorry," she muttered.

Kinsley eyed her for a moment before waving a hand. "Don't even sweat it, girl. You were standing up for your man. I get it."

"He's not my man." *Never mind that I want him to be.*

"Well, whatever. We can still be here for each other. You know I get kinda bitchy when I'm going through man-withdrawal. And I can give an encouraging word when you're kicking yourself over not giving vacation bae your number."

"Hmph. *You're* gonna give an encouraging word?"

"I can do that!"

The server brought their appetizer and drinks, and Liz steered the conversation to other things. She needed to take her mind off of Luther because pining over a man that she couldn't have was for the birds.

She managed to keep thoughts of him at bay as she went back to work for the rest of the day. In no hurry to go home and fight off thoughts of Luther yet again, she headed to Natavey, the cigar bar and lounge her brother-in-law Roland co-owned with his brother E.J. She hoped her friend and E.J.'s wife Natalia was there, fulfilling her managerial duties.

"Hey, Liz," the hostess Elaine greeted when she walked in. "How've you been? Haven't seen you around here in a little while."

"Hey, Elaine. Yeah, I was on vacation and then I dove right back into work. Is there room at the bar? I figure all the tables are probably full."

"Most of them, yeah. And the ones that aren't are reserved."

"As usual."

"But you can totally hang out at the bar. You look like you could use a drink."

"You don't know the half of it."

Elaine chuckled. "Say no more. Follow me."

"Is Natalia around?" Liz asked as she followed, absently glancing around at the décor that featured plenty of exposed brick, white oak accents and round tables, and linen draperies. The lighting was slightly muted, lending to an intimate atmosphere.

"Yeah, she's around here somewhere."

Relieved, Liz thanked Elaine as she perched herself onto one of the soft leather high-back bar stools, placing her Verano Hill clutch in her lap. The bartender came over and placed a napkin down in front of her, and Liz quickly ordered a French 75. She already felt more at ease thanks to the lighting, the jazzy saxophone music, and the grown-and-sexy vibes that permeated everything. Natavey had become one of Liz's favorite places to hang out since it opened. She loved a good cigar, but she mostly just enjoyed the vibes. And most of the time, she could just hang out, drink, enjoy the excellent menu they offered, and chill without anybody bothering her.

"Hey girl, I didn't know you were coming by here tonight."

Liz turned to see Natalia Bell standing behind her. Smiling, Liz slid off the bar stool and they shared a tight hug for a few moments before stepping back.

"Yeah, I wasn't quite ready to go home yet," Liz admitted. "I see it's jumping in here, as usual."

"Never a dull moment. Is Joel taking care of you?" Natalia asked, referring to the bartender.

Just then, Joel placed Liz's drink down in front of Liz, who chuckled as she picked it up. "It's almost like y'all planned that."

"Girl, I wish we were that smooth."

"I'm glad things are going so well because y'all can never close. This place has become my refuge."

"It would likely take an act of God to make E.J. and Roland shut the doors on this place. The waiting list for lounge membership is a mile long, and since we were featured on that local lifestyle show, the bar and restaurant portion stay busy pretty much from open to close."

Natavey was larger than the Bell brothers' other establishments, Barfly and 845. The cigar bar and lounge were members-only, and there was an intimate restaurant and bar for the general public. It was upscale, but still homey and comfortable enough to not feel stuffy or the need to put on airs. Liz actually had a membership to the lounge, but she was fine in the general area this time. She and Natalia chatted briefly about Liz's vacation (with no mention of Luther), their respective busy days, and Natalia and E.J.'s six-month-old daughter Aria, who Natalia admitted she couldn't wait to go get from her mother's, who was babysitting her.

"You having dinner?" Natalia asked as she rounded the bar, brushing her customary brow-skimming bangs from her eyes.

"Yeah, I should eat. Might just get some appetizers, though."

"You should try the lobster wontons," Natalia suggested, handing Liz a narrow laminated menu. "That's a new item on there and it is toe-curling."

"Not toe-curling," Liz laughed, reading the brief menu description of the suggested dish along with the other offered ones. She shook her head, knowing she was about to have trouble narrowing it down. "All of these look *so* good. I swear, it's like everything E.J. and Roland touch turns to gold."

"I'd like to think I had a little something to do with this particular goldmine."

Liz looked to her left to see Carlton Barber standing there. He was a billionaire who E.J. and Roland had partnered with to open Natavey after they turned down his initial offer to buy their businesses. The Bell brothers were the majority owners, while Carlton made it possible for them to have the best of everything, from location to furnishings to food, alcohol, and cigar menu items. Between his name and connections, and the stellar reputation that the Bell brothers already had, the place was a hit before it even opened.

"Have we met?" Carlton asked Liz, offering his hand. "You look familiar. I'm Carlton Barber."

Liz placed her hand in his, mildly surprised at just how soft it was. He clearly hadn't done much manual labor. "We haven't officially met, no. Liz Tate, Roland's sister-in-law."

"Oh, right, yeah. I've seen you around here several times, and over at Barfly."

"What can I say? I go where the good drinks are."

Carlton chuckled. "Well, you're definitely in the right place here. Mind if I sit?"

Liz hid her surprise as she lightly hunched a shoulder in silent approval. Natalia subtly rolled her eyes as she excused herself to go check on some things, and Joel had a Godfather placed in front of Carlton by the time he was on the bar stool.

"So since you've been coming here pretty frequently, I can surmise that you think we did a good job with everything?" Carlton asked, eying her as he sipped his drink.

"You really did. And clearly I'm not the only one who thinks so, with how this place stays full."

"It's still rather early but I'm confident that we can keep the momentum going. I'll admit I wasn't thrilled when E.J. and Roland wouldn't sell me their other clubs but partnering was a good compromise."

"Not used to being told 'no', I take it?"

Carlton smiled, and Liz briefly wondered just how old he was. She knew he was near his fifties but he must've had an amazing esthetician because his brown skin was smooth and looked as baby-soft as his hands. She wondered if his lack of facial hair was by choice or circumstance.

"I'm definitely known to get what I want," he admitted, his brown eyes sweeping over her before motioning to Joel, who hurried over. "Bring her whatever she wants, on the house."

"Yes, sir."

Liz immediately shook her head. "Oh, that's really not nece-"

"It's done," Carlton declared, considering the matter closed. "So Liz Tate, what do you do?"

"I'm a Creative Director for Azon."

"Makes sense. You're always so stylishly dressed whenever I see you."

"I've always loved clothes. And I do like to look good. I'll admit I'm one of those that puts on makeup to go grocery shopping."

Carlton laughed. "Hey, if it makes you feel good to do that, nothing wrong with it. The rest of us just get to benefit from your efforts."

No he is not sitting here flirting with me, Liz thought as she took a sip of her drink to hide her smirk. Carlton

Barber was cute, but *cute* wasn't her type. She liked grown man sexiness.

Like a certain bow-legged stack of muscles with a salt-and-pepper beard that she still couldn't get out of her head.

Still, she indulged Carlton in conversation as she ate, finding that he was actually pretty cool to talk to, mild flirting aside. Considering his status, he was quite relatable and down-to-earth. Liz didn't reciprocate or acknowledge his flirtatious comments, though, as she wasn't even marginally interested in him romantically. Aside from him just not being her type physically, the main thing Carlton had going against him was that he wasn't Luther. A large part of Liz hated that, because she couldn't put herself on a leash forever. Especially for a man she'd probably never see again. As much as she would've liked to, she didn't share Luther's optimism that their paths would cross at some point; the odds of that happening were slim to none. At some point, she was going to have to find a way to get that man out of her head.

Liz hung out at Natavey for another hour or so before finally dragging herself home. She entered her loft, kicking her heels off at the door and dropping her things onto the nearest surface, unbuttoning her blouse as she headed back to her bedroom. She changed into a sports bra and shorts and did a few rounds of squats, lunges, push-ups, and crunches before taking a hot shower. She sagged against the blue subway tiles, the long day finally catching up to her. Her mind automatically went to the shower she and Luther shared the morning she was leaving Belize, and her body instantly reacted to the memory. She groaned, unable to resist touching herself. The water pelted her, her head falling back against the shower wall as she planted herself in the corner, her hips winding against one hand while the other fondled her beaded nipples before she turned and rubbed them against the tile grooves, the sensation stoking her arousal. The closer she got to orgasm, the more vividly she could see Luther. Pretty soon she could almost hear his voice in her ear.

Yeah, let me know you're feeling this...

"Yes..." she whispered, her hand moving faster. Her eyes were squeezed shut and her brow was furrowed in desperate concentration, locked in on the image in her mind. She flattened her back to the wall again before sliding down and opening her long legs wider, her moans getting louder and her urgency increasing.

"Luther!"

When the orgasm hit, she screamed loud enough for people outside to hear, tingles running over her body at breakneck speed. She momentarily seized before sagging against the wall, spent.

"Dammit," she whispered, already kicking herself. Getting herself off while thinking of him wasn't going to help her get over him any faster.

It wasn't until the water started cooling off that she snapped out of her momentary trance and quickly pushed herself off the floor to turn the water off. Swiping a hand down her face, she got out of the shower and proceeded to get ready for bed, still reeling physically and mentally from her shower masturbation session.

"Wanting something I can't have is ridiculous," she muttered as she climbed into her plush queen-sized bed. She flopped onto her back and looked up at the ceiling. "Lord, please help me snap out of this. By tomorrow would be nice."

Chapter 4

• • • •

LIZ FELT LIKE HER SUCCINCT prayer had been answered when she started to feel back to her old self a couple of days later. The yearning and dejection from missing Luther had lifted, no longer weighing her down and leaving her with a little more spring in her step. That realization came with a ton of relief. Maybe she had finally gotten past the hard part.

Of course she hadn't forgotten him, and she figured she probably wouldn't. They really had shared a connection she hadn't experienced with anyone else, and their time together would probably stay locked in the fond memory section of her mind. But pining over him was pointless, and would only drive her crazy. There was no telling where he was, what he was doing, or who he was doing it with. For all she knew, he'd met someone else already and was moving on. She needed to do the same.

Her sister Lovey had wasted no time setting Liz up with someone, and had arranged the blind date for that weekend. But with Liz feeling better about things, she called Lovey to cancel.

"What? Why?" Lovey asked.

"Because I admit I was having a moment when I agreed to let you set me up but I'm over it now. My life is fine the way it is."

"So all the things that you said about wanting to settle down is out the window now? You're not usually prone to having random vulnerable moments; that's *my* area. What aren't you telling me, Liz?"

Liz remembered that Lovey still didn't know about Luther. She wanted to confide in her sister, but Lovey would flip out if Liz admitted to her feelings for him, declaring him and Liz to be destined soul mates and making a bigger deal out of everything than Liz had the energy for. Lovey was a huge romantic, too, and Liz didn't put it past her to bug her day in and day out about how she was going to go about finding her man.

"I've just had a change of heart, is all," Liz finally replied. "And I don't want to waste anyone's time."

"So now you're back to the meaningless flings, I guess."

"Damn, Lovey, you don't have to say it like that. I *do* have actual relationships with men. Just because my end goal doesn't happen to be marriage doesn't mean the relationships don't mean anything to me."

Lovey was quiet for a moment. "I'm sorry; I didn't mean it that way."

"I know." Liz sighed. "And I didn't mean to bite your head off about it. I'm just saying that I don't put a lot of pressure on my relationships; it's about fun and companionship for me, and whatever grows from that, so be it. But I certainly don't need a man to be happy."

"Of course not, but there's nothing wrong with having someone to spend time with. Ross is a really nice guy; handsome, funny, respectful. I think you two would really hit it off. There's no pressure for it to become anything that you don't want it to be."

Liz considered her sister's words. Going out with someone new couldn't hurt. And she knew that Lovey wouldn't set her up with just anyone. It might be nice to have someone on deck in case her newfound epiphany turned out to be temporary.

"All right, fine. I'll go and meet...what's his name, again? Rod?"

"It's Ross. Ross Westbrook. I swear, Liz, you're going to like him. And he's certainly looking forward to meeting you."

"Well, that's nice to know."

"So I need you to go there receptive and with an open mind. Be nice."

"I'm always nice."

"Liz, I love you dearly, but no you're not."

"True."

• • • •

LIZ STEPPED BACK FROM the dress form with a frown. The pinstripe halter dress was amazing, and the shoes that were chosen to go with it were to die for, but there was still something missing. Liz had tried different scarves, belts, and other accessories, trying to figure out what it was that would put this outfit over the top. Nothing seemed right and it irritated her.

"This isn't working," she muttered, yanking the scarf from the dress form. Mindlessly tossing it over her shoulder, she slowly circled the outfit, her mind whirling. Her assistants skittered in and out with suggestions, but Liz dismissed them all. She'd know the right finisher when she saw it, and she hadn't seen it yet.

"I want something *different*," she emphasized. "Something hip and funky and unexpected. All of these looks are missing that *umph* that will set them apart. And this showcase is too big a deal to settle on something I'm not feeling, so keep looking. We're not going to do this until it's right."

Tabling it for the time being, Liz went on to work on some other things, namely responding to the slew of emails in her inbox. She was just sitting down to her glass-topped wood desk when her cell phone buzzed, and her eyebrows lifted when she saw it was Ross, the guy Lovey set her up with. Lovey had insisted on them having each other's number so they could communicate before their date, and have a way to contact each other should something come up.

"Hello?" Liz answered the call, sitting in her yellow desk chair.

"Hey, Liz? This is Ross Westbrook."

"Ross, how's it going? It's nice to put a voice with the name."

"Same. I'm sorry to call in the middle of the day like this but Lovey has talked you up to me so much that I couldn't ignore my curiosity anymore. Your sister thinks extremely highly of you, if you weren't aware."

"It's definitely mutual. Lovey is the best sister a girl could have," Liz smiled, touched. "How do you two know each other?"

"I'm a former client of hers. She did my taxes and kept my business expenses in line for years. I was moved to another CPA when she got promoted, which I didn't love but I was absolutely happy for her. We chat it up whenever we run into each other there."

"Nice. And you're single? Like a hundred percent, no lurking exes or women that you're still legally bound to?"

Ross chuckled. "A hundred percent. I've never been married and I'm not in contact with any of my exes. I date on occasion but you don't have to worry about any drama with me on that front. What about you? Are there any men in the background that Lovey wasn't aware of?"

Liz thought of Luther, then pushed the thought from her mind. That was over. "Nope. I'm as single and available as they come. I know Lovey wouldn't have set us up if she thought you weren't a straight-up guy but I had to be sure, so I hope you don't mind my questions."

"Not at all. I know you can never be too sure nowadays. Feel free to ask me whatever you want."

"I hope you mean that because I will."

"Yeah, Lovey was definitely right about you," Ross chuckled. "She said you can be straightforward."

"Not everybody loves that."

"Doesn't bother me. I can appreciate a woman who doesn't beat around the bush and puts it on out there. I'm looking forward to our date even more now."

Liz couldn't resist smiling at that. "I'm looking forward to meeting you, too."

And she was. The more she chatted with Ross, the more she liked him. He seemed chill and easygoing, and had a good sense of humor. She was even more curious to see how they clicked when they finally met in person, and she hoped that they hit it off well enough to keep her attention beyond one night.

They talked for a few more minutes before Liz ended the call, needing to get back to work. She'd been a little wary still about going on a blind date but after speaking to Ross, she dared to feel optimistic. And when he sent her a picture of himself just so she could see what he looked like, her brow quirked with intrigue. He was definitely handsome, with his thick soft-looking curly hair with fresh tapered edges, maple brown skin, and lips that surely drew plenty of attention. He was bordering on 'pretty boy' with his long lashes and super-neat facial hair, but Liz was more turned on than off. And the way his chin was tilted upwards and his lips were curled in a cocky smirk was slightly endearing.

Thoughts of Ross faded out as the day went on, though, since a few other things like delayed deliveries, last-minute campaign changes, and a missing pair of $500 shoes occupied Liz's attention. By the time she was ready to call it a day, all she cared about was getting home, kicking her shoes off, and gorging on the leftover spinach lasagna in her fridge. She was tempted to go by Natavey, but decided she didn't have the energy for people anymore that day. She just needed to clear her mind, and hope that her newfound breakthrough from her longing for Luther held another day.

• • • •

LUTHER WAS IN HIS WORK space, working on his latest hat design. He'd been at it for hours, churning out sketches. It had become his happy place since he decided to hang up the bodybuilding, and in between training clients.

That had been his main thing for years, with several prominent or celebrity clients that were more than willing to pay him top dollar to whip them into shape, even flying him out to wherever they were for their own convenience. He loved it because he got to travel on someone else's dime and also keep himself in shape, and while he still enjoyed it, he'd started feeling the urge to venture into something new. He had always loved hats, donning them with almost every outfit, and took a hattery class to see if he would enjoy making them as much as he did wearing them. He fell in love with it instantly, and continued to practice and work on the craft. When he got good enough to start sporting his own designs, people constantly asked him where he got them, and he started an online shop, where it didn't take long for most of the inventory he'd accumulated to be snatched up. He occasionally sold hats to local boutiques or at craft fairs or flea markets, and it still floored him whenever someone showed eagerness or excitement over his creations.

He had just stood up to stretch when his phone rang. The groan was automatic when he saw it was Carter calling. It took him a minute to decide whether he was in the mood to deal with his brother or not, but decided to go ahead and answer it. Carter would just keep calling if he didn't.

"What's up?" Luther greeted.

"Hey, man. You busy tonight?"

"Depends on why you're asking."

"I have a date with this broad and she doesn't want to leave her friend by herself, and asked if I had someone I could bring along for her."

"Well, I hope you find somebody 'cause I'm not it."

"Come on..."

"Carter, I am not interested in going on a double date with you and some random women. Not to mention, I hate being around when you're trying to lure some woman into your bed; you become almost like a different person that I can't say I like very much. And I'm sure whoever this young lady is would think I'm too old for her, anyway."

"I bet she wouldn't. You might be fifty-five but you don't look it. And I told you, you'd look even younger if you just colored that gray out of your beard."

"I'm not doing that. I don't need to look younger."

"Even so, she's not gonna care how old you are once she gets a look at you. You're all tall and jacked and bow-legged and women love that shit."

"Yeah, well. Be that as it may-"

"It's not like we're gonna be out all night. Come on, this broad- I mean, woman – won't go unless her friend can, and she's not trying to be a third wheel. I'd *really* appreciate it if you helped me out on this, bro."

Luther glanced at the sketches he'd been working on and sighed. He'd planned on getting another couple of hours in on that before winding down with a movie and a glass of cognac. The last thing he felt like doing was forcing small talk with a woman he wasn't interested in while his brother tried to run game on someone, but he figured it wouldn't kill him. Maybe a night out would save him from sitting around pining over Liz, who he still missed and thought about daily. He hadn't let go of his belief that they would see each other again, but he knew life had to go on in the meantime. He was willing to bet Liz wasn't sitting around moping over him, especially since she thought their time in Belize was just a fleeting vacation romance. She was probably already dating; he could imagine that she got her fair share of attention given how feisty and sexy and intelligent she was. Luther didn't love the thought of her with another man but knew that it would be foolish and unrealistic to expect otherwise. He could only hope that no one else snatched her up permanently by the time they were reunited.

"All right, fine," he finally relented with another sigh. "Two hours, tops. And you're paying."

"Bet. I appreciate it, bro. And I know you're probably already dreading this but you might just end up having a good time. You never know."

"I guess."

Carter gave him the time and location details before ending the call, saying he was about to get a haircut. Luther ran a hand over his wavy dark hair and figured he could use a cut, too, and glanced at his watch to see if he had time to go by the barbershop. It might not have been a real date to him but that didn't mean he was going to go out looking any kind of way.

And as silly as he knew it was, he always wanted to stay on point for when he ran into Liz again.

Chapter 5

• • • •

LIZ TURNED IN FRONT of her full-length mirror, perusing how she looked in her teal bodycon dress that had cutouts at the waist and stopped just below her knees. It was the night of her date with Ross and she was more than a little nervous, which didn't typically happen. Liz usually looked forward to first dates and the possibilities that came with them, but they never made her as anxious as she was for this one. She knew it was because of the pressure she'd unconsciously put on it to be a hurdle over her lingering feelings for Luther. She'd managed to somewhat maintain her mindset that she was over him (or at least, over him enough), though there were a couple of times that she caught herself fantasizing about him when she was working or cooking or doing something else. She and Ross had spoken a couple more times since the day he first called her at work, and she hoped they hit it off as well in person as they had over the phone.

She was putting the finishing touches on her makeup when Kinsley called.

"What's up, girl?" Liz greeted, rummaging around for her mascara.

"Men suck."

"Uh-oh. What happened?"

"I went on this date the other night, right? *Complete* waste of time."

"What was wrong with it?"

"The guy, Trae, was nice enough. I'll even admit he was fine as hell. But we just didn't hit it off. I went home horny and frustrated."

"Damn. Where'd you meet him?"

"It was kind of a hook-up, I guess. I let my cousin talk me into it. He didn't seem all that interested in me, either, I might as well admit. At least I got a free meal out of it."

"It's just one date of many. I'm sure you'll meet someone else that's better suited for you."

"I hope you're right 'cause my find-a-boo mission isn't going well at all, so far. What you doing?"

"Getting ready to meet up with that guy Lovey set me up with."

"Oh that's tonight? Well, I hope your date goes better than mine. Make sure you wear a push-up bra; have those titties sitting right in his face. No need in *both* of us being horny and frustrated."

Laughing, Liz capped the top on her mascara tube and tossed it back into her makeup caddy. "Girl, I am not looking to sleep this man tonight."

"Oh, so you wouldn't if both of you were down?"

"I...well, I won't act like I've never done that. But I'm just hoping to have a nice time; I'm not looking for sex."

"Hell, you can do both. If y'all hit it off like that, I say get all the dick you can. You've seen him already, right?"

"Yeah. He's definitely easy on the eyes. But we both know it takes more than that."

"You know I know, especially after my last date. You need me to be on standby for an escape call?"

"No need. If I'm not feeling it, I'll just leave. Won't waste time with a ploy."

"Yeah, I can absolutely picture you leaving some man in the middle of a restaurant or wherever 'cause you're over it. Classic Liz. All right, well let me know how it goes. I'll be over here watching *P-Valley* and ordering Chinese food. Might even break into these weed brownies."

"Don't hurt yourself. Talk to you later."

"Bye, girl."

Liz gave herself a final once-over before grabbing her things and heading out. Ross had suggested they meet at Polaris, and she hoped that he hadn't chosen that in an effort to impress her. Liz liked for her men to have money but she had plenty of her own, too; flaunting usually had the adverse affect on her than men hoped it would.

But, she told herself to give him the benefit of the doubt. It was totally possible that he just liked the restaurant and that was it.

Ross was standing near the entrance when she arrived, and he was just as handsome in person as he was on his picture. He smiled as she approached, eying her appreciatively.

"Damn, just like I figured," he greeted, taking her hands in his and leaning in to kiss her cheek. "Even hotter in person."

Liz smiled, looking at him. He must've been just a couple of inches taller than her because she was almost eye-level to him in heels. Not ideal but not a deal-breaker. "I appreciate the compliment. You're not so bad, yourself. Have you been waiting long?"

"No, I just got here a few minutes ago. I made a reservation so we can go on in, if you're ready."

"Yep, let's go."

He held the door open for her and she stepped inside, her stomach immediately growling at the delicious aromas. They were shown to a table near the window and Ross held her chair for her before taking his seat across the table. After taking a minute to place their drink orders, they turned their attention to each other.

"You have a good day?" he asked her.

"Yeah, it was productive. Busy, as usual. I'm preparing for this showcase in a few months and it's a ton of stuff to get together. What about you? You're a literary agent, right?"

"That's my main thing. I also own a few dry cleaners; my sisters run them. We're getting ready to open a laundry mat in the next few months. Do you like to read?"

"Um, not really, no."

"Oh. I was gonna tell you about the book I was working on in my down time. It's my pet project that I'm not even sure I'll do anything with but it's a form of stress release."

"You can tell me about it, if you want."

Ross proceeded to talk about his Black spy thriller novel and Liz tried to stay interested. They ordered their meals and the conversation continued, and Liz's hopes for Ross being a match for her dwindled with every passing minute. It wasn't that he was boring or a bad guy, but there was no spark; they might as well have been cousins or platonic buddies, with the lack of romantic chemistry they had.

"I know you mentioned you've never been married; is that by choice?" Ross asked her as he cut into his pork chop.

"I guess you could say that," Liz shrugged. "I've never really worried about getting married. If I happen to fall in love with someone enough to want to go there, great. But I'll be perfectly fine if it doesn't happen."

"Hmm. I guess it's good that you're not pressed about it. You've never even been engaged or anything?"

"Nope. Have you?"

"Briefly. We both realized we were rushing into it and called it off, though. But I definitely want to get married one day; get a house in the country, have a few kids, all that."

"Oh." Liz's chewing slowed, disappointed. If she hadn't been sure about the low possibility of them lasting beyond that night, she was now.

Ross noticed her sudden change in demeanor. "What's the matter?"

"Ross..." Liz put down her fork. "I respect that that's what you want. But I might as well let you know that I don't want to have kids. Being a mother has never been a desire of mine and that's not going to change, so if that's a must for you, then we're just not a good match."

She could see the shift in Ross's eyes, though he managed to keep his expression neutral. Liz was used to the various reactions she got when she told men she didn't want children; some respected it, but others started treating her differently, if they didn't just break up with her altogether. One guy even cursed her out for wasting his time, calling her a selfish heartless bitch. Liz started making sure men knew her stance before things got too deep after that, hoping to avoid the drama.

"That's cool, I respect that," Ross croaked before clearing his throat, the enthusiasm gone from his voice. He gulped down half of his Jameson. "So how 'bout this weather we've been having lately, huh?"

Yeah, this is a wrap, Liz thought. *He's talking about the gotdamn weather.*

They continued to make strained small talk until Ross suddenly remembered somewhere he had to be and asked if she minded if they ended their night early. By then she was over it herself so she readily agreed. He paid the bill, walked her outside, gave her the lightest hug imaginable, then politely waited with her in silence as the valet brought her car around before turning and requesting his. Liz knew she wouldn't be hearing from him again.

"Oh well," she sighed, pulling away from the restaurant. It wasn't like it was the first time.

She was down the street when she pulled into the first available parking lot and grabbed her phone. She texted Kinsley to meet her over at Natavey, and once she got a surprisingly quick confirmation that Kinsley would be there in twenty minutes, Liz headed out.

· · · ·

"SO YOU SENT THE MAN running, huh?"

Liz shook her head. She and Kinsley were in the members-only lounge at Natavey, since Liz wanted a little more privacy as she recalled her lousy date.

"I wouldn't say all that," she replied, taking a sip of her Malbec. "We just weren't compatible."

"Did you feel like you might be compatible before the kid thing came up?"

"Not really. He was nice and I didn't hate his company but it just felt like dinner with an associate more than a date. You know how you get those tingles when you're around someone you're crushing on? There was none of that. We barely flirted with each other at all. I could've seen us hanging out platonically but I doubt he even wants to do that now."

"Damn." Kinsley tucked some hair behind her ear before taking a pull from her Padron cigar. "I'm just curious; why is it that you don't want kids, again?"

"I just don't. There's no real reason other than that."

"Don't like them? Love your freedom too much? Don't want the responsibility?"

"I love kids; I have a niece and two nephews that I'm crazy about. And I'm always cuddling up on my friends' kids. I've just never wanted to be a mother myself. Being the fun and fly auntie is more than enough for me."

"I still think you'll change your mind if you met the right man."

"Kinsley, not everybody wants children and there's nothing wrong with that. It's not about what man I'm with. Plus, girl, I just turned forty; I damn sure wouldn't want to start all that at this point in my life, anyway."

Just then, E.J. Bell entered the lounge. A couple of the other women in the room took notice, which usually happened whenever he came around. Liz would never admit it out loud but E.J. was gorgeous, with his dark brown skin, chiseled facial features, goatee, and muscles for days. Both him and Roland always drew plenty of attention because of their good looks, but they were both unrelentingly committed to their wives and never paid it any attention. And any woman that was bold enough to try any advances on them was immediately informed they didn't have a chance in hell.

When he spotted Liz, E.J. smiled and headed over. Kinsley grunted under her breath as she slowly blew cigar smoke through her brick red lips, eying his approach with an arched brow. "Umph. That man is *too* fine."

"Down, girl," Liz muttered amusingly. "That's Natalia's husband and she's not above snatching roots over her man."

"Some people get all the luck."

E.J. stood in between their butter-soft leather armchairs. "Good evening, ladies. How's everything going?"

"Just fine," Liz smiled up at him. "I'm recovering from a bad date and I brought my friend here to help me drown my sorrows. I'm not sure if you two have met or not; this is my girl Kinsley Butler. Kinsley, the illustrious E.J. Bell."

"Stop," E.J. chuckled as he shook his head, offering his hand to Kinsley. "It's nice to meet you."

"The pleasure is all mine, Mr. Bell," Kinsley replied with extra huskiness, eagerly placing her hand in his. Liz rolled her eyes.

"I'm surprised to see you roaming around in here; you're usually behind the scenes," Liz said to E.J. as he gently extracted his hand from Kinsley's grip.

"Yeah, I just swung by to see Natalia for a minute and check on a couple other things. I've gotta go pick up the baby. It's funny I'm running into you, though."

"Yeah? Why's that?"

"It appears you've made quite the impression on Carlton Barber. He's mentioned your name a few times recently."

"Really?" Liz wasn't expecting that at all. She barely even thought about the short time she and Carlton spent together. "Well, that's flattering, I guess."

"Wait, Carlton Barber, for real??" Kinsley exclaimed, jutting forward in her seat. "Liz, you've been holding out on me, girl!"

"Please," Liz waved a dismissive hand. "There's nothing to tell. He sat with me while I had a drink at the bar the other night, that's all."

"Yeah, well, don't be surprised if he tries to shoot his shot with you," E.J. commented. "I already had to tell him once to not bother trying to pump me for information or ask me to hook y'all up. You must have him pretty intrigued."

"Hmph. I doubt that."

"I'm telling you. Well, I've gotta run; you ladies enjoy the rest of your evening."

"Bye, E.J."

"Adieu, Mr. Bell." Kinsley looked after him longingly as he strolled off, even getting on her knees in the chair and turning all the way around until he was out of sight. Liz just shot her a look. "What?"

"I'm telling you, you're wasting your time with the flirting," Liz reminded. "E.J. only has eyes for Natalia. And don't get any ideas when you see his brother, either, because then you'd be trying to mess with my sister's man and I'd have to hurt you."

"Ugh," Kinsley plunked back into her seat. "I swear, sometimes it seems like all the fine men with money are taken. Then you're sitting over there with a fucking *billionaire* sniffing after you..."

"He is not sniffing after me."

"Well, unless the fine-ass Mr. Bell was lying just now, he is. Why are you trying to act like you're not interested?"

"Because I'm not."

"How could you *not* be?? Your standards must be sky-high. Look, if you don't want him, put in a good word for me."

"Kinsley, girl, would you even be interested in him if he weren't a billionaire? Do you find him attractive at all?"

"I don't find him *un*attractive. And I know you're not trying to say I'm some kind of gold digger."

"Whatever. Feel free to go for it 'cause I'm certainly not interested. He's a nice guy but I just don't look at him like that."

"I'd love to see the man that *does* make you look at him like that 'cause I'm starting to think he just doesn't exist."

Liz just drained the rest of her glass, wanting to order another but remembering that she still had to drive home. She was leaning forward to put her glass down on the cherry wood table in front of them when she happened to look up and felt like her heart stopped.

"Liz, girl, what's wrong?" Kinsley asked, looking at her friend with concern before whipping her head around to try to see what had her so suddenly stricken. "You look like you've seen a ghost or something."

Liz felt like she *was* seeing a ghost. Because that would be the only way to explain how she was staring at a man who looked *just* like Luther.

Chapter 6

• • • •

"THERE'S *no* way..."

Just then, the man turned and every part of Liz's body woke up. She pressed a hand to her chest, feeling her heart beat a mile a minute.

Then he noticed her. He froze momentarily, his face registering the same pure shock that Liz's was. He took a step in her direction and stopped, almost as if he couldn't believe what he was seeing, himself.

Their eyes were locked on each other's still when Kinsley shot out of her seat, pointing a finger. "That's Trae!"

Finally snapping out of it, Liz blinked rapidly before turning her attention to Kinsley. "Wh-what?"

"The guy I went out with. This is him!"

Having heard that, Luther swiftly made his way over to them. He could see the frown slowly forming on Liz's face and Kinsley was already glaring at him like a scorned ex.

"Liz..." He kept his eyes on her. "My mind is blown that I'm standing here in front of you right now. I have a million questions and I'm *aching* to hug you but I want to clear up what you just heard first."

"Yeah, let's do that," Liz agreed, standing and folding her arms. "Because *I* thought your name was Luther."

"My name *is* Luther. Luther Trae Monroe. I can show you my I.D. if you don't believe me."

Liz's frown cleared slightly. "So which name is it that you go by?"

"I go by Luther." He turned to Kinsley. "I only introduced myself as Trae on the date because, no offense, I didn't really want to be there. My brother hounded me into going along because he said your girl would only go if there was someone there for you, too."

"Wait, it was a double date?" Liz held up a hand. "He was basically just there to keep you company? You didn't tell me that part, Kinsley."

"What does it matter? He still lied. I don't care if Trae *is* your actual middle name; you were still basically pretending to be somebody else." Kinsley glared at Luther, her hands on her hips. "Look at all this you missed out on. We could've had it all..."

Luther just looked at her before turning his eyes to Liz. When they broke out in simultaneous laughter, Kinsley's jaw and her hands dropped.

"What the hell is so funny, dammit??"

Liz tried to compose herself. "Kinsley, you're tripping right now."

"I am not! And how do you two even know each other??"

"Believe it or not, this is the Luther I told you about; that I met in Belize." Liz returned her attention to Luther, who was already gazing at her. Her legs started to feel like jelly again. "But I never expected to see him again so I'm wondering if I'm about to wake up at any second."

"Me, too," Luther admitted. His head shook slightly in wonderment as he bit his bottom lip. "If it *is* a dream, I really hope I just stay asleep forever so I won't have to lose you again."

Liz released a shaky breath, feeling like she was going to melt where she stood. His words still had the ability to ignite her just as well as his hands did. And now that she was thinking about his hands touching her, she began aching for it.

"So you two are just gonna stand here gazing into each other's eyes like it's some kind of Hallmark movie, huh?" Kinsley scoffed, looking back and forth between them. "Right in my face."

"Kinsley, didn't you tell me that the two of you didn't even hit it off?" Liz reminded, eyes still on Luther's. "You pretty much said yourself that the best part of the evening was the free meal."

Kinsley's mouth fell open again. "Wow, really Liz? Just gonna call me out like that? You know what..." She yanked her purse from the chair she'd been sitting in. "I'm out. If you wanna stand here making googly eyes with this perpetrator, I don't need to stay here and watch."

"Drive safe, girl," Liz muttered, waving her hand absently. Kinsley just cut her eyes at her before turning and storming out.

Luther moved closer. "Liz..."

"I hope you aren't offended by that; what I said Kinsley said about your date."

"Not at all. She was correct about us not hitting it off. And her free meal came courtesy of my brother, not me."

Liz just kept staring, almost as if he'd disappear if she looked away. He looked just as delectable as he did in Belize, if not more so. "How are you here?"

"I live here. My house is a few miles away."

"B-but I've never seen you around town. *Never*. And I've lived here since I was a child."

"I moved here years ago but I was on the other side of the city, and I traveled so much I was gone more than I was here. And when I *was* home, I didn't go out much. I bought a house in this area a while back. Here," he reached into his back pocket for his wallet, fishing out his driver's license and holding it out to Liz. "See for yourself."

Liz grabbed the card with a shaky hand and glanced at it. Sure enough, his name was Luther Trae Monroe, and his address was nearby. According to his date of birth, he was fifty-five. And a Scorpio.

"This is so crazy," she marveled, handing his license back to him.

"Believe me, I'm equally as floored right now. The fact that we've been this close all this time and had to go all the way to Belize to meet each other." He took another step forward, his eyes intense. "And I've been missing you like crazy when you were mere miles away. And I *have* been missing you, Liz."

She swallowed. "I've been missing you, too."

"Can I please hug you now?"

"Yes."

The word was barely out of her mouth when he closed the rest of the short distance between them and pulled her close, wrapping her in a bear hug so tight Liz actually gasped. But she didn't care how tight it was because she was holding him with the same enthusiasm. She actually felt like she was swooning, feeling his hard body again, smelling his body oil, feeling his heart beat against hers. It felt surreal being in his arms again, and she hated that they were in the middle of a semi-crowded lounge instead of somewhere private.

"Do I get to know your last name now, too?" he asked, pulling back enough to look at her with a smile.

She blushed. "It's Tate. Liz Alexandra Tate. Since I know your middle name I guess I can tell you mine, but please don't call me that; I've never cared for that name."

"Duly noted. I look forward to calling you whatever you like. Speaking of calling, I get to have your number now too, right?"

Liz wanted to tell him he could have anything he asked for from her, but that was totally *not* a Liz thing to say. She was surprised she even thought such a thing, whether she meant it or not. "Absolutely. You're not the only one that wants to be sure we stay in touch after this."

"I'm so glad to hear that."

He looked like he wanted to kiss her. Liz ached for him to kiss her. But she made herself pull back and step out of his arms, remembering again that they were in public.

They sat down and fell into easy conversation, Luther taking Liz's hand and playing with her fingers as they talked. Their rapport was so effortless it was like no time had passed at all since they last saw each other.

"I know you probably thought I was crazy when I kept saying I believed we'd see each other again," he said. "You can admit it."

"Not *crazy*; just not realistic. I thought the odds were one in a million that it would happen. I mean, of all the places in the world...I just didn't see it. But I'm more than happy to be wrong."

"Well, even I've gotta admit that I never thought it would play out like this. I was worried that you would've moved on by the time we *did* reunite." His eyes lifted from her hand to her face. "Have you?"

"No. I admit I tried; I was driving myself crazy thinking about you when I couldn't have you. Just had a date tonight, actually. I'm even less mad now that it didn't go well."

He flashed a relieved smile. "It's comforting to know that I wasn't alone in how I felt. That our time together meant something to you, too."

"It absolutely did, Luther. Everything I told you in Belize about how I felt was a hundred percent true."

"I manifested this. I spoke it into existence daily. And now that we're together again, I want it to be known that I intend to court you, date you, and make you my woman. How do you feel about that?"

Liz had to resist the urge to dive on him. "I'm not mad at that at all."

They stayed there talking about all the things Liz wouldn't let them talk about in Belize so long that they lost all track of time, and Natalia had to come and lovingly tell them to get out. Even though it was rather late, neither of them were ready to leave each other's company so when Luther invited Liz over, she didn't hesitate to agree.

"I like your house, Luther," Liz complimented once they were in his living room. She roamed around slowly, gently running her hand over furnishings. "These are some great art pieces. Got these in your overseas travels?"

"Some, yes. A lot of them I got during domestic trips. I always try to bring something back with me, if I can."

"Yeah, I'm the same way, though my souvenirs are usually clothes or accessories. I'm still tripping that you're a hat maker. I know you've worn one every time I've seen you but I wouldn't have guessed you actually made them."

"I've always been into hats."

"Usually men that wear hats a lot are trying to hide something, like a growing bald spot or a big forehead or something." Liz strolled over to him and took his face in her hands, playfully pulling his head down so she could take a look. "Your forehead is normal, so..."

"Oh, we're doing jokes, huh?" Luther grabbed Liz by her waist and lifted her off the ground, causing her to scream with laughter. He spun her around, laughing right along with her, before collapsing onto the couch with her on top of him. She swatted his chest as she twisted in his lap, acting like she was trying to get up but they both knew she wasn't.

"You know I'm gonna get you back for this, right?" she warned with a grin.

"I hope you do. Hell, I look forward to it."

"Oh, you think so? We'll see if you're talking that talk when I tackle you. I can be pretty scrappy."

"Scrappy is good. Means you can hold your own. I happen to think that's sexy."

"You might be biased."

"I'm totally biased."

"And for the record, don't think you can just keep manhandling me, Mr. Ex-Bodybuilder. I *let* you pick me up just now, you know."

"Is that right?" His hands gripped her tighter. "What else will you let me do?"

Liz looked down at him, their smiles fading slightly. They each seemed to realize the position they were in, with Liz sitting right on Luther's groin. Her breath hitched when she felt him stir underneath her, and she quickly leaned down and claimed his lips, the intensity ramping up immediately. His arms slid around her as she pushed him all the way onto his back, twisting her body so she was laying flush on top of him. They kissed deeply, fervently, each of them perfectly content in the moment.

"I could get used to this," she whispered against his lips.

"You should."

They continued making out, their bodies gently moving against each other, hands caressing and roaming and squeezing. It was only because Liz needed to use the restroom that she reluctantly pulled away.

"Down the hall to the right," Luther offered, sensing what she needed.

She grinned as she enjoyed a few more moments of ogling his face before taking another quick kiss and easing off of him. While she went to go relieve herself, Luther sat up and ran his hands down his arms, surprised when he realized they were shaking slightly. Part of him was still in shock. Liz was there, in his house. He couldn't have imagined that a random trip to a cigar bar would lead him to the woman he'd been yearning for. He was there as Carter's guest, but Carter left him hanging when he met a woman five minutes after they arrived. Luther had been about to leave when he happened to turn and see Liz sitting there.

And the fact that she was friends with the woman he'd gone on a blind date with was crazy. It really was a small world. He was just glad Liz wasn't upset with him for how he handled things with Kinsley, and that she wasn't letting that date hinder anything between them. It meant a lot that she gave him the benefit of the doubt.

"How about a tour?" Liz suggested when she returned a few minutes later, rubbing her hands together. "And I need the hookup on whatever kind of lotion this is. The soap, too."

"I got you. On both counts." Luther stood, crossing over and taking her hand in his. "Right this way, my lady."

"Jumping the gun, aren't you?" she asked with a smile, trailing him.

"Just speaking it into existence. It majorly paid off the last time."

"Guess I can't argue with you there."

Luther led her around, showing her the galley kitchen, garage that he had converted into his gym, his meditation space, and the bedrooms. Liz's eyebrows shot up when they got to the backyard.

"I don't think I've ever seen an actual treehouse before," she noted, taking in the professionally-built treehouse that looked like a smaller version of Luther's house. "Are you a fifty-five-year-old kid at heart, Mr. Monroe?"

Luther chuckled. "I have my moments, I suppose, but I actually had this built for my daughter."

Shit! Liz thought, her stomach and enthusiasm dropping instantly. *I knew this was too damn good to be true! Shit!!*

"Oh, you have a daughter," she croaked, almost wanting to cry from disappointment. She actually wanted to sink right onto the grass beneath her feet and throw a whole tantrum. "I, um, I didn't know that..."

"Yeah, it was kind of silly to do this for her, in hindsight, considering she was a teenager getting ready to go to college when she asked for it. I had it built when I bought this house. Now that she's grown, she hardly even thinks about this thing anymore. Her mother is always saying I spoil her too much and she was right in this case."

Sheer relief washed over Liz. "She's grown? How old is she?"

"Twenty-three."

"Does she live with you?"

"Hell no. I might spoil her but not *that* much. She has an apartment with a couple of friends of hers."

Liz tried to hide her sigh of relief. She usually didn't prefer dealing with men with children, even though she knew it was hard not to, with the men she dated. But there were exceptions. Men that had young children, even teenagers, were a no-go. She wasn't trying to deal with any baby mamas or exes, because in her experience, it usually wasn't pleasant. But since Luther's daughter was grown and out of the house, Liz could deal with that.

Her fire reignited, Liz stepped in front of Luther and slid her arms around his waist, smiling when he immediately pulled her closer.

"I'm glad this happened," she murmured, looking up at him.

He smiled. "Me, too."

"I have a question for you." Her hands slid up his chest before she wrapped her arms around his neck. "Have you ever gotten frisky in that treehouse?"

"I haven't, actually. You offering?"

"Just putting it on the menu for the future. If I get to fooling around with you in there I might be over here all night, and it's getting pretty late."

"I know you didn't think I was planning on asking you to leave."

"I'm in no hurry to, but what kind of lady would I be if I slept over here on the first night?"

They both burst out laughing at the obvious joke. Luther leaned down to plant a kiss on her neck, their arms tightening around each other.

"Look at you, trying to be conventional after I've already let you have your way with me," Luther joked, giving a playful grab to her behind with both hands. "If anything, I'm the one that should be trying to protect my virtue."

"What? How do you figure *that*??"

"Uh, who was it that initiated the sex in Belize? You or you?"

"That is not fair to blame me for that! You had me so damn horny you're lucky I asked at all and didn't just take the dick, 'cause I sure started to. You set me up!"

"Oh, is that what we're calling it now?"

They shared another laugh, Luther occasionally nipping Liz's lips as he slowly walked her backwards into the house. As soon as they were inside, he backed her against the sliding glass door, deepening the kiss. Liz moaned, loving the feel of him hardening against her.

"Whenever you're ready, okay?" he told her, eyes on hers. "Seriously, no pressure. I don't just want your body, Liz, I want all of you. Most of all, this." His finger trailed to her chest over her heart. "So I'm down to get frisky when you are but please don't think it has to be the main thing between us. I just...I just like being around you. And I look forward to us getting to know each other better, over time. Because if I have my way, this won't be a short-term thing."

Liz bit her lip, looking up at him. She realized that she felt the same way about him. Usually Liz wasn't that quick to catch feelings, but Luther had managed to do in less than three collective days what other men took weeks or months to do, and that was to have her completely and totally open.

"Looks like we're on the same page yet again," she replied, her voice actually shaking slightly. Her hand caressed his face, raking her fingers through his beard. "I like you a lot, Luther."

"I like you, too."

"So I'm absolutely willing to see where this goes. As crazy as this is, it feels right. My sister will probably faint when she hears about all this; she's a big sap, like you are."

Luther chuckled. "Can't wait to meet her, then. There's no telling what my brother will say so I won't even try to guess."

Giggling, Liz pulled his face to hers for a kiss. "I'll make sure to be prepared for anything. Now, I have a vital question that has to be addressed before we move forward."

He frowned curiously. "What's that?"

"Do you have an extra toothbrush for me?"

Smiling, he slid an arm around her and started heading towards the short set of stairs leading to his bedroom. "Absolutely."

She linked her fingers with his hand that hung over her shoulder, her other arm clamping around his lower back. "I'll need one of your shirts to sleep in, too, that I might or might not take home with me tomorrow."

"Baby, I can't wait to see you walking around here in my shirt, especially if it's that and nothing else. And I'll pretend not to notice that it's missing tomorrow."

"Excellent. Are you an early riser or do you like to linger in bed? Just note, the wrong answer will result in points off your overall score."

"I get up early when I need to. I linger when I want to."

"Dammit, just when I thought it wasn't possible to like you any more than I already do at this point..."

They grinned at each other, pausing in the doorway to his bedroom for another lingering kiss that melted into a deep, panting makeout session that had Luther backing Liz against the doorjamb. Neither were in any hurry. They eventually eased to the bed, hands all over each other, whispering things about their budding feelings between kisses.

When Liz woke up the next morning in Luther's arms, she found herself snuggling up to him instead of early morning realizations sending her doing a walk of shame. She was in no more of a hurry to leave than she had been the night before, and that amazed her. She looked up at his sleeping face for a few moments before pressing her cheek to his warm chest, his arms tightening around her in response.

Yep, I'm in trouble, she thought to herself. Luther kissed the top of her head and pulled her leg that was lying on his higher around his waist, making her grin like a Cheshire cat.

But I think I like trouble.

Chapter 7

• • • •

LIZ NEVER THOUGHT SHE'D be able to describe herself as 'giddy', but she didn't know a better word that applied.

After their improbable chance reuniting at Natavey, Liz and Luther spent as much time as possible together. They spent the rest of that first weekend holed up in his house, and Liz was a little disappointed when she went back home Sunday night, which she really only did because she didn't have any other clothes with her. But she figured it would be good to get out from under him for a while; she liked Luther – *really* liked him – but she needed to get her head together. She had a lot going on at work and knew she couldn't spend all of her time fantasizing over a man; she had to focus. There would be plenty of time for fantasizing when she got home.

Putting thoughts of Luther on pause was harder than expected, though. When he called her late in the afternoon, she stopped mid-sentence on the email she was typing and grabbed her phone.

"To what do I owe the pleasure, sir?" she greeted, sitting back in her chair.

"I'll admit that I miss you," Luther revealed, his deep voice making her squirm. "But I know you've got things to do and won't take up much of your time. I wanted to ask if you were available for dinner tonight."

"Is this *actual* dinner or a colloquialism for more salacious but just as delicious activity?"

He laughed loudly, making her grin. "I love the way you think, but I was talking actual dinner. I'd love to cook for you."

"Wow. I thought men usually waited the required three days before asking a woman out again."

"I'm fifty-five, baby. Way too old for bullshit. I put it out there and whatever comes of it, comes of it."

"Ooh, I love it when you display that big dick energy. That's hot. I would love to have dinner with you tonight."

"Good. And if you wanted to bring an overnight bag or something..."

"Luther..."

"Just a suggestion, gorgeous. It's up to you."

Liz already knew she'd be taking an overnight bag. She just didn't want to seem too eager.

"I'll think about it," she replied coolly.

"You do that. Say around eight?"

"Eight it is."

It was all Liz could do to keep her mind on work after that. It surprised her, and even frustrated her a little bit. She loved what was happening between her and Luther but she'd never been one to get so consumed over a man that she couldn't handle her business. Now she was daydreaming in the middle of the day and stopping what she was doing when he called like some lovesick schoolgirl, and she told herself again to get it together. As much as she liked Luther, she didn't want to lose herself in him.

She was still trying to figure out what she needed to take the outfits for the upcoming showcase over the top. They were fine as they were, but Liz didn't settle for just *fine*. It needed some kind of knockout punch, and it infuriated her that she couldn't figure out what that was. She'd never been stumped like this, but she knew she'd figure it out. She didn't have a choice *but* to figure it out.

It was a couple of hours later when she got a call from Kinsley. Liz was in the middle of a conference call so she sent it to voicemail, but when she was wrapping things up later, she called her back, preparing herself for anything.

"What's up, Kinsley?"

"Girl..." The attitude was already heavy in Kinsley's voice and Liz rolled her eyes, sensing what was coming. "I still cannot believe that bullshit from the other night."

"Please don't tell me you're still fussing about Luther."

"Hell yeah, I'm still fussing about Luther. *If* that's even his real name. He gave me a fake one before."

"It was a real name, Kinsley. It just wasn't his first name."

"It wasn't the name he apparently goes by, so that's as good as fake, to me."

Liz sighed as she unlocked her car and tossed her things into the backseat. "Is this what you called me for? To bitch about a man you weren't even interested in?"

"Oh, what, you're riding for him because he gave you the D on vacation?"

"I'm riding for him because he's not a villain. I'm riding for him because he's the man I'm seeing. But mostly, I'm riding for him because you are blowing all of this way out of proportion. That was days ago and you weren't even feeling him so I don't know why you're acting so affronted."

"Wait, you're still seeing him after what he did to me??"

"Kinsley..."

"I'm supposed to be your girl. Are you really that hard-up that you would willingly date somebody that perpetrated about who he was to your homegirl? Would you like it if I did that to you?"

Liz paused. "I'm gonna give you a chance to walk that back before I go off."

"I don't need to walk anything back. I mean every word I'm coming with."

"Okay, then, well know that I mean every word *I'm* about to come with. Kinsley, I think your main problem is that Luther didn't want you but clearly wants me, and you need to grow up and get over it. You hate that you're on this man-finding mission and I'm getting a man before you are. A man I will continue to see, and I don't care if you don't like it. This is nothing but a pride thing for you and you need to handle it, because that's gonna be your *only* time coming at me sideways."

"Liz-"

"Now, when and if you get yourself together and start acting like the grown woman you're supposed to be, *then* we can talk. Until then, we're done."

Liz hung up and dropped the phone into her lap, shaking her head in annoyance. She couldn't believe Kinsley was acting so childishly. She had her petty moments here and there, but usually she just dismissed any man she didn't hit it off with and moved on to the next one. The fact that she was still carrying a grudge about Luther had to be sour grapes, because Liz sensed she would have let it go by now if Liz and Luther didn't have such a glaring connection and attraction towards each other.

Putting Kinsley and that whole conversation out of her mind, Liz headed home so she could shower and change before heading to Luther's. The anticipation actually gave her goosebumps, and it was just a dinner invitation. But she knew it wouldn't have mattered what they were doing; it was just because it was with Luther.

He greeted her with a kiss that had her dropping her bag at her feet and wrapping her arms around his neck, both of them getting so caught up that they didn't even close the door. When it finally tapered off, Luther pressed a kiss to her forehead before stepping around her, closing the front door and grabbing her duffel bag.

"Interesting," he commented, holding it up and perusing the images of Black women in various shades, hairstyles and lipstick colors that covered it, each image bleeding into the next. "Where'd you get this?"

"An artist I follow on social media. She has some amazing paintings and started creating merch featuring some of her most popular ones. It took me forever to narrow it down to this one."

"I bet Churi would like something like this."

"I'll give you the website. Mmm, it smells so good in here...what's on the menu?"

"Shrimp ceviche to start, paella, and jalapeno cornbread."

"Oh my god..."

"I have some peach cobbler cookies for dessert, but I admit I didn't make those. I'm a marginal baker, at best."

"I mean, I'm already smitten, Luther. You're just showing off now."

He laughed. "You've gotta eat. And I figure you probably haven't in a while."

"You got me there. I worked through lunch and just wolfed down a salad while I was doing a bunch of other stuff."

"I'd love it if you'd stop doing that."

"I'll try. Now stop fussing and feed me, handsome."

"Yes, ma'am."

Liz went to get washed up while Luther dished up the food. She kicked her shoes off and padded to the kitchen, siding up to him as he arranged the plates on the quartzite countertop.

"This looks amazing," she commented, her mouth actually watering.

"I aim to please."

"Is this a usual meal for you or is this special occasion, date night-only fare?"

"I'll make whatever when I'm in the mood for it but I won't act like I didn't want to impress you. Come on, grab a plate."

They carried their plates to the square wooden dining table, sitting side-by-side instead of across from each other. Liz vented about what she was dealing with at work, mainly regarding what she felt she was lacking for her showcase pieces, and Luther told her about the clients he'd trained earlier that day. Liz also told him about her earlier conversation with Kinsley, to which he shook his head.

"I hate to cause an issue between you two."

"You're not causing anything. She's the one that won't let it go."

"I suppose I can understand her being upset that I wasn't totally forthcoming, even if I didn't exactly lie to her."

"Yeah, I can understand her being upset, too...for a minute. Then she'd just write you off and move on to something else. But she's dragging this little grudge out because you essentially chose me over her. She just hates that she's by herself and I'm not."

"I'm sorry she's upset but I'm not apologizing for that. It's nothing personal against Kinsley but it wouldn't have mattered *who* I was on that double date with; it wasn't you."

Liz couldn't help grinning. "Well, she'll get over it."

They continued their meal, the topic veering to other things as they stuffed their faces. Luther beamed when Liz praised his food, and she insisted on helping clean up.

"That can wait, baby," he told her, gently placing his hand over hers as she went to run some water in the sink. "I'll handle it later."

"Luther, here's a thing about me; I cannot abide by a dirty kitchen. My parents would never let me and Lovey go to bed until the kitchen was sparkling clean and it stuck with me once I was out of their house. Even if it's just one dish, I *have* to wash it and put it away. And you don't even have a dishwasher."

"I get it and I respect it but I'm trying to cuddle with you, not stand in here washing dishes."

"Okay, so we'll do it together; then it won't take that long. 'Cause it's not like I'm not trying to get to the cuddling, either."

"All right, gorgeous," he chuckled, conceding. "Let's get it done, then."

After they cleaned up the kitchen while doing plenty of laughing and joking, Luther took Liz's hand and led her to the living room. He fired up the electric fireplace and grabbed a couple of blankets before turning to her.

"Couch or floor?"

"I'm good either way. You're the one that's fifty-five."

She squealed when he playfully tossed a pillow at her. He spread the thick blanket on the floor in front of the couch, the good-natured smile still on his lips. "I can get up and down just fine, ma'am. No knee or back issues over here. Knock on wood."

"That's good to know. Now I don't have to worry about hurting you when we're getting it in and things get a little acrobatic."

"Baby, I'm ready and more than willing to pick you up, toss you around, or contort into any position you want me to get inside you in." He lowered himself to the floor before reaching for her hand and pulling her down onto his lap. "That's the *last* thing you have to worry about."

"I'm glad." She turned in his arms and pressed her lips to his, taking his face in her hands. They moaned simultaneously when their tongues touched, their smacks battling with the Sade he had playing at low volume. She pulled back and looked at him, kiss-drunk and biting her bottom lip. "Will you be getting inside of me tonight? Because I want you to."

"Absolutely, baby. I'm not gonna deny you."

"Good." Their kiss resumed, this time with twice the intensity and passion. Liz readjusted to where she was straddling his lap, and Luther's hands slid down to her backside as she started to grind on him. He unzipped the front of her cropped sweater and hissed at the sight of her breasts in the navy blue push-up bra she wore. Deftly undoing the front clasp, he leaned forward and helped himself, Liz's head falling back at the first touch of his tongue to her sensitive nipples. His hands pressed into the middle of her back, keeping her in place as he took his time pleasing her, loving how she responded to him.

"Luther, baby..."

"Is this what you want?"

"I want this and everything else."

"Believe me, you're gonna get it."

In the next few seconds, Liz was on her back on the blanket and Luther was on his knees, pushing down his sweats. When he reached to get a condom, she sat up and grabbed his arm.

"I have an IUD and I was tested two months ago; I can show you the results on my phone."

"I'm good to go, too; was tested four months ago. If you're sure you want us to take this step, I'm with it, but I don't want you to just take my word for it; I want you to see for yourself. Let me grab my phone real quick."

Liz started to tell him it wasn't necessary but she knew that was just her horniness talking; she *did* want to see his test results, just like she did with any other man she got with. She appreciated his consideration for her and not letting the moment cloud his good judgment.

She retrieved her phone from her purse, ignoring the texts she saw from Kinsley, and she and Luther showed each other their test results. They felt even more at ease with each other once it was confirmed that they were both clean.

"Oh, and one more thing..." She spoke up when he started to slide her pants off. "This might not be the smoothest time to ask this but you're done having kids, right?"

His head reared slightly. "*Hell* yeah. My baby-making days were over years ago."

"Good. Because I never had any baby-making days and I don't want any. I love kids but never wanted any of my own. Does that change things for you?"

"If you were asking me this when I was in my twenties or thirties, maybe. But now, not at all. I still want to be with you just as much as I did before."

Relief caused her chest to cave in. "I'm so glad to hear that."

He pulled his shirt over his head and tossed it aside, causing Liz's grunt in appreciation, her eyes tightening as she ogled his chiseled chest and abs.

"Can we proceed?" he asked, crawling over to her with hungry eyes.

Liz quickly shed her sweater and bra before pulling him on top of her. "Yeah, we've done enough talking for now."

· · · ·

AFTER TWO INTENSE ROUNDS of sex on the floor and the couch (and for a while, kind of in between), Luther got up to get them some water while Liz tried to collect herself. She could feel herself growing more attached to Luther, and his intense lovemaking was only accelerating it.

It certainly wasn't the only thing she enjoyed about him but it was damn sure high on the list.

"Babe, your phone," she called out when Luther's cell lit up. "Someone is Facetiming you."

Luther strode back into the living room, his brow etched into a curious frown. He handed Liz her glass of water before grabbing his phone, his frown clearing. "It's just Jules, my ex-wife."

"You gonna answer it?"

"Nah. I can call her back tomorrow. She probably doesn't really want anything, anyway."

"Go ahead and see what she wants; I don't mind. I need to run to the restroom, anyway."

He eyed her warily. "You sure?"

"Yes, Luther," she chuckled, taking a few gulps of water before setting the glass on an Africa-shaped coaster and grabbing his shirt from the floor, slipping it over her head. "I'm not tripping off that. You told me the two of you are friends now; I actually think that's cool. Plus, it's not like she called when we were going at it just now."

"She definitely would've been shit outta luck, if she had. All right, then; I'll make it quick."

Luther answered the call while Liz headed off to the bathroom, him eying her the whole time.

"What's up, Jules?"

Jules took one look at him and shook her head, smirking. "Oh goodness...you're entertaining, aren't you? Or are you listening to Sade with your shirt off for no reason?"

"No, I definitely have company."

"Okay, well I won't hold you, then. I was going to tell you more about Churi's nonsense but it can wait."

"What, it's something else?"

"The little heffah actually tried to blackmail me about this school stuff. I had to put her out of my house before I hurt her feelings."

Luther couldn't help but chuckle, even though it wasn't funny. "I don't know what's gotten into that girl."

"She's spoiled as hell, thanks to you."

"You're not gonna keep blaming me for that, Jules," Luther retorted, still smiling. "It could be said that she's driven and determined."

"Yeah, okay. Call it what you want to. We'll see how much you're trying to pretty it up when she starts nagging *you* for money."

"Yeah, yeah."

"So who are you seeing now, if I may ask?" Jules asked, actually looking excited. Her long hair was pulled into a ponytail and she was nursing a glass of wine. "I didn't know anyone was in the picture."

"It's Liz; the one I met in Belize."

"What? How did *that* happen??"

"It's crazy but we just happened to run into each other at Natavey, that new cigar bar across town. Blew my damn mind; I just turned around and saw her. I still can't believe it, really."

"Damn, are you serious?? That is podcast material, right there."

He laughed, looking up as Liz strolled back into the living room. "Hey baby, you wanna meet Jules real quick?"

"Yeah!" Liz eagerly replied, hurrying over to him.

He blinked, mildly surprised that she agreed so readily, but shrugged it off. At least he didn't have to worry about his lady (or soon-to-be lady) having issues with his ex-wife.

"Damn, you are *hot*, girl!" Jules practically shouted once Liz entered the frame. "Now I see why Luther was so sprung and pining when he got back from Belize. He was claiming you from the jump and I'm not mad at it."

Liz giggled while Luther just shook his head, draping his arm around her shoulders and across her chest from behind. "I appreciate the compliment. You're gorgeous, too; whatever it is you use on your skin, I want it."

"Girl, this is black soap and shea butter, that's it. If my head wasn't so big I'd get rid of all this weave and rock a short haircut like yours. It is so nice to meet you, Liz...I'm glad I get to meet the woman that has Lu-Lu so open."

"Aww, I've got you open, Lu-Lu?" Liz teased, looking up at him with a grin as she rubbed her hand along his arm.

"All the way open, baby. So much so that I almost don't even mind you calling me that."

Jules tsked. "Shit, see there? He fusses whenever I say it. Y'all can't break up."

They all laughed before chatting for a few more minutes, with Liz and Jules hitting it off so well that Luther hardly had to say anything. Liz even took the phone from him at some point; he just wrapped his other arm around her waist and nuzzled his face in her neck as she talked.

When ten minutes passed, Luther knew he needed to step in or they'd apparently go on forever. "Okay, this was fun...Jules, good night. I'd like to get Liz back to myself now, if you don't mind."

"Don't mind at all. Sorry for hogging your woman. Liz, girl, we'll chop it up another time; get my number from Luther. Maybe we can meet up for lunch or something. I already know you're gonna be around for a while because he can't even let you talk on the phone without groping you, and you've been grinning and cheesin' the whole time he's been doing it, so you *both* are sprung. We might as well be friends, too."

"I'd like that, Jules. We should definitely hang out; would you give me the lowdown on big boy, here?"

"He's an open book; that's one thing I can say about Lu-Lu."

Luther grunted, his face still in Liz's neck.

"Fine, fine, about *Luther*, then," Jules corrected with an exaggerated eye roll. Liz chuckled. "There's honestly nothing I could tell you that he wouldn't tell you himself, if he already hasn't. So you're good there. I can give you tips on what to do if you get in an argument or something and need to get back on his good side."

"What about if he needs to get back on *my* good side?"

"Well, another thing I can say about him is that he owns it when he messes up. No deflection or denial or shifting-the-blame bullshit. Grown man energy, all the way around. I'm telling you, lock that down, girl."

When the call ended a couple of minutes later, Luther turned his phone on vibrate as Liz looked at him thoughtfully. "Why did you two break up again? I mean, I'm glad to have you to myself but Jules is pretty awesome."

"That she is. It really was nothing more than we just reached a point where we felt we'd be better as friends than man and wife. There was no cheating or deceit or anything like that; we got married right out of college and the romantic fire we had for each other just flamed out over the years. We made the decision, sat Churi down and explained it to her, and that was that. No drama; it was totally amicable."

"How did Churi take it?"

"She wasn't thrilled but she appreciated how we handled it."

"It's great that you two are still so close. Would it bother you if Jules and I hung out?"

"Not at all. Now, do you mind if we stop talking about my ex-wife and turn our focus back on each other?"

She smiled as he took her hand. "Not even a little bit."

Luther checked to make sure all the doors were secure and the alarm was set before leading Liz up to his bedroom. They entered his en suite, standing side-by-side as they brushed their teeth and got ready to wind it down for the night.

"What time do you need to get up?" he asked her, eying her in the mirror as he worked the toothbrush around his mouth.

"Ugh, seven. Dammit."

"You want to shower now or in the morning?"

"Might as well do it in the morning. We're just going to get sweaty again tonight."

He grinned. "Woman, you're gonna make me hide your keys and keep you here with me indefinitely. I think you like getting me hooked on you."

"Of course I do. I want your mind to stay on me."

"Baby, my mind *does* stay on you."

Once they were done with their ablutions, they climbed into his king-sized bed, immediately reaching for each other. They shared a few leisurely kisses before Liz pulled back, her hand resting on his bare chest.

He looked at her in the darkened room, the only light coming in through the sheer curtains. "What's wrong?"

Liz felt weird for actually being nervous about what she wanted to say. Taking a moment to gather her words (and courage), she looked up at him. "I think I want you to be my man, Luther."

She couldn't read the look in his eyes as he peered at her, but he didn't look as happy as she expected him to look. Part of her regretted her declaration already. It was the first time she'd been the one to lay down the gauntlet like that and it was sending skittish tingles all over her body.

"This isn't hesitation because you know that's what I want, too," he finally assured, putting her at ease, if only slightly. "But I need to ask you; when was your last serious relationship, Liz?"

"Uhh..." she hedged, caught off-guard by the question. "*Serious* relationship? It's been a while. Probably about six or seven years. Why?"

"Because I want you to be really ready for me and what a relationship between us will mean. Of course I can't predict the future, but it's like I told you before, I don't want short-term with you. Once we're officially together, I want it to stay that way. And there has to be a reason it's been so long since you've been committed to someone on that level."

"I...I just haven't wanted to take it there with anyone. I've dated but it was always casual."

"See, there's nothing casual about this for me. And I love that you feel you want what I want. I just need you to be sure and not caught up in the atmosphere of the evening. Because when we make that decision, I'm a hundred percent in, and I don't want that to be too much for you."

Liz started to get offended but she stopped to consider what he was saying. If she was honest, she *was* a little caught up in the atmosphere of the evening. Even from when he called and invited her to dinner earlier, she had been basking in the euphoria of the crush she had on him, and it had just intensified from there. She had even enjoyed gabbing with his ex-wife, which was something she *never* thought she'd say. Between the invite, the dinner, the sex, and the overall romantic scene, not to mention just the comfort she felt when she was with him, Liz was feeling particularly optimistic about their chances. But maybe she needed to wait until she had a clear head to make such a decision. The last thing she wanted to do was jump into a relationship with Luther today and second-guess it tomorrow.

"I can see your point," she finally admitted with a sigh. Her nails lightly raked his pecs. "Maybe we should press pause on that."

"Yeah, on that, but not on everything, right?"

"Right. I'm certainly not saying I want to stop seeing you. But like you said, I need to be sure I'm really ready and not just caught up in the moment. You deserve that much. In the meantime we can just keep doing what we're doing...getting to know each other, building our friendship, sharing and getting closer..."

"Absolutely. This is all foundation work, baby, what we've got going on now. And it's going to make our relationship even stronger. I'm just..." He took her hand and kissed it. "I'm so glad you received what I was saying and didn't take it as me pushing you away."

"And I'm glad you had the mind to recognize that I might not be where I should for us to officially start off the right way. Because I want this to work, Luther. I want *us* to work."

"You and me both, baby." His hand slid to her face, stroking his thumb along her cheek as he gazed at her adoringly. "My feelings for you are real, Liz. Since that day we met on the street in Belize, your physical beauty had me entranced. And once I spent time with you, it only deepened. And now that we're in close proximity and can *really* get closer with no barriers, I'm more and more sure that this – us – is what I want."

Her eyes roamed his, feeling her heart was going to burst in her chest.

"I want you, Liz. I want your heart, your body, your attention...and I want to give you mine. When someone hears 'Luther', I want them to automatically think 'Liz', and vice versa. That's how much I want us to be linked. But I'm not gonna rush it. So when you *know* you're ready for all that – when there's no inkling of doubt in your mind – just say the word. I'm not going anywhere."

Liz gazed at him almost as if she couldn't believe he was real. She grabbed the back of his neck and pulled him to her for a kiss, then he rested his forehead on hers.

"Thank you," she whispered. "For caring enough to be patient."

"You're worth it, Liz." He pulled her closer. "You're worth everything."

• • • •

A FEW DAYS LATER, LIZ was doing something she didn't do much of and that was sleep in. She felt more tired than usual between work and spending so much time with Luther; their late nights of talking and fooling around were finally catching up to her.

She jolted awake when she heard Lovey's ringtone. Sitting up and rubbing her eyes, she scratched her head through her silk head scarf and reached for her phone that was on the charging pad next to her bed.

"Hey sis," she yawned.

"Are you still in the bed? It's almost eleven. Are you sick?"

"No, I'm fine. Just tired."

"Work still draining you, huh?"

"That's part of it."

"Oooh..." Lovey teased. "I figured you going scarce lately was because a man had your attention. I'm glad to hear your date with Ross went so well."

Liz realized how long it had been since she spoke to her sister. "Damn, I need to get you caught up, I see..."

"What? What do you mean?"

"I haven't seen Ross since he jetted out of the restaurant after I told him I don't want kids."

"He what?"

"Yeah, he wants a wife and kids and a country house and when he heard that wasn't on my agenda, that was it. He made up an excuse and left. Haven't seen or talked to him since. My number was probably deleted from his phone before he got out of the parking lot."

"Oh wow, Liz, I'm so sorry...I had no idea it might turn out like that. I sincerely thought you two would hit it off."

"You don't have to apologize for anything. Things happen. He was a nice guy but even before the kid thing, I wasn't feeling it; we seemed to be more inclined to kick back at a bar with some beers than share a romance. It's whatever. I've actually been spending a lot of time with Luther."

"Who is Luther? I haven't heard you mention him."

Liz told Lovey about meeting Luther in Belize, their amazing time together despite her insistence that they not share anything too personal or exchange contact information, his assurances that they would meet again, and them running into each other at Natavey after her busted date with Ross.

"Oh my god!" Lovey practically screamed. "Liz, do you know how utterly romantic that is?? To meet thousands of miles away, fall for each other then have to part ways, and then discover you live in the same city? The fact that you were both at Natavey at *that* moment...I know you'll scoff, but that was fate. There's no other way to describe it."

"It...it was just a coincidence, Lovey," Liz insisted, though it was weak. She couldn't even muster up any conviction.

"You don't even believe that. Liz, there's nothing wrong with admitting you've found your soul mate. I've never known you to want to spend so much time with a man that he wears you out. It's going on noon and you're still in the bed."

"I'm not going to deny that I like him. More than anyone I've liked in a while, to be honest. It even got to the point where I told him I wanted him to be my man-"

Lovey gasped.

"But he said he wanted me to take the time to be sure I was ready for the level of commitment he wants, especially since it's been a long while since I've been in a serious relationship. And I started to feel some kind of way about that but when I thought about it, he had a point. I don't want to let the newness of everything lure me into making a premature decision."

"Why does it have to be that complicated? Either you want to be with him or you don't. And you clearly do."

"It's not that easy for me, Lovey. You know how I am when it comes to men; I have fun with them for however long and then I'm over it. Even if it's someone I'm actually dating, the novelty wears off after a while and I find myself not wanting to be bothered. I don't want that to happen with Luther. We need to get past this 'shiny new object' phase so I can see where my head is and know it's the real thing."

"I get it. But what does your heart tell you?"

Leave it to Lovey to ask her something like that. Liz's head fell back against the pillows. "It tells me he's it."

"And how often does that happen? Or has it *ever* happened? You should trust that, Liz."

Liz chewed her lip, wishing she could agree. She wanted to, but she knew her track record. And she cared too much about Luther to officially start something with him before she was truly ready.

When Liz didn't respond for a few moments, Lovey said, "How about you bring this Luther over for dinner? I'd love to meet him."

"Um, I guess, yeah. I'll ask him."

"Just out of curiosity, what's his last name?"

"Monroe. Luther Trae Monroe."

"Liz Alexandra Monroe..."

"Bye, Lovey." Liz hung up with a chuckle, tossing her phone onto the bed next to her and rolling over.

After another hour or so, she finally peeled herself out of bed and shuffled to the kitchen to see what she had to eat. She had a couple of texts from Luther, though she knew he had a client to train that morning and then he was going to be working on some hat orders. When they finally shared what they each did for a living, Luther considered their being in the same industry as only further confirmation that they were destined for each other. Liz didn't readily agree when he said it, but she couldn't help smiling at the memory.

She had just opened the freezer to see if she had any frozen waffles left when the doorbell rang. Her mind automatically wondered if it was Luther, and she felt her face flush. He hadn't even been to her place yet since they'd spent all of their time at his so far, plus he'd already told her he'd be working. Liz admonished herself as she headed for the door, fully prepared to let whoever was on the other side know that she was not in the mood.

And when she looked through the peephole and saw it was Kinsley, she *really* wasn't in the mood.

"What do you want?" she called out through the door.

"I wanted to talk to you and figured you wouldn't answer the phone."

"I'm not in a hurry to answer the door, either."

"Liz, come on. Can we not? I want to apologize. And I'd like to do it to your face so can you please open the door?"

Sighing, Liz finally pulled the door open, stepping back with a hand on her hip. She noticed Kinsley's empty hands. "A *real* apology would've come with breakfast."

"It's the afternoon."

"You know I'm down for breakfast anytime."

"Liz, look..." Kinsley closed the door behind her and followed Liz into the living room space, taking a seat on the huge overstuffed couch. "When I thought about it, you were right about what you said the other day. I *was* tripping over Luther because I was a little jealous. He *is* fine and I'd like to think that if he had shown any interest in me that night, we could've made something happen...seeing him get so awestruck over you was kind of a kick to the self esteem. Especially since I was already frustrated with how my love life has been going lately. But you're my girl and I shouldn't have come at you like I did, especially over some man. I really am sorry."

Eying her, Liz took her time responding. Kinsley might have been prone to pettiness but Liz had never known her to say anything she didn't mean, so she figured she was being sincere.

"All right," she finally said. "I accept your apology."

Kinsley smiled, relieved. "Good."

"Are you going to be able to handle seeing me and Luther together? I don't want to hear any more snide comments about the middle name shit. Hopefully you've let that go by now."

"I have. It's over with...no need in beating a dead horse. And I can't act like I've never given out a fake name. *Actual* fake names; ones that I totally made up. To this day there are a few men out there who know me as LaQuisha. So you don't have to worry about me tripping off that anymore, either."

"I'm glad to hear it."

"So you and Luther are a thing now, huh?" Kinsley asked, leaning back and crossing her legs. "You're officially boo'd up?"

"No, we're just dating." Liz didn't feel like going into the details like she had with Lovey earlier. "Taking things slow or whatever."

"Wow. With the way you two were so transfixed when you saw each other at Natavey, I wouldn't have been surprised if you told me you two had eloped by now."

"Hmph. We're nowhere near that. I like him, he likes me...we're just letting it be that for now."

"Hmm."

Liz was being purposely vague because something warned her not to tell Kinsley everything. Even though she'd apologized for it, her little tantrum and pettiness about Luther was still filed away in Liz's mind, and she didn't put it past her friend to have a repeat of all that if she got in her feelings enough. Liz chose to keep her feelings for Luther and the depth of their relationship – unofficial or not – close to the chest for the time being.

"Don't trip about me asking this, but is he seeing other people?" Kinsley asked after a few quiet moments. "Hell, are *you*?"

"I'm not and I doubt he is, either."

"Would you care if he did?" Kinsley's eyebrow arched. "Since you two are *just dating* and all."

Liz's chest burned at the thought of Luther with another woman. She felt her ears twitch, and she was glad that they were mashed under the head scarf she was still wearing so it wasn't noticeable. That was one of her tells when she got angry or agitated and Kinsley knew that.

"He's free to do what he wants," Liz replied with a shrug, trying to sound breezy despite the words leaving a bad taste in her mouth. "Like I said, we're taking things slow. If he chose to see someone else too...I'm not gonna act like I wouldn't care but he's well within his rights to do that."

Kinsley eyed Liz as if she sensed there was something Liz wasn't telling her. Liz managed to keep her face even, despite the churning in her stomach. Downplaying what she and Luther had felt wrong, like she was disrespecting him or something.

But, they weren't official. At *his* insistence. Even though Liz had agreed with his reasons, it was him that pumped the brakes on them taking things to the next level and claiming each other. So Liz told herself she hadn't done anything wrong, even if she didn't totally believe it.

Chapter 8

• • • •

LIZ LOOKED FORWARD to going to Luther's, this time for a specific reason. He had invited her over to see his work space where he made his hats, and she was excited.

"Did you have this specially built so you could turn it into your workshop?" Liz asked as he led her out to the backyard where a large shed was.

"Actually no; this was already back here. Apparently the previous owner did sculptures and the like and built it for that. It was one of the deciding factors on me putting in an offer on the house."

"Well, I feel rather privileged that you're allowing me into your work space like this. I know a lot of creatives can be very protective and wary of letting people behind the curtain of what they do."

"True enough. I don't really bring people back here but you know, you're kinda special or whatever." He winked at her as he opened the door to the shed and ushered her inside.

"Sweet-talker." Liz grinned as she entered the space, then her jaw dropped slightly as she took in her surroundings. The area was clearly designated for creating and for business. On the creating side, there was a drafting table, an area with materials such as fabrics, ribbons, feathers, and other decorative items, various steamers and irons, a sewing machine, several head forms, and a station with other things like spray bottles, shellacs, brushes, pins, scissors and cutters, sanders, and other things Liz didn't recognize. There were crafting items on the long wooden tables along the walls where he worked as well as the pegboards behind them. The opposite business side of the shed was distinctly neater and where Luther assembled his orders; there was a small desk containing a laptop and label printer, the area that contained stacks of hat boxes with Luther's logo in sexy script and other packing materials, and deep shelving where completed hats were stored upside down to protect the brims and lightly stuffed with tissue paper to maintain their form. There was even a small refrigerator in the corner with snacks and beverages for fuel during long sessions. The organized chaos of it was indicative of the time Luther spent there. It was all so surreal and fascinating for Liz because as much as she loved fashion, she didn't often get to see the creating portion of it.

But the main thing that floored her were the hats themselves. She'd only seen the ones Luther had worn around her, and those were great, but the recent designs that were displayed on hat racks actually had Liz's chest thumping with excitement. She knew instantly that this was what she was missing for her items for the showcase.

"Oh my god..." She moved over and gently touched a camel brown wool fedora with a band that resembled polished woodgrain and had a super-thin strip of dark leather along the brim, silently fawning over the design and attention to detail. Luther just stood near the door with his hands in his pockets, watching her. "Luther, you actually made all these?"

"I did."

"Baby, you are...*ridiculously* talented."

He smiled and graciously bowed his head. "I appreciate that."

"I knew you had some skills from the hats I've seen you wear but these are on another level. Are these all spoken for?"

"Not all of them. I'm shipping out those displayed ones tomorrow, and some of the others were sold to a small boutique. The unclaimed ones will go up on the site soon."

"Do people ever ask for anything specific? Or do you just design off of vibes?"

"I guess you could say that. There's only been a couple of times where I made anything customized to someone's request. Usually I just design what comes to me."

"Wow." Liz went around looking at every hat that was displayed before turning to him, her hands on her hips. "I'm sincerely blown away, and that's not just because I'm sweet on you."

He chuckled. "I take that as a high compliment, coming from a Creative Director."

"Speaking of that, I hope you'd be willing to help me out with something."

"What's that?"

"That showcase I've been working on; you know how I've been telling you that it's missing something but I couldn't figure out what? Well..." She motioned around the room. "I've figured it out. Your hats would be perfect. They're *just* the kind of vibe I'm looking for."

"Oh wow..." Luther rubbed the back of his neck, suddenly looking nervous. "Liz, I don't know..."

"You could loan them to us or we'd buy them from you. We'd still give you full credit, of course. Think of all the business you would get once more people find out about these. They're *that* good. You could really blow up."

"You know these are *men's* fedoras, right? I've barely dabbled in women's."

"Doesn't matter. I can see most of the ones I'm looking at over there with one of the outfits in the showcase just as they are. The fact that they're men's hats is actually a plus, in my head; a fly touch of masculine to top off the sexy Corporate Diva vibe. It's that extra *umph* I've been looking for all this time. Oh my god, I'm so *amped* about this!"

"Can I think about it?"

Her hands fell as her excitement melted into curiosity. "Sure, but...I'm not sure why you're hesitating. I'd think getting more recognition for your brand would be a *good* thing."

"Yeah..."

"I mean, you're already selling them so you're clearly not just making them for the hell of it. And I can't imagine that it's a self-confidence issue, from what I know of you. Are you worried about getting overwhelmed? I know you're currently doing all of this yourself but if it gets to where you need to expand, you know I'd help you. I've built up a lot of resources and connections over the years. What's the problem?"

"There's no *problem*; it's just something I need to think about. I'm very particular about business connections and I don't want that to come between our personal relationship."

"Oh. You're really worried about that? That us working together would cause an issue?"

"That's part of the reason. The main thing is the part about being mindful who I connect with, business-wise. I've had some unfortunate experiences in the past that have resulted in me being extra cautious. I hope you don't take that personally but that's the reality."

"No, I get it. A lot of things can change when money becomes involved."

"Exactly. But I sincerely am flattered that you feel my pieces would help you and I will absolutely consider your offer. And I won't take forever to do it because I know you're kinda on a time crunch."

"I am. And I promise not to pressure you about it. But would it help if you saw the pieces I want to pair your hats with? Maybe that would help you see the vision."

"Is that usually done? You showing the collection to outsiders before the big reveal?"

"Hey, you showed me yours, so I don't mind showing you mine." She smiled, going over to him and sliding her arms around his waist. "And unless you're also a fashion blogger or some other member of the press, I'm not worried about that. I know we haven't known each other that long, but I have enough trust in you to do that. Especially if it'll help put your mind at ease."

"I know how important your work is to you so that means a lot to me, Liz. We can do that. And I promise to give you an answer soon, either way. All right?"

Liz nodded, managing to keep her face even. She had hoped he would just readily agree and didn't love being put on hold while he considered whatever he needed to consider, but she could be patient. This *was* his art after all, and she didn't have to understand his reasons or methods for deciding who he shared it with.

"That works," she told him, reaching up to brush a stray hair from his cheek before pulling his face down to hers for a brief kiss. "Either way, thank you for letting me see your work space like this. I really am touched by that."

"I'm glad. You hungry?"

"I could eat."

They headed back to the main house, their joined hands swinging between them. As soon as they stepped inside, the doorbell rang.

"You expecting someone?" Liz asked.

"It might be my brother; he said something about possibly coming by today but I don't always know when to take him seriously."

"I'm just getting to meet all of your family members already. That's unusual for me, I must admit."

"Yeah? Well, I hope this doesn't sour you on it because Carter can be kind of a pain in the ass."

"Hey, I heard that!" Carter yelled through the door, making Liz laugh.

Shaking his head, Luther went to open the front door, revealing his frowning younger brother. "Come on in, Carter."

"Uh-huh." Carter glared at Luther as he stepped inside, but his expression immediately changed upon seeing Liz. "Damn!"

"Watch it, brother," Luther quickly warned. He closed the door and crossed his arms over his chest. "She's with me."

"Since when do you have a girlfriend? You've always been so damn secretive."

"I'm not secretive; I just don't tell you everything. Anyway, Carter Monroe, this is Liz Tate. We met when I went to Belize a few weeks ago."

"And you flew her out here? I didn't know you went over there looking for a wife. I've heard of brothas doing that but didn't think you needed to go there." Carter stepped closer to Liz, now looking at her as if she was some kind of science experiment. "I'm Carter. Are you Black or one of those nationalities where you can't tell? Do you speak English?"

"Oh hell..." Luther groaned as Liz laughed harder, covering her mouth with her hands. "From one, Belize is an English-speaking country, so you can quit talking like that. Two, I did not go over there looking for a bride. And three, yes, she's Black. Doofus."

"Well, I think those are all valid questions. It's hard to tell nowadays." Carter extended his hand to Liz, who was still trying to compose herself. "Nice to meet you, Liz. I won't take it personally that you're about to hurt yourself laughing at me."

"It's nice to meet you, too," Liz finally managed to reply, placing her hand in his. His grip tightened immediately. "Luther has told me a few things about you already."

"Yeah, I heard," Carter grunted, cutting his eyes at his older brother. "So that means we need to spend some more time together so I can un-do whatever he said. I'll even give you my number-"

"Man, if you don't quit flirting with my ...my date," Luther admonished, giving Carter's shoulder a shove. "And you can let her hand go now."

"Oh, yeah." Carter reluctantly released Liz's hand, unable to resist giving her another sweeping gaze. "I don't suppose you have a hot sister or anything, huh?"

"I actually do," Liz replied, still smiling. "She's happily married with three kids, though."

"Of course she is. Seems like all the fire ones are spoken for lately. You don't have any other friends that are currently unattached that might appreciate the company of a suave, well-hung-"

"Carter!"

"What?" Carter looked at his frowning brother as Liz erupted into another fit of giggles. "We're all grown. And let's not act like women don't appreciate that."

"Liz doesn't need to know how hung you are, well or otherwise."

"Uh, I think she can speak for herself, bro."

"You're right, I can," Liz agreed, winking at Luther. "I don't need to know how hung you are, Carter, well or otherwise."

"Well, aren't you two just a match made in heaven," Carter grumbled.

Unable to resist chuckling at the expression on his brother's face, Luther asked, "Man, why are you here, again?"

"You said you had some protein powder for me."

"Oh yeah. I'll run and get it."

Once Luther was out of the room, Carter turned his attention back to Liz. "That's a nice dress. Navy blue is your color."

Liz eyed him warily, unsure if he was setting her up for something. "Thanks..."

"What kind of flowers are those on it?"

"Um...I'm not sure, actually. I'm not really into flowers like that; just liked the dress."

"A woman that doesn't like flowers? Lo and behold."

"There's quite a few of us. One of my friends doesn't like them, either. You'd do better bringing her snack cakes than flowers."

"And this snack cake-loving friend...is she available? And hot?"

"Hot, yes. Available, no. She actually just got married a little over a year ago."

"Ugh. So I guess all your damn friends are cuffed, huh?"

"Actually..." Liz looked at him, brightening. "I *do* have one that isn't. But I think you've met her already."

"I did? When?"

Just then, Luther returned with a big box, setting it near the door. "Is he still in here begging?"

"I am not-"

"He kinda is," Liz interjected. "But I was just about to suggest introducing him to Kinsley."

Luther's eyebrows lifted in surprise. "Oh...interesting."

"I'm not sure how much you two interacted when you all went out that time, but she's currently unattached," Liz informed Carter. "And, per your request, hot."

"Wait, who are we talking about?" Carter asked with an upheld hand. "When did I meet her? I don't know anyone named Kinsley."

"She was the cousin of the girl you were with on the double date a while back," Luther informed him. "The one I was paired with."

"Oh..." Carter frowned as if he was trying to remember her. "I admit I didn't pay her much attention; we hardly spoke at all. All I remember is she had super-red hair."

"Yep, that's her."

"You two might just hit it off," Liz added. "It's all I have to offer in the hook-up department."

"Uh-oh. What's wrong with her?"

"There's nothing wrong with her!"

"Is she still upset about me?" Luther asked Liz. "I'd rather not invite any drama if I can help it."

Liz shook her head. "No, she's said she's over that. We hashed all that out. She might like to meet Carter for herself. Couldn't hurt to give it a shot."

"I'm down if she's down," Carter shrugged. He glanced at the box Luther brought in. "I thought it was just a couple of tubs, man. What is all this?"

"A former sponsor sent me a ton of product so I'm sharing the wealth," Luther replied. "Now, I need you to take it and go, because Liz and I were about to head out."

"Fine, okay. I can take a hint."

"It wasn't a hint."

Once Carter was gone (but not before double-verifying with Liz that she would sing his praises to Kinsley), Liz and Luther headed out. Both in the mood for fried fish, they headed to Rocky's. Luther opened Liz's car door for her and reached for her hand. But halfway across the parking lot, she eased it from his grip.

"What's wrong?" he asked.

"Nothing."

He arched a brow but let it go.

Once they were inside and waiting to place their orders, Luther stood behind Liz and placed his hands on her shoulders and gave a quick kiss to the back of her neck. She flinched and stepped forward out of his reach, her eyes on the wall menu behind the registers as if she needed a closer look. She could feel Luther looking at her but acted like she didn't.

Luther went to get their drinks while Liz made a quick trip to the restroom. When she returned, he glanced at her over his shoulder and called out, "What you want, baby? Fruit punch and lemonade mix?"

Anxiously glancing around them, Liz quickened her steps. "That was kinda loud, Luther."

"No...it wasn't. Liz, what's going on?"

"What do you mean?"

"Really? We're doing this? You've been acting funny since we got here. Do you not want people to know we're together or something?"

"No, Luther...it's nothing like that."

"Then what is it?"

"I'd really rather not talk about this right now. And really, it's nothing to get upset about."

Just then, their order number was called and Luther gave her another curious glance before going to get it. They headed to a back table, Liz carrying the drinks and Luther carrying the tray of food. She sat across the table from him, placing her purse in the seat between. He noted it but didn't comment.

The tension seemed to lift some as they ate and talked, and even laughed when recalling Carter's earlier visit. Luther was enjoying his time with Liz as usual, but he wasn't able to totally put her behavior out of his mind or take her word that it was nothing to worry about. But he sensed that it was something she wanted to address in private, so he told himself it could wait.

"You need me to take you home or can you hang out longer?" he asked her once they were heading outside.

"I'm all yours." She smiled up at him.

He glanced at her strangely but fixed his face. "Good."

Once they were back inside his car, she immediately placed her hand on his thigh. He just looked at it before pulling out of the parking lot.

"You feel like watching something?" he asked once they were at his house. "You can decide."

"Yeah, we can do that. Doesn't matter what we watch; I just want to cuddle with you." She ran her hands up his back before stepping in front of him and hugging him around his neck. "Thank you for lunch, by the way."

"You're welcome." Luther hugged her back, but now he was even more confused. She'd done another one-eighty on him, and he didn't understand what was causing the switches. He'd come to know Liz as being rather straightforward but he sensed she was holding something back from him now.

But he told himself to let it go. They were there, together, spending time and enjoying each other, and he didn't want to mar that by digging for issues. She was happy so he decided to just leave it at that.

They kicked their shoes off and got settled on the couch, with Luther throwing a light blanket over Liz's lap before pulling her close. She snuggled against him, resting her head on his chest and her hand on his stomach.

"This is nice," she murmured.

His hand rubbed her back. "Yeah, it is. Really nice."

"I appreciate you being patient, Luther."

"What, about the hats?"

"Well yeah, but I'm talking about us. What you said about wanting to make sure I was really ready for the kind of relationship you want made more and more sense the more I thought about it. I thought I was ready to jump right in headfirst but I realized I'm not quite there yet."

"I sensed that."

"But it doesn't mean I don't want to be," she quickly added, sitting up to look at him. "I want this, Luther. Really. I'm feeling you more than I've felt anyone, and I refuse to disrespect you by agreeing to a commitment I'm not ready for. But I'm not scared of it. This has nothing to do with me trying to run from what we have; I hope you know that."

His lips lifting in a half-smile, he nodded. "I believe you, baby."

"Good. 'Cause I don't want you to go anywhere. I can admit I'm...I'm falling for you."

Luther felt himself warming at her words and the sincerity painted all over her face. His earlier frustration was forgotten as he leaned forward and grabbed her chin before giving her a lingering kiss.

"I fell for you in Belize," he reminded her, their lips inches apart. "And I already told you, I'm not going anywhere. We might move at different speeds but as long as I know we're trying to get to the same place together, I can be as patient as I need to be."

She slid her arms around his neck, giving him a tight hug. Luther buried his face in her neck, holding her just as tightly. This was the woman he wanted, and he believed she was sincere in wanting him back. Being secure in that was all he could do for now.

• • • •

"DAMN, IT'S BEEN A MINUTE since we've all hung out, hasn't it?"

Liz looked over at Natalia thoughtfully as she, Lovey, and their friend Desiree Mashburn-Wade assembled their various goodies on Desiree's kitchen counters. "Yeah, I guess it has been. We've all got so much going on now."

Lovey had insisted on them scheduling a girl's night and Liz surely needed it. She looked forward to a night of drinking and getting caught up with her girls while they stuffed their faces. There was sushi, mini chicken salad sandwiches, pita chips and hummus, and fresh fruit. And since Desiree had a sweet tooth out of this world and considered no meal complete without them, she made sure there were plenty of mini cheesecakes and red velvet brownies.

"Are these vegan desserts from your man or are they the real deal?" Natalia asked Desiree, referring to her husband Lorenzo. He had a talent for making vegan desserts that were so good that you (usually) couldn't tell they weren't the sugary, fattening versions.

"No, Lorenzo didn't make these. He's been so busy at the firm he hasn't had time to bake. I've made sure whatever free time he has is spent on me."

"Of course you have."

"Well, hell. I need my attention, too. I'm sure you and Lovey know what that's like."

"I mean, yeah, E.J. does have his hands in a lot of things, but we made a promise to not let work interfere with our time as a couple. We make time for date night once a week, which isn't always easy with a newborn in the house."

"And Roland delegates as much as possible so he can spend time with me and the kids," Lovey added. "Or he'll work from home. With three young children and us both having busy careers, we don't get a ton of alone time but we're not complaining. The family we have is what we prayed for so we make it work."

"Y'all done baby-making or is Roland trying to put some more buns in that oven?"

Lovey giggled, grabbing one of the mini sandwiches. "We thought we might like to have one more but I think we're done. We talked about it and we're both good with three. But, you never know."

"Yeah, she's gonna get knocked up again," Desiree surmised, nudging her before taking a couple of bottles of wine out of the refrigerator. "Y'all know how she and Roland are always all over each other."

"As if you and Lorenzo aren't the same way. You *stay* humping that man."

"I'm not gonna deny it."

"Hell, I wouldn't be surprised if I'm the one that got knocked up next," Natalia commented. She put several pieces of sushi on her plate. "E.J. has gotten greedy since we had Aria, already talking about having another one and she's not even a year old yet."

"Do *you* want another one?" Liz asked her. "How are you dealing with motherhood so far?"

"Not to mention changing careers, going from being a software engineer to managing Natavey," Desiree added. "That's gotta be a lot."

"It is, but I actually love it more than I thought I would. Y'all know how wary I was about having kids at first because of the affect I thought it would have on my marriage but it's only made it better and stronger. I wouldn't trade my little nugget for anything; Aria is my heart. And fatherhood has brought out a whole different side of E.J.; he's whipped already."

They all laughed.

"And as far as the career change, it was right on time. Managing Natavey has been an adjustment but I enjoy that so much more than being stuck behind a computer all day. I overhauled the websites for all the clubs and I just sold an app, so I'm still using my skills. Of course E.J. wants me to develop one for them now, too."

"Hell, I'm surprised he hasn't asked you to do that already," Desiree snorted, filling up her wine glass. "Well, business is good for me, too. Aside from handling events and promotion at Barfly, 845, and Natavey, I've also been contacted recently by a couple of celebrities to do some stuff for them."

"Yeah? Who?" Natalia asked excitedly.

"I'm not supposed to say yet. But one plays ball and one is a real housewife. Who happens to not even be married."

"Congratulations on that!" Lovey exclaimed, giving her bestie a brief hug. They'd been best friends since they were barely teenagers. "I'm so happy for you."

"I appreciate it. Between that and the fine hunk of man I married, I'm really living the dream right now."

"So what's been going on with *you*, Liz?"Natalia asked. "You've been kinda quiet."

"Oh, I'm just letting y'all hog all the limelight," Liz joked, drawing laughs from her friends. "No, but I'm good. Work is work; busy as ever. Getting ready for a big showcase in a few months. And..."

They all looked at her expectantly. "And what?"

Liz hesitated slightly. She loved her friends but didn't usually dish about her relationships; she gave vague details, at best. But she wanted to blab about her own love life like they did about theirs.

"I've been seeing someone," she admitted.

"Oooh, the one you met in Belize?" Lovey piped up, grinning. "Luther, is it?"

"Yeah."

"Is that the one you were with when I had to kick you out of the lounge at Natavey?" Natalia asked. "They were trying to close the damn place down, y'all. I must say, though, girl, I can see why. Buddy was hot."

"Yep, that's him." She got Natalia and Desiree caught up on how she and Luther met overseas and then reunited back at home by chance. "We've been pretty much all over each other since then. I'm really, really feeling him. Like, on-the-verge-of-falling, feeling him."

"That's wonderful!" Lovey squealed, grabbing Liz's hand.

"Why do I sense a 'but' coming?" Desiree asked, eying Liz. "What else aren't you telling us? Are you trying to fight the feelings or something?"

Liz shook her head. "No, it's not that. Well...Luther is very affectionate and when we're alone, I love that. But when we're out in public...not so much."

"Oh..." the ladies chorused in realization.

"Not big on the PDA, huh?" Natalia surmised.

"Not really. And I can see this being a potential issue; he's already asked me about it once but thankfully let it go. I don't expect him to keep doing that, though."

"Well, what's your issue with it? Is he trying to grab your ass when y'all are out?"

"Slob you down?"

"Fondle you under the table?"

"Grind on you while you're waiting in line?"

"Titty tweak?"

"Are y'all done?" Liz asked, amusingly rolling her eyes as her friends laughed their heads off. "He hasn't done any of that and I doubt he would. It's just been stuff like holding hands or putting his arm around me."

"Oh hell. That's it?"

"That's plenty, for me. I've never been one for putting my affections on display like that. Back in the day, my parents were always doing that stuff whenever we went anywhere and it always creeped me out. I found it embarrassing."

"Seriously? I found it romantic," Lovey noted. "It was an example of the kind of relationship I wanted to have for myself. I *loved* seeing them show their affection for each other. It was beautiful to see, them so in love."

"You can be in love without being all over each other in public."

"Liz, girl, holding hands isn't 'being all over each other,'" Natalia informed. "Kids do that."

"Yeah, but who's to say that Luther will keep it at tame stuff like that? What if he gets comfortable and tries to...I don't know...do that mess where you encircle your arms around each other's while you drink champagne? Or do some of the stuff y'all mentioned just now?"

"Oh brother," Desiree rolled her eyes. "Okay, one, if you're together, he's probably already comfortable. Two, you *just* said you doubted he'd do the stuff we said. And three, hardly anyone does the corny-ass arm-tangling drink thing."

"Liz, if this is a sincere concern of yours, you need to talk to him about it," Lovey advised. "I'm sure he wouldn't do it if he knew it made you uncomfortable. He can't read your mind."

"Yeah, that's true, but I also think Liz needs to loosen up a *little* bit," Natalia chimed in. "I get it; PDA isn't for everybody. But it's not like he's trying to sex her against the car in the mall parking lot."

"I've done that," Desiree grinned. "It's fun."

The three of them just shook their heads at her before Natalia continued. "I'm just saying, Liz. If you're not even willing to hold hands with your man in public...I don't know."

"Well, I more than make up for it in private," Liz defended. "That should count for something."

Lovey came over and put an arm around her sister. "Again I say, talk to Luther. Don't stew and fret over it and keep him in the dark. If he's your man, you have to be able to communicate with him."

"We're not *official*-official yet. But I know you're right."

"Take it from me, you don't want the kinds of problems that come with not being straight up with your man," Natalia warned. "You saw what happened between me and E.J. last year."

Natalia and E.J.'s marriage had been in serious trouble after he found out she'd lied about wanting children when she didn't, not to mention some other things she hadn't been honest about. They even separated for a while. Natalia was a mess, worrying if she'd driven her husband out the door.

"That's a good point," Liz mused, remembering that situation all too well. She certainly didn't want anything like that happening with her and Luther. The thought of losing him wasn't one she enjoyed.

When her phone chimed, Liz pulled it from the pocket of her jumpsuit. She couldn't help the grin that broke out across her face when she saw it was a text from Luther letting her know he missed her.

"Oh, that is so sweet!" Lovey gushed, getting a peek at the text. "I so can't wait to meet him."

"Yeah, I've never seen you blush like that so he must have you good and sprung," Desiree added. "Hang onto this one."

"I wouldn't be surprised if you come up in here with an engagement ring before too long," Natalia predicted. "Though I know you're gonna deny it."

Her friends knew her well because she certainly *would* deny that. Liz was in no hurry to get married, but she was absolutely sure she didn't want to lose Luther. She'd like to believe that he'd be understanding about the PDA issue, especially once he heard her reasoning, but she couldn't be sure. If it was something he insisted on, it could create an issue between them that they might not be able to fix. She didn't want their relationship to come to a screeching halt over something like holding hands or sharing a smooch in public. She'd have to nip it in the bud and let him know, and just hope to high heaven it didn't stop their relationship when it was just getting started.

• • • •

CHAPTER 9

• • • •

IT HAD BEEN A LONG day that began at seven a.m., and Liz still had to go get her dry cleaning and run by the store. She couldn't wait to get home, take a ridiculously long hot shower, and collapse on her couch with the remote.

She had just gotten to Home Goods and grabbed a basket when she got a frantic call from Kinsley.

"Can you come get me?" she hissed. Her voice was muffled slightly.

"What? Where are you?"

"I'm on a date and it's...it's hell on earth, pretty much. And I stupidly let him pick me up instead of driving my own car."

"Wow, it's that bad?"

"It's that bad, girl. Can you *please* come get me??"

"All right, all right," Liz sighed, returning her basket to the stack. She figured she could get the things she needed the next day. "Send me your location and I'll be on the way. I'm heading out to my car now."

"Thank you, thank you, *thank you*! I *so* owe you for this."

"Yes, you do."

Kinsley sent her location to Liz a few moments later and Liz was relieved to see she wasn't that terribly far away. When she arrived at the address, though, she wasn't expecting it to be a house. It was faded green and looked rather plain, and no lights were on, and she started to wonder if she was in the right place when Kinsley came sprinting from around the side of the house. Liz hooted with laughter when Kinsley tripped on something and face-planted into the grass, but tried to contain herself as Kinsley fumbled to her feet and skittered over to yank open the passenger door.

"Okay, step on it!"

"Really? We being trailed by the mob?"

"Liz!"

"Okay, okay." Liz pulled away from the house just as a husky beige brown man stepped onto the porch and looked after them, throwing his arm up in frustration. Kinsley turned to watch until he was out of sight before plopping onto her bottom in her seat with a sigh.

"Ma'am, what is going on?" Liz demanded.

Before Kinsley could respond, her phone started going off. She glanced at the screen and let out a long exasperated (and loud) grunt of frustration. "This punk-ass..."

"Kinsley."

"I met dude on a dating app and he invited me to a party. We'd been chatting for a while online and then over the phone and I thought he was cool so I was down. He neglected to tell me it was a damn swingers party."

"What??"

"Everything was chill at first and then a couple people started kissing. I didn't think anything of it but then they started really going at it...like, *really* going at it. Growling and shit like some animals. Then clothes started coming off and once *they* kicked it off, everybody else joined in. I've never seen folks get naked so damn fast."

Liz pulled her lips in, trying her best not to laugh.

"Then my date pulled *his* shirt off. Not only did he expect me to participate in that shit, turned out the picture he'd used on his dating profile was hella old, unless he gained sixty pounds recently. I don't mind big men but don't lie about it. Then he started reaching and grabbing on me."

"And that's when you snuck off and called me?"

"Uhh...well, I *started* to. But somehow he coerced me into letting him go down on me-"

"Oh damn..."

"Well! I figured since I was there I might as well get something out of it! But he did not know what the *hell* he was doing! Dude put his entire face in it which might *sound* like a good thing but it is so, so not."

Unable to hold it anymore, Liz burst out laughing, actually jerking the car a bit before pulling into a nearby fast food parking lot so she could compose herself. Kinsley just glared at her.

"I'm glad you think this is funny."

"I'm sorry, girl, but you know you would be clowning me if the roles were reversed."

"Whatever." She sucked her teeth as her phone rang again. "Lemme go ahead and block this joker..."

"He didn't tell you where y'all were going?"

"He said his friends were having a casual get together. I mean, really. Who the hell thinks it's appropriate to take someone to a swingers party on a first date and not tell them?"

"Kinsley," Liz's face was actually red from laughing so hard, "Let's not act like you wouldn't still be there enjoying yourself if he knew how to munch that muffin."

"Munch that muffin? Are you twelve?"

"Don't try to turn this around on me."

"Whatever. Can we go?"

"You sure? I can run you back over there if you need to work off all this frustration you have going on right now. Since it's a swingers thing you can try someone else there to get you off; I'm sure *one* of those men there knows what they're doing. Or if it doesn't *have* to be a man-"

"Are you done?"

Liz fell back against the seat in another fit of laughter, tears rolling down her face. Kinsley just folded her arms in a huff, tapping her foot and waiting.

"Okay, okay, I'm done," Liz finally assured a couple minutes later, wiping her eyes before putting the car in Drive. "I must say, I don't even mind that I had to put off my errands for this. *Well* worth it."

"Hilarious. Ooh, pull around to the drive-thru so I can get some fries. The punk didn't feed me, either."

Once they each got some fries and orange Hi-C's and were back on the road, Kinsley asked how things were going with Luther.

"They're fine," Liz replied casually. She plucked some fries from the bag in her lap.

"Just fine?"

"I mean, I like him a lot. But we're not a couple or anything still. It's...casual. We're just dating and seeing where it goes, like I told you before."

Liz wished she didn't still felt the need to downplay her feelings for Luther to Kinsley. But she had the inkling that her friend wouldn't be as supportive as she'd hope. Kinsley had already admitted to being jealous about Liz and Luther hooking up, and even though she'd apologized, Liz didn't believe all that jealousy was gone. And she didn't want to have to curse her friend out for saying the wrong thing.

Kinsley was eying her, again sensing that Liz wasn't being totally forthcoming. Liz kept her eyes on the road, periodically stuffing fries into her mouth or sipping her drink.

"I hope you don't mind my saying this but...Luther is mad sexy. I kinda hate that we got off to the start that we did because if I'd met him in any other situation, I would've shot my shot."

Liz's ears twitched instantly and her face felt like it was going to snap, it tightened so much. "Is that right?"

"No disrespect. I'm just stating facts."

"It's fine. Luther *is* incredibly sexy. Can't fault you for noticing that."

"Would you fault me if I tried to shoot my shot now?"

"Excuse me?" Liz's head whipped around, her anger instant.

Kinsley didn't look fazed. "I asked if it would bother you if I were to step to Luther."

"Are these hypothetical questions?"

"Would it matter?"

"Why the hell would you do that?" Liz snapped. "And why would you think it was even okay to ask after what I just told you?"

"Uh, I *believe* what you just told me was that you aren't a couple and you're keeping it casual. If you're just dating, it shouldn't be a problem if he saw other people, right? If I recall correctly, you told me when I asked about you two the first time that he's free to do whatever he wants."

Liz blew a long breath through her nose, biting her bottom lip so hard she could almost taste blood. She now hated this blasé path she'd chosen to take; true enough, she and Luther weren't an official couple, but there wasn't anything casual about how she felt about him. And she certainly didn't want him seeing anybody else, whether he was within his rights to do so or not.

"Still, Kinsley, it's pretty jacked up for you to come at me with this knowing I'm dating him," she finally pushed out, cutting her eyes at her. "We're supposed to be friends and you're scheming on my man?"

"Oh, he's your man now? You weren't saying that before."

"You know what, Kinsley-"

"No, Liz, just forget I said anything," Kinsley held up a hand. "I'm not trying to be at odds with you over some dick."

Liz's nostrils flared as she jammed a little too hard on the brakes at a red light. "He's not just *some dick*. He's a whole man with a mind, body and soul. And it sounds to me like you're still jealous that I got him and you didn't."

"You're awfully snippy over someone you're just seeing *casually*, girl."

Forcing herself to take a breath, Liz tried to calm down. Part of this was her own fault for not being upfront about the nature of her and Luther's relationship. But while she didn't necessarily buy into the whole 'girl code' thing, she thought it was pretty messed up that Kinsley had the nerve to lust over Luther right in her face, whether she thought he was actually her man or not.

But she decided she'd make Kinsley put her money where her mouth was. She wanted to see just how much nerve Kinsley had.

"Okay, fine," she said bitingly, glancing at her friend who she wasn't feeling very friendly towards in the moment. "If you're feeling Luther that hard, go for it."

The shock on Kinsley's face was evident. "What?"

"Shoot your shot. Make your move. If you're bold enough to put it out there, go for yours. I just hope you can handle whatever comes from it."

Kinsley was quiet for a few moments before she slowly reached for her cup and took a long sip, her plump blackberry-colored lips closing over the straw. She eventually returned the cup to the holder and let out a noise that Liz couldn't decipher, her long black coffin-shaped nails tapping the lid.

"Well, since you're okay with it, I will."

Liz's eyebrows lifted slightly but she fought to keep the frown from bursting through on her face like it wanted to. She half-expected Kinsley to back off once she called her bluff, if for no other reason than she and Liz were friends. But apparently, Kinsley really had intentions of going for Luther, which burned Liz's gut.

But Liz reminded herself that it wouldn't matter. Luther wasn't interested in Kinsley, anyway, so no matter what she did, he wouldn't entertain any advances she tried. Liz didn't usually put anything past anyone, especially men, but she truly believed that.

"Good luck with that, then."

"Mmm-hmm."

• • • •

LIZ WAS STILL SMARTING over that whole scene with Kinsley the next day. She fully expected for Kinsley to call and tell her she wasn't serious about trying anything with Luther, but that didn't happen. Apparently, Kinsley's jealousy and frustration over being single was blocking out her loyalty.

"Whatever," Liz muttered to herself with a frustrated sigh. She hated that she was even stressing over this. She'd never let herself worry about competition over a man before. If he chose to be with someone else, then to hell with him and he became dead to Liz. But she already knew it wouldn't be as easy to write Luther off if he ended up succumbing to Kinsley's advances.

Making herself put it out of her mind, Liz concentrated on the meeting she was supposed to be paying attention to. She slyly glanced at her watch and was glad to see that almost an hour had passed and it was almost time to wrap it up. It was a budget meeting, which she always enjoyed as much as she enjoyed trigonometry back in the day (which was not at all.). As soon as the final roundtable was done and they wished everyone a good day, Liz was shooting out of her chair and heading back to her office.

She had to go and meet with a jewelry designer whose pieces she was going to include in an upcoming campaign and possibly the showcase, which she usually didn't have a problem with, but this particular designer was super particular about how her work was going to be used.

"Is there going to be nudity?" Summer, the jewelry designer asked for the second time. "I can't have my pieces in a nude showing. The human body is beautiful and all-"

"There won't be any nudity," Liz insisted, summoning patience. "I've told you, this is going to be a sexy but classy aesthetic."

"Okay, good. That does make me feel better. I'm not a prude but I prayed over these pieces, had sage going when I made them. I even covered my hands in purified soil. I want them to be seen in the light in which they were created."

Liz resisted the strong urge to roll her eyes, reminding herself not to mock anyone's creative process, not matter how utterly ridiculous it sounded.

"I get it. And I absolutely respect that, Summer. I've shown you the storyboards for what we're going to do," Liz reminded her. "You can trust that we'll use your pieces with the reverence that you require. And you've seen what we do at Azon; everything is high-level. Believe me, as amazing as your work is, there's no way we'd do anything to disrespect them or you."

Summer beamed, her thick chunky locs hanging over her face. She rubbed a hand over her arm that was completely covered in a myriad of tattoos. Liz didn't think she'd ever met anyone in person who was so thin; she could literally see Summer's bones poking through her halter top. But that wasn't what she cared about; she just needed to get her on board for this campaign so she could get on with her day.

After a little more back and forth, Summer finally agreed to let Liz use her pieces and Liz breathed a silent sigh of relief. Once they finalized everything, Liz headed out, intending to grab some lunch before heading back to the office.

Craving waffles and hash browns, she headed to Waffle House. She placed her order and checked messages and emails as she waited. Luther had sent a couple of texts earlier, and Liz's desire to see him surged, especially when she realized it had been a couple of days since she had. They communicated every day but she was easing into the space where she wanted to actually *be* with him every day. Maybe not all day every day, but getting to be around him and see that face and feel his touch at some point would be ideal. She wondered if that was abnormal to feel so early on. It surely felt strange to her.

Once she got her order, she was heading back out to her car when she happened to look up and do a double-take. She could've sworn that was Luther across the parking lot, and when she took several hurried steps closer, she realized it was. But what had her ear twitching was that he was with some other woman, laughing.

Liz stood there slack-jawed for a moment before turning on her heel, intending to just leave and not sweat it. It wasn't like they were hugged up, kissing and grinding. They were leaning on opposite cars having what looked to be a perfectly platonic conversation. Liz wasn't so insecure that she would trip off that.

So why were her feet taking her right back over there?

The click of her heels seemed extra loud as she stalked over. Luther noticed her when she was a few feet away, and the smile he was already sporting grew twice as wide. He pushed himself off his car as she approached.

"Hey, baby," he greeted, clearly happy to see her.

"Hey." She stopped where she was too far away for him to touch her but close enough to where she could get a look at his laughing companion, overtly of course. Big boobs, voluptuous, long black hair, brown skin. Figures.

"I didn't expect to see you over here," Luther said, apparently not noticing her simmering ire. "I would've invited you to lunch, if I had. Thought you'd be super busy all day."

"Ehh, I kinda am. Just leaving a meeting and wanted to grab something while I was out." Liz was waiting on an introduction and wondered if she'd have to initiate it or if he would.

As if sensing this, Luther shook his head. "Oh damn, my bad...it's actually cool to run into you, baby, 'cause now you finally get to meet Jules in person. You remember talking to her on the video chat a little while back?"

Liz felt immediate cold wash over her body as she turned to the smiling woman, finally taking a good look at her face. Now that she was paying attention and not going off pure attitude, she absolutely recognized the pretty round-faced woman that she'd hit it off with so well. Instantly, she felt ridiculous.

"Hey, girl," Jules greeted her with a brief wave. "I see why Lu-Lu talks about you so much. We can't have a conversation without him working you in there somewhere. You're even prettier in person."

Relaxing, Liz smiled. "I can say the same about you. It's good to officially meet you, Jules. You two had lunch or something?"

"Not together. I actually had a lunch date and saw Luther coming out of the farmer's market over there," she said, pointing across the parking lot. "We were just cutting up for a minute, being silly. But I need to get going, actually, so I'll leave you two lovebirds and get on my way. Lu-Lu, talk to you later. Liz, here," she fished a business card from her Coach purse and held it out. "I was serious about us meeting up for lunch. Feel free to text or call me sometime."

Liz took the card, nodding. "Absolutely. Hope you enjoy the rest of your day."

"I surely will once I'm back in my living room with a big ol' glass of wine and some edibles. It's been a day. Bye, y'all!"

"Drive safe, Jules," Luther told her.

Liz moved closer to Luther as Jules got in her Audi and drove off with a wave. Once she was gone, Luther turned to Liz and started to say something but she held up her hand.

"Here's where I need to admit that I totally jumped to conclusions when I saw you and Jules over here because I didn't immediately recognize her, and was fully prepared to show my ass. But I'm glad I didn't because I feel stupid enough right now. I'm sorry about that."

He looked at her for a moment before stepping closer and taking her hand. "I see we still have more to learn about each other, huh?"

"Seems so."

"I appreciate the apology. Consider it forgiven and forgotten."

"Just like that? Wow."

"You made a mistake. You apologized. No need in making it a bigger deal than it needs to be. I'd much rather focus on how glad I am to see you."

She grinned but when he leaned down to kiss her, she automatically eased back. He straightened and dropped her hand, looking at her evenly.

"I'm glad to see you, too," Liz emphasized, hoping to avoid a tense exchange. "I hate I have to get back to work...what are you about to do?"

He took a moment before answering, still eying her as if trying to figure her out. "I have a consultation with a potential new training client and then I was going to work on some designs. If you're free later I'd love to see you."

"Absolutely," she agreed, hoping she didn't sound too eager. "I already know I won't be in the mood to go out, though, so I'll just come over after I get a chance to go home and change when I get off. And I'll bring dinner."

"You don't have to do that, baby. I like cooking for you."

"I know you do and I appreciate it, but you're always doing stuff for me; I want to do something for you, even if it is just buying something someone else made."

He chuckled. "All right, then. I don't think I've mentioned it but I don't care for Chinese food. Just putting it on your mind; that's really the only cuisine I don't mess with."

"No Chinese food. Noted. Do you have a taste for anything in particular?"

"Just you."

Liz almost forgot about her PDA aversion because she wanted to jump him right in the parking lot. It still amazed her how this man made her feel like the most priceless thing walking.

"How do you always manage to scramble my brain and make me lose my breath, Mr. Monroe?" Liz mumbled with an uncharacteristically shy smile, smoothing her hand down the back of her tapered haircut.

"I'm just being me. And in case you need reminding, 'me' is only interested in 'you.'" He tweaked her chin. "But I'll show you better than I can tell you."

"I believe you. Though I still look forward to it."

"And maybe you should consider leaving an outfit or two at my house," he continued. "And some toiletries. Just so you don't always have to carry a bunch of stuff back and forth."

Her eyebrows lifted. "You want me to leave stuff at your place?"

"Why not?" he shrugged. "As much as I love having you there, I want you to be comfortable. And for things to be easier for you."

"Wow...I guess that means you'll have to make room for my facial products in your bathroom and clear out a drawer."

"I'll do you one better. I'll make room in my closet, too."

When she released a dramatic gasp, he laughed. "You're silly, you know that?"

"I have my moments," she hunched her shoulders with a smile. "I need to get back to work but I can't wait to see you later. I'll give you a call when I'm on the way."

"Cool. Am I allowed to hug you?"

Liz blinked as her smile flattened a bit, because she could hear the slight testiness in his tone. Since she felt like refusing wouldn't be smart, she stepped into his arms. The hug was brief and their bodies were mostly separated, but it was a hug. Luther was looking at her with a slight frown, rubbing his lips together.

"See you tonight," she mumbled as she patted his chest, turning and heading back to her car before he could respond. She felt a little silly and wondered what Luther was thinking of her right then. This couldn't keep happening without her addressing it with him; she knew they needed to have a talk when she went over later that night.

• • • •

THE LAST THING LIZ was expecting when she got to Luther's a few hours later was for him not to be alone again. Though this time, the unexpected guest was his daughter, Churi. And unlike her mother, she didn't look happy to see Liz at all.

"Liz, this is my baby girl Churi," Luther introduced, looking back and forth between them with a smile. "Churi, this is Liz Tate, the lady I'm seeing."

Liz plastered on a smile even though Churi was looking her up and down with clear distaste. "It's nice to meet you, Churi. Your dad is surely proud of you. What is it you were studying in school, again?"

Clearly in no hurry to respond, Churi rolled her tongue around her teeth. It wasn't until Luther gave her a pointed glare that she finally muttered, "Sociology."

"Interesting. What do you want to do with that?"

"Don't know yet." Churi rolled her eyes and turned her attention to her dad, her body language clearly indicating she was done with Liz. "Daddy, we were in the middle of a conversation."

"I told you when you showed up unannounced that I was expecting someone, Churi. We would've had plenty of time to talk if you'd shown up for our brunch this morning but you flaked on that. Again."

She huffed. "I'm sorry about that, Daddy, but-"

"And anyway, I already gave you my answer. I put you through undergrad. Your mama put you through grad school. If you want something more than that, apply for a grant or get a loan."

"A loan?? You want me to go into the real world you're always talking about already saddled with *debt*?"

"I want you to go into the real world, period."

"I'm already paying for my apartment!"

"Good for you. So you already know how to pay for everything else you need, too."

"Mama told you to say this stuff, didn't she? That sounds like something she'd say."

"Nah, this is all me, baby girl. You're twenty-three; it's time for you to get your hands out of our pockets."

"Daddyyyyy..."

Liz just stood quietly and listened to this exchange, slightly amused. It was interesting seeing Luther in this element. The hot dad who dealt with a loving but firm hand. It was endearing.

And Liz could see both Luther and Jules in Churi; she had Jules's big expressive eyes and Luther's chiseled features.

The rest of her was teeny-tiny, though, and Liz would have never believed she was twenty-three if someone hadn't told her. Churi definitely didn't get any of her father's height, as she couldn't have been more than 5'3. She sported a gold ring in her nose and in her exposed bellybutton, and there was a tattoo of a string of hearts going around her waist. Her hair was straight, black, and currently being twirled around her finger as she turned on the puppy dog eyes for her dad.

Luther was unfazed though. He ended their back and forth with a final and emphatic 'no', which resulted in an exaggerated pout that Liz almost giggled out loud at. Churi cut her eyes at her, as if she was to blame for Luther denying her wishes.

"I see we should talk about this when you're not distracted," Churi muttered bitingly. "Because I think your *company* is influencing you treating me like this."

Liz reared, not appreciating that comment at all. She wasn't going to be blamed, however indirectly, for anything Luther decided when it came to his daughter. Churi clearly had already decided she didn't like Liz, which was too bad, because Liz had no plans on kissing the butt of a twenty-three year old.

Apparently, Luther didn't appreciate Churi's comment, either. With a stern expression he ordered, "Look at me, Churi."

Churi's sneer that she'd flashed at Liz melted into a look of chastisement as she slowly turned towards her dad.

Standing at full height, Luther stood directly in front of her and said, "Get this straight: that is the *last* time you will disrespect Liz. Not just in front of me, but period. Like

I said, my decision was all me. You don't get to be grown when it comes to doing what you want and then want to come running back here like a child when it's time to be an *actual* adult and handle your shit. You wanna act childish? You have your own apartment for that. But when you're in *my* presence, you will behave like the woman your mother and I raised you to be. And that does not include being disrespectful to someone who has done nothing to you. Apologize." His finger extended in Liz's direction as his eyes stayed locked on Churi's. "*Now.*"

Sufficiently checked, Churi swallowed and turned towards Liz, who didn't try to erase the displeasure she still felt at the young woman's earlier statement from her expression. Liz wasn't just going to brush that off just because Churi was Luther's daughter. Just because she was the size of a child didn't mean she had to act like one.

"I apologize," Churi said with as much pleasantness as she could manage. "I shouldn't have said what I said."

"True," Liz couldn't resist agreeing. "But I accept your apology. Hopefully we can get along, Churi, because I'm really into your dad. And that's it. I'm not here to be your enemy."

Pursing her lips, Churi just gave her a short nod before looking back up at Luther as if waiting to see if she had served her penance.

"You're not done," he informed, his arms folded across his chest.

Confusion flitted across her face for a brief second before realization replaced it. "I apologize to you, too, Daddy."

When he simply nodded, she breathed a short sigh of relief.

"I'll leave you two alone," she said, stepping forward to hug her dad around the waist. "Bye, Daddy."

Returning her embrace, Luther kissed the top of her head. "Bye, baby girl. I love you."

"I love you, too." Churi stepped back and grabbed her purse from the kitchen counter. Knowing better than not to, she turned towards Liz and muttered a goodbye before turning for the door. Luther followed her to make sure she got off safely before rejoining Liz, and was surprised when she literally jumped into his arms and gave him a deep, impassioned kiss.

"Is it weird that watching you check her like that turned me the hell on?" she asked once she finally pulled back.

"I don't suppose so." His hands that were cupping her bottom squeezed. "And I'm not complaining."

"I appreciate you defending me."

"Always."

They shared another kiss before Liz reluctantly slid back to her feet, though she kept a lingering hand on his chest, her expression morphing into a pensive one. "Hey, can we talk?"

His face sobered as he nodded. Liz took his hand and led him to the living room, taking a seat next to him that was close but not touching. She turned towards him and rested both hands on his thigh, tangling her fingers as the nervousness over what she had to say returned.

"Luther, I know you've noticed how I'm not as affectionate in public."

Now knowing the discussion topic, Luther sighed and leaned against the back of the couch. "Kinda hard to miss. Especially since you're all over me when we're alone."

"Yeah...I'm not really big on public displays of affection. It just makes me skittish."

He slowly nodded, his lips twisting thoughtfully. "Any particular reason?"

"I hate to say it like this but I blame my parents. They were wonderful, don't get me wrong, but they were *not* shy about stuff like stopping in the middle of the sidewalk to hug, or start kissing while we're waiting in the drive-thru, or copping feels when they didn't think anybody was looking. It always embarrassed me. Clearly I'm not frigid or a prude but it's because of that that I prefer to keep my amorous activities behind closed doors."

"I see. So you saw your parents showing affection to each other as a bad thing?"

"When it was on display for any and everybody to see? Yes. It was like they were putting on a show, Luther. It always mortified me when people would stop and look at them. Or when they kept people waiting or held people up because they were too busy acting like some horny-ass teenagers."

"Wow, Liz. Don't you think you're putting a rather negative spin on it? Of course I wasn't there, but did they do anything *that* egregious? Occasional hugs and kisses and pats on the butt between two people in love doesn't sound that bad to me."

"They might not have been grinding or grabbing genitals out in the open but that doesn't mean I loved seeing it."

"And you've carried that into your own relationships and you want me to adhere to it, I take it."

Feeling like she was being baited, Liz hesitated, her eyes narrowing slightly. "Is that a problem?"

"I don't just love behind closed doors, Liz. I'm an affectionate man and I'm into you. And I don't want to have to act like your brother when we're out in public."

"I didn't say all that..."

"That's what you're telling me, though. Hell, you've already shown it. You won't even let me put my arm around you, let alone kiss or hug you when we're out and about. But as soon as we're alone, it's on. That's not how I roll."

Her breath quickened. "Luther, this isn't anything personal. I've been the same way with every man I've been with."

"I thought I've made it perfectly clear; I'm not trying to *be* like every man you've been with. You left them. I'm not in this for it to be temporary."

Her face flushed with a mix of astonishment and arousal. "I'm not either..." she confirmed carefully, trying to choose the right words. Her fingers gripped his thigh. "Luther, you *know* I wanna be with you. Or at least, I hope you know. I'm not saying we can't act like we're together in public. There are just some things I'd prefer to wait to do when we don't have an audience."

"Where was all this when we were in Belize? Because I recall several times where we held hands or hugged right out in the open and you didn't seem to have a problem with it. Our first kiss was right in the middle of the hotel lobby."

"I know this is gonna make me sound flaky but it was different there. It was like we were in a whole other world and I admit I was caught up in the euphoria. Plus, I never expected to see you again. It's not the same now that we're back in the quote-unquote 'real world.'"

He just peered at her for a moment before looking away.

"Luther." She waited for his eyes to return to hers, feeling her heart beat a little faster. It felt like she might be losing him and the thought actually frightened her. "I don't want this to become a major issue between us. I'm asking you to please try to understand where I'm coming from. You mean a lot to me, and that doesn't change just because I refrain from doing certain things when we're in public."

When another few silent moments passed, Liz started to feel frustration creep in. Why was he making such a huge deal out of this? It wasn't like she was saying she didn't want him. How was she wrong for wanting to keep private things private?

"I'd like to think you'd know that I would never purposely do anything to embarrass you," he finally said, his voice a rumble. "But clearly this is a major point for you, so I'll respect it. I'm not thrilled about it, but..." He threw up a hand, sighing. "Like I said, I'll respect it."

Liz relaxed some now that she knew it wasn't a deal-breaker for him, but she was still wary because he clearly wasn't happy. She could only hope that this didn't become a point of contention that eventually drove them apart, or made him resent her.

"Are we gonna be okay?" she asked.

His hand covered hers, and she smiled.

"You mean a lot to me too, Liz," he told her, his fingertips stroking her soft skin. "I'd like to think this won't come between us. Showing affection is important to me and I'm conceding on this because it's so important to you. So we can just consider it settled and move on from here."

"Do you think you're going to be happy with this long-term, though?" Liz couldn't resist asking. "I appreciate you bending for me but I don't want you to resent me for it."

He hunched a shoulder. "I can't predict the future, Liz. So I guess we'll just have to see."

Chapter 10

• • • •

"LADIES, CAN WE FOCUS? As much fun as it is to be regaled with the latest trysts of our former member, we can't keep getting sidetracked. We're supposed to be deciding on a theme for this year's adult prom."

Liz sighed and glanced at the time on her phone. This was why she should've been in charge. They'd have been out of there an hour ago because she would have shut down all the side gossip.

She was at a meeting of her local sorority chapter, and the president, Hilary, had lost control of the meeting yet again and was letting gossip overtake what they were supposed to be discussing. Liz could appreciate a good gab fest with her sorority sisters sometimes but on this particular day, she just wasn't in the mood.

She didn't want to obsess over a man, even if it was a man she was steadily falling deeper for by the day. But she couldn't stop thinking about the last night she spent with Luther, when they came to a begrudging agreement about the PDA issue. They'd gone on with their evening, playing a few games of cards before he read poetry to her as she laid in his lap, but there was an undercurrent of tension. It didn't take a genius to sense the shift between them. He didn't treat her any differently; he didn't try to be petty or slip in any sly remarks, or withhold any of the private affection she loved out of spite. He'd said he would respect her wishes and left it at that. But Liz could just feel that things weren't quite the same between them, and would've given anything to know what he was now *really* thinking about her.

Not to mention the tepid assurance he'd given when she'd asked if they'd be okay.

"Liz, can we count on you to co-plan things with Delilah?"

"Huh? What?" Liz's eyes snapped back to Hilary, who was standing at the head of the long table in the banquet room of Geneva's Tea House where they were holding their meeting. The rose silk wallpaper, the cushioned Victorian dining chairs, and the glass chandeliers were all very pretty but not really Liz's style. Another choice she wouldn't have made if she'd been in charge.

"You're going to head up the planning with Delilah. You gave the deciding vote."

When the hell did I do that?

"Oh. Yeah, sure." Liz shrugged, reaching for her mimosa.

"Great! I'm so looking forward to this event; this is going to raise a lot of money for Black Entrepreneurs of Tomorrow and it'll be a ton of fun, too. It'll be like going back to our high school days, except we can have all the alcohol we want and don't have to sneak kisses with our dates on the dance floor."

Everyone laughed. Liz thought about facetiously suggesting implementing a rule about keeping things chaste at the adult prom as a playful homage to their high school days (or at least hers), but she figured that wouldn't go over well. She didn't want anyone throwing their salads at her for stifling the fun.

Truth be told, Liz was not in the mood to be in charge of such an event at all, but she'd been skirting the last few meetings and hadn't participated much in the ones she'd attended before that, so she figured she was due to step up. And she wouldn't be doing it alone, though she couldn't say she was over the moon about having to plan with Delilah. She was all right but she tended to be a little too friendly and open with Liz.

"Liz, darling, I'm *so* glad that we're going to be working together on this," Delilah said once the meeting had finally adjourned. Several of the ladies were still lingering around, engaging in hushed, giggling conversations as they polished off their drinks. "It's been too long since we've spent any time together."

"Yeah," Liz tried to force *some* enthusiasm into her voice, choosing not to remind Delilah that they'd never exactly been the best of friends. They got along fine, but that was it. "When do you want to get started with the planning?"

"It needs to be ASAP. When you think about everything that needs to be done, four months really isn't a lot of time."

Liz blinked. They were expected to plan a whole adult prom in four months? She really *had* been zoned out during the meeting because she surely would have pushed back on that timeline had she been paying attention. With everything she had going on at work with getting ready for her upcoming showcase - which was far from the only thing she had on her plate - she really didn't have time for this.

But she had already agreed, so she'd have to find a way. This was what she got for daydreaming. She'd never sat around doing that before she got with Luther.

But no man had ever affected her like he had, either.

"I know a woman as stunning as you probably has no shortage of gentleman callers but I'd love to set you up with my brother-in-law Cole for the prom," Delilah commented, placing a hand on Liz's arm and snapping her out of yet another round of musings. "You two would make such a cute couple. And you could ride in the limo with me and Zander. We'd all make such an enviable foursome, don't you think?"

Liz's face tightened. "Thanks but I'm seeing someone, so I already have a date. Let's just focus on starting to get everything together for this prom. When are you available?"

They set up a time to meet the next evening before parting ways, with Delilah giving her a firm hug that lingered longer than necessary and a kiss on the cheek that was a little too close to her lips. Before Liz could call her out on it, though, she tossed up a wave and scurried away, suddenly having to dash.

"I can tell already..." Liz muttered, throwing back the rest of her mimosa before grabbing her things and leaving herself, waving goodbye to her sorority sisters as she passed. At least being forced to focus on getting this adult prom planned and swatting Delilah's subtle flirtations would give her something else to think about besides her relationship with Luther and whether or not she'd put a nick in it.

· · · ·

LIZ WAS LOOKING OVER some storyboards for an upcoming marketing campaign with a couple of her assistants when there was a knock on her office door.

"Yes?" she called out, frowning slightly at the interruption.

Wendy, the receptionist, poked her head in. "Sorry to interrupt, Ms. Tate, but you have a delivery."

Her frown clearing, Liz stood from the gold leather couch in the corner of her office she'd been huddling on with her assistants. "Oh?"

Wendy fully entered the office carrying a huge bouquet of jewel-toned roses and hydrangea in a crystal vase, leaving her assistants in awe and murmuring how beautiful they were. Liz's jaw dropped slightly, her hand drifting to her chest. Had Luther sent those?

But she figured that didn't make sense. Luther knew flowers weren't her thing. And she didn't take him for the type that would forget such a detail or send her something he knew she wouldn't enjoy to the fullest. So if they weren't from him, who could they be from?

"Thanks, Wendy," she muttered, rounding the cracked glass table they were working at and moving over to her desk where Wendy left the bouquet before strolling back out. Digging through all the flowers, Liz plucked out the card. When she read it, she almost couldn't believe her eyes.

> You've done what few women have: distracted me. I'd love the pleasure of your company again, in whatever capacity you wish.
>
> Carlton Barber

Liz was floored. He'd even left his personal cell number. If she was honest, Liz never even thought about her encounter with Carlton Barber, or the fact that he was apparently taken with her, according to E.J. She hadn't been interested then and, though flattered by the gesture, she still wasn't. But she'd be sure to thank him for the flowers out of courtesy.

She had to put it out of her mind and get on with her day, which wasn't going swimmingly. Several things had gone wrong; late shipments, damaged clothing pieces, frustrating meetings, and having to replace a photographer for a photoshoot last minute thanks to an untimely slip in the shower. They were making progress on finalizing the outfits for the showcase, but Liz still wasn't totally satisfied with the overall looks. She knew Luther's fedoras were what she needed to get the vibe she wanted, but he still hadn't given her an answer about whether she could use them or not. She'd been trying to give him his time to mull it over but time was running short. Hopefully he wouldn't deny her out of spite.

While she had a minute, she sent him a quick text, reminding him that she was still waiting on his decision. And she figured she'd go ahead and call Mr. Barber to thank him for the flowers.

"Carlton Barber."

"Wow, I wasn't expecting you to answer so quickly."

"Not many people have this number so I had a feeling it was you. How are you, Liz? Did you get the flowers?"

"I did, and they're really, really nice, Mr. Barber. However-"

"What am I, your teacher? You don't have to be so formal."

"Just trying to show you your due respect, I guess."

He actually chuckled. "I appreciate the thought but I'm just a man with money. I'm not your boss or superior in any way. So just call me Carlton, please."

"All right, Carlton. Thank you so much for the flowers. I have to admit, though, that the only flowers I really enjoy are the ones imprinted on clothing."

"You know, I actually suspected that. Forgive me for succumbing to the cliché and settling for convention. I didn't want to go totally high school and pump E.J., Roland, or Natalia for information about you – though E.J. already declared he wasn't telling me anything, anyway - and I figured you wouldn't appreciate me using other resources to dig, though I surely could have..."

"You figured right."

"So I went with the safe choice. It won't happen again. Now go ahead and tell me you aren't interested in me."

That caught Liz slightly off-guard, and she chuckled. "You sensed that, huh?"

"Well, when a woman calls you *Mr. Barber*..."

"You're surprisingly cool and I enjoyed meeting you but another man has all my attention."

"A lucky man, indeed. I hope he realizes how fortunate he is."

"That's sweet of you to say."

"So, I get that you're not willing to run off and elope but that doesn't mean we have to completely part ways. Like I said in the note, it can be whatever capacity you wish. No pressure. And you don't have to worry about me disrespecting your relationship because that's not what I'm about. I find you refreshing, Liz, and endearing. And there's something to be said for being treated like just another man instead of the billionaire people can try to get something out of. I'd hate to lose that."

"With great blessings come great headaches, they say."

Carlton laughed. "Catchy."

Liz couldn't help but join in, feeling unexpectedly comfortable with him. It almost felt like she was talking to a buddy, and she didn't hate it.

"No, but for real, I can't even imagine what it must be like to be in your shoes, with everyone always wanting something from you."

"That's one reality but the more important one contains way more positives. My family is taken care of. I employ a lot of people. I can support a myriad of causes I believe in. I can do more than my part to help the economy and make improvements in the city I grew up in and still love, and plenty others. I could keep going. My life is damn good and I don't dare complain. Sorry for slipping into 'soapbox' mode but, hey."

"No worries. I found it endearing."

"Touché."

They talked for a few more minutes before Carlton had to go. Liz felt surprisingly refreshed after that conversation. What she didn't tell him was that even if she wasn't spoken for, she probably still wouldn't have gone out with him, because Carlton Barber had quite the reputation with the ladies. Nothing unpleasant; he just seemed to have a different one on his arm whenever she saw him on this blog site or that social media posting or in whatever article. Apparently since his divorce years earlier, he'd settled on variety and while Liz didn't want to judge, she also didn't want to be one of many. But she figured having Carlton Barber as a friend wouldn't be the worst thing.

• • • •

LUTHER HEADED TO THE juice bar after wrapping up his morning training session. It was barely noon and he was already wiped. He'd been up since eight so he could get in his own workout before starting his first training session of the day with a new client, but he knew his fatigue wasn't just physical.

He'd told himself to let the whole PDA issue with Liz go; that it wasn't that big a deal. She wasn't trying to keep him or their relationship under wraps; she just wanted to mute the affection when they were out in public. On some level he could understand it, but despite himself, it still irked him. It wasn't like he'd licked her neck like an ice cream cone or grabbed handfuls of her ass while they were out, nor would he. He didn't love having to restrain himself because she was still carrying around some issues from childhood.

But, he'd promised to adhere to her request so he knew there was no point in stewing about it. He couldn't help that his fire was a little bit dimmed, though. He couldn't quite pinpoint exactly why this was sticking in his craw so much, but he hoped he figured it out before it became a real issue between him and Liz and caused a rift they wouldn't be able to mend.

When Carter showed up for his session, Luther was actually glad to see him, hoping he'd come with his usual silliness to help take his mind off of Liz.

"Let's get me swole, man," Carter greeted him after they slapped hands in greeting. He frowned slightly, noting the flatness of Luther's expression. "What's wrong with you?"

"Nothing." Luther's response was immediate.

"Please don't be in one of your moods today. I had a crappy date last night and I was counting on you to cheer me up."

After Carter put his things away, Luther had him start warming up. "What happened on your date?"

"Ugh. She invited me over, right...made me dinner, then took me to her room where she had this whole setup for a freaky-ass evening. Handcuffs, vibrators, highlighters, the works."

"I'm sorry...highlighters?"

"Don't ask. Anyway, we were getting into it, clothes coming off, things getting hot and heavy with Prince playing in the background. Then all of a sudden I hear the front door slam and some dude yell out that he was home. Freaked me the fuck out."

"Whoa, she had a man?"

"According to her, he was her ex. They'd been broken up for a couple of years but both loved their house, since they went half on it and decorated it together and all that shit, and decided to just share it. I was thinking I was about to have to fight a brotha but she insisted that he didn't care and we could just keep doing what we were doing. And I was so horny by then that I was gonna roll with it."

"Really, Carter?"

"Yes, really. Not everybody has a girlfriend they can hit up when they need some lovin' like you do."

"I technically don't...never mind, go ahead."

"Anyway, I was all set to forget dude was even there but then he started knocking on the bedroom door. *And she actually stopped sucking my dick to go answer it!* Blew my damn mind! But even *that* wasn't as bad as her actually letting him in and them having a whole-ass conversation while I'm sitting right there."

"Where do you find these women??"

"Then he actually comes over and tries to dap me up like it was the most normal thing in the world. And I'm like, bruh...I'm naked! We're not shaking hands right now!"

Luther ran a hand down his face, resting it over his mouth and dropping his head as he tried to refrain from bursting out laughing like he wanted to. Only his brother could get into this kind of foolishness.

"Long story short," Carter sighed, "I ended up leaving pissed off and horny."

"They asked you to leave?"

"Oh no...I don't think she would've minded buddy sticking around while we did our thing. They were just way too chummy for me and I'd bet a hundred bucks they picked up where me and her left off once I hightailed it out of there."

"I'd bet a thousand. Wow, Carter."

"Don't make fun of me. I'm still reeling from all that. I swear, I have the worst damn luck when it comes to the ladies lately. My arsenal is dwindling."

"Maybe all of your playboy shit is coming back to haunt you. Even the fact that you feel an *arsenal* is necessary..."

"Please don't start with the preaching. Cheer me up."

"I'm not sure what you want me to say. Maybe you should change the quality of women you pursue."

"I don't want no choir girls. Ugh, I'm still too wound up to talk about this. What's going on with you? How's Liz?"

Luther hesitated. Part of him wanted to confide in his brother but the other part wasn't sure he wanted Carter's feedback. But he ultimately decided it couldn't hurt.

"Liz is fine. Though she and I did recently hit a small snag."

"Already? What happened?"

"It turns out she has a major problem with PDA. Even stuff as tame as hugs and holding hands. But it's a completely different story when we're alone."

"You're really that bothered by that?"

"I don't know; something about it just seems...disingenuous. Especially since none of this was an issue when we were in Belize. I'm trying to respect where she's coming from but it's been bugging me since we had that conversation. Usually I can deal with things and move on but this has been harder to let go of, for some reason."

"I get it, man. You should be able to do whatever you want to your woman – I mean, within reason - whether you're in public or not. It's just like these broads nowadays to let you get used to things one way and then flip the script once they've got their hooks into you. This is exactly why it's flings over relationships for me."

Luther regretted mentioning it. He should've known Carter wasn't the ideal audience for this particular conversation.

"Let's just get over to the bench for these chest presses, man," he mumbled, closing the subject. They continued on with their session, Luther managing to push his and Liz's issues to the side for what he knew was only a limited time.

• • • •

GROCERY SHOPPING WAS the last thing he felt like doing, but Luther grudgingly headed to Trader Joe's for more fresh produce. He liked to have it on hand for snacking as well as for his green smoothies, and he only bought so much at a time. He could have had the groceries delivered but he didn't trust anyone else to choose his produce for him.

He had just grabbed a basket and was perusing pints of blueberries when he happened to glance up and see Kinsley a little ways away. Not planning on speaking, he went back to what he was doing, hoping she didn't notice him.

"Luther?"

He sighed.

Turning as she approached, pushing her half-full cart ahead of her, he gave a polite nod. "Kinsley, hello."

"How's it going?"

"All is well. In a *slight* hurry, though..."

"Well, I'll keep it brief, then." She stepped around her cart, stopping a couple of feet in front of him and tucking some hair behind her ear. "I wanted to apologize to you directly for my attitude towards you, with the name stuff on our date. I'd told Liz I'd chill out but since I'm running into you, I wanted to tell you to your face, too."

Her brown eyes held such sincerity that Luther loosened up some. "Thank you for that. And I'll own my part in it; I should have been more forthcoming. In hindsight, it was pretty immature of me to handle it the way I did."

"Once I came up outta my feelings, I could admit I might've done the same thing, though, if I was stuck going on a date I didn't want to go on. Hell, I've done worse. It was a blind date and you just can't be too careful nowadays. People are crazy."

"You're right about that."

"So we're good?"

"Consider the matter forgotten."

"I can see why Liz is so sprung over you, regardless of how cool she tries to act about it. You're one of the decent ones. I know it's been a while for her as far as having an actual relationship and I hope she appreciates what she has."

Luther managed to keep his face even. He wasn't eager to talk about Liz or their relationship to Kinsley. "I appreciate the compliment."

"I know you have to go but if I could get your advice on something real quick...my mama has been on me about not eating so much junk and getting more fruits and veggies and shit, and convinced me to try that green smoothie diet-cleanse thing. Liz told me you're a trainer – not that she'd *have* to tell me 'cause, look at you – and I was wondering if you could give me an idea of which is better to use, flaxseed or chia seeds?"

"There are slight differences but they're kinda neck-and-neck, nutrition-wise. It's mostly a matter of preference with that. Personally I tend to go with flaxseed, usually."

"Got it. And does it matter what kind of greens I put in there? I'd be fine with just spinach but she says I should rotate some kale and collards and stuff too, and both taste like feet to me. Can you enlighten me on that enough so I can tell her I know what I'm doing and don't need her damn advice?"

Luther found himself laughing at that. Shrugging, he proceeded to give Kinsley his recommendations, and they ended up talking for several minutes. Kinsley was actually easy to talk to, not to mention funny, and Luther found himself not minding their conversation. When they parted ways, he was just glad that they were now on good terms, since he didn't love the idea of being on the outs with Liz's friend, even if he lost no sleep over it when he was.

He finished his shopping and headed back out to his car, looking forward to getting home, getting showered, having some lunch, and then getting some hat work done. He had some orders to ship out, some emails to return, and then he could get to the fun stuff and spend the rest of the day holed up in his shed creating.

It surprised him that checking to see what Liz would be up to that evening didn't occur to him as it usually did. His feelings for her certainly hadn't disappeared, but something had clearly shifted for him with this whole PDA issue. Luther sincerely wished he knew what he needed to do to get past it because he hated that it was consuming him like it was. This wasn't like him.

As if he conjured her up, she texted him.

Hey, you. Are you able to come over tomorrow night? We haven't spent time at my place yet. Plus, I miss you.

Liz

Smiling because he couldn't help it, Luther wasted no time responding:

I miss you, too. And you already know; I'd love to see you and see your space. Looking forward to it.

Luther

Luther meant the words, but he noticed the level of anticipation that was usually there when he knew he was going to see Liz wasn't quite as high, and it was a realization he didn't love.

Chapter 11

• • • •

AFTER WAY MORE ANALYZING and overthinking than he liked, Luther felt a lot better about his future with Liz. He decided that PDA was not something that he was willing to let come between them. He believed her when she said that it had nothing to do with her feelings for him, or about hiding their relationship. And who's to say that she wouldn't loosen up over time, the longer they were together. Maybe once they got more comfortable and secure with each other, she wouldn't be so quick to shy away or skirt his touch when they were out in public.

Once he'd come to that realization, he was able to breathe a lot easier. He spent the rest of the night and the next morning working, able to concentrate a lot easier now. Speaking of his hats, he realized he never gave Liz an answer as to whether he'd allow them to be used in her showcase. She'd sent him information about it and the stills of the outfits that she wanted to pair them with and he could definitely see his fedoras adding to the overall looks. Seeing the level of quality and attentiveness that had gone into it already put the final nail in his decision.

Unwilling to wait until he saw her later that evening, he called, hoping she wasn't too busy.

"Hey, handsome."

His grin was automatic and that familiar heat rushed to his face. Just hearing her voice affected him.

"Hey, baby," he returned her greeting, the smile still lingering. "I know you're probably busy but I wanted to give you a response on the hats. I admit I've been a little sidetracked with recent...developments between us."

"Oh...I hope that doesn't mean what I think it means..."

"If you think anything other than it means that I agree to your request, then it doesn't."

She gasped, then let out an excited shriek. He could hear her clapping her hands and it made him laugh. Making her so happy meant everything to him.

"Luther, baby, thank you so, *so* much!" she exclaimed. "You have no idea what this is going to do for me!"

"It's nothing, Liz."

"No, it is not *nothing*. Those are your creations; your babies. Your name is on them. And you have every right to be selective about how they're used. So the fact that you're trusting me like this means a ton. I promise you won't regret it."

Luther's hand played across his chest. "I absolutely trust you because I've seen how seriously you take what you do. Can't wait to see how everything turns out."

"It's gonna be so hot! I almost can't believe I'm working with a man I'm seeing; being with you is just a mountain of firsts."

"For you and me both," he agreed. "Look, I won't hold you...get back to work. I'll see you later tonight."

"Can't wait."

• • • •

IT WAS ALL LIZ COULD do to concentrate during the rest of her work day. She couldn't wait to see Luther that evening. Even though it hadn't been, it felt like so much time had passed since she last got to see him and feel those muscled arms around her, or feel those lips. She missed him immensely but she was also relieved that it seemed they were still okay. Part of her had been worried he would decide that he couldn't get past the PDA issue.

She rushed home to get everything ready, actually feeling giddy. Her place was neat already so she didn't have to do a lot in the way of straightening up. Outside of lighting a few candles and fluffing a few pillows, she was set. What she needed time for was going from office-sexy to for-her-man sexy, and to make some homemade waffles to go with the chicken she picked up. She mixed up the batter and let it sit while she went to go take a shower, doing a quick leg shave, and then slathering on her almond sugar body oil that had her smelling like a pastry. It actually made her tingle, imagining him burying his face in her neck like he enjoyed doing so much.

When she pulled open her lingerie drawer, she paused. She absolutely wanted seduction to be part of their evening but did she really want to be so cliché and answer the door in a nightie? Would he think she was overcompensating because of the PDA thing? That she felt like she owed him for agreeing to let his hats be used in her showcase?

"I'm *seriously* trippin'," she muttered, pushing the drawer closed with a thump. The last thing she needed to start doing was questioning herself or her relationship with Luther. Up until the PDA issue, they were rock solid. And Luther wouldn't still be with her if he didn't want to be.

Her confidence back in place, she fished out a clingy satin lounging dress with a super-high slit up the side;

comfortable enough for wearing around the house but sexy enough to send his jaw to the floor when he saw her. The deep v-neck showed off a good amount of cleavage, and Liz smirked when she imagined his tongue sliding down the middle of it.

I am so far gone over this man.

Once she touched up her hair and applied some lip stain, she scurried back to the kitchen to get the waffles going. Luther had sent her a text letting her know he was on his way, and the tingles skittering over her body had picked up the pace. By the time he was at her door, she had a stack of buttermilk waffles, chicken wings warming in the oven, and several bottles of wine chilling in the wine fridge.

"Damn."

Liz grinned at Luther's reaction upon seeing her. She reached out and grabbed the front of his shirt, pulling him inside her loft. Luther pushed the door closed before they wrapped themselves around each other.

"I was going to say how delicious it smells in here but now that you're in my arms..." He licked from her shoulder to her ear, making her shudder, "I see that it's you and not the food."

"Mmmm," Liz moaned, her head falling to the side as he continued to savor her soft skin with his tongue. "You smell damn good, too. And if you keep licking on me like this we won't be eating any dinner."

"Just tell me to stop."

"Shit..." Her hand slid to the back of his head. "I hope you don't mind reheated waffles, then."

They stayed in that same spot making out and enjoying each other before finally parting. Liz held onto his hand as she led him further into her loft, glancing back at him as he took everything in.

"This is beautiful, baby," he complimented, taking in the exposed brick walls, lush greenery and colorful, abstract artwork. "I didn't think you liked plants, though."

"They're fake. I love the look of the Monstera and Fiddle Leaf plants but don't have the green thumb to maintain them. Just have to keep them dusted."

Chuckling, Luther nodded. "Understandable. How long have you lived here?"

"Ooh, probably about eight years now. I was in a nice condo before but it never felt like home to me. This is way more my style."

"It looks like it. It's homey but it still has that stylish flair to it. I feel like I know the answer to this but you decorated everything yourself, huh?"

"You already know. Nobody can capture my style but me. Come on, I'll show you around."

After Liz gave him a brief tour, the two of them sat down to a meal of chicken, waffles, and sparkling cider. Liz was glad that Luther didn't seem to be holding a grudge and hated to ruin the vibe, but she couldn't resist addressing what was on her mind.

"Luther," she wiped her mouth with a cloth napkin, "Are you *sure* we're okay? I know you said you would respect my wishes on the PDA stuff but I can't help but wonder if there's any part of you that resents our agreement."

Luther looked thoughtful as he finished chewing the bite of chicken he'd just taken. Wiping his hands on his own napkin, he sat back in his seat. "I've told you what I thought, Liz. I didn't keep any of it from you."

"So nothing has changed since then? Because I'd rather know now instead of thinking we're good only to be hit out of the blue later after you've let any lingering frustration build up."

"All right, if I'm honest, it *has* been bothering me since we had that conversation," Luther admitted. "More than I expected it to, really. But I decided I could deal with it. My feelings for you are way too strong and real to let opposing PDA stances come between us. As long as we respect each other's feelings on it, we're good. I can be patient."

Liz frowned slightly at that. He could be patient? Did he think that she was going to change her stance over time? Was he planning on trying to wear her down? Her mind was made up, and as into him as she was, it wasn't changing for him.

But instead of challenging his statement, she let it go. The last thing she wanted to do was keep digging until she struck contentious oil. He said they were good, so she'd take his word for it.

After they ate, Liz broke out a deck of conversation cards that she'd gotten at a bachelorette party some time ago, and she and Luther parked it on the couch, taking turns asking each other questions from the deck that sat between them.

"'Is there anything that you would change about your childhood?'" Liz asked, reading from the card.

"Hmm..." Luther's eyes drifted up, his hands still massaging Liz's foot that was in his lap. "I was blessed with a great childhood. Hardworking, loving parents, God bless their souls. Had everything I needed. I guess if I could change anything it would be the point in my life when Carter was born."

"What do you mean?"

"I had always wanted a sibling, but after a while I figured it wasn't in the cards and resigned myself to being an only child. By the time Carter came along, I was seventeen and only a year away from going off to college. We didn't get much time together and I've always kinda hated that."

"But you're close now, right?"

"Ehh. We're kind of close, but my being out of the house and the vast difference in our ages caused us to not start *really* getting to know each other until we were both adults. And I love my brother dearly but we have next to nothing in common."

"I know I only met him that one time but he seems like he'd be a hoot to hang out with."

"Yeah, that's one way to put it," Luther chuckled. He smirked when he earned a moan from Liz with his foot manipulations. "Carter is more playboy while I've always been the romantic. And I can't say I always love his mentality when it comes to women. But he's a good man, at the core. We might not be best buddies but I'd run through a brick wall for him. All right, my turn." He plucked a card from the deck. "'What's the worst thing an ex could say about you?'"

"Ugh, I don't like that question," Liz scoffed, scrunching her nose and drawing a laugh from Luther. "Draw another one."

"Answer the question, woman. Or I'll shut down this massage."

"Well, I can't have *that*, so..." Liz laid her head on the back of the couch. "I guess the worst thing an ex could say about me is that I'm heartless."

Luther's head snapped to her. "You? Why would anyone say that?"

"Because I admit it's never been very hard for me to walk away from men or relationships, and it can come across the wrong way, especially if they're not as ready for it to be over as I am. They'll be upset over the breakup or trying to rekindle the flame and I'm already over it. And the fact that I don't want kids is another thing that has earned me that title."

"You've been deemed heartless because of that?"

"That's one of the nicer names I've been called."

"That's unfortunate that those men weren't more mature than that. Everything isn't for everyone. And I bet those same men wouldn't bat an eye if one of their male friends said they didn't want children."

"Oh, you know they wouldn't. Us women are supposed to be willing to pop out as many babies as their men want, apparently. But I've gotten used to it. If they trip, it's just further confirmation that they aren't for me."

"I hate you had to put up with that."

"Me too, but I'm glad I'm with the right one now."

He looked over at her, and smiled at the look of adoration in her eyes as she gazed at him. His own eyes softened as he sunk against the back of the couch, feeling like he was falling under her spell but not minding it at all. "You've got that right."

They continued to ask each other questions from the deck until Luther's massage started moving from her foot to her calf, then her thigh. Liz was whimpering softly by then, squirming the closer his fingers got to the wet heat between her legs. She gave herself a mental pat on the back for not bothering with any panties.

"Is this for me?" he whispered, trailing a light finger between her folds as he eased off the couch and knelt between her legs. He lifted one of her long limbs over his shoulder, gripping it in his strong hand as he gave a tongue-filled kiss to her inner thigh, making her shudder violently. "I'd hate to devour what isn't mine."

"It's yours, baby," Liz breathed, her chest heaving in anticipation. "It's all yours."

"That's what I want to hear."

He continued kissing and nipping up her inner thigh until he got to where they both wanted him to be. He pushed her dress up to her hips as he swirled his tongue around her clit before trailing the tip from bottom to top, causing her to cry out in pleasure. When he angled his head and slid that long tongue inside of her, Liz thought she was going to pass out.

"Luther, oh my *god*..." she whispered, clutching his head with both hands. "*Fuck*, you're amazing at this..."

"Just amazing? I clearly need to up my game, then."

And that he did. Pretty soon, Liz's head was whipping side to side so fast it's a wonder she didn't strain her neck, and her curses and moans were running together into erotic gibberish. Luther had both of her thighs in a death grip, holding them right where he wanted them as he suckled and teased her ultra-sensitive clit until she saw stars.

"Luther Trae Monroe, *shit*! Fuck it, marry me! I don't want nobody else getting this shit but *me*! Just eat my pussy forever! *Fuck!!*"

She felt the orgasm in every inch, every cell, every nerve of her body. Her legs trembled for several moments before her energy gave out and she collapsed onto the couch, moaning in satisfied exhaustion.

"Did I say anything crazy just now?" she whispered, eyes closed. "'Cause I *think* I might need to clarify..."

"Not necessary, baby," Luther smiled. "Anything is liable to come out at the height of orgasm. I know which parts to gloss over." He didn't mention that he wasn't planning on ignoring *everything* she said.

"Good. That's good."

Luther eased back, licking her flavor from his lips as he watched her, a hint of hunger still in his eyes.

"Don't look at me like that," she muttered when her eyes finally pried open.

"Like what?"

"Like you're ready to tear me apart."

"That's one way to describe what I want to do to you."

"Ooh..." Despite her momentary fatigue, the thought of some aggressive sex from Luther was like an espresso jolt. "I just might be calling in sick tomorrow."

"I need to be sure to give you sufficient reason, in that case." Grinning, Luther planted a kiss to her stomach through her dress before standing and heading to the kitchen. By the time Liz managed to push herself up to sitting, he was standing in front of her with a glass of peach mango juice.

"I need you replenished."

Her eyes didn't leave his as she took the glass from him, her hungry gaze now matching his. She felt her energy renew as she drank, looking forward to that sexy body of his being naked on top of hers.

"To my room, mister," she announced, plunking her empty glass onto the end table and standing. She grabbed his hand and took urgent steps to her bedroom, pulling him behind her. Once they were in front of her bed, she turned to him with every intention of pulling him in for a kiss when she paused, noticing the strange look on his face. "What?"

"We might have a problem here, baby."

Liz frowned, glancing around at what might possibly be considered a problem. Drawing a blank, she looked back up at him. "What are you talking about? What problem?"

"This." He pointed to her queen-sized bed. "Have you had other men in here?"

She reared at the unexpected question. "You know I've been with other men, Luther."

"Yes, but have you been with them in *this* bed?"

"Yeah, so?"

"That's what I thought. I'm not trying to make love to you in the same space other men have. It's not happening."

Not believing her ears, Liz stepped back. "Are you serious with this?"

"I'm beyond serious, Liz."

"You act like I haven't washed the sheets."

"You can boil the sheets. Wouldn't matter."

"Luther, that's ridiculous. What damn difference does it make? We both have pasts."

"My issue isn't with your past. I thought I was clear in my reasons."

Her attitude ignited at his tone and she folded her arms, shifting her weight to one leg. "So you can have me up in your bed but you can't be in mine?"

"I haven't had any other women in my bed, Liz." His tone was firm but calm, his eyes unwavering and undeterred from her growing scowl. "When I bought my house, I bought a new bed, also. And you're the first woman I've shared it with. So you'll have to come with something else."

"Why? Apparently it doesn't matter what the hell I say. You're set on this foolishness-"

"Did I call it *foolishness* when you told me I couldn't hug you or hold your damn hand in public because you're still fixated on stuff that happened between two other people *years* ago?" Luther interjected, his voice slipping into a biting tone he rarely used. "Just like you wanted me to respect that, I need you to respect this. Because it's just as important to me."

Liz seethed. She was beyond frustrated not only at the fact that he was denying her the loving that her body still desired, but that he was making such an issue out of the fact that other men had graced her bed. Did he expect her to replace it every time she had a new lover?

But mostly, Liz hated that he had a point. He hadn't loved agreeing to tamp down the PDA but had done so for her. She couldn't now dismiss his concerns just because she didn't see the logic in them.

Her pride wouldn't let her come out and say that, though.

"You know what? I really cannot believe you're ruining our evening over something this damn trivial," she snapped. "Were you worried about other men when you were just eating my pussy out there on the couch? Or when you were sitting in my kitchen chairs? Other men's asses have surely been on those. Why don't I just throw out all my damn furniture so you won't be so affronted and can be the only one spoiled and privileged enough to touch it, because we certainly wouldn't want you soiled with my past dirty deeds, would we?"

Luther just stood there looking at her, his breaths even and eyes slightly narrowed. His expression was even but the angry fire in his eyes was as clear as day.

"How 'bout this," he finally said, holding up his hands. "I'm gonna go before one of us lets our anger lead us to say something we'll regret."

Liz knew she'd gotten carried away, but she was too angry to acknowledge that. She just huffed and turned away from him, rolling her eyes. And for an extra dose of petty, she dropped onto her bed, kicking then crossing her legs and putting her bare thigh on display through the high slit.

Luther eyed the motion but didn't take the bait. He just shook his head as he stepped back. "Call me when you're ready to talk about this rationally. And when you're done with this," he waved a hand at her defiant pose, "Come lock the door behind me."

He left, and Liz had to make herself stay put and not go after him. That had gone way left when it didn't need to.

Flopping onto her back, she released a long frustrated groan. She and Luther had disagreed before but this was their first fight, and over something like a bed. She still didn't agree with his rationale, but she knew she could've handled it better. Usually she didn't even bother arguing with men at all, never really caring enough to do so. But this was just another example of how Luther was different than any other man from her past.

She finally got up and trudged out of her bedroom, going to secure the front door before heading to wash the dishes she'd been too enamored to worry about earlier. She picked up a plate before plunking it right back onto the table and rushing to find her cell phone. Glancing at the time, she figured it was too late to call Lovey like she wanted to. Her sister tended to go to bed kind of early, and she also had three young children wearing her out. So Liz called Kinsley instead.

"What's up, girl?" Kinsley greeted, wide awake. A Jay-Z song played loudly in the background.

"I need to vent."

"What's wrong?"

Liz recalled her argument with Luther, leaving out what they'd done on the couch just before it. Her frustration prevented her from considering just who it was she was venting to; Liz had temporarily forgotten the whole scene in her car where Kinsley was musing about making a play for Luther. If Liz had been thinking clearly, she definitely would've called Desiree or Natalia instead.

"I know you won't want to hear this, girl, but I can see where Luther is coming from with that," Kinsley finally admitted. "And it's not like you haven't had quite a few men up in there."

"It hasn't been *that* many."

"It's been enough. And some people believe in stuff like transferring spirits or however you say the bullshit. Just because you don't buy it doesn't make it invalid."

"So I'm seriously supposed to replace a perfectly good bed just because he's in his feelings?"

"Or don't. There's other places y'all can get it in. Or maybe this is a sign that you two aren't as compatible as you thought. 'Cause I'm sure this won't be the last time you butt heads over differences in values. Might be something to think about, girl."

That cooled some of Liz's fire. She dropped onto the couch, in the very spot Luther had her losing her mind not too long before. "I'm pissed right now but I don't want this to come between us."

"Well, unless one of you is going to walk back what you said, I'm not seeing how you can move past it. You should try seeing someone else; I'm sure there are plenty of other men that would gladly grace your bed and wouldn't give a flying fuck about who'd been there first."

"I don't want anyone else; I still want Luther."

"You wouldn't be calling me if you didn't feel like you had something to fuss about. You're usually pretty rational. But just like his feelings are valid, so are yours. And this issue might just be the tip of the iceberg. I'm just saying it wouldn't hurt to get out while you still like each other, at least."

"Fuck this," Liz muttered, standing and looking around for her keys. "I'm going over there."

"What?"

"I'm going to see him. We don't need to let this fester and become a bigger issue than it needs to be."

"Why don't you just run down the middle of the highway with a bullhorn yelling how wrong you were, then, 'cause that's what it'll be like if you go running over there now. Hell, at least give him some time to reconsider *his* part in all this; for all you know, he might realize what an asshat he was being and come to you."

"I thought you said you understood where he was coming from."

"Doesn't mean I agree with it. I'm telling you, stay where you are. Have a couple glasses of wine, take an edible."

"I don't have any of those."

"You want me to bring you some?"

"No." Liz was suddenly exhausted and out of energy for the whole evening. "I'm not even gonna bother. I'll just finish cleaning up the kitchen, take a shower, go to bed and try to forget how damn horny I still am."

"I'm telling you; Luther isn't the only man that can help you with that. I'm sure you still have your dial-a-dick file."

Sighing, Liz swiped a hand up her forehead, pushing her short hair back. "Good night, Kinsley."

Ending the call, Liz dropped her head and tried to ignore the sense of dread that was knocking at her consciousness. What Kinsley said about this bed issue just being the tip of the iceberg of problems with Luther worried her. Liz didn't want anything coming between her and Luther, but how many compromises were they each going to have to make before one of them got tired of it? Was it possible that they weren't as good a match as Liz thought?

She looked at the phone in her hand and considered calling him. But her head was still all over the place, and she figured Luther was probably still heated at her, too. It would be better to wait, and she could only hope cooler heads would prevail and they would be able to come out of this.

Chapter 12

• • • •

LIZ TRIED TO PUT THE whole argument with Luther out of her mind and go to bed, but sleep didn't relieve her like she'd hoped it would. Her mind kept replaying the argument with Luther, not to mention what happened on the couch right before they argued. She alternated between aching for Luther and fuming at him.

She'd never heard of someone not wanting to sleep on a bed that past lovers had used. Try as she might, she couldn't make herself see where he was coming from with that. But he'd been unyielding, and Liz knew he felt strongly about it. There wasn't anything she could do but respect it.

But if she gave in on this, what about the next time he came with some irrational demand that she didn't agree with? Was she going to be expected to cave on that, too? Was that what this relationship was going to be like, her bending to his preferences just because of how attracted she was to him? Liz knew there was no way that would work for her.

But then she had to check herself. Just like she'd remembered earlier but let her anger brush aside, this wasn't any different than the PDA issue. Luther hadn't seen the logic in that any more than she saw the logic in this. But he'd acquiesced, and he'd done it without losing his temper like she had. She was glad that he'd left before things got too heated, because Liz wasn't sure she wouldn't have in fact said something she would've regretted later. It wasn't like she was proud of the stuff she *did* say.

Her mind kept going back and forth about this, and Liz punched her pillow in exasperation. Rolling over to her side, she eyed her phone on the nightstand, partially appalled that Luther hadn't reached out to her already. Not even to give assurance that they were okay, to check on her, anything. That little voice reminded her that he'd said for her to call him when she was ready to talk rationally, since she was the one who flew off the handle earlier. Sometimes she hated having to be so damn mature.

It was late but she had a feeling Luther would still be up. They'd spent many nights on the phone into later hours than this, talking about any and everything as they continued getting to know each other and strengthening their bond. She could imagine him lying in bed as she was, staring up at the ceiling...shirtless. He only wore briefs to bed. Imagining that had Liz biting her lip and gripping the sheets in both hands.

Her urge to work things out flaring, she grabbed the phone and called him, working out what she'd say as the phone rang. But when it rolled to voicemail, she frowned and actually looked at the phone as if she was mistaken. He was ignoring her calls now? Luther wasn't that heavy of a sleeper so she couldn't imagine that he didn't hear the phone, even if he was asleep. He'd said to call when she was ready to talk and then he doesn't answer the phone? The thought turned the dial back up on her irritation.

Kinsley's advice about calling someone else flashed through her mind and Liz found herself scrolling through her contacts. Usually once a man was out of her life he was out of her phone, too, but to her surprise and relief, one of her former fling's names had managed to skirt deletion. Raj. Before she could stop herself, she had sent him a text inviting him over and he'd sent quick confirmation accepting her invitation.

Liz didn't let herself think about what she was doing as she sprung out of bed to yank off her headscarf and make sure she was still presentable. She no longer wore the sexy lounging gown she'd worn for Luther and was now in a midriff-baring camisole and some shorts. Figuring that was enticing enough, she decided she looked fine the way she was and waited for Raj to arrive, ignoring her common sense that was screaming how bad an idea this was.

She jumped when Raj knocked on the door, and she rushed to answer it. She hated the tiny part of her that hoped it was actually Luther coming back to make up with her.

Before Raj even had a chance to say anything after she opened the door, she yanked him to her and stuck her tongue down his throat. They stumbled to her bedroom, her unzipping his hoodie revealing his bare chest underneath, pushing it from his shoulders as he groped her with firm hands. Liz had forgotten Raj liked it a little rough.

"I am so glad you called," he grunted once they'd fallen onto her bed with him on top of her. He was already grinding on her, his hand squeezing her breast. "Always hated how we fell out."

Liz didn't even know what he was talking about. She couldn't remember exactly why it was that she and Raj parted ways and in the moment, she didn't care. She just wanted to feel better.

In seemingly no time, they were both naked and Liz was on all fours, with Raj enjoying her from behind with his mouth. She puffed air through her lips, trying to get into it. Then he suddenly flipped her over and buried his face between her legs, greedy and doing a lot of talking in between licks and sucks. Liz writhed, her eyes squeezed shut as her hand gripped his thick soft hair. It only reminded her how different he was from Luther. Luther kept his hair in a neat low-cut, black waves fading into tapered sides and back. Raj's hair was thick and bushy, graying at the edges, and he usually kept it in cornrows but apparently was letting it hang free this evening. It never bothered Liz when they were fooling around before but it didn't have the same appeal now.

And neither did his cunnilingus skills. His technique was loud and sloppy, not like the quiet intensity Luther was a master of. He whispered or gave sexy taunts here and there, but he mostly let his skills do the talking. Liz loved that.

But she wasn't supposed to be thinking about Luther; Luther was mad at her. She was enjoying Raj now.

"You ready for this, girl?" Raj asked her, his teak brown skin glowing in the dim light of the room. "Ready to get what you've been missing?"

Liz looked at him, noting the absence of anticipation that usually came before good dick. But whatever; she didn't need to be in love to get off.

"Yeah," she muttered, wishing he would hush and get on with it.

"Damn, those titties look good," he licked his lips. "I've missed sucking those nipples and making you cum, girl. You want me to suck those-"

"Just do it, Raj!" She was starting to remember why she'd left him alone. He talked too damn much.

He dove on her, seemingly trying to stuff her whole 36D into his mouth and sucking from the back of his throat.

Has he always been like this?

Liz tried to scrape up all the arousal she could as she wrapped her legs around him and matched his rhythm as he grinded against her. Raj managed to calm down enough to lighten up a little on what he was doing, and it actually started to feel pretty good. Liz moaned, more into it, and threw her head back as she arched her back a little.

They were sharing a deep sloppy kiss when Liz felt a strange feeling wash over her. An image flashed of Luther sitting in the corner of the room, watching them. Her eyes popped open and her head whipped towards the spot, but of course no one was there. Raj didn't seem to notice her sudden distractedness; he just kept kissing all over the side of her face and neck.

You're tripping, she assured herself, turning her face back to Raj's and resuming their kiss. She felt the tip of his dick nudging at her opening, and she was just about to open her legs wider when Luther's face flashed through her mind again. She imagined him sitting there, a foot crossed over his knee, chin in his hand, eying them with that intense gaze of his. Liz couldn't help but wonder what he would say if he knew what she was doing. What would he think of her for running to another man just because they had a fight?

Even if they weren't technically a couple yet, this might be something he walked away from her for. She certainly wouldn't have been thrilled if he'd done the same thing, official couple or not.

The thought cooled her jets significantly, and Liz suddenly pushed Raj away, her hands against his chest.

"What's up?" he asked, looking down at her in panting confusion.

"I changed my mind about this. You need to go."

"What the hell? Are you serious?"

"I'm absolutely serious. Please get up."

"What just happened, Liz? You called me over here and now when I've barely got my dick wet, you're shutting me down?"

"You nailed it. And I'm sorry you're frustrated but I have every right to change my mind about having sex with you, and I have. Now you can either move willingly or I'll get you off me in my own way, and I hear the ER is a bitch this time of night so I suggest you go with the former."

Raj's eyes widened slightly before narrowing, and Liz prepared herself for anything. She might've been in a compromising position, but she hadn't taken years of self-defense classes for nothing. If she needed to, she could absolutely defend herself.

Thankfully, it didn't have to come to that. Raj was clearly pissed but he did as she asked, yanking his clothes back on and stomping out with plenty of curses and muttering about his time being wasted. Liz didn't care about him being angry. She was plenty angry at herself. The realization of what she just did started to wash over her, and she rushed to the shower, hoping to wash Raj's scent as well as the memory off her.

Losing her head with Raj made Liz realize how much she wanted to straighten things out with Luther. After a quick shower, she threw on a jumpsuit and some fuzzy boots and grabbed her keys. In what seemed like no time, she was ringing Luther's doorbell, shifting her weight anxiously.

Luther didn't seem surprised to see Liz show up out of the blue. He just eyed her for a moment before stepping aside.

"Come in."

Liz's keys pressed against her palm as she squeezed them in her hand, nervous about what was going to happen. She took a breath and told herself to calm down; they were mature adults who were into each other. And the whole point of her going over at almost two in the morning was because she was ready to stop being stubborn and own her part in things.

Instead of them going to the living room or his bedroom, Liz was mildly surprised when Luther headed out to his backyard. It was a cool evening and a clear sky, and Liz figured Luther had been out there thinking and sipping cognac as he sometimes did. She eyed him from behind, unable to help appreciating the view of his tall bow-legged form walk ahead of her.

"Treehouse?" he turned and asked, jerking his head towards it.

Slightly thrown off, Liz nodded. "Sure."

He held out his hand for hers, preceding her up the ladder and gently pulling her up once he was inside. Once

Liz had crawled onto the small wooden landing and followed Luther through the door, she marveled at what she was seeing. She'd always pictured treehouses to be rickety things that you barely had room to move in, but they were both standing in it at full height. It was actually like a tiny house that one could sleep in, complete with a twin-sized bed, a short cushioned bench and a fold-down table, and a snack area. Liz couldn't believe her eyes.

"Wow, you had this built for your daughter? I expected just a big empty box in a tree but this is actually livable."

"I figured if I was going to do it, I'd do it up. It's actually not as fancy as it could've been; there's no toilet or anything. Thankfully I had enough sense to resist the urge to do all that, considering how little she ended up using it."

"So *you* use it now?"

"I do. When I want to clear my head. It's kinda like camping, in a sense. You can have a seat."

They sat next to each other on the bed, and Liz wondered if he would be able to tell she'd just been underneath another man not even an hour before. She was nervous about his reaction but she knew she had to be honest.

"Luther, I came over for two reasons." She turned to face him, feeling she owed him eye contact. "One, to apologize for the things I said earlier. Whether I disagreed with you or not, that was no way to handle it and I acknowledge that."

He nodded, eying her. "Agreed. And the other reason?"

"To..." She felt her heartbeat quicken. "To admit that after you left, I called another guy over there to finish what you started. And I'm sure I don't have to tell you that it was largely out of spite. I was pissed at you and ignoring my rational mind reminding me that you didn't fly off the handle when I told you something you didn't like, and that I was being childish. Now that I'm thinking clearly it's actually embarrassing that I let myself go there."

Luther didn't look pleased, but he also didn't look pissed. His lips curled in as he looked away from her. "I see."

"It's just...when I called ready to talk and you didn't answer..."

"I was in the shower. And I called you back."

"Oh." Liz's body went cold, feeling even more ridiculous. She hadn't even thought to check her phone after her foolish petty booty call to Raj. "I, um...I didn't realize that."

"Hmm."

"I'm *so* sorry for the way I handled things. If it makes any difference, I thankfully came to my senses and stopped it before it went too far, but letting him come over and put his hands on me at all was too much. I want you to be able to trust me and my feelings that I say I have for you and I know my doing stupid shit like this doesn't help that."

He cleared his throat. "I'm not gonna say I'm not disappointed, Liz. To be honest, I'm really trying to hold it together at the thought of you inviting another man over to touch you like I'd been doing earlier just because we had an argument."

Her face burned. "I get that. I know I'd feel the same way if the roles were reversed. Luther, this is not how I usually handle things. I'm not typically one to let my emotions dictate my actions. The depth of my feelings for you have taken me into a new area that I'm still trying to navigate, and in this instance, I slipped up. But nothing has changed about my wanting us to be together, despite us being at odds over a couple of issues."

"So you've really never felt for anyone what you feel for me?" His brow arched. "I'm not saying you're there yet but you've never been in love?"

Releasing a sigh, Liz rested her back against the wall. "I have," she replied, looking thoughtfully out of the treehouse window. "And I thought that was real – and maybe it was – but this, us, *far* surpasses whatever I felt back then. And I admit I'm not used to it. I wasn't kidding when I said being with you is a mountain of firsts, Luther. It just turns out not all of them are good."

"This is new for both of us, in a way," Luther admitted, resting his own head against the wall. A doo-rag was covering his waves. "I've absolutely been in love before but how you and I came about and the intensity of what I felt for you almost immediately has definitely been a new experience. One that I'm still reeling from at times. I might fall hard but I don't fall easily."

Liz was mildly surprised by that; Luther always seemed to be so self-assured. "Really?"

"I'm not expecting perfection, Liz, from either of us. How I came at you about the bed thing...it could have been better. I own that. Of course I sensed that we'd likely end up getting physical when you invited me over there...I should have addressed my concerns before things got intense. When you mentioned how long you'd lived there, it popped into my mind then but I kept quiet, and that was a mistake. So I apologize for that."

"And I apologize, again, for my part. I just...I hope this doesn't change anything between us."

"It's absolutely changed things between us, Liz."

His words were like a bowling ball to the gut. Just like that??

Daring to look over at him, she could feel the unfamiliar tears stinging her eyes and her face crumbling, her attempt to keep her emotions in check failing. "So we're over?"

His head swiveled to her, a slight frown marring his handsome face before sitting up and turning his body towards hers.

"I want us to be looking right at each other when I say this to you," he began, his voice holding no hesitation. "Us disagreeing doesn't deter me. You making mistakes won't send me running. And I'd hope it would be the same for you. We're building and growing together, Liz, and even though it oftentimes feels the opposite, we haven't known each other that long. There are going to be bumps along the way because as we both just admitted, we're each navigating new territory with each other. That's going to require us giving each other some grace."

Liz looked at him in wonder. She'd truly never met a man like him.

"It's easy to assume that we'll both just automatically have it together at our ages but I guess we're never too old to learn." She ventured a small smile, relieved that he wasn't throwing in the towel on them. "But I'm willing to."

"As am I. And when I said things changed between us, I meant that we've moved beyond the sometimes blinding euphoria of a new relationship and into the real. Stuff like this is what's going to really test us, baby. How we handle it when our opinions or stances clash, when we get pissed at each other, or when other unpleasant things come up. It'll happen again. We just have to be committed to handling it together."

"And not let our emotions get the better of us," Liz added. "Having enough respect for each other to step back and take the time to figure out how to handle things so that we come out of it stronger."

"Together."

"Absolutely together."

He grabbed her hand, kissing it. "Liz, know that I forgive you for tonight. I didn't love hearing about what you did after I left your place but the fact that you came over and was up front with me goes a long way. It would have pissed me off if you were still being petty or making excuses about it."

"I could say the same about the bed issue. One thing I love about you is that you can take it as well as you give it. It gives me more assurance that I wasn't wrong about you or us."

"Same. But tonight also just reaffirms that you're still not ready for me in the capacity that I need you to be. And that's okay. If I didn't feel you weren't sincerely trying to get to where I am in regards to us, I wouldn't waste my time. But I do so I'm still all in. I still want you, Liz. My heart wants you. If I'm alone in that-"

"You're not." Liz took his face in her hands, needing to touch him. She'd never felt as close to another man as she did to Luther in that moment and she didn't want him to think anything was one-sided. "I'm crazy about you, Luther. I'm not used to this level of emotions, let alone expressing them, but I don't want there to be any doubt about how serious I am about us and how much I want to be with you. I want this to work. I've never said this to another man, but my heart wants you, too. If I'm honest, you had it before we even left Belize."

Luther's large hand slid up her arm and across her shoulder to the back of her neck, gripping it slightly with conviction. The emotion in his eyes at her words were clear even in the muted moonlight in the treehouse. It touched Liz that she could say anything that would have him looking at her like he was, and she was already addicted to the feeling that it gave her. And she'd never disrespect him by saying anything she didn't mean.

"Come here," he whispered, already pulling her towards him. Liz willingly closed the rest of the distance between them and their lips locked in an invigorated kiss, both of them relieved and reassured. Luther pulled Liz onto his lap as the kiss deepened and intensified, neither in any hurry. It didn't matter that it was late and they both had to be up in just a few hours. They couldn't let go of each other, and didn't try to.

Liz ended up spending the night, though they eventually moved from the treehouse down to Luther's bedroom. They didn't make love but did plenty of kissing and heavy petting, rolling around his large bed. It wasn't lost on either of them that the issue about Luther sharing Liz's bed still wasn't resolved, but it could wait. In unspoken understanding, they each knew they'd work that out at some point.

A few short hours later, Liz woke up to Luther leisurely kissing the back of her neck.

"Wake up, baby," he said softly. His hands roamed her hips from behind. "Your alarm just went off."

"Ugh," Liz groaned, hating the thought of having to leave Luther's bed and his arms. "How is it time to get up already??"

"We were up pretty late. I'd say I was sorry for that but I made a promise not to lie to you."

"I'm not complaining about anything other than the fact that I can't stay here in bed all day with you. Which I think is yet another first. Playing hooky because I want to stay up under a man has never been a thing for me but I'm seriously considering calling my assistants and letting them know I won't be in today."

"I'm surely not going to push you out of here; I'm in no hurry for you to leave. But I understand if you need to. Are you able to do work from home?"

Liz tried to recall what she had on her calendar for the day. "Probably. Though I admit I don't do that often."

"Feel free to go get your things and work from here. I'll make room in my office."

She wiped any remaining sleep from her eyes before turning in his arms. "You have clients today?"

"No, not today. I'll either be in the office myself or out in the shed working on some more hat designs. Got a custom request yesterday that I need to get started on."

"And you really wouldn't mind me being here while you're working?"

"Baby," he leaned back slightly so she could see his face, "Of course not. I love you being here; working, chilling, lounging in my bed, whatever. You are always more than welcome here with me, Liz."

Liz felt warmed at Luther welcoming her into his space like that. Most men made her feel like she was invading or crowding them after a while, so she got used to leaving before she was asked to leave. And anyway, she never wanted to get too comfortable in a man's space but that wasn't the case with Luther. She felt at home on her first visit.

And as he'd promised, he'd cleared out a drawer for her and made space on his bathroom counter and in his closet for her. It was a simple gesture to him but it touched her beyond belief.

"I'll run to the house and get my things, then," she informed, placing a kiss between his pecs.

He grinned. "Good. And I'll get some breakfast going while you're gone. I'd offer to make you some coffee but I don't have any; never got into the habit of drinking that."

"Neither did I. Never loved the taste of it, no matter what I put in it. I'll be all right once I'm up and moving around."

After another few minutes of cuddling, they got up and took turns in the bathroom before heading out to the living room. They were discussing what Luther would make them for breakfast when the doorbell interrupted them, their expressions morphing into confused ones.

"You expecting someone?"

"Not at all." Luther closed the door to the refrigerator that he'd just opened. "What time is it?"

Liz glanced at her phone. "Almost seven-thirty."

His frown deepening, Luther strode to the living room and glanced at the small monitor by the couch that showed the security camera over his front door, since his phone was still in the bedroom. He sighed when he saw who the unexpected guest was.

"It's Churi."

"Oh…" Liz straightened slightly. "Want me to go in the other room?"

"For what?"

"Just to avoid any drama that might start from her seeing me here this early. Believe me, I'm not running or anything; I just want to save you the headache."

"Churi is *my* child; I'm not hers. She doesn't run anything over here. And she knows better than to behave any way but respectfully after I've already had to tell her about herself once. So stay right where you are."

Convinced, Liz just folded her arms and waited.

Churi wasted no time making the point of her visit known as she breezed inside once Luther let her in. "Daddy, they raised my rent! And my roommate's hours got cut so I'm probably gonna have to pay for her part *and* mine! The other one already said she's not paying anything extra."

Luther shook his head as he closed the door. "Hello to you too, baby girl."

"I'm sorry; hi Daddy." She started to go over and give him a hug but stopped, looking at him with a slightly scrunched nose. Her finger twirled in the direction of his bare chest. "Um, can you put on a shirt?"

"My house. So no."

"Ugh. *Anyway-*"

"We're being rude, Churi." Luther nodded towards Liz, who was standing across the living room. "I have company."

Churi whirled around, her eyes instantly narrowing upon seeing Liz. Her mouth opened but as if catching herself, she glanced at her father before taking a beat and forcibly clearing her expression. "Good morning."

"Good morning, Churi," Liz responded politely. "Nice to see you."

"Yeah...I guess I wasn't expecting anyone to be over here with Daddy...at this time of morning."

Liz hoped she wasn't expecting an apology or an explanation, because she was owed neither. "I'm sure you know how it is when you're with the person you're head over heels for. You can't get enough of each other."

Luther smiled and winked at Liz, who winked back with a flirty smirk. Churi looked back and forth between them, floored that they were flirting with each other right in front of her.

Apparently choosing not to acknowledge Liz's statement, Churi turned her attention back to Luther. "Anyway, Daddy, can you help me out? I'm almost out of that money you gave me the last time."

"And I believe I told you when I *gave* you that money that it was going to be the last time I bailed you out," Luther reminded her. "I already footed your rent for the first six months you were in that apartment, against your mother's objections, and you swore up and down you'd take it from there. I'm the one that had to convince Jules that you were responsible enough to handle getting that place and yet this is the second time you've come over here asking for money."

"That was for school."

"Doesn't matter. You have a job, Churi."

"It's only part-time!"

"You'd better up those hours, then. Is this all you came over here for?"

Churi's jaw dropped. "I didn't know I needed a reason to visit you but...kinda."

"Call before you come next time. And just to avoid us having this conversation again, know that I'm not paying your bills at all, be it for rent, school, or whatever else."

"Daddy, how am I going to work full-time and go to school? *And* pay for all that?"

Liz subtly shook her head. Jules wasn't kidding about how spoiled Churi was.

"People do it all the time, baby girl," Luther informed his daughter, undeterred. "You'll find a way if you put this energy towards that instead of trying to get someone to bail you out."

"It's not like I'm asking you to pay for *everything*; just to cover my rent increase for a couple of months." Churi turned towards Liz with pleading eyes. "Can you tell him, girl? Maybe he'll listen to you, since you're his girlfriend or whatever. You see where I'm coming from, right?"

Oh I'm your 'girl' now, huh?

Luther started to respond to that but Liz motioned to him that she had it covered. "Churi, I get it. Living on your own for the first time is tough and a huge adjustment. I went through all this that you're going through now. But I agree with your dad. You'll be a lot prouder of yourself if you stand on your own two feet." Her brow arched pointedly when she added, "And just call me Liz."

Churi clearly didn't like that response but knew better than to show it. She just subtly rolled her eyes and turned back to Luther. "Can I at least get something to eat? It's been a while since we've had breakfast; just the two of us."

"I believe that's on *you*, baby girl, not me. You've stood me up for our brunches more than once. And you're more than welcome to stay and eat but Liz will be here, too," Luther let her know, refusing to entertain Churi's blatant attempt to exclude Liz. "We were already planning to have breakfast together when you showed up."

"Oh, well I wouldn't want to get in the way. I'll just go home and eat some cereal or something...if there's any left."

Churi paused as if she was waiting on one of them to insist that she stay, and when she got nothing but silence, her face actually flushed in either anger or embarrassment. Or both. Liz tried her best not to laugh.

"Ugh," Churi yanked the strap of her purse higher on her shoulder and started to stomp towards the door, but one warning glare from Luther softened her steps. With her hand on the doorknob, she turned to him and said, "Oh yeah, Daddy, Mom broke up with that guy she was dating. Maybe you can call and let her know you're still there for her, since she's single again and everything."

She was out the door in a flash, and Luther just shook his head.

"Sorry about that, baby," he said to Liz, going over to the window to watch Churi get in her car and drive off. "My daughter can be something else when she wants to be."

"I see. And I probably should have refrained from giving my opinion about the whole money thing but I guess I couldn't resist."

"No, I actually appreciate that. Some women might have taken her side in an effort to win favor with her. Especially since it's no secret she's not a huge fan of yours, for whatever reason."

"I think the reason is that I'm not Jules. Given her parting remarks, she wants you two to get back together."

"She tries that every few months, as if we'll have magically changed our minds. We've both told her it isn't going to happen. But Churi can be selectively forgetful and relentless when it comes to something she wants."

"That can be a good thing, in the right capacity. And I'd like to be cool with your daughter but I'm not going to suck up to her. Hopefully she'll realize that I'm not the enemy at some point."

"I'd like to think she will. Despite the couple of examples you've had the misfortune of witnessing, Churi is actually a sweetheart."

They resumed their tasks from before they were interrupted, with Liz running home to get her things as Luther got breakfast going. Once she had returned and Luther helped her get set up in his office, they sat down to a meal of omelets and turkey bacon.

"Do you want to get re-married?" Liz asked suddenly.

"That's out of the blue," Luther chuckled, wiping his mouth. "Why?"

"Just curious. I was thinking about what Churi said earlier and realized that's something I don't know; if you have intentions of marrying again."

"I wouldn't mind it. Marriage is a beautiful thing with the right person."

"So I've heard."

He eyed her. "You disagree?"

"Oh no, not at all," Liz quickly assured. "I have nothing against marriage."

"I know you said before that you weren't that hyped about it, though. So if we continued to progress in our relationship to where I wanted you to be my wife...would you be happy about that or are you wanting to just date indefinitely?"

"Luther," she reached over and took his hand. "Knowing the kind of man you are and how intensely you invest in relationships, there's no way I'd get involved with you expecting to keep things at dating forever. I'm not running from anything. If we get to the point where we want to spend our lives together, nobody could beat me down the aisle."

"That's good, Liz. I'm glad to hear that. Because..." His hand squeezed hers. "I love you. More than that, I'm *in* love with you."

Liz's breathing deepened as she took in his words, her body warming from head to toe. Luther was looking at her with such sincerity that she couldn't look away. His admission touched her but it didn't totally surprise her; he'd made the depth of his feelings clear several times, and had admitted to falling for her before they'd even left Belize. Usually an admission of love so early in a relationship would have sent her running but from Luther...it only cemented what she already knew.

He was it for her.

"I know I've alluded to it before but I've kept the full declaration to myself because I didn't want to freak you out," he continued. "But-"

"I'm not freaked out and I don't need you to keep anything to yourself," Liz blurted. Suddenly needing to be closer to him, she stood and rounded the table to straddle his lap, draping her arms over his shoulders. Just looking into his face sent her heart racing. "Luther, I love you, too. I'm *in* love with you, too, baby."

"Are you sure?" His hands roamed over her warm body everywhere they could reach. "I need you to be sure."

"I'd never say something like that if I wasn't. Maybe we still have plenty to learn about each other and still have some kinks to work out in our relationship, but...there's not a doubt in my mind what I feel for you. If anything freaks me out, it's how intense it is...I honestly didn't think I was capable."

"I thought you said you'd been in love before?"

"It was nothing like this. This is *so* beyond that...it makes me realize I've probably never experienced it like I thought. But like I said, I'm not running from it. I'm a hundred percent in and you are pretty much stuck with me."

He grinned, which only made her grin. She loved making him smile like that.

"I guess that's enough said, then," he concluded, leaning in for a kiss. "I'm relieved to know we're on the same page but I also want you to know this doesn't mean I'm going to try to rush anything. Like you said, there's still plenty more we have to learn about each other and things we still need to iron out-"

His words were interrupted by Liz's sudden kiss. She just couldn't help herself, and grabbed his face in both hands, laying it on him. Luther certainly wasn't complaining, though, and eagerly matched her energy.

"Can we make this new development between us official?" Liz asked against his lips.

"We're already official, baby. At least, as far as you having my heart. I know we said we were going to hold off on declaring us as actually *official*-official until-"

"Okay, let me put it this way: make love to me, Luther."

He immediately pushed his chair back and stood, lifting her with him and drawing an excited squeal out of her. He smiled and then groaned at how she nibbled on his ear, her hand sliding up and down the side of his face and neck. His feet moved quicker towards his bedroom.

"Yes, ma'am."

Chapter 13

• • • •

IT WAS HARD FOR LUTHER to keep the smile off his face as he sat at the bar at Natavey, nursing his drink. He honestly felt like a schoolboy who found love for the first time.

It had been a couple of days since he and Liz professed their love for each other, subsequently declaring their relationship as official and exclusive after a couple rounds of lovemaking, and he was still riding high from it. Knowing that Liz was officially his woman now actually made him a little giddy, which floored him. He didn't even feel like this when he fell for Jules. Liz truly felt like one in a million, and the issues he knew they still had to work through didn't faze him. Getting her assurance that she was as all in as he was put his mind at ease, because part of him had started to wonder if maybe he was too much for her and she'd come to tell him that she wasn't ready for something quite so deep.

He hadn't planned on telling her he loved her so soon. He'd admitted to falling for her, though that wasn't quite the same as saying it flat-out. But he hadn't been able to hold it in anymore. In truth, Liz had him captivated since the moment he laid eyes on her in Belize. And when they reunited by chance in the Natavey lounge, he knew there was no way he was letting her go again. They would only part ways if she told him she didn't want him anymore, or if he realized he was totally mistaken about their connection and compatibility and it turned out they were wrong for each other. And while they differed on some things, he didn't believe that to be the case.

There *was* the teeny tiny voice in the back of his mind that reminded him not to get too comfortable too fast, however. As great as Liz was, she still practically recoiled at his touch if they weren't behind closed doors. Luther had convinced himself he could deal with it but that didn't mean he didn't wish it was different.

And aside from that, Luther had to remind himself to not let his feelings overshadow his good sense. He really was a romantic to his bones, and had made the mistake before of letting himself be blind to issues in his relationships that were clear to everyone else because he was riding the infatuation wave. That's why he was trying to measure his steps with Liz, despite jumping the gun on revealing his love for her. He readily embraced love when he felt it, but he wasn't going to let it turn him into a fool, either.

"How's it going this evening?"

Luther snapped out of his musings and looked at who he recognized to be one of the owners standing opposite him behind the bar. He knew it was a pair of brothers but he didn't know which one was which.

"Everything is great, thanks, man," Luther replied. "This is becoming one of my favorite places to hang out."

"I'm glad to hear it. E.J. Bell."

"Luther Monroe." They shared a brief handshake across the bar. "Your wife is the manager, right? I think she's the one that put me and my date out of the lounge a little while back."

"Oh that was you?" E.J. chuckled. "Yeah, she told me about that. Apparently you and Liz were really enjoying yourselves."

"Yeah, admittedly we weren't thinking about the time," Luther admitted with a smile. "But we'll be more mindful from now on."

"It's all good. I'd rather have the problem of getting people to leave because they're enjoying themselves that much than having to beg them to come in here."

They chatted for another minute or so before E.J. moved on and Luther continued enjoying his drink. He had decided to come in after wrapping up some errands. Liz was working and he didn't know if he'd be seeing her that night, since she said she had to meet with her sorority sister for an event planning session once she got off and it would probably take a while.

"Well if it isn't my unofficial nutritionist. I think you were on point about the flaxseeds."

Luther glanced over his shoulder to see Kinsley standing there, smiling at him. He flashed her a polite smile of his own. "Good evening, Kinsley. You going to the lounge?"

"I was but now that I see you here...you mind if I hang?"

He did, and tried to think of a nice way to say so. "I just came in to veg out for a while and have a drink or two; I wouldn't be great company."

"I'm not trying to talk your ear off; just don't really want to sit by myself." Kinsley eased onto the barstool next to him without invitation, flagging down the bartender.

Luther resisted the urge to sigh. He and Kinsley were cool now but that didn't mean he was particularly eager to hang with her one-on-one. She was Liz's good friend and he mainly only wanted them to be on good terms because of that.

"I'll have a..." Kinsley paused and swung her eyes to Luther's tumbler. "What's that you're drinking, Luther?"

"A Black Manhattan."

"I'll be daring and try that; haven't had one of those," Kinsley announced with a brief nod to the bartender, who got right to work preparing her drink. Kinsley watched him for a moment before turning her attention back to Luther, briefly placing a hand on his arm. "So what's been up with you?"

"Just staying busy," Luther replied succinctly, not in the mood for small talk. Yet he still felt obliged to ask, "What is it you do?"

"I'm a judicial clerk. And before you ask, no I don't love it but the top two things I care about as far as a career is that it pays my bills and I don't dread doing it every day. It meets those criteria so I'm good."

"Well, hey, as long as you're happy with it."

"I'm satisfied with it. I don't look to my career for happiness. I get that from the other areas of my life."

"Interesting perspective," Luther mused, meaning it. He couldn't imagine not loving what he did every day for a living and honestly didn't think he'd met anyone else with Kinsley's mindset.

"So how are things between you and my girl, Liz?"

Luther looked at her evenly, sensing the motives behind that question weren't as innocent as she tried to make it seem. "I'm sure she's told you, since you two are such good friends and all."

"There's two sides to every story, right?"

"Hopefully you can understand why I'm not going to discuss my relationship with you, Kinsley, but the short answer is, things are great."

"Great, huh? So you've progressed from casual to exclusive, I guess...you're not seeing other people like you were before?"

Luther felt his ears go hot. When were they seeing other people? Is that was Liz had told her?

But Luther kept his face even. He wasn't going to fall for whatever bait it was Kinsley was trying to lure him with. "My answer remains the same."

"Well, then I'm glad to hear that." Kinsley lightly bumped his shoulder with hers, smiling at him as she picked up the drink the bartender just put in front of her. "I know Liz had her...*concerns* about things but it looks like you two have worked everything out. I'm not surprised she was so drawn to you; you just have this aura that screams 'patience' and 'tolerance' and that's what she needs. Mmm, this drink is good! What's in this?"

Luther was too busy processing her earlier words to hear her, but thankfully the bartender was still nearby and offered the answer she was looking for. He and Kinsley went back and forth a couple times before Kinsley turned her wide smile back to Luther. "You're two-for-two on recommendations, Luther. I see you have a knack for knowing just what I need...and want."

A silent alarm going off in his head, Luther smoothly swallowed the last of his drink and set down his glass, standing. He didn't have to look directly at her to know how she was eying him. "Excuse me a moment."

"I'll be here."

Not responding, Luther turned and headed off towards the men's room, his long legs moving swiftly. There were a couple of other men inside and he gave them a brief nod before closing himself in one of the stalls, just standing there to get his thoughts together.

Kinsley was flirting with him, however slyly she tried to do it. That was bad enough considering her relationship to Liz, but what bothered him more were her comments *about* Liz. Luther was hardly one to fall prone to gossip, but he couldn't make himself dismiss Kinsley's words. He couldn't help but wonder how Liz had portrayed their relationship; was she painting it as some casual thing while he was treating it with devoted reverence? Had she been dating other men? She told him about the one she invited over after their argument, but what about before that? Even if they hadn't been official-official, Luther hated the thought of being that far off about how he thought Liz felt about him. Just like that, he started to regret telling her he loved her so soon.

Shaking his head, he tried to check himself. He didn't like to think of revealing his true feelings as a mistake. And it wasn't like he'd never been wrong about a woman before, but he just couldn't buy that Liz wasn't as all in as he was; that she was faking any of the times they shared, even a little bit. It would be foolish to start doubting her just because her friend was trying to be slick. If Kinsley was bold enough to flirt with him knowing he and her friend were dating, then he couldn't put anything past her, including embellishing or straight lying to do the very thing he was allowing to happen now, which was doubt Liz. He didn't want to be that easy.

But the voice in the back of his mind reminded him not to be a fool, either. What if there *was* some merit to Kinsley's words…then what? Luther had been all about Liz since they met, and maybe Liz believed she could do as she pleased, since he'd made his devotion clear. It would crush him if what he thought he had with Liz turned out to be a sham.

"Stop this," he muttered to himself, lacing fingers behind his head and looking up at the ceiling. He rarely succumbed to self-doubt, and he didn't want to start now. He'd trust Liz until he had reason – *concrete* reason – not to.

Marginally encouraged, Luther stepped out of the stall and washed his hands out of habit, even though he hadn't done anything. He dried his hands and helped himself to some of the complimentary hand cream before exiting the bathroom, rubbing his hands together and hoping Kinsley had left by then.

She hadn't, but now she wasn't alone. Luther knew from the way his heart automatically quickened that the tall woman with the short sassy haircut having what looked to be a heated conversation with Kinsley was Liz, even though her back was to him. His brow furrowed in curiosity, he headed over to them.

"Hey, hey," he greeted, standing next to his vacated stool and placing a hand on the supple leather. Liz turned to him with heat in her eyes and Kinsley's dimmed ones quickly averted.

"Hey, yourself," Liz greeted. Luther didn't miss the bite in her voice.

"Um, I just remembered something I need to do so I'm gonna go," Kinsley muttered, placing some money on the bar and easing off the stool. "I'll talk to you later, Liz. And Luther...I'll see ya."

Luther gave her a polite wave while Liz just turned and glared at her. After Kinsley had scurried out, Liz turned her attention back to him.

"I thought you had to plan your sorority thing," Luther commented. "Did you all wrap up early or something?"

"No, not even close." Liz's mouth was in a tight line, her right hand gripping her left forearm in front of her, her weight shifted to one leg. "I had to cut it short."

"Why is that?"

"Because I found out my friend and my man were over here getting a little too close."

His frown deepened. "Excuse me?"

"Why are you over here letting Kinsley flirt with you, Luther? Why were you even entertaining her?"

"Um, I wasn't *letting* her do a damn thing nor was I entertaining anything other than polite conversation. I came here by myself and she just showed up, striking up harmless conversation. You can't honestly think I'm interested in Kinsley."

"No, but she's interested in *you*. And when you sit around here shooting the breeze and sharing drinks together-"

"Whoa, whoa, hold up," he interjected, holding up his hands as his frown spread to match hers. "I'm not appreciating the way you're coming at me right now, Liz. And unless you've implanted some kind of bug on my person without my knowledge, how do you even know what was said at all?"

"I know Kinsley," Liz retorted. "And I'm telling you, she's trying to make her move."

"And this is supposed to be your best friend?"

"I never called her that. She's a *good* friend; at least, most of the time. If anyone is my *best* friend, it's my sister."

"Whatever adjective you want to use, you seem strangely calm to be so sure about your girl apparently trying to step to me. And I'm still curious as to how you managed to know anything might be happening, anyway. Last you told me, you were going to be across town planning and I likely wouldn't be seeing you at all tonight. Don't tell me you have some kind of sixth sense."

"Don't make jokes, Luther."

"Do I look even remotely amused right now?"

"How would you feel if I was in here grinning in some other man's face?"

"If it was with any intentions beyond the casual, I'd hate it. That's exactly what my intentions towards Kinsley were. I can't speak to hers for me. But since you broached the subject of you and other men..."

Liz's hand slid to her hip. "Yes?"

"*Have* you been seeing other people? Because your friend intimated as much. Or at the very least, that you claimed you were within your right to."

Liz's ears twitched, and her jaws clenched so hard they ached. Had Kinsley really thrown her under the bus? Liz hadn't dated anyone else but she *had* repeatedly told Kinsley that she could if she wanted to, and that Luther could, also. It burned her to think that her friend would use that against her.

Before Liz could respond, though, Natalia strolled up to them with a painted smile. "Is everything okay over here?"

Liz and Luther both looked at her before their eyes drifted back to each other. Each seemed to remember they were arguing about their relationship in a public place and loosened their combative stances.

"Everything's fine, girl," Liz assured her, forcing a smile. "Thanks for checking."

"No problem. What about you, Luther?" Natalia looked up at him, a sharpness in her brown eyes under her bangs. "Are you good, also?"

"I am, thank you." Luther made himself take a breath and step back, his earlier ire now cooled. He hated that he'd lost his composure like that; he'd never been one to air his private issues publicly.

Once Natalia stepped away, Luther wasted no time saying to Liz, "I'm not sure how we got to this point but this isn't the place to discuss it."

Liz nodded. "I agree. Are you about to head to the house?"

"Yeah. I have a headache I didn't have when I got here that I need to tend to."

"I see." Her face flushed at the possible double entendre. "I have to get back to this planning session, as much as I wish I didn't. If it's not too late, I'll call you when I get home."

"Please do. I'd like to know you made it home safely."

"Don't forget about dinner at Lovey's on Thursday."

"I haven't. Nothing has changed over here."

Liz searched his eyes that were looking steadily into hers. She knew he wasn't pleased, but neither was she. And it wasn't lost on her that there was likely more meaning behind his statement about nothing changing on his end; and the fact that he didn't insist that there was no hour too late for her to call or even come by like he usually did wasn't lost on her, either. Her desire to wring Kinsley's neck flared.

"I'll talk to you later," she announced, suddenly eager to make her leave. She hated the tension between them and figured they could each use a little time to clear their heads.

"All right."

Hesitating, Liz quickly stepped forward and grabbed his chin, leaning up and placing a quick peck to his lips before turning and quickly strolling towards the exit. Luther just looked after her, as confused as ever, before sighing and turning back to the bartender to settle his tab so he could go home and try to figure out how the hell things had taken such a turn all of a sudden.

• • • •

BY THE TIME THURSDAY night rolled around, Luther had calmed down considerably from the uncomfortable scene with Liz at Natavey and was feeling better about things. He and Liz did in fact talk once she got home later that night, and while neither had the energy for an emotional conversation, Liz did assure him that he was the only man she was seeing and had been since they met, save for her one admitted lapse in judgment. Luther was relieved, though there was a dull ache that remained in his gut. Something still felt off, and he hated not knowing what that something was.

Liz wasn't feeling much better. She'd been on a high after she and Luther admitted their love for each other and cemented their status as an official couple, but now things felt precarious. And Kinsley was suddenly avoiding her. Liz knew she wasn't blameless; she'd stirred the pot in this soup of confusion and uncertainty by not being totally honest with her friend and also by challenging her to make a play for Luther. Regardless of her rationale that she didn't think Kinsley would actually do it because of their friendship, Liz should have never put it out there. If she had just admitted to the depth of her feelings for Luther from the beginning, this wouldn't be happening.

But despite this rough patch, Liz told herself that she and Luther would get through it. That his recent cooling off towards her was just temporary. They'd talked, but hadn't seen each other since their face-off at Natavey. Liz realized how used she was to being in his bed and in his arms at night because being in her own bed at home just didn't feel right, and before Luther, one of her favorite places in the world to be was her own bed.

They arrived to Lovey's separately, but Liz waited for him in her car before going inside. She hoped they could at least put their still-unaddressed differences aside for the evening. Luther wasn't the petty type and she knew he'd act maturely, but Liz wished this cloud wasn't hanging over them at all and that their rapport wouldn't be something they had to force to save face.

When she saw his car pull up, Liz felt the usual tingles of anticipation and excitement that usually came when she knew she was going to see him. She got out of her car and waited, leaning against the door while giving a last quick check to her outfit. Her cream fitted turtleneck, wide camel leather belt, faux leather pants of the same shade, and camel thigh-high boots were intentionally chosen to entice, and she wasn't ashamed to admit it. Everything in her woke up as she watched him approach, her hand absently adjusting her huge white gold hoop earring.

"Hey, baby," he greeted, walking right up to her.

Liz felt relief that he seemed to have warmed back up to her. She smiled. "Hey, handsome. Did you have any trouble finding the house?"

"Not really. Just seemed to get caught by every red light, is all." His eyes swept over her. "You look beautiful."

Her smile widening, she pushed off the car and stepped closer to him, sick of the emotional and physical distance between them. Her hand touched his face before she snaked her arm around his neck, feeling encouraged when he instantly pulled her closer.

"Thank you, baby. You're looking as hot as usual."

"I appreciate it." Luther himself had taken extra care when he dressed for the evening, wearing a tan button-down with the top couple of buttons undone, chocolate brown slacks, and shiny brown oxfords. And of course, he was donning one of his custom fedoras.

Between his look, his cologne, and the fresh haircut and beard trim he'd clearly had, Liz had the strong urge to pull him into the backseat of her car. But she knew Lovey probably already knew they were there thanks to their security cameras, and Liz didn't want to give her sister reason to blush upon meeting Luther by seducing him in the driveway. She could only hope that they'd be getting back to their intense amorous activity later that evening.

Luther leaned in to kiss her but, catching himself, he just tweaked her chin and stepped back. Liz looked up at him in disappointment.

"We're out in the open," he reminded her. His voice didn't sound snide or resentful; just matter-of-fact. "And I'm sure they're expecting us so we should probably get inside."

Pursing her lips, Liz just nodded and turned to lead him up the driveway to the house. Even though he was just adhering to the boundaries she insisted on, she still felt a little slighted.

"Hey!" Lovey greeted when she opened the door moments later. She stepped back to allow them inside, immediately giving Liz a big hug before eagerly turning her attention to Luther.

"Lovey, this is Luther Monroe," Liz introduced, unable to resist a proud smile as she turned to him. "Luther, my awesome sister, Lovey Bell. And if you get to know her well enough, you can call her by her government name, Est-"

"Liz!" Lovey lightly smacked her arm, though she was smiling. "Don't do that. I'm sure Luther isn't interested in my boring details." She playfully pushed her big sister aside and stepped closer to Luther, arms extended and grin on full blast. "It's so nice to finally meet you! Welcome!"

"Same, Lovey," Luther replied with his own wide smile, readily receiving her hug. She had such an obvious warm spirit that he liked her already. "And I see why Liz brags on you so much. You seem to be just as beautiful on the inside as well as the outside."

"Oh, Luther," Lovey ducked her head slightly, her fair brown skin immediately flushing. "That's so sweet of you to say, thank you. Liz is just as taken with you, I hope you know. I swear, I have *never* seen her so sprung over anyone. Honestly, I wouldn't be surprised if she has your name scribbled all over her-"

"Um, Lovey! Don't you have to go check on the babies or something?" Liz asked pointedly, making both Luther and Lovey chuckle.

"They're spending the night with Mama Elyse," Lovey informed, giggling. "Roland is upstairs taking a phone call but he should be down any minute. Oh, and Desiree and Lorenzo are coming. Have you met them yet, Luther?"

"I haven't, no. I've heard about them, though."

"Just be forewarned; Desiree is likely to say anything. Especially since this is the first time we've gotten to have a gathering like this, meeting Liz's man. It's a privilege we don't get so you must be mighty special."

"That's good to know," Luther mused, looking over at Liz, who he could tell was blushing but trying to hide it. "And I'm the one that's privileged because Liz is definitely special to me."

The raw tenderness in his voice made Liz lift her head, their eyes locking and holding. Lovey was standing there with her hands over her mouth, looking back and forth between them and practically squealing behind her hands.

"You two are so *beautiful* together!" she gushed. "I love it!"

Just then, Roland came down, smiling when he saw their guests. "Hey, I didn't hear y'all come in. What's up, Liz?" They shared a brief hug before he turned to Luther, hand extended. "Hey, man, I'm Roland. You must be Luther. I've seen you around Natavey a couple times."

"Yeah, that's my spot. My brother Carter turned me on to it and now I'm up in there more than he is."

"Dig that; I love to hear it. Wow, I honestly didn't think I'd see the day when Liz brought a man over to meet the family. You must have the magic touch or something."

Luther couldn't resist a chuckle when Liz threw up her hands. "Is this what I'm gonna have to look forward to all night? 'Cause I'm already rethinking this whole little gathering, if it is."

"Too late, girl; it's already happening," Lovey teased. "And you know it's all in good fun."

"For *y'all*."

"Well believe me, it's all mutual," Luther assured, winking at Liz. "Can I help with anything?"

"You're a guest; don't be silly," Lovey gently scolded. "You can come on in the dining room while we finish getting everything together. Would you like anything to drink? And I meant to ask Liz to see if you have any dietary restrictions or allergies or anything..."

"No allergies or restrictions. And unless you made Chinese food, I'm good to go."

"Oh, great," Lovey sighed with relief, her hand on her chest. "I would've felt *so* guilty!"

"Get used to this, man," Roland quipped, sliding an arm around his wife's shoulders and kissing her temple. "My baby can be incredibly accommodating. Or should I say *overly* accommodating, at times. She'll make herself sick over it, if you let her."

Lovey just poked him in the stomach before they shared a laugh and a tender kiss to the lips, grinning at each other. Luther couldn't resist watching; the love they had between them was so glaring it warmed him both with admiration and jealousy. That was the kind of bond he wanted.

And when he turned his attention to the woman he wanted it *with*, she quickly averted her eyes, as if knowing exactly what he was thinking.

Thankfully, Desiree and Lorenzo showed up just then, and Liz was spared from Luther's intense silent scrutiny. Lorenzo and Luther hit it off immediately, and Desiree was looking at Luther almost in wonderment.

"I have to say, part of me didn't believe you were actually real," she joked as everyone headed to the dining room. "Especially since Liz doesn't really do cute couple selfies or social media posts bragging on her boo. I just thought of you as some kind of mythical being that existed only in her mind. But here you are. I'm gonna have to mark this on my calendar 'cause Liz does *not* bring men home; I hope that doesn't mean the good Lord is coming already."

"Ha ha," Liz rolled her eyes as everyone laughed. "Everybody has jokes tonight, I see. If y'all are gonna roast somebody, it should be Luther; *he's* the new kid on the block."

"It's more fun to roast *you*."

"And we definitely wouldn't want to do anything to run Luther off," Roland added.

"I'm sure I could handle it," Luther commented good-naturedly. "I'm just glad to be welcomed so if this is what comes with it, bring it."

Desiree grinned. "I like you already just because you're not a stick in the mud. Liz, marry him tomorrow."

Liz chuckled along with everyone else despite the immediate flush to her cheeks. She knew Luther was looking at her, but she pretended to have to inspect something on her boot.

"It's so funny to hear you pushing anyone to get married, baby," Lorenzo teased his wife, lovingly rubbing her shoulders before he pulled out her chair for her. "Considering how you used to feel about it."

"*And* that you turned your man down the first time he asked you," Liz reminded, unable to resist getting in a jab of her own. "Don't think we forgot about that."

"Hey, this isn't *my* night to be roasted," Desiree reminded, pointing a finger at Liz before taking her seat. "And anyway, people can change. I might not have wanted anything to do with marriage before but it took meeting the right man to change all that."

"That's right," Lorenzo concurred before leaning down to place a light kiss to her lips, though Desiree grabbed his face and deepened it before he could retract. Lovey just grinned at them as she and Roland brought the food in from the kitchen.

Usually Luther loved being in the presence of so much amazing and genuine Black love, but now it just felt like he was being tortured. He wanted to be able to share a kiss with Liz or hold her hand or even play footsie with her under the table. But they hadn't touched since they entered the house, and the fact that his hands were proverbially tied agitated him.

But he reminded himself that he had agreed to Liz's stipulations so there was no use getting upset about it now.

As the dinner continued, though, and the other couples continued to freely display their affections towards each other while he and Liz just sat side by side barely brushing elbows, his frustration blossomed and he stopped trying to keep it from doing so. It wasn't that Luther needed to show off or prove anything to anyone else by showing affection to his woman, but being restricted because of Liz's unresolved issues was stifling almost to the point of making him itch. He regretted agreeing to this no-touching rule of Liz's, and he felt his resentment take root.

Thankfully, he was genuinely enjoying getting to know Liz's family and friends, and it helped to soothe his frustration. For the moment, at least.

"Do you have children, Luther?" Lovey asked him, holding her glass as Roland poured her more wine.

Luther nodded, taking a moment to finish chewing his steak. "Yes, I have a daughter, Churi. She's twenty-three and spoiled rotten."

"Oh, I can already say that about ours, especially our daughter," Lovey glanced at her husband. "*Somebody* tends to give her special treatment, and it's *not* me."

Roland just hunched his shoulders with a convicted smile. "Hey, I love my boys but there's something about my baby girl. And she's the spitting image of her beautiful mama, so you really can't blame me."

"Real smooth save, man," Lorenzo chuckled as Lovey blushed with appreciation.

Grinning, Roland winked at his wife. "It's true, though."

"I know what you mean, though, Roland," Luther spoke up. "I can admit I'm mostly to blame for Churi being so spoiled. She's my only daughter and I was a goner as soon as I laid eyes on her."

"Absolute same."

"Have you met his daughter, Liz?" Desiree asked.

"Yeah," Liz gave a playfully exaggerated sigh. "Unfortunately, she's not a fan."

"Why, what did you say to tick her off?"

"Believe me, it's all Churi," Luther jumped to Liz's defense, even though he knew Desiree was only kidding. "She's still keeping hope alive that her mother and I will reunite, though we've been divorced for years and have told her repeatedly that all we'll ever be from here on out is friends."

"I'm sure I'll win her over soon enough, though," Liz stated. "People don't usually hate me forever."

"She's doesn't hate you, baby."

"She certainly doesn't *like* me. Y'all should've seen the look on her face when she saw me at Luther's house early in the morning the other day. And it probably didn't help that I was wearing his shirt."

"Homegirl doesn't appreciate you getting it in with her dad, huh?" Desiree tsked. "Oh well."

"I'm sure once she gets used to the idea, she'll warm up to you, Liz," Lovey added. "At least she's an adult and it's not a child that can't understand how relationships can go."

Liz refrained from saying that they wouldn't even be there if Churi were a child, because Liz would've bailed immediately. Instead she just replied, "True enough. I just want us all to get along. I've had enough of the drama for a while."

Luther couldn't help but wonder if she was at all talking about him in that statement. He placed a hand on her leg under the table and felt it immediately tense. When he looked at her, she treated him with a pointed scolding look, her brows furrowing slightly, reminding him where they were.

He removed his hand, his jaws clenching briefly.

The dinner continued with mostly good vibes. Luther readily answered whatever questions he was asked, and was grateful that he genuinely liked Liz's people. He knew her parents were deceased, as were his, and how important her sister and friends were to her. And he was serious about feeling privileged to be there, especially since Liz's suitors apparently were usually kept hidden behind the scenes, according to everyone's earlier teasing.

After gobbling up the dessert of mixed berry cobbler, everyone congregated in the den for more wine and conversation, having too good of a time to cut the evening short. When Luther asked where the restroom was, Liz offered to show him.

"I'm timing y'all," Desiree teased, sitting up slightly from where she was snuggled under Lorenzo's huge arm. "Lovey, girl, maybe we need to turn on some music or something, just in case. You know, to drown out any *spontaneous activity* they might get into on the way to the bathroom."

"Hush, Desiree." Liz admonished as she stepped over her feet, giving her an 'accidental' kick in the ankle as she did. Desiree yelped, causing everyone to laugh. "It's not gonna be any of that."

"Uh-huh."

"If there is, though, just keep it downstairs and don't tell me where you did it," Roland requested. He nodded towards Desiree and Lorenzo. "I'm still trying to get over hearing these two in the kitchen pantry that time."

"Ohhh..." Lorenzo hummed, hiding a smile behind his fist.

"You heard that, huh?" Desiree muttered, sinking a little in her seat.

Roland playfully shuddered. "Unfortunately."

"Anyway," Liz shook her head with a smile, heading towards the hall leading to the guest bathroom with Luther close behind. "We'll be right back."

Once they were outside the door, though, Luther suddenly grabbed her and yanked her to him, drawing a surprised squeak from her. He quickly leaned down and closed his mouth over hers, backing her against the wall and pressing their bodies together. Liz returned his kiss, readily responding to him, until she suddenly pushed him away.

"We can't do this here," she whispered, panting slightly.

He kept his hold on her hips. "Why not?"

"Because we're in my sister's house. Somebody might catch us."

"I don't think it would matter if they did, baby. You heard what Roland said."

"That doesn't mean I want it to happen." Her hands gently pushed again at his chest, urging him to step back. "Getting caught having sex is no fun, believe me."

"Okay, let's go in the bathroom and lock the door, then."

"Luther."

"What? I've been keeping my hands to myself all evening and I'm aching for you, baby. I miss you."

Liz released a small breath at his words, her chest caving in slightly. She lightly grabbed the front of his shirt. "Luther, I miss you, too. But a quickie in the bathroom isn't the way for us to handle that."

"Why? Because you're too worried about what someone else will think?"

He couldn't help his sharp tone. His frustration had been building all evening. Seducing her in Roland and Lovey's house wasn't something he planned but he couldn't resist the opportunity once it was right in front of him. Everyone else was a ways away talking and drinking in the den, and he was certain all that would happen if anyone *did* happen to catch them was some good-natured teasing.

"Are you really trying to go there right now?" she asked, folding her arms.

"Tell me I'm wrong. They're all in the other room, not even thinking about us. And everybody here is grown and committed to who they came with. There's nothing we need to hide or be ashamed of yet you can't loosen the hell up enough to even kiss me in an empty hallway. Though I guess

I shouldn't be surprised, since you practically turned to stone when I dared to touch your leg under the table earlier."

Liz's ears twitched, and her face tightened so much she felt it might rip in half. She looked away, taking a moment to gather herself.

"Can we not do this here?" she finally requested, keeping her voice low. "And why are you tripping about this, anyway? I thought we came to an agreement. You said you understood my concerns, Luther."

"I said I'd *respect* your concerns, Liz; I didn't say I understood them. Because I don't. And I'll fully admit that I made a mistake when I agreed to this no-PDA bullshit because..." He swallowed and stepped back, telling himself to calm down. He knew it wasn't the time or place to have that discussion. Holding up his hands, he grunted, "Let's table this. I'm not trying to get riled up right now."

"But you were willing to fuck in the bathroom?"

Standing straighter, his jaw set before he stepped closer, invading her space. Her intake of breath and chest that was suddenly rising and falling with increased speed revealed the effect her had on her despite her frustration towards him.

"Yes, I was," he confirmed, his lips grazing her ear. "I absolutely wanted to fuck you and I wouldn't have cared who heard me do it. And I'm willing to bet that once I was inside you, you wouldn't have, either."

A shudder overtook Liz's body at his words. Now she was hating that she'd refused him because she was aching for him, too, not to mention sufficiently wet.

"But I guess we'll never know," Luther finished, putting distance between them that Liz immediately hated. "Since you're so uptight. You can go on back in there with them; you don't have to wait for me. Wouldn't want them thinking we were doing anything illicit back here 'cause that would be absolutely tragic, huh?"

He stepped around her and entered the bathroom, closing the door with force. Liz heard the lock click immediately. Her body was still buzzing from both his affect and his words, and her arousal had now taken the lead on her frustration. She turned towards the door and placed her hand on the knob, lifting the other to knock. If nothing else, she wanted her and Luther to come to a truce, however temporary, so neither of them would have to fake anything when they were back around everyone else.

But her hand ended up just resting on the door, her head eventually following suit. She couldn't hear anything on the other side, so she figured Luther was probably collecting himself, too. Liz hadn't been blind to the fact that there was an underlying tension between her and Luther that had started right after they declared their love for each other days before. At the time, she'd been over the moon. But maybe they'd been a little premature in that declaration, sincere or not.

Figuring she'd give him the time away from her he clearly needed, she straightened and moved away from the door. Touching her flaming cheeks and smoothing her hands down the back of her hair, Liz took a deep breath, pasted on a smile, and rejoined the others in the den.

After another hour or so, Liz and Luther were back at her place, not even bothering to sit down before resuming their earlier argument.

"Luther, why the hell would you tell me you were okay with the PDA thing if you didn't mean it?" Liz demanded, hands on her hips. "We could've avoided all of this if you'd just been honest."

"Nobody was being dishonest, Liz. I sincerely thought I could be okay with your requests. And I've tried. But it's not as easy as I thought it would be." He rested his linked hands on top of his head, looking at her. "And I wish you would try to respect my side of this as much as you want me to respect yours."

"I am!"

"You're not. You want me to just get over it because it's what you want and it just doesn't go like that. Like I've said; I'm not your damn brother."

"I'm aware of that, Luther. It's not like I act like you are. Just because I'm not grinding on your lap at the dinner table doesn't mean I treat you like a sibling."

"See there, how you always go to extremes with it?" He extended an incredulous hand. "I think you do that to justify your position. I would never, ever do anything to embarrass you, baby, and you know that. But you won't even let me hold your damn hand. Can you at least *try* to imagine how that makes me feel? Do you even care?"

"Come on! Of course I do!" She crossed the room towards him, stopping a couple of feet away. "Baby, this isn't me trying to control everything or make you feel any kind of way. You can't seriously think that."

"All I know, Liz, is that it's not a good feeling when your woman only acts like she wants you behind closed doors." Luther looked exhausted suddenly, his arms falling to his sides. His eyes pleaded for understanding. "Being there tonight with your people and seeing them be so openly loving towards each other...I'm not gonna lie, I want that. I want that with *you*. But you won't give me anything."

Liz sighed. "Luther..."

"Think about tonight. When we were all standing around, you stood opposite me instead of beside me. At the table, you scooted your chair away instead of closer. When we were all hanging out in the den, you hugged the arm of the couch harder than you did me. I can't even get the barest minimum amount of affection from you. Maybe, *maybe* if I was at least getting that, it would be easier to deal with. But I get *nothing*!"

Liz hadn't even realized she'd done all that. It had become so ingrained since she began dating that she didn't even think about it anymore. And apparently her intense feelings for Luther didn't alter her tendencies.

"Luther, I really wish I could get you to understand this," she pleaded, her hands pressed together in front of her chest. "I get it; it's not ideal. And I *know* it's asking a lot. But I don't want something like whether or not we touch each other in public to come between us. Maybe I could loosen up a little but...it would help if you didn't overreact every time things don't go the way you want."

He chuckled sarcastically, looking away as he marveled at her statement. "Believe me, you haven't *seen* overreacting, Liz."

"What does *that* mean??"

"I want you to consider how it would feel if the shoe were on the other foot." He turned challenging eyes to her.

"If you wanted to get closer to me, even in private, and I recoiled as if it were the last thing I wanted. If I moved away when you tried to touch me, all the while claiming to be in love with you. How do you think you would like that?"

Liz started to immediately declare how unbothered she would be but she knew that wasn't the truth. "Okay, fine, I wouldn't love it. But let's not forget that I kissed you at Natavey the other night. And *that* was out in the open."

"And why did you do that?"

"What do you mean, why did I do it?"

"Was it a genuine show of affection or an awkward attempt to cover up the fact that we'd just been arguing in clear earshot of other people? To the point where your friend had to come check on us?"

Huffing, Liz groaned as she covered her face with her hands. "Does it matter??"

"Does it..." Luther shook his head. "The fact that you even asked that says a lot, Liz. It says a hell of a lot."

They stood there, facing off and staring at each other, each unyielding in their positions. Liz felt an eerie feeling start to creep over her, and she feared that the distance that had formed between them over the previous days was only spreading wider.

"So where does this leave us?" she finally asked, unable to take the silence anymore. "Just tell me."

His eyes squeezed shut briefly before he hung his head. His voice was low when he answered, "I think we need to take a step back."

Her hand clenched as her body went cold. "A-a step back?"

"To determine if this is really what we both want. If we can be what we need for one another."

Liz tried to blink back the tears that automatically burned her eyes. "Luther, I get that this is something we need to deal with but...I *want* to. I love you; I don't want us to be over."

"Neither do I," he immediately insisted, looking at her. His eyes were glassy. "I still love and want you as much as I did before, baby. But we both know that love and desire aren't enough. Compromise, adjusting, respecting each other's positions even if we disagree with them...all of that is necessary, too. And if either of us doing that is only going to result in unhappiness or resentment, that's not healthy. And as much as I love you, Liz, I cannot be in an unhealthy relationship. I sincerely thought I could deal with the PDA thing; I really, truly did." His hand was on his chest as he moved closer to her, his other hand grabbing the side of her face. "But the kind of man I am doesn't align with this, and I guess it took me trying it to recognize that. And I *did* try, Liz. I just wish you could do the same for me."

Her hand gripped his wrist. "Luther..."

He pressed his lips to hers, silencing whatever she was about to say next. "I don't love having to say any of this. But I also don't want to get to where I resent you. I'll walk away from you and us before I do that."

They stood there with their foreheads pressed together for several moments, Liz sniffling and holding onto him, before Luther separated himself and quickly walked out. Liz looked after him, the sound of the door closing breaking the dam on her sobs as she crumbled onto the couch and cried over a man for the first time.

Chapter 14

• • • •

IT HAD BEEN FOUR LONG days since Luther walked out of Liz's place and they hadn't spoken or communicated at all. Luther was summoning all of the strength he had to stay away from her, because he missed Liz like crazy. But he'd meant what he said about needing to reassess things. They were at an impasse that they weren't moving beyond, and clearly, somebody had to make a move, even if it wasn't the one his heart wanted.

Luther managed to continue about his business, training clients and making hats, though he was practically a robot going through the motions. His heart wasn't in any of it, but he couldn't sit around stewing in his feelings and driving himself crazy. But late at night, when he had nothing else to occupy his mind, he sat in his meditation space or up in the treehouse thinking about his relationship with Liz.

He sincerely loved her and was more than willing to compromise, but he needed the same in return. That was what burned him; that he was the only one that apparently had to bend and make all the concessions. As much as he wanted to make his woman happy, it couldn't be to the detriment of his own happiness. And Luther knew that even if he could roll with being restricted from public affection from Liz for a while, it wouldn't work in the long term. And long-term was what he wanted with Liz but if they weren't on the same page, he didn't want to waste his time.

When his alarm went off one morning, he reached over and silenced it before rolling onto his back, his arm over his eyes. His body felt heavy as he made himself get on out of bed and prepare for his workout. He tried to keep his mind from wandering as he dressed, warmed up, stretched, and grabbed the heaviest set of dumbbells he could, positioning himself in front of the mirror as he began a set of curls. Usually Luther was good about staying focused on what he was doing, but his mind pictured Liz there in his home gym with him, doing her workout as he did his, wearing a tank top tied in a knot underneath her breasts and leggings that showed off the musculature of her long legs. Occasionally, they'd spot each other or help each other stretch. And after they were done, they'd shower together and trade massages, easing each other's sore muscles. Then Luther would sit between Liz's legs and she'd rub beard oil into his beard as they talked about whatever. Everything was so natural between them. He ached at the thought of losing that intimacy.

And when he finished his breakfast dishes, he immediately washed them, as he'd gotten into the habit of doing since he started seeing Liz. Even doing that put a slump in his shoulders, simply because it reminded him of her.

When his phone rang and he saw it was Jules, he wasted no time answering, grateful for the momentary distraction. "Hey, Jules."

"What's up, Lu-Lu? You busy?"

"Not at all."

She paused. "What's the matter? And don't insult me by saying 'nothing.' Don't forget I know you better than just about anybody."

Unable to deny that, Luther sighed. "Things aren't great between me and Liz."

"What happened?"

"Long story short, she has a major problem with PDA. And you know the kind of man I am; I'm out in the open with my affection. I don't overdo it but I don't hide it, either."

"I know. So, what, she won't kiss you in public?"

"She won't do anything. I can't hold her hand, put my arm around her, nothing. Yet when we're alone, it's a complete one-eighty. She has her reasons and while I tried to respect them and acquiesce to make her happy..."

"It's making you *un*happy," Jules concluded.

"Exactly." Luther sighed, leaning against the kitchen counter and running a hand down his face. "I met her people the other night; her sister, brother-in-law, and another friend and her husband. Everyone was so loving and affectionate with their mates and there Liz and I were, acting like acquaintances. I was actually jealous that I couldn't show her the affection that I wanted to. It was then that I realized that we just might not be right for each other."

"Do you really believe that?"

"I don't *want* to believe it. I'm in love with Liz, Jules. And I believe it's mutual. But I can't see myself being happy or satisfied with things the way they are long-term. I don't want to get to where I resent her."

"I'm not trying to get too far in your business but is this the *only* thing that's causing a problem between you two? Churi called herself trying to tell on you two to me, by the way, as if. I had to tell her about herself yet again."

"Churi's feelings towards Liz aren't an issue at all; she hasn't even tried to get to know her. The PDA is the main thing. You should've seen the look Liz gave me when I touched her leg at the dinner table."

"Well, Lu-Lu...you have to remember that not everyone loves as hard as you do. Did you ever think that Liz is loving you the best way she knows how?"

"Maybe she is, but...I'm not sure it's good enough. I'm not going to be the only one making concessions, nor am I going to keep having the same argument over and over. I could see if Liz was at least *trying* to bend a little but she isn't and that just doesn't work for me."

"I get it. And that's fair. So how are things between you two now?"

"We're on pause. I told her we needed to each take a minute to see if this relationship is serving us like we both need and want. We haven't communicated at all in four days and I hate it."

"You're not any closer to making a decision?"

"My head and my heart aren't exactly in agreement right now."

"I've seen you two together. You don't want to walk away from her, Lu-Lu. You'd be miserable if you did."

"But I'd also be miserable if I stayed in a relationship where I felt stifled and couldn't express myself. Everything is great when we're in the privacy of our homes but we can't stay locked inside forever. I mean, if I'm being unreasonable, please tell me."

"I wouldn't say that. And knowing you like I do, you've given genuine assessment of your own actions as much as you have hers. Only you know what you can deal with and what you can't. But I want to ask you...are you sure this is *just* about PDA?"

Frowning curiously, Luther folded an arm across his chest. "Meaning?"

"I'm no shrink or relationship expert by any means but I don't think PDA is a sole indicator of a relationship's success or failure. I can understand it being a factor, to a degree, especially if she's ten toes down in her position and insists it's not changing, ever. Has she said that?"

Luther paused, thinking. "No, not in those words..."

"Okay, so who's to say it wouldn't change the longer you're together and the more comfortable she gets with you? Look, I'm definitely not saying you're in the wrong. I just want you to really look at the big picture. You love this woman. She loves you. Is not being able to hold hands in public really worth throwing that away over?"

• • • •

MEANWHILE, LIZ WASN'T doing any better than Luther. She'd started to call him several times and stopped herself because she didn't know what to say.

The last thing she wanted was for her and Luther's relationship to be over. She'd never been in love before like she was with him and it would tear her heart in half to lose that. But she couldn't resist the burn she felt at him for questioning her and their relationship just because they had different stances, and about something as relatively minor as PDA. She knew not everyone was as staunch about that as she, but she sincerely couldn't understand why it was such a huge deal to him. From what she remembered about being in love, it wasn't supposed to be this complicated. And Liz had enough headaches.

With *any* other man that said they needed to 'take a step back', Liz would have just saved them the trouble and walked away altogether. But this was Luther. And Luther was different. There was no walking away from him and what she knew they meant to each other just like that, even though the defiant part of her *did* consider it for a second. She wondered if battling with him over something like public displays of affection was worth it.

But almost as quickly as that thought appeared, it vanished. Luther was absolutely worth it. She just wished he wouldn't take her stance so personally.

It wasn't like she didn't ever *want* to be affectionate with him in public. There were several times when they were out that she wanted to reach for his hand or snuggle up beside him. And when he kissed her in the hallway at Lovey's, she legitimately forgot where she was for a second and gave into it.

And when he told her how he wanted to sex her in the bathroom, every part of her wanted to let him.

Every time these temptations came up, though, Liz remembered a time when her parents had one of their public displays and how she felt when she saw it. More specifically, how she felt when *others* saw it. When they'd frown in disapproval or scrunch their noses, or mutter under their breath. It always humiliated Liz, and that aversion to public affection got stronger as she aged and entered into her own relationships. Luther wasn't the first man to have a problem with it but none was as strongly against it as he, and none were held in as high regard as him, either. Liz barely felt it when those other men left but she knew it wouldn't be the same if she and Luther parted ways for good.

She couldn't let that happen.

When Desiree invited her, Lovey, and Natalia out shopping with her so she could find something for a special night she was planning for Lorenzo, Liz jumped at it. She needed the distraction, and when they eventually headed for the lingerie store, she decided to plan her own surprise evening for her man.

"You think this is too slutty?" she asked Natalia, holding a red sheer teddy close to her body.

"When it comes to your man, no such thing."

"I'm just wondering if he'll think I'm trying too hard…" Liz mused, taking another look at it.

"Why would he think you're trying too hard?"

"There's nothing wrong between you two, is there?" Lovey asked with a frown of concern, turning from the green silk negligee she'd been perusing. "If anyone should be worried about that, it's me. This stuff is a little racier than I'm accustomed to."

Desiree sucked her teeth. "Girl, please. With that video vixen body of yours, anything in here would look stupidly amazing on you."

"Stop," Lovey blushed, as she usually did when complimented. "And I'm still carrying some baby weight from when I had the twins…"

"Doesn't matter. You know Roland would lose his mind if you strutted into the bedroom wearing one of these nighties and some stilettos."

Lovey's eyes lit up at the suggestion.

"Go ahead and pick that negligee back up, Lovey, so you and Roland can make baby number four," Natalia teased. "'Cause I'm surely getting some of these thongs to wear for E.J. I *love* how he rips them off me."

"*Girl*, isn't it a turn-on when they do that??" Desiree exclaimed, a couple pieces of lingerie already hanging over her arm. "Lorenzo's strong ass is good for that, and picking me up and tossing me around like a sex doll. I love it. Damn near every night I'm climbing him like an oak tree."

"We know. With your horny ass."

"Like you aren't the same way with E.J. And so is Lovey with Roland, even though she tries to act all bashful. And from the looks of it, Liz has met the one that brings it out of her, too."

"Yeah," Liz sighed, feeling uncharacteristic jealousy listening to her friends talk about their men. "I'm not gonna deny it. Luther is definitely the match I never thought I'd find. Let's just hope that's still the case."

"Why wouldn't it be the case?"

"You two having issues?" Lovey asked, coming over to stand next to her sister.

"We're..." Liz hated to even say the words. "We're kinda on pause right now."

"What? Why??"

"Already?" Natalia marveled.

"What could've happened?" Desiree asked. "Y'all seemed good the other night at Lovey's."

"It's the PDA stuff," Liz admitted. "He's tried, but he's tired of it. And it didn't help being around y'all's affectionate asses and he felt he couldn't be the same with me."

"I hope you're not expecting an apology."

"We hope we didn't make him uncomfortable," Lovey jumped in, shooting a look at Desiree. "But that's just how Roland and I are together; it's natural. And it's certainly not intended to rub in anyone's face."

"I know, sis," Liz assured, smiling. "I'm not saying any of y'all did anything wrong. It's just that seeing that only reminded Luther of what he can't do with me. When I showed him to the bathroom, he tried to kiss me and...I stopped him. He got pissed. We argued about it after we left and neither of us was trying to budge. That's when he said we needed to take a step back from our relationship."

"Oh no..."

"Is that what you want?" Natalia asked, flanking Liz's other side.

"No." Liz shook her head, fighting the emotion that was starting to swirl in her chest and behind her eyes. "It's absolutely *not* what I want."

"I admit, I thought something was up between you two when you were at Natavey. You could cut the tension with a knife. But I thought it was because of that heffah that was pushing up on your man at the bar."

"Oh, we had words about that, too, believe me. Thanks for the heads up on that, by the way."

"You know I've got your back. Especially since I thought that was supposed to be one of your girls. If I wasn't in my 'manager' role I'd have had some choice words for her."

"Who was this??" Lovey inquired.

"Kinsley," Liz informed her.

"Oh. I have to say, I'm not all that surprised to hear that about her. I know that's your friend, Liz, and I certainly respect that-"

"I get it, Lovey. I can't say I'm all that solid about my friendship with her right now, either. But I'm woman enough to admit it's not totally her fault."

Liz explained how she'd foolishly downplayed the intensity of her relationship with Luther to Kinsley, and Kinsley's subsequent request for permission to step to him and Liz (again foolishly) telling her to go for it.

"I didn't think she'd actually *do* it," she concluded, feeling herself get heated at the very thought. "I thought she was just messing around. Or even if she *was* serious, that us being friends would be enough to make her fall back. But clearly, I was wrong."

"I don't know whose ass I wanna beat more, yours or hers," Natalia muttered, giving Liz a small shove to the shoulder. "Girl, you don't *ever* give another woman the keys to your ride."

"Yeah, some women see a fine man and all loyalty goes out the window," Desiree added. "And she apparently wanted your man more than she cared about her friendship with you."

"Apparently. I get it; I messed up on that. But she's not my main problem. She can drool over Luther all she wants;

that doesn't mean it's mutual. I never once worried about him giving in to her. The PDA issue is what's standing between me and Luther."

"You're still not budging about that, huh?"

"It's not like I'm doing it to be difficult," Liz felt the need to defend herself. "This is just the way I am. But I absolutely don't want to lose him. These last four days of us not talking have been hell for me, and if I need to make the first move to get us back on track, then so be it."

"I hear you, girl, but I don't think some sexy lingerie is going to fix this," Natalia gently advised. "Sex would be a distraction, not a solution."

"If anything, it might have the opposite effect, because you're resorting to seduction privately to get back into his good graces, and that's the heart of his issue," Lovey added. "I so want you two to work this out but I agree with Natalia; this isn't the way to do it."

Liz's shoulders slumped. She hadn't thought of that but she could see Lovey's point. Luther might not appreciate it if she tried to seduce him at the point they were at then; even if he gave in, their issues would still be there when they rolled off of each other.

"Dammit," she whispered, practically throwing the teddy she was holding into the panty bin in front of her and covering her face with her hands. Frustration at not knowing what to do made her want to break down, and she hated doing that in public almost as much as she hated public affection.

"Oh, Liz…" Lovey immediately wrapped her arms around her big sister. "I hate to see you like this."

"I'm *shocked* to see you like this," Desiree commented. "In all the years I've known you, I've never seen you pressed over any man. Luther must be really special to you."

"He is," Liz assured behind her hands.

"Then maybe you need to reconsider this PDA ban you have, and if it's worth losing the man you love over," Natalia suggested. "He at least tried to do it your way. Don't let it be said that he's the only one who put forth any effort." She gently pried Liz's hands down and turned her face to hers, looking right into her eyes. "As the one here who's been married the longest and who almost lost her husband because she was only thinking about herself and what she wanted, believe me...it can't work like that. And you *will* regret it."

• • • •

WITH NATALIA'S ADVICE fresh on her mind, Liz called Luther when she parted ways with her friends and asked if she could come over.

She still didn't have the magic solution to their issues, but she needed to see him. The ache in her gut that hadn't budged since he walked out of her place the other night had hardened into a boulder at Natalia's warning. Liz wasn't trying to be selfish or make things all about what she wanted, and if that's what Luther was thinking, she needed to alleviate that.

When he opened the door and she finally laid eyes on him, Liz felt everything in her body clench. Uninterested in pretense or trying to play it cool, she quickly stepped inside and threw her arms around his neck, squeezing her eyes shut in relief when she felt him hug her back just as tightly.

"Damn, I've missed you," she whispered.

"I've missed you, too." He buried his face in her neck as his arms tightened around her even more. "You have no idea."

They stood there like that for several moments before finally loosening their holds on each other and stepping back. Luther closed the door before leading Liz to the living room, offering her something to eat or drink before they took a seat on the couch.

"Luther," Liz began, "I wanted to come over here not just to see you, but to ask if you feel like I'm being manipulative or selfish with the PDA issue."

He drew in a long breath, contemplating her question. His fingers played in his beard. "I wouldn't use the word *manipulative*. And maybe there's a little selfishness but I don't believe that's your intention."

"It's really not. Believe me, I *hate* those women that only care about what they want in relationships and expect the man to always acquiesce to them, and I admit I didn't think about how I was coming across when I was so unyielding about the PDA stuff. And like you said, you *did* try. I guess I was too in my feelings to realize I wasn't putting forth the same effort."

"I appreciate the acknowledgment. So what does this mean?"

"I'd like for us to move forward and get our relationship going again."

"As would I. How, though?"

"I mean..." She lifted her hands before dropping them, stumped. "Can you help me out a little here?"

"You came over here so I figured you had an actual solution, Liz."

"I told you the two main reasons I came over. I guess I'd hoped that would lead to us working through the rest of it *together*."

Luther eyed her for a moment before dropping his hand from his beard and scooting forward a little on the couch, his elbows resting on his knees. "Let's start with this, then. Say we resume things right now. We go out somewhere. Would you still resist me if I tried to kiss your forehead or put an arm around you?"

"I..."

"That's what I thought."

"I didn't say *no*!"

"You hesitated. That makes me think nothing has really changed."

"God, Luther..." Liz flung herself against the back of the couch in a huff.

"I'm not sure why *you're* getting frustrated..."

"I just wish this didn't have to be so hard." She looked at him. "Why is this so hard?"

"You tell me. Why *is* it so hard for you to let your guard down?" He aimed pointed eyes at her before shaking his head and looking away. "You know, Liz, I've been going back and forth about this for four days. I've tried, *sincerely* tried, to recognize if I'm being unfair to you at all. So I'll ask you...do you think I am?"

Liz sighed, making sure to think before she spoke. "No. We might not exactly be on the same page but I wouldn't say you're being unfair."

"I'm glad you confirmed that. So we're still at this impasse. And this is my thing...we're each the way we are but people can change if they make the effort to. And if you're unwilling to yield even a little bit on this, it makes me think you'll be just as stubborn about anything else that might come up down the line if it requires doing something you don't really want to do."

Her jaw practically to her chest, Liz sat forward. "I take offense to that, Luther. I told you I'm in love with you, and that was real. *Everything* I've ever said about how I feel for you is a hundred percent real. I'm ready and willing to give everything I have to you and *us*...why is that not enough?"

Luther's chest constricted at the catch in her voice. She sounded so impassioned that part of him wanted to just forget his concerns and say everything was okay. But he knew they'd be right back where they were as soon as they went anywhere together. And as he realized, the issue wasn't just about PDA at all.

"I wish it was," he finally responded, his throat suddenly feeling like it was coated in sand. "I want nothing more than to move on from this and just be with you. You have no idea how much I want to take you in my arms right this second and spend the rest of the night reacquainting myself with every inch of your body. I love you just as much as I did before, baby, and I need you to believe that this is not even a little bit easy for me." He dropped his head, running both hands over his waves. "Like I said, the whole PDA thing might have started this but I think it just lends to a bigger issue. When things come up – and they will, as I'm sure I don't have to tell you – how are we going to get through them together? We can't even get past this *one* issue. It doesn't inspire a lot of confidence."

Liz just sat there. As much as she hated to admit it, she saw his point. And she hated that it was because of her that they were already skidding to a stop right when they'd been picking up steam.

She eyed him sitting next to her, and felt every part of her body go warm. Not just with sexual arousal, but just for the overall love she had for him. As if she couldn't control herself, she grabbed his arm and yanked him around to face her before taking his face in her hands, pulling him to her for a kiss, her tongue immediately tangling with his. He hesitated, his hands hovering before finally grabbing her as aggressively as she was clawing at him. They went at it, taking turns pushing each other against the back of the couch, their kisses full of breathy moans and pants and smacks of their lips.

Liz felt like she was going to explode, being with Luther again like this. She pulled at his shirt, tugged at the waistband of his sweats, grunting in frustration that she couldn't get as close to him as she yearned to be. When his hand grabbed her breast, she screamed at the intimate touch and wished she could snap her fingers and make their clothes disappear.

Luther let himself get caught up in the moment because he wanted to. He needed to feel Liz's lips and her touch again. Everywhere her hands went left a trail of tingling heat on his body. He felt his restraint slipping with every second they went at it and something blared in his head that if he didn't stop, right that second, he'd confuse things even more than they already were.

"I can't," he whispered, forcing himself to pull away. He rested his forehead to hers for a moment before plopping next to her, panting and repeatedly scrubbing his hands down his face. "I can't do this, baby."

"Why not?" Her hand kept its hold on his shirt as she sat up next to him, the yearning still blazing in her eyes as her chest heaved with still-pent up need and arousal. "We both want it..."

"Wanting each other isn't our issue, Liz. And having sex isn't going to change anything. As much as I *wish* I didn't have to resist you right now-"

"You *don't*!"

"*I do!*" He shot off the couch, the frustration from their situation and forced restraint overtaking him. "Liz, I want it all with you. I want us to be best friends, lovers, soul mates, partners. And that requires something I don't think you're willing to give me. As much as I hate to say it...maybe we just have to face facts. You're *so* unwilling to even try to let go of your issues, *knowing* how much it means to me, though I was willing to try for you. I can't make myself ignore that."

Liz looked up at him, seeing his pained expression. Her own face started to crumble, realizing what was happening.

"So that's it, then."

He stopped pacing and looked at her, summoning calmness despite the chaos that was going on inside of him.

He was both pissed off and devastated that they were at this point.

"Seems so."

She drew in a sharp intake of breath at the confirmation, her hand going to her stomach. Her eyes dropped to the floor, unable to look at him anymore.

Without another word, Liz blindly grabbed her purse from the floor, stood, and made her feet move to the door, her tears practically blinding her by the time she was on the other side of it.

Chapter 15

• • • •

LIZ TOLD HERSELF IT was for the best.

Luther clearly wasn't the man for her, despite everything in every part of her body and soul still believing he was. It wasn't like she'd never been wrong about men before. It had been a week and a half since their breakup and Liz forged ahead, throwing herself into work and getting ready for her showcase. That's when Lovey wasn't trying to comfort her.

"Lovey, sis, I appreciate the concern but as I told you when you called an hour ago, I'm fine," Liz muttered as soon as she answered the phone, shuffling through the design sketches on her desk.

"And as I told *you*, I know that's horse puckey."

"You're thirty-seven. You're allowed to cuss."

"Stop it, Liz. You're deflecting and I'm not sure why. If you can be real with *anybody*, it's with me."

Liz sighed. "What is it you want me to say, Lovey?"

"Be honest about how you're feeling. Admit that you're hurting over you and Luther breaking up. You've been working loads of overtime, closing yourself off and refusing to hang out with us, your friends. We're worried about you."

"You don't have to worry about me. I was in a relationship and now I'm not. Breakups happen. It's not the end of the world."

"And there it is. I was waiting on it."

Liz's hands stopped. "What are you talking about?"

"The old Liz that acts like she doesn't care about anything. Like she's above feeling hurt over a man."

"What am I supposed to do, fall apart? That's not gonna change anything. Luther made his decision and...that's that."

"So you're just going to leave it at that? You said you loved him."

"Yeah, well, love clearly wasn't enough, was it?" Liz slammed her hand onto her desk before sighing and running it wearily across her brow, hating she lost her cool even for a second. "I totally opened myself up to that man and was willing to ride with him until the wheels fell off, and it wasn't good enough. So, whatever. Look, I have to go; I have a meeting coming up."

"Sure you do. Just know I'm here whenever you're ready to quit this tough act you're putting on."

"Bye, Lovey."

Liz missed Luther terribly, and if she allowed herself to, she'd pine over him to the exclusion of everything else. But she refused. Maybe he was right; maybe they *weren't* as right for each other as they thought. If he wasn't willing to accept her for who she was, then he wasn't the man she needed to be with.

If only she could make her heart buy what her head was trying to sell her.

At least things for the showcase were finally coming together. They'd hired all the models, nailed down all the looks down to the color of Jazlyn Ellis nail polish that would be used, everything was all set with the venue, the music had been chosen, pretty much all the RSVPs were in...Liz felt like she could start to breathe a little easier. There were still a few odds and ends that needed to be tucked in, but her and her team would get that handled in plenty of time.

"Liz, these looks are *perfect*!" Viola, Liz's superior, exclaimed, clasping her hands together in front of her chest as she looked at the row of boards showing the completed looks. Liz was presenting them to the board and the designers, and even though she'd been confident in what she'd pulled together, she could never be sure that others would love it as much as she did. It gave her huge relief that she'd been right. Viola beamed, her shiny dark brown skin glowing in the bright lights of the conference room and her always purposely-tousled hair framing her face. "You've done it again."

"I'm glad you're pleased with everything," Liz smiled proudly. "It took some doing to get everything spot-on and I'm glad we were as diligent as we were; I wasn't going to settle for 'good enough.'"

"When do you ever? You're part of the reason these designers even came on board for this showcase; they know your reputation."

"You've really knocked it out of the park with this entire campaign, Liz," Geoffrey, another board member, spoke up. "Everything, from print to social media and now this showcase. I know it was a ton of work but we knew you could handle it."

Liz nodded graciously. "Thanks, Geoffrey. My team was a huge help. I'm just glad everyone is happy with how everything came together."

"I must say, the hats you chose really set all of this apart," one of the designers whose name Liz could never remember spoke up. "And I never would've even thought to put a hat with my designs at all, specifically a *man's* fedora. Maybe some fun hair accessories, if anything. But between the colors and the design, these hats make a world of difference. They're so sleek."

"Where did you find these, again?" Viola asked, moving closer to one of the boards.

Liz fought to keep her expression even. "I came across an amazing hat maker when I was in Belize. Once I saw his inventory, I knew they were just what we needed for this showcase."

"And you were right. Luther Monroe, huh?" Viola read from the displayed list of designers and contributors. "I'm not familiar with him but he certainly knows what he's doing. Look at you, snagging this amazing find when you were supposed to be on vacation."

Liz chuckled along with everyone else but she felt like her throat was closing up. She really *had* snagged an amazing find in Belize, but it had nothing to do with hats.

"I can't wait to meet him," Geoffrey commented. "With talent like this, he can go a long way in this industry. These are high-end designs. And the quality is excellent."

"Well, you'll get to meet the man behind the hats at the showcase. I mean, most likely; he...might not be able to attend due to a conflict." Liz cleared her throat, hoping no one noticed the slight hitch in her voice.

"Well, try to see to it that he's there. Use your powers of persuasion. One of the reasons we're confident in putting you in charge of so much is because you get things done and don't take no for an answer."

Oh god. Can we please wrap this up??

"I'll do my absolute best," Liz assured, though she had to force the words out. Her professional association with Luther thanks to using his hats in her showcase was something she'd temporarily forgotten about in the midst of their breakup, and she was willing to bet it hadn't been at the forefront of Luther's mind, either. Forgetting about using his hats and finding another alternative hadn't even been considered; letting her personal affairs interfere with business wasn't something she did. And she couldn't now even if she wanted to, with how everyone loved them.

Liz hated to admit it, but a tiny part of her was giddy at the realization that she still had this tie to Luther, even if it wasn't the one she wished for. When the meeting wrapped, she started to call him to let him know how everything had gone with her presentation and everyone's reaction to his designs, but she stopped herself. She didn't want to come across like she was trying to scrape up any excuse to reach out to him.

But she knew she'd have to at some point to make sure he was coming to the showcase. He'd said he'd be there when she initially asked him, but that was when they were together and he would be there by her side as her man, not just as a hat maker. Accessory designers surely weren't under any obligation to attend, though Liz wanted to stay in favor with her superiors. Luther didn't owe her any favors but maybe he'd still show up just because of that.

The fact that she was no longer reason enough for him to attend burned her throat like a shot of aged whiskey.

Speaking of whiskey, Liz knew where she'd be going as soon as she got off work.

• • • •

SURE ENOUGH, SEVERAL hours later Liz was moping at the bar at Natavey. She wanted to drown her sorrows but if she was honest, she also hoped Luther might show up.

When she'd been there an hour and he hadn't made an appearance, her spirits sunk even lower. She couldn't help but wonder if he was avoiding Natavey because he knew it was one of her favorite spots, too. Liz hated being so paranoid, and her resentment towards Luther and at herself for falling so hard for Luther flared like a prodded fire. She wished she could just snap her fingers and be over him. It certainly hadn't been this hard to move on from any of her other men.

But as Luther had told her more than once, he wasn't trying to be like any of them. And clearly, mission accomplished.

Not in the mood for the growing crowd in the bar area, Liz made her way to the less-crowded membership-only lounge. She headed to the corner section in search of the closest thing she could get to seclusion in public, and ordered another drink as well as a cigar from the sharply-dressed waitress. If she was going to mope in a cigar bar, she was going to utilize everything they offered to do it.

When she saw Kinsley enter a little while later, Liz groaned and turned away, hoping she could blend into the wall despite the bright yellow cropped jacket she had on. It was one time she didn't want to stand out.

No such luck, though. When she smelled the familiar gourmand perfume suddenly blend with the cigar smoke, Liz knew she'd been spotted.

"Hey, Liz."

"Fuck."

"Guess that means you're not glad to see me."

Liz turned and looked up at her, her brown eyes like slits. "Did you think I would be?"

"No." Kinsley sighed, her shoulders slumping slightly. Her freshly-done fiery red hair fell in her face and she hastily pushed it behind her ear, showing off an array of silver piercings. "Look, can we talk?"

"For what? So you can give me some bullshit excuse for being a shitty excuse for a friend? Or maybe you'll apologize again only to go and do some more fucked up crap later. I'm good."

"Liz." Kinsley leaned in, frowning with concern. "How much have you had to drink?"

"I know what I'm saying. But...I've lost count."

Heaving another sigh, Kinsley went ahead and plopped into the leather armchair across from Liz, unfazed when Liz rolled her eyes and swiveled away, taking another sip of her drink.

"Liz. Look at me."

"I don't wanna look at you."

"Liz."

"Ugh!" Liz swung back around, her scowl on full blast. She didn't even seem to notice when a tiny bit of her drink sloshed over the rim of the glass and onto the sleeve of her jacket. "What?"

"I need to let you know what was up with me trying to push up on Luther a while back."

"I know what was up. You made it more than clear that you wanted to shoot your shot with him and hmph...you certainly did *that*."

"That's not the whole story, though, Liz. I-"

"You know what? I don't need to hear this," Liz interjected, holding up her hand. "And it doesn't matter now anyway 'cause me and Luther broke up. So shoot all the shots you want."

Kinsley frowned, leaning forward to put a hand on Liz's chair and stop her from swiveling away again. "What the hell happened? Why'd you break up?"

"Because I'm a selfish uptight bitch, that's why."

"What??"

"I pushed him away," Liz continued, her words starting to blend together thanks to all the alcohol. "I don't like being affectionate in public and he does. He couldn't get with that. So he dropped me. Story over."

"Oh damn..."

"So go ahead, make your move again," Liz suggested with a dramatic sweep of her arm. "We all know you have *no* problem getting touchy-feely in front of an audience."

"Still not too drunk to forget some stuff, huh?" Kinsley muttered. "Look...clearly you're not okay with this breakup. You wouldn't be in here getting wasted if you were. Fight for your man, girl...do whatever you need to do to work this out."

"There's no point. He made his decision." Liz's face fell at those words, the reminder of her hurt busting through her drunken stupor. Her eyes fell to the almost-empty glass she held in both hands in her lap. "I'm *not* gonna beg."

Kinsley sucked her teeth. "You gon' have to put that pride up. I know you're the queen of dismissing men but you can't tell me you're not miserable right now. I've never seen you go in like this after it was over with *anyone*, even if they were the ones that walked away from you. I've been telling you for years that you need to get over that PDA shit. So your parents were all over each other; so what?"

"Don't 'so what' me. You don't know what it was like or how embarrassing it was."

"Yeah? Well *you* don't know what it was like to have parents that fought day in and day out because they couldn't stand each other. Who always put me in the middle of their shit. Who couldn't even attend school functions together because they were too immature to be in the same damn room without starting an argument. You didn't have to decide between two separate events for birthdays or graduations because they couldn't be cordial enough for a few fucking hours to have one together. Now you tell me; which one of us had it worse?"

Liz knew she couldn't say anything. She'd had no idea. Kinsley had never been eager to talk about her parents, always just saying she didn't really get along with them nor did they get along with each other. She only saw them occasionally, because they were still each so bitter about the other despite having been divorced since Kinsley was eleven years old, and Kinsley was just sick of their negativity.

"I guess you've got me with that one," she admitted meekly. She slowly set her glass on the small wood table between them before briefly pressing her fingertips to the corners of her eyes. "Hearing that, I actually feel kind of ridiculous for all the pouting I've done about my situation."

"Look," Kinsley sighed. "Your situation is your situation, and your reaction was your reaction. I'm not here to tell you how you should've felt about it then. But I *can* say you need to quit letting it dictate what you do now. It's all in your head, girl...believe me, nobody is gonna give two flying fucks about you walking down the street holding hands with your man or sharing a kiss out in the open. Who cares? Yeah some people are nosey but most people are too caught up in their own shit to worry about yours. Not to mention, there are plenty out here doing *way* more overt stuff than that. However you need to do it, you need to let that shit *go*. You're forty and still looking at it from a child's perspective."

Liz felt the prickles of conviction stab her right in the gut. She'd never thought about it like that.

Still, she replied, "If he really loved me, he would've stayed."

Her eyebrows shooting up, Kinsley jutted forward in her seat. "Love? Y'all were there already? What happened to 'we're just dating' and 'it's casual' and all that?"

"I lied, all right?? I didn't want to tell you how deep things were between us so quickly but clearly, I fumbled that just like I fumbled everything else with this damn relationship. I miss Luther but I'm pissed as hell at him, too. He made me fall in love with him and then left me high and dry because I wasn't perfect. I'm supposed to be perfect..."

"Nobody is perfect, Liz, come on. Don't start downing yourself."

"Why not? If I can't even hang onto someone as decent and level-headed as Luther, then..." Liz slumped against the seat as if having run out of energy to finish the sentence. "I'm just...I'm all over the place right now."

"Yeah, you are. Have you eaten anything with all this alcohol you've been tossing back?"

"I don't know. No."

"I'm gonna order you something and then get you home."

"You don't have to do all that."

"It's happening. I know you're used to being the one that always has it together and fixes everything but you're having a moment right now, girl, and it's understandable. Even if you go back to being mad at me once you sober up, I'm still going to have your back." Kinsley signaled for the waitress. "If it makes you feel any better, nobody has to know that you're so in your feelings that you got slithered because of a man but you and me."

• • • •

LUTHER WASN'T USED to being so angry. He'd gotten rather good over the years at meditating and praying so that when something upset him, he could deal with it, make his peace with it, and move on. But that wasn't happening this time.

He'd been in a mood ever since Liz walked out of his house almost two weeks earlier. His head told him he'd done the right thing; that they just weren't on the same page as much as he needed them to be. But his heart was admonishing his impatience. Just because she was one way in the early stages of their relationship didn't mean she'd stay that way throughout. He'd said when the PDA thing initially came up that he could be patient, but that all went out the window after one dinner party.

But Liz was *so* steadfast in her position, unwilling to bend even a little bit. Was he supposed to stick around for months or years, holding out hope and gambling with his time? What if she decided there was no need to change, since she'd gotten him to commit, anyway?

And *then* Luther considered if he was wrong to expect her to change at all. There was nothing inherently wrong with disliking PDA; he knew several people that weren't fans of it. But he wasn't in romantic relationships with any of them. Physical touch was one of his love languages, and he'd do best with a woman that received that readily, whether in public or private. And as much as he wished otherwise, that just wasn't Liz.

All these conflicting thoughts only added to Luther's agitation. He usually prided himself on being self-assured and confident in his decisions, however unpleasant. But this situation with Liz really had his head messed up. He missed her so much that it disrupted his usually peaceful sleep, disturbed his concentration, and delayed his productivity. He didn't have the same energy for things that he used to enjoy, and he prayed that this part of the post-relationship grief cycle would be swift so he could start getting back to his old self.

Luther had never been one to just lounge around all day but after a quick trip out of town for some special hat fabrics he wanted and taking on more new training clients than usual to fill his time and attention, he was looking forward to doing exactly that. He made himself do his own workout, as halfhearted as it was, and prepared to park it on his couch with a bottle of cognac and a couple of James Baldwin novels. When a reminder popped up on his phone about a workout session with Carter, he wanted to throw something.

"Fuck!"

He'd forgotten that Carter had rescheduled one of their earlier sessions. Every part of Luther wanted to cancel, but he knew Carter's fitness competition was coming up rather soon; he wouldn't feel right leaving his brother hanging just because he was in his feelings over a breakup. The booze and books would be there when he got back.

"In another one of your moods again?" Carter quipped once they met up at the gym.

"Not today, Carter," Luther muttered, not even looking at him as he pushed a weight plate onto the bar with way more force than necessary. "Let's just get this done."

"You're becoming kind of a grouch, man. The last few times I've seen you, you've been all snappy and shit. You're sucking the fun out of these sessions."

"You're paying me to get you ready for your competition, not entertain you."

"Okay, yeah, but still. We used to at least shoot the breeze some but you hardly wanna talk unless it's to bark out orders. What is wrong?"

Luther hated that he hadn't given in to his temptation to cancel or reschedule. The gym was the last place he wanted to be. "Look, I can go home and you can work out by yourself. I'd like to get this over with. Can we focus, please?"

"Luther." Carter's face turned serious, his light brown eyes locked on his brother. "What's up? This sour shit isn't you. Come on, you can talk to me. I don't like seeing you like this, man, for real."

Luther started to let his guard down a little before suddenly shaking his head. "Nope. I'm not in the mood for any of your stupid jokes."

"I'm not gonna do that. As evil as you're looking right now, I don't put it past you to try to throw me through the front window."

"That sounded like a joke to me."

"It was the kind that's based on truth, though, so it doesn't count as a real joke. You really would try to do that shit if I pissed you off enough."

Despite himself, Luther felt his lips twitch the tiniest bit in amusement. "Fine. But we need to talk and move; I'm not having a heart-to-heart standing idle in the middle of the gym. Plus, I really am itching to get back home."

"Bet." Carter sat on the incline bench and adjusted his weightlifting gloves before taking a hold of the loaded bar, Luther standing over him. Once Carter was into his set, Luther started talking, still silently counting his brother's reps.

"I ended things with Liz. You better not stop; keep going," he quickly admonished when Carter started to return the bar to the stand before he was done. "I realized that Liz might not be willing to invest as much of herself into the relationship as I am."

"Wait a minute," Carter huffed, finishing his set. He turned to look at Luther as soon as the bar was back on the stand. "Is this about that PDA stuff you told me about?"

"That's part of it. It's not the sole reason."

"I thought y'all were solid."

"So did I. But I apparently misjudged."

"Wow...you really broke up with her over that?"

"I told you, it wasn't just the PDA. That might've started it but I realized the bigger issue was her unwillingness to compromise for me the same as she expects me to do for her. If she won't do that about this, why would I expect otherwise when more things that we disagree on come up later? That's not the kind of relationship I want."

Whistling softly, Carter's gaze dropped to the black hard rubber floor, pondering."How did she take it? When you broke it off?"

"She was upset. We both were upset. But she basically thought I was overreacting and making a bigger deal out of it than necessary. *I* was supposed to be the one to acquiesce, *I* was supposed to be the one to come to grips, *I* was supposed to be the one to fix everything, and within the boundaries she insisted on keeping."

"I guess I can understand why you had to back up, then. If she's causing all the strife *and* isn't willing to help fix it..."

"To be fair, she *did* acknowledge that she could've handled it better. But at the end of the day, nothing really changed, unfortunately. It was one of the hardest things I've had to do in years, walking away from her. I'm in love with her and even now, part of me wants to question my decision.

But I know it was the right one for me despite how much it hurts right now."

"Is the hurt worth it?"

"What?"

"What you're feeling right now; is it worth it?"

Luther frowned, crossing his arms. "What are you trying to say?"

"Look," Carter stood from the bench and faced his brother. "Believe it or not, I get where you're coming from. If I was going to be in a committed relationship, I'd hate to have my hands tied, too. Hell, even flings don't sweat it when I give them a little pat on the ass or a quick smooch when we're out on a Waffle House run."

"Lucky you. At least, as far as the affection part."

"But I know you, bro. You don't just fall in love like it's nothing. You had to have seen something real in Liz to go there with her. If *I* were to get with somebody, I'd hope that she'd hang in there with me while I learn the ropes of this relationship stuff, 'cause I'm damn sure no expert. Maybe Liz isn't, either. I don't know, I just..." Carter tugged at his ear. "I just hope you didn't throw in the towel too quick, that's all."

They resumed their training, but Carter's words stayed etched on Luther's mind throughout and as he headed back home afterwards. He had total confidence that his reasoning for ending things with Liz was valid but...*had* he been too premature?

He managed to quiet his thoughts enough to enjoy his evening of leisure when he got home, but they were renewed and refreshed the next day when he was back to business and working on some hat designs. Several times he had to stop himself from wondering what Liz was doing at any given moment, or torturing himself wondering if she was struggling as much as he was. He thought about calling to check on her, but felt that might come across as condescending.

When he got an alert on his security camera and saw Churi's Mini Cooper in the driveway, he groaned; not because he wasn't glad to see his daughter, but because he didn't have the energy for her usual drama. Then his phone rang, her name flashing across the screen.

At least this was something to take his mind off Liz for a while, he figured.

"Hey, baby girl," he answered the phone, putting down the handheld steamer he'd been using.

"Hey, Daddy. You busy?"

"Kind of but you know I'll make time for you if you need it. What's up?"

"I was wondering if I could come by."

"Oh?" Luther's eyes remained on the security camera, watching his daughter as she sat in her car talking to him, eating a huge burger and taking occasional pulls from a vape pen. "Everything all right?"

"Everything's fine, Daddy. I'm just here at work putting in some extra hours and thought about getting off early to come see you, that's all. We need some father-daughter time."

Luther didn't usually tolerate being lied to but he couldn't help being amused at Churi digging her own hole while he stood there and watched.

"How are things at work?" he asked her, leaning down to rest his elbows on the table where the small security monitor was. "Jules said something about you possibly getting a promotion soon."

"Oh yeah, that," Churi muttered. She flicked something out of her car window before taking a swig from a bottle. "Nothing is set in stone yet. I'm actually about to go talk to my manager right now and see if he's made a decision; he's been keeping me on ice for days. I need him to quit playing and let me know what's up."

Shaking his head, Luther stood up straight, over this act his daughter was putting on for whatever reason. "What have I told you about smoking that vape shit?"

"H-huh?" Churi coughed, having been mid-puff. "What are you talking ab-"

"And I hope to high heaven that whatever it is you're drinking isn't any kind of alcohol."

"How do you know this??"

"Churi, you *know* I have security cameras. I've been watching you sit in my driveway lying to me this whole time. And whatever you tossed out the window a minute ago, pick it up."

He could see her sheepish embarrassed expression as clear as day on the camera as she meekly pushed open the car door and retrieved the balled-up napkin she'd tossed out. Her big eyes looked in the direction of the camera, apparently now remembering where it was. "I'm sorry, Daddy."

Luther just sighed. "I'll come unlock the door."

"Is it all right if we just keep talking like this? I'm kinda embarrassed to face you even more now."

"What's going on, Churi? You know you never have to lie to me about anything and it pisses me off when you do."

"I'm sorry!" Churi plunked herself back into the driver's seat, closing the door with a thud. "I guess I didn't know how to admit that I...got laid off today."

"You what?"

"I had an argument with my boss about my hours and he canned me. Said I'd had one too many times being insubordinate. Can you believe that??"

"Wholeheartedly."

"Ugh. Anyway, I wasn't in the mood to go home and have to deal with my roommate, and I knew Mama would just cuss me out. I wanted to come talk to you but I remembered I had this vape somebody gave me and I was only taking a few hits off it to calm my nerves before I did, because I knew you'd lecture me, too. And I'm drinking root beer; I'm upset but not stupid enough to drink and drive."

"I'm glad to hear it. Though I'm not happy to hear you got yourself fired. What do you plan to do now? I hope you didn't come over here with the intentions of trying to sweet-talk me into giving you some money because it's not happening."

"I figured. Though that would be nice..."

"No ma'am. You got yourself fired knowing you have responsibilities. So I suggest you get on the grind and find something else, because those bills are going to keep coming whether you're employed or not."

"Ugh. Can I go back to being a kid? I don't think I like adulthood."

Laughing, Luther perched himself on his work stool. "It's not so bad, baby girl. You just have to stop running from it."

"I guess. You don't have to go, do you? Talking to you like this really is making me feel better. Unless your...girlfriend is there. I always seem to interrupt you two lately."

Luther wasn't going to bother letting Churi know he and Liz broke up; he'd barely managed to make the teeniest progress towards pulling himself out of his funk and had no interest in allowing his sullen mood to completely overtake him again. He knew it was easier said than done, and he was still a long way from doing so, but he needed to start to get past it. He'd made the decision he made for a reason.

"Don't worry about Liz. I'm all yours, baby girl."

When he saw Churi's grin on the monitor, he couldn't help a grin of his own. He might not have Liz anymore, and he hated that, but there was still plenty in his life to smile about.

Chapter 16

• • • •

LIZ COULDN'T WAIT FOR this damn adult prom to be over with.

She and Delilah were still working on pulling all the details together, scrambling to make it as epic an event as they could in the short timeframe they'd been given. Liz was no more over Luther after almost three weeks than she'd been the night after he ended it, but she was starting to accept their reality. Thanks to her unavoidably endless pondering, not to mention her conversations with Lovey and Kinsley, Liz had come to several realizations, and could acknowledge the part she played in how her and Luther's relationship ended up. If she was honest, she couldn't say she wouldn't have done the same thing if she were in his position. Hell, she'd dumped guys for less many times before.

Letting down her guard and taking that accountability was helping her deal with the hurt she still felt. She still missed Luther and wished things could be different; there were a couple of times she'd started to call him to let him know she now saw where he'd been coming from, but felt it wouldn't make any difference. He hadn't reached out to her once since they broke up, so clearly he was trying to keep the distance between them. As hard as it was, she had to respect that and keep her game face on.

Dealing with Delilah wasn't exactly fun, though, especially when she continuously insisted they meet in person whenever possible instead of just over the phone or Zoom. Liz had to constantly summon extra patience.

"Are you sure you won't reconsider?" Delilah asked her as they sat in the living room of Delilah's home, which was decorated in ivory and rose colors and full of lush greenery. And none of the fake stuff like Liz had at her place. "Zander and I would *love* to have you."

"Delilah, for the last time, I do not want to do a damn threesome with you and your husband. And I wish you would quit asking me that."

"What's the big deal? It's just a night of fun. Several of our other sorority sisters have joined us. I bet you'd love it if you loosened up. You've had threesomes before, right?"

Liz refrained from asking which of their sorority sisters had been in Delilah and Zander's bedroom with them. It was best that she not know. "*Anyway*, back to this prom...we still need to decide on a DJ since the first couple we contacted are already booked. Did you hear back from the caterer? Please tell me it's good news, if you did."

"I *do* have good news on that front, actually. Since the one we chose previously fell through, I reached out to a couple companies with somewhat similar menus and thankfully, one of them is able to fit us in. They've gotten their deposit, they have the desired menu, so we're good to go on that."

"Thank *god*," Liz muttered in relief, glad to finally check that off her list. It had been one roadblock and headache after another since she and Delilah started planning this event, either with vendors or with she and Delilah being unable to agree on certain things. Liz had been ready to throw up her hands and let Delilah have her way with everything, but she had too much pride in her sorority to do that. There was no telling what Delilah would plan with no one to answer to. "My assistant was kind enough to help me get all the promo stuff together, and the newsletters and invitations have already started going out. Thankfully folks aren't taking forever to RSVP."

"I keep telling you not to worry; that everything will come together as it's supposed to," Delilah purred with a smile, placing a brief hand on Liz's leg. "You're too pretty to let yourself get so stressed out."

"I'm not trying to hear any bitching about subpar planning. You know how our sisters can be."

"Very true. But you still don't need to fret about it. We've had some hiccups but things are finally starting to come together. It looks like we'll have everything in place so we can have an amazing adult prom and raise lots of money for Black Entrepreneurs of Tomorrow."

They discussed a few more items before Liz checked the time, preparing to leave. There were some work emails that had come in during her time with Delilah, and she needed to check those as well as get a jump on some other things that were coming down the pike at work. Staying occupied was still a good strategy for her, as far as keeping her mind off Luther as much as possible.

"Before you rush off, what would you say to drinks with me, Zander, and his brother Cole?" Delilah asked as Liz popped the last of the finger sandwich she'd been nibbling on into her mouth. "I've told him about you and he's intrigued."

"No thanks."

"Oh come on. It's just drinks. And he really is a looker, if I do say so myself." Delilah looked over her shoulder before leaning in slightly. "If I'm being a hundred percent transparent, he's almost sexier than my husband. He might just be someone you can have some fun with, if nothing else."

It was on the tip of Liz's tongue to ask Dellilah if she'd had any *fun* with Cole herself, but she decided she didn't want to know. She knew too much about Delilah's sex life as it was.

Liz actually didn't hate the idea of meeting someone new, as long as it was just casual. It might do her some good.

"All right," she conceded. "As long as he doesn't expect anything. I'm really in no frame of mind for anything deep or serious...*just* drinks, right?"

"Just drinks." Delilah grinned, excitedly patting her hands on her thighs. "I'll set it up. I'm telling you, you're going to *adore* Cole. He owns vending machines all around this city."

"That's...neat. Well, I have to go so just let me know when y'all want to meet up." Liz grabbed her things and scurried out before Delilah could give her another one of her overly-aggressive hugs. She headed back across town to her loft, forcing herself to keep her eyes straight and not look at the road leading to Luther's house when she passed it, her fingers tensing slightly on the steering wheel as she did.

• • • •

LIZ HAD MANAGED TO steadily convince herself that agreeing to meet this Cole guy was a smart move. While she was at work the next day, Delilah sent her a text letting her know the time and place the four of them were to meet the following evening.

"Damn, that was quick," Liz muttered. She could only hope Delilah's eagerness was just out of desire for wanting Liz to have a good time and not some kind of sexual ulterior motive or setup. She was glad she'd be driving her own car.

She was knee-deep in fleshing out the details of an upcoming campaign rollout when her receptionist Wendy buzzed through, letting her know she had a visitor. Distracted, Liz told her to send them in without asking who it was. She had cleared some time on her calendar because an artist she'd been trying to get a meeting with was possibly stopping by after several scheduling conflicts, and she figured they'd finally made it over to see her.

Her heart dropped to her stomach when she saw Luther standing there.

"Luther?" she asked, as if she couldn't believe her eyes.

"Hey." He stood tall and sexy in her doorway, his clothes hugging that beautiful body of his and his cologne hugging her like she was already wishing he would. "I apologize for just dropping by like this but I needed to talk to you, if you have a minute."

"Um, sure, yeah." Liz stood, smoothing her shaking hands down her navy and white pinstripe slacks. "You can close the door."

Doing as suggested, Luther fully entered the office, seeming to fill up the space despite the room being sizeable. Liz rounded her desk but stopped a few feet away from him, willing her body to calm down. Their breakup and the time apart had clearly no effect on her physical desire for him.

They quietly faced off, eying each other for several moments. Luther's expression was unreadable as he stood there with his jacket over his arm, trying to mask the internal chaos happening within him. Seeing Liz instantly reignited his fire for her, despite the reason he wound up in her office unannounced.

"What's up, Luther?" Liz finally asked, though she was in no hurry to rush him along. She now actually hoped that artist *didn't* show up, because she didn't want them to be disturbed. She only broke the silence to keep herself from jumping him.

"I need to know what game it is you're playing, Liz."

Blinking, Liz's brows twisted into a frown as she folded her arms. "Excuse me?"

"Did you tell Kinsley to ask me out?"

Her building heat immediately freezing over, Liz's mouth opened slightly in shock. She couldn't believe it. After the talk they had where Kinsley encouraged Liz to try to get Luther back, she then goes and asks him out? "When did this happen?"

His head tilted slightly as his eyes narrowed at her question. "Why does *that* matter? Did you tell her to do it or not?"

"I...okay, yes, but it's not what you think-"

"Oh it's not? The woman I'm in love with and who I *thought* was in love with me actually encouraged her friend to ask me out on a date, and it's not what I think?"

"Luther, if you would just *listen* to me!" Liz took a beat to calm herself, holding up her hands. "I was drunk. Kinsley showed up and when I eventually told her about our breakup, she tried to encourage me to work things out with you. But I foolishly encouraged her to make her move, since Kinsley has made no secret of her attraction to you. I didn't mean it, nor did I think she'd actually do it."

"And that makes it okay?"

"It was a stupid thing I said when I was drunk and hurt; I admit that. But that's why I wanted to know when she asked you because when I told her the first time that she could step to you-"

"I'm sorry, what? This happened more than once?"

"Equally as bad a decision, and I can't even blame alcohol that time. It wasn't too long after we started dating and Kinsley was...look," Liz sighed, not having the energy to explain when she knew Luther wouldn't understand her reasoning, anyway, which she couldn't blame him for, "Again, I might've told her that but I thought she was just messing with me; trying to get a rise. It's one thing to think your friend's man is fine but another to actually try to act on it."

"Was I ever really your man, Liz? If you could even think to let encouragement to another woman to step to me come out of your mouth, I'm wondering what that says about your supposed feelings for me."

"Supposed??"

"Yes, Liz. Because either what you said you felt for me was bogus or you're playing games since I'm the one that ended things. Either way, you don't come out looking too good to me."

Instantly affronted, Liz stalked closer to him, giving him a light shove to the chest as she looked up at him in heaving anger, her ears twitching like crazy. "How fucking dare you."

"How fucking dare I, what?"

"Let yourself try to believe that what we had was anything but real. Don't you ever in your *life* question my feelings for you, Luther Monroe! Yes, it was stupid to involve Kinsley, but don't try to make yourself feel better about throwing away what we were building by making me look like the bad guy. Oh my bad; you were probably doing that already, right?"

He stood over her, his scowl now matching hers. "So that's how you're gonna try to spin it, huh? You know what, Liz? You really are a piece of work. If what you felt for me was so deep, then why couldn't you meet me halfway on something that you *knew* was important to me? Why did you have to be so damn stubborn? I'm not the only one that threw us away so don't even *try* putting it all on me! Because I wanted us, Liz, and you *know* I did! From the first time I laid eyes on you, I wanted this! And I was willing to do my part but it can't just be me!"

"I *know* that, Luther! I get it! But if you think I don't miss what we had you're wrong, just like you're wrong if you for one second believe that I want you with any other woman but *me*!"

When her hand lifted to shove his chest again, he caught it and yanked her body to his, their lips crashing into each other's in the next moment. Their grunts and moans filled the office as their intense, desperate kisses intensified by the second. Luther's jacket fell to the ground before he grabbed the back of Liz's thighs, lifting her and placing her on her desk. She immediately clamped her legs around him, grinding against the hardness that was throbbing against her. His hand gripped the side of her face while the other took a handful of the fleshy part of her hip, aiding in her frantic gyrations against him.

"I still don't want anyone but you," he whispered between kisses. He tweaked her nipple through her shirt, loving how she shuddered in response. "Fuck, I've missed you, Liz..."

"I've missed you, too. Luther, please..."

She wanted him to sweep everything off her desk and ravage her. She wanted him to declare they would get back together; that their three weeks apart had been as agonizing for him as they had been for her. She wanted to be over her PDA hang-ups. She just wanted her Luther back.

Luther wanted everything Liz wanted and more. Having her in his arms again, kissing her, was almost surreal. He'd been agitated when he showed up at her office but when she said the things she said with that angry but pleading look in her eyes, whatever restraint he'd managed to force when he arrived snapped like a dry twig. He couldn't *not* kiss her, *not* touch her. As much as he'd told himself he accepted their breakup, his need for Liz hadn't waned in their time apart even a little bit.

Her hands gripped his shirt, trying to pull him even closer to her. The clothes that were keeping their bodies from touching like she wanted them to were frustrating her to no end. One hand slid down to his butt, pulling him harder against her.

"Can we please..." she panted, temporarily losing her words as Luther sucked his way down her neck as his hand found its way inside her shirt. "I need you."

Luther wasn't sure if she was talking sexually or in general, but it didn't matter. He was right there with her, on both counts.

But before he whipped it out and gave it to her on top of her desk, he made himself step back.

"What's wrong?" she asked, looking dazed.

He turned away, pressing his fists against his eyes as he willed himself to calm down. He was frustrated with himself for how he lost control, and also frustrated that he even needed to have any at all. Liz was supposed to still be his woman. Remembering that she wasn't cooled the fire that had been roaring inside him just moments before.

"I can't do this," he muttered. He dropped his hands to his hips but kept his face averted.

"Why?"

He blew a breath through his lips before looking over at her, then suddenly taking two long strides and ending up between her legs. "Because fucking you on your desk right now is only gonna piss me off since we still won't be together when we're done."

"What if I said that didn't have to be the case?" Liz urgently asked, taking fistfuls of his shirt again. "What if I said I was ready to do my part for us? I want you back, Luther. And I want you back *now*."

"I want you, too, baby." He took her face in both hands. "But we're both too wound up to have this kind of conversation right now. I'm still thinking about being inside of you and totally forgetting that we're in your place of business and...I can't..."

He released a frustrated huff before abruptly pressing his lips to hers again. Liz immediately responded to him, clutching his shoulders as she matched his fervency.

But Luther suddenly released her and stepped back, running a hand down his face as he peered at her through squinted eyes.

"I need to go, Liz," he muttered, his expression clearly relaying that he wanted to do the opposite. But he still made himself scoop up his jacket from the floor and hurry out of the office, closing the door behind him.

Liz just sat there on her desk, horny and confused, not sure if they'd just taken a step forward or backward.

• • • •

LIZ KNEW SHE SHOULD'VE cancelled the meetup with Cole. Casual or not, she was in no mood.

Luther's visit to her office had stayed heavy on her mind since he left her wanting and panting on her desk the day before. As sexually frustrated as she might have been, she could understand his point about not having a discussion about their relationship when their emotions were so high and raw. She certainly didn't want either of them to say something they'd need to walk back once their heads were clear.

But over a day had passed, and Liz's declaration about wanting Luther back hadn't budged. She wanted them to take another go at it, but she needed him to give her the benefit of the doubt. She could sense he still had his reservations, and she couldn't blame him. And if she was honest, she wasn't sure how she'd react once they went out together for the first time and he tried to show her some kind of affection. If her old issues flared up, they'd be right back where they were, if not worse.

Choosing to temporarily put it out of her mind, she made herself focus on where she was. She, Delilah, Delilah's husband Zander, and Zander's brother Cole were seated around a small table at some restaurant Delilah had chosen across town. Liz had almost suggested E.J. and Roland's club, 845, but she didn't want to risk being seen with another man by anyone she knew, regardless of the fact that she was no longer with Luther and wasn't doing anything wrong.

"Isn't this lovely?" Delilah asked, holding up her glass of champagne and smiling, her eyes flitting across everyone. "I'm so glad we could all get together like this. Cole, doesn't Liz look just yummy in that dress?"

Liz cut her eyes at Delilah and ignored Zander's concentrated stare over his wineglass as Cole gave her a polite sweeping perusal. "Yeah, she does. That's a nice dress."

"Thanks."

When the conversation petered out there, Delilah cleared her throat and sat forward a little in her seat, determined. "I see a former client over there that Zander and I need to say hello too; the hobnobbing never stops, you know. You two talk amongst yourselves." She drained the rest of her drink before grabbing Zander's hand and standing, giving Liz a pointed look and subtly jerking her head in Cole's direction. Liz wanted to yank Delilah's meticulous bun right off the top of her head.

Cole didn't look any more thrilled to be left alone with Liz and she had to wonder why he even agreed to come out if he didn't want to be there. Delilah had said he was intrigued to meet her but he surely wasn't acting like it. Still, she figured they might as well make the most of it, since they were there. And Delilah and Zander were footing the bill for the drinks.

"So..." she hedged, rubbing her right palm over the back of her left hand, "Delilah said you own several vending machines. That's pretty cool. Is it like a whole company you have or..."

"Um, yeah, you could say that." Cole stroked his clean-shaven jaw. His skin reminded Liz of toasted peanuts. "I wanted a nice side hustle and just started out with one. Built on that over time. Now it's my main thing, though there are a couple other small ventures I have my hands in."

"Nice. It's practically necessary to have multiple streams of income these days."

"True. What about you, Lucy? What do you do, again?"

Liz cleared her throat, calming her budding agitation. "It's Liz."

"My bad."

"I'm in fashion; Creative Director. And my sister and I co-own a couple of chicken franchises; we got into that about a year and a half ago."

"Cool..." Cole subtly checked his watch before turning his hazel eyes back to her. "Any siblings?"

"Besides the sister I *just* mentioned? No."

"Oh...sorry. I guess I'm a little distracted. I really don't mean to be rude."

"It's all right," Liz assured, some of her tension loosening. She placed a hand on his forearm and he actually twitched at the contact. She retracted, looking at him strangely before shaking it off. "We all have a lot going on, I guess."

"Yeah. You're right about that." He glanced towards where Delilah and Zander escaped to before expelling a tiny sigh and turning his attention back to Liz, giving her another perusal. "You really do look nice tonight. That haircut really suits you."

She smiled. "Thank you, Cole." She could certainly say the same about him. His dark hair with sprinklings of gray was cut into a smooth taper with an expertly-edged hairline and sides. And she wasn't blind to how juicy his lips looked or how nice his hands were.

Strangely determined, she scooted a little closer. "Are you and Zander really close?"

He shrugged, barely glancing at her. "I wouldn't say *really* close; we're close enough. We have different mamas so we didn't really grow up together."

Liz's knee brushed his under the table and she wondered if he even noticed, as unaffected as he was. "Do you get along well with Delilah?"

Taking his time responding, Cole took a long swig of his drink before slowly returning the glass to the table, his eyes locked in on that rather than her. "Yeah, we're good. You two are sorority sisters, right?"

"Mmm-hmm. We're putting together this year's adult prom; it's a charity event. I figure she probably told you about it, though."

"She mentioned it, yeah."

"Are you going?"

"I might. I'm not usually keen on making plans that far in advance."

His aloofness was throwing Liz off. He was facing forward while her body was angled towards his. Even though she hadn't been interested in meeting him and had no desire to be his woman, she found herself determined to get him to loosen up. She again wondered how Delilah had managed to get him there.

"So, Cole," she leaned slightly towards him. "Tell me something fun about yourself."

He immediately shrugged, barely contemplating the request before he droned, "I can't think of anything."

"There's gotta be *something*. A man as enterprising as you, not to mention handsome..."

"I appreciate that. But there's not a lot to tell about me, really. I just handle my business and stay to myself, pretty much."

Her leg brushed his again and she was mildly shocked when he shifted away from her. Her eagerness to get him to engage with her rapidly began to morph into indignation.

"So you're always this apathetic?" she asked with a tiny bit of bite to her voice. She leaned back in the booth, putting more distance between them. "Or am I the only one that gets the pleasure?"

Cole finally turned fully towards her, his eyebrows lifted at her tone. "Whoa, what's up with that?"

"Seriously? You're gonna act like you don't know what I'm talking about? I didn't come here expecting a love connection, Cole, but I didn't think I'd be totally wasting my time, either. And *this*," she stood, snatching her clutch from her seat, "Is a waste of time."

"Liz, look..." He shook his head as if he couldn't believe her nerve, "Like I said earlier, I'm not trying to be rude. But I'm not in the headspace for this tonight and I told Delilah that. But she can be pretty persistent, as you probably know. And I'll admit I'm not used to such aggressive women, with all the touching and innuendo you were giving off-"

"What damn innuendo? And so I barely grazed you a couple of times; you're trying to say that's the reason you're being so standoffish? You act like I grabbed your damn dick under the table."

Cole glanced around, his face flushing at the nearby couple that heard her. "*And* you grabbed my arm. You were just coming on a little strong, is all I'm saying," he hissed, leaning closer to her and lowering his voice. His pointed glare pleaded with her to chill out. "Can you just sit down and finish your drink, please? I'm sure Delilah and Zander will be back any minute now-"

"Why would I want to keep spending time with someone that clearly doesn't want to be here?" Liz picked up her glass and gulped down the last of her French 75, resisting the urge to toss it in his face. "I'm out."

"Liz-"

She was already heading for the door. She saw Delilah and Zander standing near the bar talking to someone and look at her with questioning eyes, but she just brushed right by them without acknowledgment.

Liz got into her car in a huff, slamming the door and tossing her clutch to the passenger's seat. She was frustrated but she was also a little embarrassed. Cole had acted like her touch repulsed him; like he was just tolerating her to fulfill a promise to Delilah. When she thought about how he actually leaned away from her to avoid any more contact...Liz had never felt so affronted like that from a man. She wasn't even doing anything that egregious.

She started her car and then froze.

This must have been how Luther felt.

Except his frustrations were likely worse because they were actually dating and claimed to have feelings for each other. But whenever he tried to touch her, however innocently, she acted like he was committing some cardinal sin. Just the way Cole did with her tonight.

The conviction made her eyes burn with tears. If Luther felt anything like she was feeling right then, she could absolutely understand his frustration with her. Cole wasn't even someone she was interested in and yet she still felt slighted. It had to have been ten times worse for Luther, who was in love with her.

Before she knew it, she was pulling into Luther's driveway.

The footsteps were immediate as soon as she softly knocked on the door, and she knew he probably saw her pull up on the cameras and was probably already headed to meet her. Her nerves accelerated the closer he got to the door; she was sincerely afraid he'd turn her away.

But he didn't. Luther didn't even look surprised to see her when he opened the door for her; he just stepped aside and allowed her to come in. Liz stopped just a few feet past him, not even leaving the front entryway before she turned to him. Luther locked the door before turning his intense eyes to her, advancing as their gazes locked. He stepped in front of her, pushing her against the wall with his body. Liz's heels clicked against his hardwood floor, the only sound in the uncharacteristically quiet house.

Luther's finger grazed her lips before trailing along her jawline, around her ear, down the side of her neck, along her collarbone, and to the valley of her breasts. Liz's breath hitched, the anticipation leaving her extra jumpy. Their eyes never left each other's as he slowly began to unzip her dress, and Liz's hands slid inside the waistband of his sweats and began to push them down.

Before too long, all of their clothes were on the ground next to their feet, both naked except for Liz and her heels and jewelry. Luther swooped down and trailed his tongue along the same path his finger had taken, and Liz's eyes fluttered closed as she leaned her head back to assist his seduction, shaky breaths puffing out in an uneven staccato rhythm. Luther's long tongue snaked between her heaving aching breasts, his hands taking firm but gentle hold of them as he continued licking down her body. When he was kneeling in front of her, he nipped and savored her warm brown skin as his hands kneaded her breasts and his thumbs flicked her beaded nipples. Her body snaked in a slow body roll she almost had no control over. Her arms slowly drifted upwards, palms flattening against the wall, her breaths and whimpers extending like a long musical note.

Luther slid his hands down her torso to her hips, momentarily gripping before he lifted one of her legs over his shoulder, then the other. Then he suddenly stood to his full height, sending Liz shooting straight up and screaming as her hands clutched the back of his head.

"Luther!"

Liz's head was near the ceiling and her upper back was braced against the wall, but one touch of Luther's tongue had her forgetting her precarious position.

"Ooohhh *shiiiiit*..."

"Mmm-hmm..."

It was a toss-up as to who was enjoying it more, with Luther savoring Liz's pussy like it was coated in dulce de leche and the erotic element for Liz being ramped up to a million with Luther having her hoisted up as she was like it was nothing. She ground against his mouth, feeling her leg muscles tighten as the pressure valve on her orgasm started to loosen. And when it erupted, it erupted *hard*.

"HOLY *FUCK* I LOVE YOU, LUTHER TRAE MONROE! *YOU ARE THE KING OF THIS SHIT!!*"

Luther smiled as he took his time lowering her. Her arms landed on his shoulders and her legs encircled his waist, taking a moment to look at him in lustful amazement before they shared a slow, erotic kiss, him sharing her taste with her and her loving it.

He began to slowly walk towards the living room, her hand caressing the back of his head as she whispered in his ear exactly what she wanted to do next, and the result she wanted from it. Grunting in approval, Luther laid her on her back on the couch, nestled in the corner, making sure she was good and propped up on some pillows behind her head before mounting her. Liz licked her lips as she eagerly grabbed his hips and pulled his dick to her mouth, Luther hissing as he slid inside.

"Damn, baby..." he whispered, slowly moving his hips back and forth, one hand braced against the back of the couch and the other on the arm. "I love face-fucking you, Liz, *shit*..."

Liz just winked at him, humming as she sucked him off. She kept her eyes on his, loving seeing his strong dark body on top of her and the various expressions of pleasure wash over his face, and how his firm ass clenched under her fingers as she gripped him, pulling him into her.

"Liz," Luther's head dropped, his speed starting to increase.

Liz just encouraged him by strengthening her suction and pulling him into her mouth faster. And when he was ready to cum, per her instructions, he pulled out and did it on her face. He'd gotten head plenty of times but no other woman had specifically requested that like Liz had. The sight of her pretty face covered in his release revved him right back up.

As soon as he got them cleaned up, he was right back inside of her, between her legs as they kissed deeply and slowly. They couldn't get enough of each other, and for the time being, nothing else mattered.

It was a long while later when Luther finally picked Liz up and carried her to his bedroom. Once they were under the thick covers of his bed, they instinctively met in the middle, him pulling her into his arms.

"I hate to be cliché, but what does this mean?" she asked softly, her head against his chest. "Because I meant it yesterday when I said I wanted you back."

His arms tightened around her. "I want you back, too, Liz."

She leaned back slightly to look up at him, sensing the unspoken ending of his sentence. "But you still have reservations?"

"I'd be lying if I said I didn't." He smoothed a sweaty lock of hair from her forehead. "I don't want to keep doing the breakup-to-make up thing. If we resume our relationship, I want it to be for good. I just..."

"Luther. Look...you probably won't love hearing this but I had drinks with another man tonight. It was along with my sorority sister Delilah and her husband and I made it clear from the jump that it *wasn't* a date, but I admit I partially agreed to go to try to get over you."

The furrow between his brow was evident even in the darkened room. "I see."

"But I got a taste of my own medicine when the guy started acting like I probably acted with you, as far as touching. And considering I wasn't even doing anything anywhere *near* the level that you tried with me, it was pretty offensive. I left him sitting at the table and came here because in that moment, I needed to be with you. In *most* moments, I need to be with you, Luther."

His chest swelled at her words. "And you're sure this isn't just your bruised pride talking?"

"You know what..." She hunched a shoulder. "Maybe a little bit of it is. But the majority of it? All sincere."

"I appreciate the honesty. And 'paranoid' isn't usually something that applies to me. But with this," he rolled on top of her, nestling between her legs as he looked lovingly at her face, "I don't want any uncertainty, from either side. So when we're both at a hundred percent, we'll lock it down. Does that sound fair?"

Liz nodded, feeling surprisingly okay with the suggestion despite her usual impatience. When she thought about the myriad of emotions she'd experienced over the three weeks they'd been apart, she knew that she'd rather have Luther in her life than out of it.

Both Liz and Luther knew they'd be fine on their own, if it came to that. But they each also knew that being on their own wasn't what they wanted.

Chapter 17

• • • •

LIZ WAS WONDERING WHAT the hell Carlton Barber was doing in her office.

"Carlton," she blinked, standing from the loveseat she'd been sitting on to shuffle through some storyboards. "I'm sure you can understand how surprised – and confused – I am right now."

"My apologies for just showing up out of the blue like this." Carlton roamed around the office with his hands in the pockets of his expensive suit like he was a potential buyer. "I'm sure you're a very busy woman."

"And you're an even busier man, so I'm sure you don't have time for pointless visits. So what brings you here?"

"I love how direct you are." Carlton stopped his roaming around and moved over to Liz's desk, perching himself on the edge and looking right at home. "I'd like for you to accompany me this evening."

"Pardon me?"

"You have to eat dinner, right? No reason we couldn't do that together."

"You're seriously asking me out? I thought we had this conversation already."

"I'm asking you to dinner, Liz, not to the Maldives. This isn't anything romantic, as I fully recall you mentioning having a man already. I'd just like the pleasure of your company, that's it. Hell, bring your man with you."

Liz scoffed as she wandered to her desk and dropped into the chair with a sigh. "If he and I were actually still together, I'd probably do that."

Carlton peered at her, noting her change in countenance. "So it sounds like you could use a friend *and* a good meal. I'm more than happy to provide both."

Liz found herself intrigued and even grateful for the offer. Especially since her evening plans only consisted of working late, grabbing some takeout from Waffle House, getting in a short workout, and then going to bed and watching CSI until she fell out.

So later that evening, she met up with Carlton at a rooftop restaurant that she knew was almost impossible to get a reservation to, yet it appeared she and Carlton had the place to themselves. She didn't even want to think about how much it must have cost to reserve the entire thing for the night.

"Hope you're hungry," Carlton said once they were seated. "This place has great food."

"I've heard. Never thought I'd get to try it, though."

"I surely hope it lives up to your expectations, then. Nothing like thinking something is going to be amazing and then realizing it wasn't worth the hype. Feel free to order whatever you want; I get the feeling you probably haven't eaten in a while."

Liz looked at him in amused amazement. "Did you sneak a camera into my office when you were there earlier?"

He chuckled. "Just a hunch. I got the sense that you might be one to use work to distract you from whatever you're dealing with. And since you mentioned no longer being with your man..."

"Ugh."

"We can talk about it. Or not. Your call."

Once they placed their orders, Liz found herself spilling her guts to Carlton, telling him all about how she and Luther met in Belize, how she instantly felt for him like she had no other man, their reuniting at Natavey, and how everything started falling apart once they said 'I love you.' And of course, the whole PDA issue that caused the initial wedge between them.

"I'm fully willing to admit that I've made the mistake of letting past issues have too much power over me now," Liz admitted, taking a sip of her wine. "With every man I've been with, it's been the same thing...keep our hands to ourselves in public, go all in in private. And there were a couple men that didn't love that but it wasn't a deal-breaker for them like it was for Luther."

"So it wasn't just an issue of public affection; you got used to getting your way."

Liz blinked. "Wow..."

"Hey, I'm used to getting my way, too," Carlton assured, briefly holding up his hands. "But I know how to compromise when I need to. And when it comes to personal relationships, I'd like to think getting what I want is secondary to what's best for both of us."

"I never thought of myself as selfish before, but..." Liz shrugged as she tapped her nails against the base of her wineglass. "Maybe I was."

"Admission is the first step to recovery."

"The thing is, though, I know Luther still has reservations about our compatibility, despite how much we both want to get back together. That's what's keeping him from resuming our relationship; even after I admitted to my recent realizations, I don't think he trusts it."

"Should he?"

"I meant it when I told him my mindset had changed, after talking with my friend Kinsley and the drink outing I had with that guy. But I get that it's one thing to say that and another thing to actually change. I know it seems like it would be an easy thing to fix but..."

"Let me ask you," Carlton paused as the server brought out their appetizers. Once she was gone, he turned his attention back to Liz. "You said your aversion to PDA is because of your parents. Did you ever let them know how their being so affectionate in public embarrassed you?"

Liz pursed her lips. "No."

"Any particular reason?"

"I...guess I didn't know how to approach it. My parents were wonderful people; great parents, always happy, ridiculously in love. I didn't want to be the Grinch that had the problem with them being affectionate with each other."

"So you kept it to yourself and let it build over the years, then carried it into your relationships."

"Pretty much." Liz sighed, eying her shrimp cocktail.

"Liz, if you just don't care for PDA because you don't care for it, that's one thing. That's just your preference and there's nothing wrong with that. But if you're *solely* basing everything on the actions of your parents over twenty years ago, that might be something to deal with. Especially if it costs you the love of your life. I'd hate to see you end up like me."

She looked at him, intrigued. "What do you mean, like you?"

"You may or may not know but I was married before," Carlton informed her, taking a bite of his lump crab cake. "I was fairly young and still making a name for myself, and had it in my head that everyone knowing I was married would somehow be a detriment. So I kept her hidden."

"Oh...and she left you because of it?"

"She did. It wasn't an immediate thing at all, though; lots of arguments, lots of tears, ultimatums, a brief separation. All this went on for a few years. I was *way* more stubborn and bull-headed than I am now but I finally started to come around when she began dropping hints about leaving."

"That's when you started letting people see her?"

"Basically. But it was too little too late. By then, she didn't trust my reasons. It didn't help that someone who I thought was a friend was whispering in her ear behind my back, telling her that I was only relenting for business reasons, saying that I cared more about work than I did her, all kinds of stuff. Even hinted that I'd been unfaithful."

"Oh my god..."

"It was all bullshit. I never once cheated on my wife, nor was I even tempted. But by then, she'd accumulated so much doubt that it didn't take much to shake her belief in me. We ended up divorcing, somewhat amicably. It was years ago but I can't say I totally got over it."

"So that's why you just casually date now? Don't want to put yourself out there again?"

"I'd like to think that if I met someone I was intrigued by enough and it was mutual, and genuine, that I'd take that leap. I'm not anti-relationship by any means. About my ex-wife, though, it took me years to realize that even though I thought I was fixing things with the about-face I did regarding her wishes, it wasn't enough."

"How could it not have been enough? You were doing what she asked, right?"

"It wasn't the 'what', it was the 'why.' I was relenting so she wouldn't be upset, not because I sincerely wanted to. And she sensed that. I'm wondering if Luther feels the same about you and that's fueling his hesitancy about reuniting."

"Oh...damn." Liz sat back in her seat, pondering Carlton's words. "That's new...I admit I never thought of that. If I'm honest, I expected him to take me back when I went to his place the other night after having drinks with that guy and getting my face cracked. While I accepted what he said at the time...I won't lie, I felt some kind of way afterwards that he was *still* hesitating. And he did flat-out ask if I was only coming to him because my pride was bruised."

"From the way you've described this Luther, he seems to have his shit together and his head on straight. If he loves you as much as he seems to, and has said he wants you as much as you want him yet isn't ready to jump back in, there has to be a reason. I don't know the brother but I'd be willing to bet that's at least part of it, if not the main thing."

Liz considered that. Luther being the man that he was, she knew he wouldn't accept anything that he felt was less than sincere or genuine. He wouldn't want her doing anything just to appease him, or simply to get back into his good graces. It made so much more sense to her that he insisted they wait now.

"I must say, this has been really enlightening," she admitted. "Here I was thinking I had it all together and Luther was just being paranoid. But it makes more sense now which is...pretty refreshing, actually."

"Again, I'm only surmising. It's certainly something you should address with him to be sure. Now, eat that food, girl...this stuff isn't cheap."

Laughing, Liz finally picked up her fork. Their conversation paused as they each dug into their appetizers and soon after, their entrees. Liz marveled at how good everything was, and she began telling Carlton about what else was going on with her, including the showcase she'd been working so hard on and the adult prom.

"Is Luther going to be your date for the prom?" Carlton asked her once their dinner plates were whisked away.

Liz shrugged. "I'm not sure, actually. With everything else we've dealt with, we haven't even talked about it in a while."

"Well, hopefully it'll be him twirling you around the dance floor but if not, I'm more than willing to accompany you."

"Carlton, that's really sweet of you to offer that, but I'm sure you have better things to do."

"Know that I don't make offers I don't want to make. Even though it wouldn't be romantic, I'd damn sure enjoy an evening with a beautiful woman that I'm building a friendship with. More importantly, you said it was a charity event for Black Entrepreneurs of Tomorrow and I admire that organization, and always like to do my part. And this would be more fun than just sending a check, though I'll absolutely do that, as well."

"Well, hell, let me quit trying to be polite, then, and just make sure you know what color dress I'll be wearing so we don't clash," Liz grinned. "You know, just in case."

Carlton laughed. "Yes, please. We wouldn't want that."

"And don't expect to get in my panties at the end of the night, either."

He threw his head back, laughing even louder. Liz couldn't help but join in, and they spent the next couple of hours cutting up like old chums and ordering more things off the expensive menu.

• • • •

LUTHER HAD SPENT THE day running errands, getting a checkup, and rescuing Churi when she got a flat tire on the highway. She was so frazzled that he couldn't resist paying for new tires for her car and treating her to lunch. Once they were seated, Churi wasted no time ordering the biggest margarita on the menu.

"I know you're of age but it's still weird to see you ordering alcohol right in front of me," Luther admitted with a chuckle.

"At least they didn't give me grief like most places do. I'm always getting questioned about if my ID is fake or not, since nobody seems to believe I'm really twenty-three. Can you believe that?"

"Yeah."

Churi gasped and Luther shook his head, still smiling. His daughter could be extra dramatic when she wanted to be. "Daddy!"

"Churi, you know you look young for your age. It's not a secret."

"Hmph. Well, thank you again for coming to help me out. I tried to call my roommates but they didn't answer, though they might not have even known what to do anyway, now that I think about it. And Uncle Carter would just grill me about every little thing I'm doing so I'm glad I didn't have to go there."

"You know I'll always have your back, baby girl. I'm not gonna have my daughter sitting on the side of the road with two blown tires."

"This is something a boyfriend *should* be helping me with but of course I can't seem to get one of those," Churi muttered, snatching some bread from the basket that was just brought to the table. "My love life sucks. I can't even tell you the last time I had any-"

"Feel free to save this particular conversation for your mother."

"Aww, Daddy. We should be able to talk about anything, right? We're supposed to have that kind of relationship."

"All right..." Luther sat forward, resting his forearms on the edge of the table. "Perhaps you can tell me why you have such a problem with Liz, then."

Churi grunted and stuffed her mouth full of bread. "I don't know."

"You're too educated and intelligent for that response. Be honest with me, Churi."

She sighed, putting the rest of her yeast roll on her saucer. "Daddy, you know I want you and Mama to get back together."

"And *you* know that's not gonna happen. We've told you that a hundred times. And from what I hear, you don't give the men your mother dates a hard time. So what's the *real* reason?"

She fiddled with the tablecloth, taking her time. "I don't want her replacing me."

"What?"

"You're different with her; I see it even in the few times I've been around y'all. It's like I'm a bother or something if I'm there. It's never been like that with any other woman you've dated since you and Mama split up. Maybe it's silly and childish but I don't want to get pushed to the side because you're in love with her, and I know you are."

"Churi, are you serious?" Luther reached across the table and grabbed her fiddling hand, shaking it gently until she turned her big brown eyes to him. "Baby girl, please know that no woman can replace you. You're my daughter. I love you more than I love anything."

"Has she been in my treehouse?"

"*You've* barely been in that treehouse, Churi. Don't act possessive of it now. But to answer your question, yes, she has."

"See there. I knew it."

"Churi."

"Daddy, there have been times I've wanted to talk to you about how freaked out I am about this adulting stuff, having to do everything on my own and how stressed I get. I know you and Mama think I'm just making excuses or trying to skirt responsibility and that's really not it. But I don't feel like I can call you like I used to now because I think you'll be with *her*. And it's not like she seems that eager to get to know me, either, and that doesn't seem to bother you. I just feel like she's already coming between us and...I hate that."

Luther looked at his daughter's forlorn expression and felt his heart break. The last thing he ever wanted was to make his baby girl feel unwelcome or that she couldn't come to him, whether he was in a relationship or not.

"Baby, if I've ever made you feel like a bother, I apologize. You know you're my heart and that's not changing. I love our relationship and Liz or no other woman will break that but you also have to understand that we're in different phases now. I'm your father but I have a life, too. And when you decide to show up to my house unannounced, you can't get upset over what or who you might find when you get there. And it's wild that you're upset about our lack of time together when you've cancelled our brunches the last few times, and we've been having those since you were a child. I didn't love that but figured you'd outgrown it or were no longer interested."

"No," Churi insisted immediately. "It's not that. And I know I'm wrong for flaking. I guess it got too easy to let other stuff get in the way. And if I'm honest, maybe I was taking you for granted a little, figuring you'd make time when I was ready. That's why I just stopped by your house whenever."

"Well, that's not a good plan. Would you like it if I just showed up out of the blue when you were in bed with some guy?"

Churi's cheeks immediately flushed and she looked away. "Daddy!"

"We're not gonna do the thing where we pretend you're a virgin, are we?"

"I...um..."

"You're grown, Churi," Luther chuckled at his daughter's mortified expression. "You're gonna do what you do. As long as you're being smart, safe, and careful, I have nothing to say about it. But I hope you get my point, in regards to Liz."

"I guess." Churi took a long sip of her drink, then flipped her hair over her shoulder. "I'll be nicer, I promise. Do you think you're gonna propose to her?"

Luther didn't want to get into the current state of his relationship with Liz, trying to explain how they weren't really together even though they both wanted to be. He still had his reservations, as much as he wished he didn't.

"I don't know what's gonna happen, baby girl," he replied honestly, now doing his own fiddling with the tablecloth. "I've certainly thought about it but it remains to be seen."

"If you need me to, I can help you pick out a ring," Churi offered. "That can be my olive branch. And since you don't really wear jewelry you'll probably need some help, anyway. Wouldn't want you trying to do that by yourself."

Luther shook his head though he couldn't help but laugh. His daughter was something else. "Thanks a lot."

• • • •

LATER, LUTHER WAS FINISHING his meditating when he got a couple of texts. One was from Carter, letting him know he had a date with Kinsley, and the other was from Liz. She shared several pictures with him from the showcase looks where she used his hats, and even though he might not have thought to put his designs with those outfits, he couldn't deny they looked great. Liz even included a short video showing a few designers and executives raving about his hats and how they were just what was needed, which made him smile. He couldn't help being flattered. And it made him feel good to be able to help Liz out like that.

A little later, Liz sent one more video. She was sitting on the loveseat in her office, and it appeared to be late afternoon, given the muted sunlight coming in from the windows. Her expression was somewhat pensive but he could see the warmth in her eyes as she spoke into the camera.

"I just wanted to thank you again, Luther. Not just for the hats, though that was huge for me. I'm just thankful for *you*. The impact you've had on me since you came into my life is...it's immeasurable. And I hope that mine has been just as positive for you."

Luther placed a hand to his chest, leaning closer to the phone.

"When I sat and really thought about it, I realized I haven't been in many serious relationships at all," Liz continued. She looked so poised in her navy, gold, and orange silk striped blouse and gold hoops, her makeup light but flawless. And as usual, her short hair looked like she'd just left the salon. "It's mostly been flings and casual dating situations that only lasted until I got tired of them. And if they were the ones to leave, I didn't even care. I wasn't bitter but I *was* dismissive of men and relationships and the whole notion of love; figured that was great for everyone else but not in the cards for me.

"But that's not the case with you, and I hope you know that. I need you in my life, Luther. And I get what you've been saying, and why you hit the pause button on us getting back together. I truly do. And though I miss you and the impatient part of me wants you back yesterday, you deserve my hundred percent. And I'm working on it. Just know that I'm not going anywhere and I hope you don't, either, because I really can't see myself with anyone but you. I love you, Luther Monroe."

When the video stopped, Luther just kept staring at the screen, Liz's words sinking into his head and his heart. Everything in him wanted to go to her right then. It meant a lot to him that she gave him that reassurance, because he honestly had moments where he wondered if he was being too demanding. But he knew that was mainly his own impatience flaring, because he missed her and what they had as much as she did. But if there was one thing Luther always did, it was stand on his convictions. And the fact that Liz understood and respected where he was coming from meant the world to him.

Luther chose to respond to Liz's video in kind, even though he almost never made videos himself. He wracked his brain for the perfect things to say, but ended up just gazing into the camera, picturing Liz's beautiful face as he said:

"I love you, too, Liz Tate. With my whole heart. And I'm not going anywhere, either."

Chapter 18

• • • •

LIZ HAD BEEN PUTTING in so many extra hours on the showcase and the other campaigns she was working on that when Jules reached out and invited her to a spa day, Liz jumped at it.

"Girl, I can't tell you how much I needed this," she commented once they were in side-by-side pedicure chairs, adorned in the fluffy robes in the spa's signature sky blue color. "I needed some pampering and relaxation in the worst way."

"I sensed that. The last couple times we talked, you were kinda frazzled."

"That's one way to put it. It's been pretty much nonstop these past few months between getting everything together for the showcase and planning this adult prom, and things are only more hectic the closer we get to it, with all the damn last-minute hiccups and changes. So I surely appreciate this."

"Girl, please, I got you. We all need to unplug every now and then."

They each rested their heads back on the comfortable pedicure chairs, giving in to the relaxation from the chairs' vibrations and the skilled hands of their pedicure technicians. Liz sighed, glad to put everything she had on hold for a while and just chill.

Their pedicures were almost finished when she turned to Jules and asked, "Speaking of the prom, you're going, right?"

"Yep, I bought my ticket the other day. I'm looking forward to it; it's been a while since I've had occasion to get all fancy and do it up for a night. And I'm always down for an excuse to do more shopping. I found a hot dress; gonna need some Spanx but I don't even care."

"Can't wait to see it. I'm still trying to narrow down what I'm gonna wear, myself. I just hope no one will start acting all extra when I show up with Carlton Barber."

Jules's head whipped around, the long tendrils she'd left out of her loose ponytail flying. "Carlton Barber? You're not going with Luther?"

Liz kicked herself. She figured Luther had kept Jules updated on how things were going, at least to a degree. "No, I'm not. We're not back together yet."

"Yet. So you *do* want to be."

"Yeah, of course. But Luther wanted to wait and without going into all the reasons for that and getting myself worked back up and erasing this zen I've managed to fall into, I get and respect it. So we're...kinda giving each other space, though we're still somewhat in contact. I'm surprised he hasn't told you any of this."

"He actually hasn't been that eager to talk about it. Whenever I ask how things are going with you two, he changes the subject. The most I got out of him was that y'all were 'fine.'"

"Hmm. Well, I can't say me and Luther being apart is my favorite subject, either."

"He did tell me about the whole PDA thing. Not to be dismissive or judgmental but-"

"You think it's stupid that I'm hung up on that."

"I wouldn't say *stupid*. I'm sure you have your reasons. But I actually asked Luther if he was really willing to let you go over that. When he stopped wanting to talk about it, I figured…"

"It's a long story that I just don't have the energy to get into."

"I get it. I'm the ex-wife, after all; I'm not entitled to the whole story. Just want Luther to be happy. So since you're going to the prom with Carlton Barber, I guess that means you and Luther are seeing other people."

"Umm…that's not something we discussed. And this thing with Carlton isn't a *date*-date; we're just two friends going to an event, that's all."

"And you didn't consider asking Luther?"

"I did but I figured he wouldn't want to go while we're in limbo like this. And instead of hearing him tell me 'no', however politely, I just didn't bother asking."

Jules just peered at her, and Liz could only imagine what she was thinking. But before either of them could say anything else, someone came in to usher them to their respective rooms for their facials. Liz was partially relieved but she couldn't help but wonder what was going through Jules's mind, or if she'd go back and tell Luther that Carlton was her escort to the prom. Liz imagined Luther would be as mature about it as he was about most things, but she didn't want him getting the wrong idea. Especially after they exchanged those heartfelt videos to each other. Liz had watched the one Luther sent her more times than she could count.

But the thought of Luther misinterpreting her ateending the prom with Carlton made Liz want to call him right then and let him know, just so things were out in the open.

She hadn't even considered how Luther would react when she accepted Carlton's invitation, which didn't make her feel great. The tension crept back into her shoulders as she continued to agonize over this during the remainder of her spa day.

Well, there goes my zen.

. . . .

"I HAVE TO SAY; I'M still getting used to seeing you in 'mommy' mode."

Natalia glanced at Liz with a giggle as she finished cleaning applesauce from her daughter Aria's face and hands with a baby wipe. "If I had a dollar for every time I've heard that since Aria was born..."

"I actually thought Lovey was going to be the only one of us popping out babies but then you switched up on me," Liz joked. She leaned back on the couch in Natalia's den, having come over to see her friend after she left the spa. "Now it's just me in the 'no baby' crew. I'm still tripping that Desiree is pregnant."

"I know, right! I thought she was just fucking with us when she put that in the group chat the other day. But I guess all of her climbing all over Lorenzo did it."

"Have you talked to her? Is she happy about it?"

"Girl, she's thrilled," Natalia confirmed, placing Aria between them on the couch with one of her light-up toys. "She's still a little freaked out because she never thought she'd be having any kids but mostly, she's over the moon to be carrying Lorenzo's baby. She's already picking out names and everything."

"I can only imagine how her baby shower is gonna be," Liz joked.

"Oh, you already know. These nine months will be full of any excuses Desiree can think of to throw a party. Besides the gender reveal and the baby shower, she'll probably have something when she and Lorenzo decide on a name, when she starts to show…"

"I wouldn't be surprised if she throws something to celebrate being knocked up in the first place."

Liz and Natalia laughed. Aria looked up at them momentarily before going back to her toy. She looked like she'd have Natalia's bronze brown skin but Liz could definitely see some of E.J. in her features, too.

"Lorenzo is gonna be an amazing father, though," Natalia commented. "From what E.J. told me, he's *so* excited. You know him and E.J. mentor teenage boys who are all off at college now; they're both thrilled to finally have kids of their own."

"Is E.J. already talking about having another one?"

"Girl, you know he is. I wouldn't mind having one more but *whew*, between work and this little nugget here," Natalia pinched Aria's chubby cheeks, making her squeal, "I told him we need to wait another year or so first. I'm still getting used to all this."

They continued to play with Aria and chat about various things, eating the sushi Liz brought over. When Natalia asked how things were going with Luther, Liz's expression grew somber.

"Whoa, what's wrong?" Natalia asked, noticing the change in demeanor. "You two still having issues?"

"Something like that."

"What's going on?"

Liz got Natalia caught up on everything that happened since they last spoke. Part of her couldn't even believe she and Luther had dealt with so much in the relatively short time they'd known each other.

"Let me ask you something," Liz hedged, absently running a nail back and forth along her scalp. "I know you love your husband more than Monolos. But when you were going through all that drama with E.J. last year, was there ever any moment when you thought it was too much? That it might be better to just...let it go while you both at least still loved each other?"

"Nope." Natalia's response was immediate and accompanied with an emphatic shake of her head. "Not one. I can say that I would have accepted it best I could've if he decided *he* wanted to fall back, but there was no way I was willingly giving up on my husband or my marriage. No way in hell."

"That's what I thought you'd say."

"Are you thinking of giving up on Luther?"

"Hell no." Liz's response was almost as immediate as Natalia's had been. "When I say I love that man, I *mean* that. I just feel like I'm so bad at this that...I don't know...even though he says he loves me – and I do believe him – that he might get sick of my shit. I can't expect him to have endless patience. *I* surely wouldn't."

"I get it. You think he'll feel some kind of way about you going to the prom with Carlton instead of asking him?"

"I wouldn't blame him if he did."

"You won't know unless you ask. You could always just tell Carlton you changed your mind. He'll get over it."

"The fact would still remain that I didn't ask Luther in the first place. But I honestly thought he might not want to go."

"You shouldn't have assumed that, though. And I must say: this lets me know just how much you're into him because I've never known you to be apprehensive about saying *anything* to a man, or how he might react. Luther is the one. And that's not something you just let go of just because things get rocky, girl." Natalia looked at Liz pointedly as she eased Aria back from inching towards the edge of the couch. "Love like I have with E.J. and how it seems you have with Luther is worth putting in some work for. So dig those stilettos in and tough it out. Trust me, you'll be glad you did."

Liz felt encouraged when she left Natalia's. She needed that reassurance from someone who had been through some major relationship adversity, and that was Natalia. Tiny sprigs of doubt tended to pop up in Liz's mind despite herself, and they shot up after her conversation with Jules earlier. It felt good to rip those weeds out.

Speaking of weeds, Kinsley was waiting in the parking garage of her building when she got there.

"What the hell are you doing here?"

"Damn, that's how you greet me?" Kinsley marveled. "What did I do now?"

"Are you serious? After all that apologizing you did and encouraging me to try to work stuff out with Luther, you still went and asked him out. Don't try to act like you don't know."

Kinsley sighed as she followed Liz to the building's entrance. "Are you going to let me come up so I can explain all this?"

"No, thanks."

"You owe me that, Liz."

Liz whirled around, her incredulousness on full blast. "I *owe* you what?"

"I tried to explain this last time I saw you at Natavey but you weren't trying to hear it. And not to mention, maybe if you'd been honest with me from the beginning about you and Luther, we wouldn't be going through all this."

"Ugh." Liz rolled her eyes but she could (internally) concede that Kinsley had a point. And she was curious as to what her explanation could possibly be, anyway. "Fine, come on."

Once they were inside of Liz's loft, Kinsley got right to it. "I only asked Luther out to prove a point. You kept insisting from the beginning that the two of you were just chillin', though I didn't really buy it. Then you again told me to go for it with him when you two broke up, and I knew you didn't mean that shit, either. I'm not an idiot; I know Luther doesn't want me. I only asked him out to call your bluff and show you that you don't want anyone with that man but you."

Liz glared at her friend. "And you couldn't think of any other way to make that point? We're supposed to be friends, Kinsley. I considered you one of my girls. And you doing all this talk about how fine my man is and asking me if you can step to him...that's foul, regardless of your intentions."

"Maybe it is. And if you wanna be mad at me over it, I get it. But I'd like to think you know me well enough by now to know that I'd never betray you over some dick."

Liz's fist automatically clenched. "I've told you about referring to him like that."

"See there? You're always *so* quick to defend him and get up in my face yet when it comes to going all in and just being with him, you can't seem to do it. Yeah, part of me was fucking with you because I knew you weren't being straight-up with me, and I didn't appreciate that. As long as we've been down for each other, you should know you don't need to fake the funk with me about anything, regardless of how you think I'll react."

Liz nodded, her eyes falling to her hands. "True enough."

"But mostly, I was trying to show you what could possibly happen if you kept dragging your feet. I'm sure Luther really does love you but no man is gonna wait around forever."

"I'm aware of that. Do you think I'm *trying* to be so bad at this? I'm not! I'm forty years old and in that old school R&B-type love for the first time, and I keep shooting myself in the damn foot."

"Why, though? What are you so scared of?"

"I'm not *scared*, I'm just-"

"Quit fucking playin' me, Liz, damn! Why can't you just keep it a hundred with me for once??"

"Go home, Kinsley."

"You're not running me off. And you don't get to have it both ways. Either you want Luther or you don't. Either you want to do what it takes to be with him, or you don't. But don't repeatedly tell me a bunch of bullshit then clam up when it's time to get to the real. What the hell is the problem??"

"I'm not sure I'll be good enough!" Liz exclaimed, her restraint exploding like a shaken can of soda. She hadn't even realized that was the issue until she said it. Squeezing her eyes shut, she linked her fingers behind her neck and let her head fall back in emotional exhaustion.

Kinsley was quiet for a moment. "Why would you even say something like that?"

Lowering herself onto the couch, Liz shook her head, trying to process her jumbling thoughts. "It's not that I don't think I'll measure up as a person. I'm not sure I'll measure up as a partner. Luther deserves...everything. And I want to give him that. I want to be the kind of woman for him that Lovey and Natalia and Desiree are for their men. Hell, as much as I bitched about my parents being all over each other all the time, if I'm honest, I always hoped that, if I ever seriously ended up with someone, it would be a love like theirs. And I can't help but wonder if I'm even capable of that."

"And you'd hate to give yourself over to him only for him to eventually leave because you fell short despite how much you love him, huh?" Kinsley surmised, joining her on the couch.

"Yeah." Liz released a dry chuckle, shaking her head and looking absently at her seldom-used fireplace. "This is so crazy; I never thought I'd find myself here. I didn't even really get the depth of what was really holding me back until now. I thought the PDA stuff was my biggest problem but that was just a front for my basic-ass fear."

"Okay, and there's nothing wrong with that. You're human, Liz. And now that you know, you can do something about it."

"What?" Liz whirled around to look at her. "What can I do about it?"

"You can be honest with Luther. Tell him what's keeping you from going all in. Then at least he'll know and won't have to come to his own conclusions or assumptions. I'd bet just about anything that he'd stick in with you." Kinsley rubbed Liz's back before pulling her in for a side hug. "But he can't ride with you if you won't let him in the car. Tell him everything you just told me. Then let him prove himself to *you* by showing you he can be patient and love you through those fears. And I know he would, girl."

Liz knew Kinsley was right. She placed a hand on her friend's knee. "I'm still mad at you. But thank you for that."

"I keep telling you I've got your back. See all the wisdom and insight you've been missing out on by not keeping it real with me? We could've avoided all of this. Oh, and I have a date with Carter tomorrow night."

"I pray your strength."

• • • •

WHEN KINSLEY LEFT A little while later, Liz grabbed her phone. Hesitating only for a second, she called Luther.

"Hey," he greeted, his voice sending the tingles through her body that it usually did.

"Hey. How are you?"

"I'm cool. Took Churi out earlier to celebrate her new job. Just working on some hat designs now. I heard you and Jules went to the spa today."

Liz wondered if Jules already told him about Carlton being her escort for the prom. "Yeah, we had a good time; I really needed that. Um, I wanted to ask if you were still going to the adult prom or not."

"Yeah, I'll be there."

Liz had wandered into her bedroom and sat on the bed, falling onto her back and fiddling with her gold necklace. "Are you...going alone?"

"I wasn't planning on it."

Her grip on her necklace tightened. "I don't suppose this is some cute way of letting me know you were planning on taking *me*, is it?"

"I wanted to go with you. But I heard through the grapevine that you have a date already."

Liz's ears twitched so hard it almost hurt. So Jules *had* told him. She certainly didn't waste any time; Liz had only told her about that earlier that day. Part of her couldn't help but feel betrayed; she thought she and Jules had developed a friendship but apparently she was wrong.

"I should've told you about that," she admitted, her voice suddenly hoarse, "But it's not like a real date. Carlton is just a friend; that's it. I've made it perfectly clear to him that-"

"Liz, you don't have to do all this; it's fine," Luther interjected. "I get it. I can't say I loved hearing about it – and from someone other than you – but I had to check myself. Technically, you're free to do what you want."

"Yeah, but I don't want you to think that I *want* anyone else but you," Liz quickly insisted, sitting up slightly and resting on her elbow. "I should've told you I was going with Carlton and I apologize for that. Hell, I should've locked you in as my date from the beginning. I wasn't even sure if you were still going and if you were, I honestly felt like you wouldn't want to go with me in the state we're in."

"You were mistaken." Luther's voice was strong but there was no anger to be found. "I was actually going to ask if you still wanted to go together when I heard that you were already spoken for. So, I asked someone else to accompany me."

Liz didn't like hearing that. She didn't like hearing that at all. "You're actually taking someone else?"

"As are you."

"I'm not sure how I'll handle seeing you with another woman at my event, Luther."

"Should I just stay home, then? I'm not trying to make you uncomfortable."

"No!" Liz hated how desperate she sounded and rubbed a frustrated hand down her face. "No, I'm not saying that...what if we just ditch our dates and go together?"

"Liz, we're in the same position, here. My escort is just a friend, too, so if you're worried about something happening, you shouldn't. I'm sure we're both mature enough to handle being in the same ballroom with each other. We've talked and now we both know what the deal is. It doesn't have to change anything between us."

"And what if whoever you're taking doesn't see it that way?"

"That's the least of your concerns. My feelings for you haven't changed."

"If that's the case, then why are you denying me?"

Luther was quiet for a moment. "If you and I go together, will I be allowed to hold you like I want to? Place a kiss on that beautiful neck or those lips I miss every day? Hold your hand in mine? 'Cause if not, it'll be almost like the platonic dates we're already going on."

"Y-yeah...I want to let you do all of that, Luther."

"You want to let me. Not you *will* let me. This is progress, though; at least you didn't hesitate or inundate me with excuses as to why you can't."

"Luther-"

"Let's just leave things as they are, Liz. It doesn't have to be a big deal. Look, I need to go...but rest assured that I still love you and I look forward to seeing you. I know you're going to look gorgeous."

He gently hung up, and Liz just sat there, feeling she'd fumbled again.

Chapter 19

• • • •

THE EVENING OF THE adult prom had finally arrived. Liz was a ball of anxiety and nerves as she got ready. She needed the event to go well but she was more nervous about seeing Luther there with another woman, and him seeing her there with another man. Platonic or not, Liz already knew she wasn't going to like whoever his date was.

But she reminded herself that them taking friends to an event didn't have any bearing on their relationship. Instead of kicking herself for how she handled everything, she just wanted to focus on having a successful prom and a good time. She refused to spend the whole night obsessing; at least, that's what she told herself.

Of course, she had to make sure she looked extra fabulous. If Luther was going to be there with another woman on his arm, she wanted to make sure he wished he was with her, and she didn't care if it was petty.

"Pardon my language, but got*damn*!" Carlton exclaimed when he got the first glimpse of Liz in her navy slip sequin patchwork dress with the back that dipped low and the slit that went high. The satin Jimmy Choo ankle strap heels with crystal embellishments made her long legs even more enticing. Large rhinestone hoop earrings hung from her ears and silver bracelets adorned both wrists. Shimmery body oil made her brown skin pop and her makeup had her face looking like it belonged on a fashion billboard. "I might have to rethink this 'just friends' thing."

Grinning, Liz did a sassy turn, her arms out. "So I chose well, huh? I fell in love with this dress as soon as I saw it."

"And I'm sure every man is gonna fall in love as soon as they see you in it."

Liz only cared about that happening with one man in particular.

"Thank you, Carlton. You're looking mighty dapper, yourself. Shall we go?"

"After you, my incredibly gorgeous sexy..." At Liz's arched brow, he grinned and finished, "Pal."

"Uh-huh."

They rode to the venue in Carlton's Phantom, chauffeured, of course. Liz was glad he hadn't done the cliché thing and gotten a limo. They sat on opposite sides of the backseat and chatted about various things during the drive, which helped put Liz at ease some. Thanks to Carlton's conversation and a shot of whiskey, the ball of nerves that had been sitting like a boulder in her stomach all day was now reduced to a small rock.

Delilah rushed over to her as soon as she and Carlton stepped foot inside.

"Liz, honey, look at you! You look absolutely delectable!"

Liz stifled a laugh at Carlton's expression before she quickly bypassed Delilah's comment and started making introductions, but Delilah scoffed and waved a hand at her.

"Girl, everybody knows who Carlton Barber is," she insisted, turning her megawatt smile over to Carlton, extending her hand as if she expected a kiss to her ring. "Delilah Wakefield. We're honored to have you here."

"A pleasure to meet you," Carlton bowed his head graciously as he gently took her hand, but smoothly avoided the kiss. "And I appreciate it but I'm just another guest."

"Nonsense. You deserve all the recognition for everything you've accomplished, and all the good you've done in this city. If you don't mind saying a few words, we can fit you in before we-"

"Delilah, chill out," Liz interjected before she had him doing a mile-long list of things to show off. "He's here as my friend, not to be showcased. Just know that he's made a huge contribution to the charity that pretty much surpasses our goal for the evening on its own, so be happy with that. Now, how is everything looking? Is everything all set?"

"Yes, everything turned out wonderfully. Zander and I got here early to make sure. I'd make some quip about you not being here when we were but given how you look, all is forgiven."

"There's nothing to be forgiven, Delilah. I'm here at the time we agreed on. If you chose to come early, that's you."

"Right." Delilah cleared her throat, her smile growing tight as her eyes flitted to Carlton. "Well, here's to a wonderful evening. Oh, and Cole is going to be here. I think he's looking forward to seeing you."

Liz found it funny that Delilah practically sang that as if Liz should care. She didn't know what Cole had told them after she left him sitting at the table in the restaurant that night, and she hadn't answered any of Delilah's calls once she left. And when she and Delilah did meet up about the prom after that, she made it clear that Cole was a non-factor that she wasn't going to discuss.

The venue started filling up quickly with well-dressed people ready to party. There was a red carpet, and just about everyone was all too eager to take their turn posing for the professional photographers. The ballroom was decked out in periwinkle and crystal, with white taffeta drapery on the ceiling, crystal curtains along the walls, iridescent spheres hanging throughout, and a floral wall for pictures. There was also a photo booth, an open bar, and several tables adorned with tablecloths and centerpieces in corresponding colors. More than a few people noticed Carlton or ventured over to introduce themselves or commend him for something he did, but for the most part, he was able to enjoy the evening like everyone else.

Liz grinned when Lovey, Natalia, and Desiree showed up with their husbands. Kinsley arrived on Carter's arm, to Liz's mild surprise. She had to admit, they looked cute together. When almost forty minutes had passed and she still hadn't seen Luther or Jules, she wondered if they'd changed their minds about coming. Maybe Luther had thought he'd make her uncomfortable and Jules was avoiding her after telling Luther about Carlton being her escort for the prom.

But both of those theories evaporated when they showed up together.

"Girl, who is that with Luther?" Kinsley hissed in Liz's ear, a slight frown in her freshly-threaded brows. She was eying Jules as if she was already considered the enemy.

It took Liz a moment to respond because her mouth had seemingly filled with cotton. She watched Luther...her tall, hot, bow-legged Luther...looking mouth-wateringly sexy in his black tux that looked like it was tailored specifically for his muscular body, his hair freshly cut and his salt-and-pepper beard as neat as could be, stroll into the ballroom with Jules's hand tucked into the crook of his arm. Liz hated to admit how amazing Jules looked in her winter white mermaid dress and her hair swept to a low side ponytail and adorned with a rhinestone clip, and how they looked a little too much like a bride and groom for her imagination.

"That's his ex-wife, Jules," Liz finally muttered, clearing her throat.

"They look awfully chummy."

"They're still friends. It's no big deal."

"Uh-huh." Kinsley didn't look at all convinced. "Homegirl looks a little too smug, if you ask me. Not to mention how she hasn't let go of his arm since they walked in here."

Liz surely noticed that, too. But she wasn't going to let herself get worked up.

"I'm not sweating that, Kinsley," Liz made herself say, forcing a smile onto her face. "I met Jules a while ago and we've even hung out a couple of times. Luther already told me he was bringing someone. Not to mention, I'm here with Carlton."

"Don't even get me started on *that*."

"I'm not trying to."

Liz was determined to enjoy her night; she danced with Carlton, laughed with her friends, and mingled with her sorors and the other guests. There were a couple of speakers, and Delilah made sure to grab the microphone to encourage everyone to pump up their donations. Liz had noticed Luther eyeing her a few times but had managed to keep her distance, though she knew she couldn't avoid him all night. And she didn't want to give Jules the satisfaction of knowing her little ploy had gotten to her.

Before she could make her move, though, Luther made his way over to her. When she turned and saw him approaching, eyes fixated on her, she felt every pore of her body wake up and do the jitterbug.

"Hey." He stood in front of her, openly perusing her from head to toe, the approval in his dark eyes clear.

"Hey." Liz was surely enjoying her up-close view, as well.

"You look..." His hand drifted to his stomach as he dragged his bottom lip between his teeth. "Breathtaking."

Liz's breaths deepened and she hoped her pebbled nipples weren't visible through her dress. "I admit it's been hard to keep my eyes off you since you got here."

"I was wondering if we'd get a chance to talk." His hands slid into his pockets. "It almost seemed like you were avoiding me."

"I didn't want to interrupt you and your...date."

Luther scoffed, giving her a *you know better than that* look. "Come on, Liz. It's just Jules. You know we're only friends."

"Hmm. Is that why she-"

"Hey Liz!" Jules appeared next to Luther, piercing their little momentary bubble. Liz's face tightened at Jules's arm that was around Luther's waist. Luther looked down at his ex-wife curiously, but her attention stayed fixated on Liz.

"This is an amazing event. Y'all did a great job. And you are looking too hot!"

"Thanks," Liz pushed out, her eyes dropping to Jules's arm again. She also noted how close Jules had her body pressed to Luther's. Liz's skin began to feel hot and she started to fan herself but stopped. She refused to let them know they were getting to her. "It's really big of you two to come and support."

"We're always down to support a good cause. Right, Lu-Lu?" Jules grinned up at Luther, who arched a brow at her. Her other hand landed on his chest.

"Right. Well, enjoy. I have to go and check on...something." Liz turned and hurried off, dodging people and trying to manage walking in heels when her legs felt like jelly. Carlton caught her before she could escape the ballroom, looking at her with concern.

"What's wrong?" he asked discreetly, stepping closer to her. "And don't try to tell me it's nothing."

"You're right, it's not, but I don't want to get into it here." Liz shook her head, telling herself to get it together. She wasn't going to let Jules and her antics throw her off. "Come on, let's dance."

Carlton let Liz pull him back to the dance floor, his eyes on Luther and Jules who were several feet away. Jules was talking rapidly to him while Luther's attention was on Liz.

"Is that him?" Carlton asked Liz as she stepped into his arms, turning to where her back was to Luther and Jules. "The one that's looking like he wants to club me over the head and then sweep you into his arms?"

"Yeah. Though I don't know why he cares, since he's here with somebody, himself. I even offered to ditch you so I could come with him."

"Nice to know. But I get it."

"What are they doing now?" Liz couldn't resist asking.

"He actually started to come over here but she stopped him. Now a pretty red-haired woman and a man that seems to live in the gym are approaching them."

Kinsley and Carter. Liz could only hope that Kinsley didn't cause any kind of scene on her account. "Is he still looking?"

"Sure is. It looks like the two of you need to talk, Liz. This is the man you're in love with, right?"

"Yeah, but...there's no use in us talking right now. I'm just trying to enjoy my evening. Just stop paying them any attention."

"It's ingrained in me to stay keen on anyone that might be coming for me and that man wants my blood. I imagine he doesn't like the sight of another man dancing with you."

"Not sure why he's acting like that. I told him you and I are just friends. Not to mention, his date certainly hasn't been keeping her hands to herself. That's his ex-wife, you know."

"Interesting. Well, I'd be willing to bet my fortune that he's regretting bringing her and not you."

Carlton was right. Luther couldn't help the agitation he felt upon seeing Liz in another man's arms, even if they were just friends as she claimed. Their bodies weren't even that close, but Luther didn't care. Everything in him wished he and Liz were there together; when they were talking earlier, it had taken all of his restraint not to pull her into his arms. He had to put his hands into his pockets to resist the urge.

He'd been about to ask Liz to dance when Jules interrupted them, acting all clingy. Luther hadn't missed the look on Liz's face, and he hoped she wasn't thinking that anything was going on between him and Jules. Luther hated confusion and wanted to clear the air, but first he had to see what was going on with his ex-wife.

"Jules, what are you doing?" he asked, gently grabbing her arms when she started to slide them around his neck. "This overly-affectionate thing isn't what we do and you know it."

"I'm having a good time."

"Jules, I'm not in the mood. Now, what's up with all this, for real?"

She sighed. "I'm just trying to help you out."

"How is you pawing all over me helping me out? There's no telling *what* Liz is thinking right now and I'm telling you, Jules, if whatever it is you're trying to do backfires, you and I are gonna have a major problem."

"You know good and well I would never do anything purposely to cause problems for you. *Or* Liz. I've been rooting for you two since I met her, remember? But for whatever reason both of you are here with other people when it's clear you want to be with each other and I'm just trying to show you both what idiots you are."

"I can think of ten better ways you could've gone about this. And nobody is an idiot; you don't know everything we're dealing with."

"I understand that. But I *do* know that you both are miserable without each other when you don't have to be. Now you tell me how much sense that makes."

Jules sauntered off and Luther just stood there a moment before whirling around and searching the ballroom for Liz. He didn't see her anywhere and his chest almost caved in at the thought of her leaving because of a misinterpretation about him and Jules. He started to go look for her, but Carter called him over, wanting to introduce him to someone. Luther gave one more sweeping hopeful glance around the room before going over to them, hoping he didn't get roped into some long conversation.

Liz was actually out in the hallway, at the far end near the double-doors leading out to the garden, trying to compose herself. Her constant self-reminders that Luther and Jules were 'just friends' were no longer working, and when she happened to turn and see Jules start to wrap her arms around Luther's neck with a huge grin on her face, Liz couldn't take it anymore. She excused herself from Carlton, telling him she needed a minute, and hurried out of the ballroom. Lovey, having seen her scurry out, was right on her heels. Desiree and Natalia weren't far behind.

"Liz, what's wrong?" Lovey asked, gently grabbing Liz's shoulders. "You actually look like you're about to cry."

"Is it because Luther is here with that woman?" Natalia asked, looking stunning in her floor-length strapless silver dress with a middle slit that was like a curtain reveal for her bronze legs. "Who is that, anyway?"

"Yeah, she's been hanging all over him all night," Desiree added. Her thick natural hair was slicked back into an elegant afro puff. "Though I couldn't help but notice he didn't look too happy about it."

"That's Jules, his ex-wife," Liz informed them, anger flashing through her eyes. Her hands were actually shaking. "They've been friends since they divorced years ago and I *thought* she was mine, too, but clearly, I was wrong. I made the mistake of trusting her and telling her I was coming with Carlton, and she hurried up and told Luther so she could snatch him up as her date."

"Why would she behave like that now?" Lovey asked. Her long thick hair was a mass of sexy tousled curls and held from her face with a satin headband that was the same shade of emerald as her body-hugging halter dress. "It seems to be really suspicious timing, to me."

"I don't know. I'd hate to think she's been scheming this whole time, but..."

"Liz, girl, do you want me to go handle that?" Natalia offered, ready to attack. "E.J. stopped me one time but he's not out here to do it again."

Liz didn't put it past Natalia to do exactly that; she had never been one to bite her tongue and was always down to stand up for her loved ones. "As tempting as it is to set you loose on her, I can't have that going on here. I don't want what this night is supposed to be about to be overshadowed by drama and besides that, Delilah and my sorority sisters would never let me hear the end of it. They're already tedious enough to deal with."

"You should go talk to Luther," Lovey suggested. "From what I've seen, he'd much rather be here with you, as much as he's been ogling you all night. Roland actually got onto me for paying you two more attention than him."

"He already tried to say that they're just friends still. I know I've handled some things wrong with Luther but this was the last thing I was expecting. I knew he'd be here with somebody but...I'm not used to feeling this kind of jealousy and...ugh!" Liz covered her face with her hands, and Lovey immediately wrapped her arms around her.

"Liz."

They all looked over to see Jules approaching, her strut so confident that it was almost taunting. Liz just sucked her teeth and turned away, Lovey shielding her, while Natalia and Desiree quickly stepped up and blocked Jules's path to their friend.

"You might wanna back up," Desiree warned her.

"It's only because Liz told me not to that I'm not tearing you apart right now," Natalia seethed, looking like she wanted to pounce on Jules. "The same friend that you stabbed in the back just saved your life."

"I didn't stab anyone in the back," Jules insisted, though the wariness in her eyes was clear as she gave Natalia a wide berth. "Liz, if you'd just give me a minute, I can explain all of this."

"There's nothing to explain," Liz snapped, forgetting her momentary plan to just ignore her. She stepped out of Lovey's arms. "You acted like you were my friend, told on me to Luther, snagged him for yourself, then made it your mission to rub it in my face. I must say, you're a hell of an actress 'cause I really thought you were supportive of me and Luther together."

"I *am*. Liz, girl, I am not trying to get Luther back; that ship sailed years ago and even if I *was* still feeling him like that, I wouldn't humiliate myself making any kind of move because that man is ridiculously head over heels for you." Her eyes pleaded with Liz to believe her. "And believe me, he wasn't any happier about my groping and flirting than you are."

Liz felt as if the screws on her tension had been loosened and her body relaxed somewhat, though her frown remained. "And why would you even do that?"

"Like I told Luther when he was going off on me, I was only trying to show you both what you're missing by being apart. I get that I don't know all of the intricacies of why you and Luther aren't together, but it's clear to anyone with eyes that you want to be. You wouldn't be out here near tears with your posse ready to kick my ass on your behalf if you didn't want Luther, so why aren't you getting your man? There's never gonna be a 'perfect' time. ..whatever issues you're trying to work out, y'all can do that shit together. Girl, time is too precious to waste with whatever it is you two are doing, I'm tellin' you."

Jules reached out and squeezed Liz's arm, giving her an encouraging smile before turning and sauntering back to the ballroom. Liz just stood there, unable to say anything.

"She's right, you know," Desiree muttered, nudging Liz's shoulder with her own. "She pretty much said what I've been thinking for a while now."

"Yeah, it might not have been the ideal way to go about it, but I can see where she's coming from, too," Lovey added.

"You have to stop letting your reservations or whatever is holding you back keep you from the man you love, sis."

"Yeah, Liz, there's always gonna be something else that pops up in your head to make you think you're not ready," Natalia spoke up. "You're holding yourself back when you need to just jump in and let him catch you. You're not going to be perfect and neither is he but it doesn't mean you're not perfect for *each other*. You've gotta get out of your own way, girl."

"Don't miss out on your blessing. You love each other, you both know what each other expects, you've felt the pain of being apart...like Jules said, you can work through everything else together." Lovey gave her big sister a nudge. "Go to him."

Liz glanced at Lovey and their friends, her resolve strengthening. Not even bothering to protest, she took off for the ballroom, hurrying to where she was just short of running. Seeing Luther with someone else was a foreshadowing of what could happen if she kept trying to wait to be 'just right' for a relationship with him. She wasn't flawless, and she wasn't going to be flawless. And if she was sure of nothing else, she was sure that she did not want to let another day pass with her and Luther apart.

Luther was looking mildly frantic as he made his way towards the exit of the ballroom, and his relief was evident when he saw Liz. He started to say something, but Liz halted his words with a heated kiss, right in plain view of everyone.

He was clearly thrown but quickly recovered and wrapped her tightly in his arms, returning her intense kiss with all the pent-up desire he'd been harboring for her. Liz's hands slid from his face to the back of his head to around his neck, totally lost in the feeling of being in his arms again. She could hear her friends pass by them muttering variations of "Get it girl!" before going to find their husbands.

Several long moments passed before the kiss finally tapered off, and she caressed his face as she pulled back, his hands clamped to her waist as if he feared she might run off.

"I don't want to keep wasting time, Luther," she told him, her voice impassioned. "This, us, is what I want."

"It's what I want, too." Luther pulled her even closer. "I know you said Carlton was just a friend but it drove me crazy seeing you here with him."

"I didn't love seeing Jules hanging all over you, either. I thought that she ran and told you about me coming here with Carlton because she decided she wanted you back."

"Jules didn't tell me Carlton was going to be accompanying you, baby. I was at Natavey and Carlton was there; I happened to overhear him mention it to Roland."

"Oh." Liz felt bad for jumping to conclusions; she'd been sure Jules had concocted a whole scheme to get Luther back and rub it in her face. She'd apologize to her but it wasn't her top priority at the moment. "Well, I feel ridiculous..."

"I can see how you would jump to that. It's not like I wasn't doubting what you said about you and Carlton being just friends, and you two weren't even doing anything like Jules was trying with me. I just...I want to be the only man on your arm, holding you." His hand cupped the side of her face. "I need you, Liz."

"I need you, too. And I'm done running or doubting myself or blocking my own blessings. And that's exactly what you are to me, baby. I'm a thousand percent sure that I'm ready for you and us."

"That's all I need to hear, then." He lowered his face to hers, reclaiming her lips again. Thankfully their respective escorts were happy to see them together because from that moment on, Liz and Luther were all about each other.

Chapter 20

• • • •

"LUTHER, YES..."

"Liz...baby, you feel so good..."

They were back at Luther's place, having left the prom way before it was over, and were all over each other as soon as they were through the door. In truth, they were all over each other in the car on the way to his place. But neither could wait to get their fancy clothes off and take advantage of the passion that had been building since they each first saw each other in them earlier that evening.

"It's me and you, right?" Luther panted, nipping her lips as he moved in and out of her with firm strokes.

"Me and you." Liz held him close to her, her matte blue nails digging into his strong back. "For good."

He leaned back and looked into her eyes. "Say that again."

Her arousal shot through the roof at the intensity in his expression. "It's me and you for good."

"*Again.*" His hips moved faster.

"Shit..." She gasped, her hips meeting his. "It's me and you for good, baby."

He lifted her legs higher around his waist before bracing his hands on either side of her, pounding into her so hard her jaw went slack. "One more time."

"M-me and you for goo*aahhh*! Luther, I'm coming! Fuck, I'm coming! Luther, *shit*, I'll marry you *tomorrow*! This pussy is *all yours!*"

"Damn right it is," Luther grunted as he kept stroking into her, loving how expressive she got when orgasms hit her. And he planned to spend the rest of the night taking her there.

She pulled him down for a hungry, sloppy kiss as her body shuddered through the wave of pleasure crashing into her. Her hands grasped his face, humming and moaning as she sucked on his tongue, jerking with occasional aftershocks as he continued to twitch inside of her.

They went a couple more rounds before they finally calmed down, tightly snuggled on the right side of Luther's bed, which just happened to be where they ended up.

"You remember what I told you in Belize about our connection?" Luther asked, his voice low in her ear as he held her from behind.

"I do. And I thought you were out of your mind," Liz replied with a chuckle.

"Uh-huh. And what do you think now?" His arms squeezed her.

"I think that I'm glad you believed it for the both of us, like you said. I'm glad I had that crappy date that made me want to go drown my sorrows at Natavey that night we ran into each other. I think I can finally relate to my sister and friends when they gush over their husbands." She turned in his arms, looking into his eyes and feeling the love she felt for him wash over her for the hundredth time that evening. "I think that you're the love of my life and I never want to be without you again."

"Liz..." His finger traced her eyes, down the bridge of her nose, around her lips, and up to her ear before his hand clasped the back of her neck and he pressed his lips to hers. "You had my heart before I walked out of your hotel room in Belize. I truly believe you're my soul mate and we were made for each other. I never thought I'd find a love like this at this point in my life and now that I have you...baby, I thank God every day for bringing you to me. And I damn sure never want to be without you again, either."

Liz ginned, her eyes shining with blissful tears. "I love you so much, baby."

His forehead rested against hers, their heartbeats falling into rhythm. "I love you, too."

• • • •

LIZ COULDN'T BE MORE relieved that it was finally the day of the showcase. She was more than ready for it to be over with after working on it for months.

It was a super-hectic morning with lots of running around, organizing, and putting out last-minute fires. Liz almost wished she drank coffee because between the late nights leading up to the showcase and whatever time she had left over spent with Luther, she was practically running on fumes. But she wasn't complaining because even though she was tired, she was still excited. This was one of the main parts she loved about her job, seeing how everything came together. She looked forward to seeing everyone's reactions to all of the looks, and most importantly, Luther seeing up close how his hats fit in with everything and why she'd been so insistent and excited about using them. He'd seen pictures but there was nothing like seeing the live models wearing your creations in front of you.

Just a few more hours, she reminded herself as yet another person shrieked her name about something. *Then this will all be over with.*

"Liz, this is magical!" Summer, the formerly-reluctant jewelry designer exclaimed, rushing up to Liz backstage and throwing her thin arms around her. "I just saw a couple of the models and I love how you've chosen to use my pieces!"

Liz smiled. "I'm glad you're pleased, Summer. I knew you would be."

"Is there time for me to burn some sage? I want to bless all of the looks and the runway before the public comes in with their various and conflicting energies."

"Uhh, I'm not sure sage-burning can be done in here but there is a spot over there in the corner you can do some meditating in."

Summer clasped her hands together, bouncing slightly at the knees. "Perfect! It'll help calm and center me before everything begins. I've been a little jittery."

"Well...go for it."

Liz was so glad when she was finally able to change out of her jeans and hoodie and into her strapless dotted mini dress and matching cropped blazer, because it was finally almost showtime. Luther texted to let her know when he arrived, and she rushed out to find him, throwing her arms around his neck.

"Whew, am I glad to see you," she breathed, keeping her tight hold on him.

"Busy morning, huh?" His hands rubbed up and down her back.

"Extremely."

"Hang in there, baby...you're almost to the finish line. How's everything looking?"

"Everything is *great*." Liz pulled back, flashing an excited smile. "I can't wait for you to see how everything came together in person."

"I can't, either. It's still kinda wild that something I created is going to be in a professional showcase. Churi actually wanted to come but she couldn't get off work. She asked me to tell you congratulations."

"That's surprising but flattering. It would've been nice for her to be here but I look forward to spending some time with her and us getting to know each other; I know I need to do my part on that as much as she does."

"True. I'd love for my favorite girls to get along. Oh, and Jules also wanted to come and support but thought you might still be upset with her. She said you haven't returned her last couple of calls."

It had been two weeks since the adult prom and while Liz appreciated overall what Jules did to try to push her and Luther back together, there was a small stubborn part of Liz that was still holding a grudge over how she went about it. Liz knew she'd get over it at some point, though, because she knew Jules was just trying to help.

"I'll call her back soon enough."

"I know you aren't thrilled about what she did and believe me, I wasn't either. I told her about herself for that, but I can't be too mad because at the end of the day, whatever she said to you that night pushed the accelerator on us getting back together. I just choose to be grateful that she cared enough about the both of us to do that."

Liz knew he had a point and gave a conceding nod. "I strive to have your maturity one day."

"You know she's seeing Carlton Barber now. Apparently he offered her a ride after we both ditched them at the prom and they hit it off."

"I didn't know that but good for them. Carlton called the next day but we didn't get to talk that long; he was mostly just making sure I was good. I'll pump him for information eventually. Come on, let me show you to your seat."

She grabbed his hand and ushered him through the many people milling around to the cushioned chair that she'd reserved for him right by the runway. Once she was done with all of her running around, she planned on sitting right next to him instead of hanging out backstage like she usually did. With a quick parting kiss, she told him she'd be back soon and scurried off backstage to make sure everything was all set to kick off.

It was almost laughable to Liz how readily she showed affection in public to Luther now when she'd been so extremely adverse to even the smallest display of it before. But after she kissed him on the dance floor at the prom, she realized she wasn't even worried about what anyone else might think about it. All she cared about was Luther. And whenever they'd been out since then, she realized there was no anxiety or paranoia to be found when Luther took her hand or put his hand on her waist. Luther never took it too far. And she found herself initiating the affection sometimes by hugging him from behind or even sitting on his lap one time when they were waiting to be seated at a restaurant one night, though she could admit to herself that was partially due to making sure the women eyeing her man knew he was spoken for.

Once the lights lowered and it was finally time for the showcase to kick off, Liz shuffled to the front and plopped into the chair next to Luther. He immediately put his hand on her thigh as they both turned their attention to the runway.

Everything went off without a hitch. The models hit their marks, the looks were just as Liz envisioned, the music was on point, and the crowd ate it all up. Liz watched Luther as he watched the models stroll in front of him wearing the various hats he created, and he actually looked a little emotional. She placed her hand over his, giving it an encouraging squeeze.

Barely a couple hours later, it was over. Liz often marveled at the tons of work and preparation that went into these things only for them to last such a short amount of time, but that was just how it was. So many people wanted to meet Luther once they found out he was the creator of the hats that were featured, and Liz left him to it while she went about all of her post-production duties. By the time they were finally ready to leave, Liz just couldn't wait to get from around all those people and be alone with her man.

"I'm glad you talked me into participating in that," Luther commented as they headed outside. "That whole experience was rather surreal."

"I'm glad you enjoyed it. And I thank you again for even doing it because as you can see by how everyone raved, the looks wouldn't have hit like they did without your creations.

I hope you're prepared to get a lot busier because there will be a *lot* of hat orders coming your way, watch what I tell you."

"I'm not mad at it." His phone chimed and when he glanced at it, he chuckled. "It seems your girl has my brother's nose wide open. He actually sent me a picture of them and that has *never* happened."

He held his phone out for Liz to see the shot of Carter and Kinsley at some amusement park, sharing a huge cloud of pink cotton candy. Both of them sported big goofy smiles. Liz's eyebrows shot up in surprise.

"Wow. Now I see why Kinsley has gone kinda scarce lately. I knew she had gone to his physique competition thing with him and was the loud and proud girlfriend when he placed second. I can just imagine those conversations because those two are wild enough separately. Love the happy ending for them, though."

"Same." Luther tucked his phone back into his pocket. "You coming to the house?"

"Actually, I was thinking we could go to my place." She smiled flirtatiously, swinging her shoulders slightly with her hands behind her back. "I have a surprise for you."

"Does it involve me getting to see some new piece of lingerie you got or lick some kind of dessert topping off your body?"

"Ooh, see...that can definitely happen after I show you what I need to show you."

"Okay," Luther shrugged, his curiosity piqued. "I'll meet you over there after I stop to get us something to eat. I know you've gotta be starving after the long day you've had."

"Thanks, baby."

Once they got to Liz's loft a while later, she linked her fingers with his and led him to her bedroom. When she turned on the light, Luther blinked, wondering what it was he was supposed to be noticing. Everything looked the same as he remembered it, from what he could tell.

"What am I missing?" he finally asked, looking down at her.

"Right in front of you," Liz informed, nodding her head towards the bed before moving over and sitting on top of it, excitedly drumming her fingers on the bedspread. "Brand new bed."

Luther's head jerked, his eyebrows practically up to his sharp hairline. "Seriously?"

"Seriously. I might not have totally understood where you were coming from on the whole bed thing but I respected that it was a big issue for you. That bed was old, anyway, and it gave me an excuse to shop for a new one. Most importantly, though, I want you to be as comfortable here as I am at your place-"

"Until we're both living under the same roof, that is," Luther interjected, moving over and leaning down so his fists were braced on either side of her legs. He moaned as he took a leisurely, tongue-filled kiss. "Because that's the plan, I hope you know."

"Oh I know. And I'm totally on board with that plan. In the meantime, though, you will be the only man that shares this bed with me, just like I've been the only woman to share yours with you."

Luther gazed at her for a moment before pushing her onto her back with his body, lowering himself on top of her. "Thank you for that, baby. This really does mean a lot to me."

"I always want to be sure I do my part in this relationship, Luther. That's an ongoing lesson I'm learning."

"There's going to be a lot of that on both our parts the longer we're together, baby. We might've had relationships but we haven't had one with each other. And I'm all in to learn and master everything I can about my lady Liz Alexandra Tate."

"Well, Mr. Luther Trae Monroe, you're well on your way. I know you stopped and got us Waffle House on your way here. You know I love me some Waffle House."

"Your preference for breakfast food was something I picked up on early. Just like navy blue being your favorite color. Just like how you wear heels damn near everywhere. How you prefer to work out at night instead of in the morning like I do. Just like there's no telling *what* will come out of your mouth when I make you cum-"

"Luther!" Liz gasped, laughing as she playfully shoved his chest.

"That damn sure wasn't a complaint."

She bit her lip, lifting her leg around his waist and purring when she felt him harden on top of her. "Do you like the bed?"

"I do. Feels quite comfortable. Now let's test how sturdy it is."

"I thought you'd never ask."

• • • •

THE END

That's it for *Liz and Luther*! I was thrilled to get to write another story in this character universe; this might be the last one, it might not. I'm not forcing or fighting it.

Please consider leaving a review or at least a rating; they're so vital to us indie authors. And if you want to go the extra mile, share that you read it on social media! ☺

You can find me on Instagram, Threads, FB, and TikTok at @authorjessicaterry. And don't forget to subscribe to my email list at jessicaterry.com.

Also by Jessica Terry

Discussion Questions:

1. With Liz and Luther, it was instalove. Do you believe feelings can develop as quickly as theirs did for each other?
2. Was Kinsley a good friend to Liz?
3. Whose side were you on when it came to the PDA issue, Liz or Luther's? Could you understand their points?
4. If you were Liz, would you have had a problem with Luther and Jules's friendship?
5. Was Luther unreasonable regarding Liz's bed?
6. What did you think of Churi and how she reacted to Liz? Did you think her reasoning was justified? Did you feel Liz made enough of an effort to get to know her?
7. Speaking of Churi, did you feel Luther was too hard on her?
8. Was Luther too forgiving of Liz's encounter with Raj?
9. Did you find Carter to be immature?
10. Things came to a head at the adult prom. Did Jules's actions and her reasoning for them make sense to you?
11. Liz clearly fumbled some things with Luther; in what ways do you feel he handled things poorly?
12. Do you think Jules and Carlton are a match and would stay together beyond this story? What about Kinsley and Carter?

Did you love *Liz and Luther*? Then you should read *Couple's Night*[1] by Jessica Terry!

[2]

When four couples decide to play a relationship question-and-answer game on couple's night, all hell breaks loose:

Serenity and Taj might seem like the perfect couple but one of them is harboring a secret that is affecting their intimacy, and the other is losing their patience.

Lavinia and Ricky are on the brink of divorce thanks to Lavinia's tendency to bulldoze and Ricky tiring of giving her so much leeway just to keep the peace.

---

1. https://books2read.com/u/3knPxg

2. https://books2read.com/u/3knPxg

Charmaine and Ace's pending nuptials might not happen if Charmaine decides she can't deal with his irritating ways. Or if neither of them can deal with the other's mistakes.

Iman and Rasheed suck at communicating how they feel about each other, and their relationship might be doomed before it can evolve beyond friends-with-benefits.

It's not only the romantic pairings that are in jeopardy but some of the friendships, too. And at least one of the couples won't be able to come out of this together.

Read more at https://www.jessicaterry.com/.

About the Author

Jessica Terry caught the writing bug at a young age and loves little more than holing up at home in Douglasville, GA, cranking out contemporary novels. And eating. www.jessicaterry.com

Read more at https://www.jessicaterry.com/.